Broken
Pieces
Shine

KASSANDRA MULLAN

To all of you who supported me with my first book -

This is all your fault

CHAPTER 1

The tavern located in the center of the township bustled even though it was late at night. The building still stood on its own volition, however it bore scars that told a horrific story. Attempts had been made to repair the damage, including patches that covered holes from deterioration and munition explosions. One wall had been supported internally by tree trunks of different lengths and treated for the severe fire that had scarred it. None of the furniture matched, as salvaged chairs, tables, and even dishes were frugally utilized. Even the two doors that led back into the kitchen were different sizes, styles, and type of wood.

In contrast, along the back wall were three rather luxurious booths. The booths on each end had bench seats that ran parallel to the table, with a small nook inside the wall. The middle one was shaped like a horseshoe, with a small round table that wasn't original. The wooden foundation of the booths was left unscathed, but the cushions which used to line them were gone and patrons now sat directly on the hard wood.

Men and women of different ages milled around, settling into booths or grabbing seats at tables clustered together haphazardly in the middle of the dining area. As seating became unavailable, stragglers leaned against the bar and doorframes. They were common folk, gaunt from poor nutrition and wearing patched clothing. Their skin tones, hair color, and eye color varied, while familial traits like noses and ear shapes told an onlooker who was related.

Near the bartender's nook stood a man who did not fit in with those who gathered. Kentar was a polished, lightly armed man. He wore fine clothing, not one silk thread nor one black hair out of place. But the fact he didn't blend in mattered little to Kentar, he was better than this rabble near him.

Looking around the room, his chest puffed up with pride. The size of the group was a testament to his advertisement and it only confirmed his power over the people. He glanced across the room at his man-servant, Pendaff, and nodded. Pendaff, a small young man with short red hair and clothing not as fine

2

as his master's, locked the pub door and guarded it. Then Kentar made a loud discordant sound, causing everyone to quiet down.

"Good of you all to come," Kentar said. "You are a pride to your country."

"What's left of it," someone along the wall muttered.

"Yes, that is the travesty we are here to discuss," Kentar admitted. "The King of Grenan, who had promised to help us, has done nothing but take from us. To the point where we have nothing left but our anger. I say we move on that anger! It is time to regain our pride, our resources, and our country!"

Everyone started murmuring amongst themselves, surprised.

"But how?" a frail, older woman asked.

"Each community has been assigned a leader, a general, to be the decision maker on what steps to take toward this goal. Your leader is I, Kentar."

"Who voted you our leader?" another woman demanded.

She was different. She sat in the horseshoe booth in the far back, a hand holding a cobbled together mug. Her brown hair was pulled back in a crooked bun, with small leather gauntlets encircling her wrists and holding down the sleeves of her well-worn tunic. She had a broad sword sheathed in a weathered leather scabbard attached to her belt and it ran the length of her leg as it disappeared under the table. Her pants were hidden by the table's shadow but light touched her leather boots, showing how old and worn in they were. The men sitting next to her, one on each side, were similarly dressed and armed.

"Each general comes from the royal line," he replied, straightening himself to look intimidating. "I am a distant relative of our late honorable royal family." He looked around the room, challenging someone to say something. No one argued his nomination. "Our first step is to gather what weapons we can. Therefore, I will lead a raid on the weapons depot near the port tonight!"

Some cheered, most hesitated.

"Wouldn't replenishing our food sources not be a better move?" the well-armed woman asked, leaning her elbows on the table in front of her. "We've nothing but moldy crusts in our cabinets and infested meats in our cold storages. That won't sustain us enough to hold our own against the King's Castle Guard."

That made Kentar's eyes narrow. "We need weapons to fight! To overthrow the tyranny and to take back our country."

"But who has the energy to do so? I sure don't. I need to eat before I can fight."

"Then you are useless and you do not need to join us."

The well-armed woman, Sreana, smirked. Then she glanced at her two friends, Pirco and Duncar, then nodded. "Fine by me."

Kentar sniffed. "All those who are capable, meet me in the kitchen immediately."

Some stood and moved to the kitchen, but the majority stayed. Those who didn't move looked worried. Kentar sniffed again then started toward the kitchen, his servant by his side. However, before he could get very far, Sreana and her two friends intercepted him.

"This is a foolish endeavor," Sreana snapped. "You're going to get everyone killed."

"Says who?"

"Someone who understands the enemy. Fought with them against a common scourge. Someone who has seen conflict, which is what your actions will ignite again."

Kentar scoffed. "Great, just what we need. Another gods-forsaken war hero."

"Not a hero, just someone who has seen enough death in their lifetime."

"That's right, you're not a hero," Kentar replied. "The true heroes died."

Sreana heard Pirco start to draw his sword and she grabbed his hand without looking at him.

"At least we fought," she retorted. "Unlike others who hid with the weak and feeble-minded." This time Kentar grabbed his sword hilt, glaring heatedly at Sreana, who only smiled wickedly. "Please, do challenge me." He let go of his hilt and she raised an eyebrow. "Go die. We'll hold the line."

With that Sreana, Pirco, and Duncar walked back to their table. They listened as the two men left the room, the mismatched doors to the kitchen creaking as they swung open.

"So now what?" Pirco asked, disheartened.

"Well, their fool's errand actually gives us something we've needed," Sreana answered.

Duncar raised his eyebrow. "A diversion?"

"A diversion," Sreana agreed. Then she raised her voice, "Anyone else interested in eating?" The remaining men and women in the tavern's dining area looked up and answered positively. "Good, let's get going. As usual, we'll need some covered carts and horses. They will be switching guards soon and, lucky for us, there shouldn't be that many to begin with. By the time we get to the food storage units, our mighty general will be entertaining the troops at the weapons depot." As people prepared, Sreana whispered in Pirco's ear, "Let the other communities know about the distraction. They might as well use it to their advantage as well."

A mischievous smile flashed and Pirco disappeared out the front door.

~   ~   ~

The food storage units appeared more heavily guarded than necessary. However, enough volunteered to make short work of the Castle Guard. They were all under strict orders: disarm but do not kill. Sreana didn't need to worry too much; most of her group were veterans of the invasion and had already participated in similar raids alongside her. With that, they split up into smaller groups, sneaking up on the oblivious guards.

After stealthily climbing up on a short stack of pallets, Sreana laid down behind the lead guard's head. She slid her dagger along the lieutenant's throat, whispering in his ear, "We are not here for blood."

Stiffening with fear, he asked, "Then what are you here for?"

"Just a visit. And your keys, please."

He huffed, then handed the keys over. "Not you again."

"Ah, you do look familiar. Haven't they demoted you yet?" Amused, she watched as his eyes narrowed with annoyance. "You know the drill. We will need to blindfold you so you cannot identify us later. And may we borrow your restraints?"

He pursed his lips, then handed over the cuffs. Sreana secured the lieutenant, then looked around and confirmed that the others were taking similar actions with the other guards. No one was injured, no one was killed. Just as planned.

They unlocked the building and took account of the food and supplies inside. They moved toward the ingredients they could use more readily and those that they could store, while leaving behind things like sweets and other items not traditional to the Sedoran diet. They again broke off into groups per her instructions, loading up their wagons quietly and efficiently. They kept any speech to a minimum so their voices wouldn't be recognized later, in other settings, which could lead to arrests or worse.

Sreana moved among her people, checking the supplies being collected. "Leave the pallets. And any bags or containers you can."

Her friends nodded acknowledgement.

Beside her, Duncar snorted. "To think that self-proclaimed general looked at you as if you were mad."

"Am I not?"

"You are definitely crazy. But you're not supposed to show it."

"Too much is wasted hiding it." Then she pulled a small bag from her sleeve and it jingled with the sound of coins. Duncar glared at her, knowing she had palmed it off the lieutenant. "What? He won't miss it."

From the back of the complex, Pirco peeked out and waved Sreana and Duncar down. They strode across the delivery yard then Pirco led them to another unit in the far back, hidden amongst all of the other containers. Pirco and his group had already taken care of the more-than-necessary sentries when they first descended on the area, but the lock appeared to have been picked.

Sreana looked into the storage unit and metal flashed in the torch light. "Weapons? Here?"

"A lot of weapons," Pirco answered. "Enough to arm a fort's worth of men."

"So, what's at the armory?" Duncar asked.

Sreana sighed. "A trap."

"What do we do?" Pirco inquired.

"There is nothing we can do. The others are either dead or arrested. We will take these though. It was an eventual need. We should take advantage of this unpleasant surprise."

"And then what?"

"Move the guards over to the far gate, so they can run quickly." Sreana glanced around the outside of the structure, taking stock of the bags and pallets they were planning on leaving behind. "Throw all of this inside. Then burn it down."

~   ~   ~

The group returned to the tavern, their covered wagons full of contraband circling to the back alley. The tavern owner, a woman named Trealle, opened the cellar doors and let them fill it with food and supplies. The confiscated weapons were also hidden there, for the time being.

By the time they finished, Kentar's servant had returned. Pendaff arrived alone, with a bloody strip of his master's embroidered shirt in his hand. Tears poured from his eyes and no words escaped his lips. Sreana felt Duncar brush past her and she watched helplessly as he approached the young man. He gingerly took the boy by the elbow and led him inside, towards the kitchen. Pirco followed with a flask of his strongest homemade spirits in hand. Sreana turned away, taking a few breaths to steady herself. She had seen plenty of death during the invasion, but to see the look in Pendaff's eyes… she hadn't seen that in a long time. Voices snapped her out of her despair and she finally moved to help shut and lock the basement's doors.

~   ~   ~

Down the street from the tavern, behind the actual township hid a small lea that bumped up against the river. There, a firepit and the felled trees encircling it greeted her. The little hidden place of respite allowed anyone to sit, relax, and visit with others away from prying Grenan eyes. The fire burned usually every night, but after their mission tonight, it would continue to burn but the group would lay quiet for a while as a safety measure. They didn't need to make the Grenans' job any easier by congregating together if they did decide to arrest anyone.

Sreana walked to the far edge of the lea, to a hornbeam tree with a lush canopy. She touched the trunk reverently and whispered greeting. She closed her eyes briefly, then saw a flash of leaves to her right. A woman, with gray bark-like skin and leaves for hair, peeked around the trunk. Her knees and elbows looked like knots while her more private body parts were covered by the same moss that grew along her tree's trunk and limbs. Her serious green eyes worried Sreana.

The jahla rushed around the tree and hugged her tightly. "We could only watch," the other woman whispered.

"I know, Jya. I tried to talk them out of it, but they didn't want to listen. They made their decision and suffered the consequences." Sreana dreaded asking, "How many?"

"Not as many as in your group. The young one was the only survivor because he was told to stay back." Jya sighed, an angry sound. "Why do they want to fight again? Don't they understand what they do makes things harder for others? Haven't we lost enough already?"

Sreana found it difficult to answer immediately. "Those who did not fight, those who did not suffer like we did, they believe they know what should be done. But us? We know what works and what doesn't. As always, we will continue to do what needs to be done." She squeezed the other woman. "Rest. We've all had a taxing evening. Thank you, and thank your sisters, for keeping an eye out for us."

Jya nuzzled Sreana's neck, her jaw finally loosening up. "Thank you for keeping us safe."

"Always. Good night, Jya. May the gods keep your nightmares to themselves."

"And may they give you dreams worth dreaming," she responded automatically.

The jahla finally let her go, disappearing behind the hornbeam tree. Sreana turned away and walked toward a clump of moss and rock on the other side of the lea. If one did not pay attention, they would miss the small door and the light from the small window off to the side.

Most of the homes in her community were buildings: walls, roofs, doors, and windows. Sreana's hovel was built into the side of a rock face that bumped up to the back of the township. Inside was a bed off to the left of the door, huddled under the small window. Her bed was modest, mostly random stuffing she had shaped into a mattress. A well-used pillow laid at the head while a patchwork quilt covered the rest. Next to her bed hung a broadsword in one slot, while the other remained empty until she retired her sword for the night.

A small wood burning stove with a vent bent to exit the crooked roof sat in the middle of the room. Near the stove was a small table for dining with two mismatched chairs. A reflecting glass sat on another small table, propped against the rock wall, with a wash bowl beside it and a patched chair in front of it. A pair of shelves were attached to the front wall: one with canned foods and snacks and the other for her treasured books. Two books were family related while the last one was her handwritten copy of Dranar's teachings.

Her clothes were hidden away in an antique cedar chest, one of the few things she kept of her family's. She had a few tunics, patched and darned carefully, two pairs of leather riding pants, and a few pieces of underclothes. She had two pairs of gauntlets, the small stylish ones she wore that night and longer ones that had seen too many campaigns, and one belt that she wore daily that fit her scabbard perfectly. She had one pair of good boots, that laced up the sides and covered her from toes to knees. She also had a pair of beat-up sandals for use around the house.

She slipped out of her clothes, swapping the layers for the oversized undershirt and undershorts she wore to bed. She brushed her hair out and splashed her face with what water was left in the wash bowl. After drying her face with a small towel, she stared at herself in the reflecting glass. Her walnut brown hair already had a gray streak along her left ear. It was a nice highlight, setting off her gray eyes, but it hid her youth. She wondered often how long it would take before she was completely gray. She had a scar along her eyebrow and eye, where a soldier got lucky, but her face was mostly unblemished even after her long list of altercations with the invaders. Her only other visible scar was on her lower lip, down the middle, from a childhood dare that did not go well… and sometimes when a change in weather occurred, her elbow still ached due to the corresponding break.

Her mind wandered to Pendaff, Kentar's servant, hoping the boy would find peace with the slaughter at the armory. She sighed, hard, and walked up to the bookshelf. She touched the spine to the book of Dranar's teachings and whispered a prayer for the boy. Then she climbed into bed.

CHAPTER 2

The warrant hung on the tree, swaying sweetly with the spring wind as it offered money for information that led to the arrest or death of the criminals who set fire to the food storage unit. No mention of the theft, the missing weapons, the raids on the other food storage units, or even the attempted assault on the weapons depot.

The three friends stared at the announcement solemnly until Sreana started laughing and shaking her head. The gossip had already spread throughout the townships about the polite woman, with her group of mute thieves, ensuring the safety and survival of the guards after the fire broke out. And considering their actions and what they stole, no one would willingly turn them in.

"How many warrants does this make, Sreana?" Duncar inquired.

Duncar watched her with his dark blue eyes that reminded her of kyanite. His blonde hair had similar streaks as Sreana's, however the touches of gray and silver ran throughout. He kept it trimmed short, but one lock always grew faster than the rest and would slide down his forehead to interfere with his eyesight. It gave him a shy, boyish facade that contrasted with all the experiences gained during and after the invasion. He was a little taller than her and Pirco, but not as muscular as most of her fighters.

Sreana shrugged, playfully wiggling her fingers. "I've ran out of fingers and toes to count with."

"Doesn't this make things messier?" Pirco asked.

Sreana stared at Pirco for a moment. His dark brown hair made hers look fair and those jasper hazel eyes, which usually gleamed when he was up to no good, were dulled with worry as he regarded her. He wasn't much taller than her and more muscular than one would assume at first glance. Even though he hid his physique well under his clothing, he was one of the strongest fighters in her ranks. And even after everything he survived during the invasion, he could always find a joke in any situation.

She sighed. "Everything we get caught doing or are accused of doing always

9

makes things messy."

"But it hampers our movements, does it not?" Duncar demanded.

"The day we allow these things to bother us," and she raised an eyebrow, "is the day we retire."

Duncar and Pirco grinned at Sreana's comment, because they knew it was very true.

"So, we do nothing to correct the rumors?" Duncar prompted.

She furrowed her eyebrows. "Which ones?"

"That there is a leader of the miscreants? A rebel as he is called?"

"The more they incorrectly assume, the better, I say. Especially since I am not a leader. Just an instigator."

Pirco made a face at that, causing Sreana to tap his elbow lightly. "So what now?"

"Well, we have enough food to last us a while," she answered. "We'll lay low on the raids."

"But?"

"I have a feeling that the Castle Guard needs to be reminded of how lazy they have gotten," she replied, walking away from the tree and into the forest.

"Who's all going?" Duncar asked, concerned, as they followed close behind her.

"Just me as always." She saw their disappointment. "The less the better. Anyway, if I get in a bind, I'll only have to worry about myself."

"We'll wait outside the walls then."

Sreana grinned, touched by their devotion. The old adage rang true: it was better to have some friends, then have too many enemies.

~   ~   ~

The siege itself seemed like a lifetime ago. The Carmanic Empire's army did damage not just to the Sedoran land but also the structures. Castles, manors, even small outhouses that stood on the edge of a township were either burned, trashed, or used as target practice by the invaders.

The castle nearby had been a victim of such abuse. It still bore the mutilated scars, including a wound to the northeast wall. It had probably been done by fire sand, creating a crack big enough for a slim person to slip through.

And for Sreana, it was the best entry point.

She climbed through the crevice, trying not to slip on the loose bricks, while Duncar and Pirco watched for trouble from the tree line. Once through, she ran along the wall of the outer bailey. Hidden in the darkness, she kept out of the guards' sight as they protected the delivery gates. She jogged through the open postern and into the inner bailey, which led her into the main courtyard and the doorway to the great hallway. That guard was nowhere near his post.

She caught sight of him near the stables, flirting with one of the stable hands. With him distracted, she snuck into the main hallway, staying in the shadows, until she found the side hallway that led to what was the castle staff's workrooms.

There, she entered the Captain of the Castle Guard's office. He had already retired for the evening, but left his fireplace going. She rolled her eyes. He always left it for the household staff to deal with, just like the pile of used dishes. She walked to his side of the work desk and scanned the documents sprawled out. She tried not to touch anything so as not to leave a noticeable disturbance that gave away her snooping. Then she recognized the closed ledger that had dates and times of supply transfers.

As she reached for it, the sound of voices made her pause. The voices got louder, which meant the owners were getting closer, and Sreana looked for a place to hide. She slipped under the settee that nestled beneath the bay window, allowing the throw blanket that draped over it to hide her as she balled herself up. Two women entered, she could tell by their sandals, and they continued to chat.

"I heard him again," one woman admitted, her tone dark with pity.

"Another night terror?" the other woman asked, then sighed, probably in response to the first woman nodding. "Poor man."

"It was before sunrise, when I started to draw open the curtains. His cries were..." and she exhaled, sadly. "They feel nightly even though I'm sure they are not."

"Have you said anything to the healers?"

"I have and they said they would talk to him. But they will not tell me anything said in private."

"Well, of course not."

"Whatever they are doing doesn't seem to be helping."

Once the women finished collecting the dishes, they extinguished the fire and left, still speaking softly about the man.

"I overheard them discussing his injury the other day. They didn't sound hopeful but... He just needs time. All we can do is not embarrass him..."

Sreana stayed hidden for a few more moments, to ensure they didn't forget anything and return. But their voices dissipated and when she felt it was safe, she exited her hiding place. She stood in the darkness, her curiosity piqued. Night terrors? Who were they talking about? Her mind wandered upstairs. The Grenan King? She shook her head, dismissing the idea of the Grenan King being a man with such an injury let alone emotions.

She decided then to leave without anything in hand before she got caught. She already had a few ideas of what her next theft would be and knew she could sneak back in if needed.

As she made her way down the great hallway to exit the castle, her curiosity got the best of her. She had an idea where the royal chambers were, considering it had been home to a member of the Sedoran Royal Family, and the architecture mirrored other castles throughout the country. Before she could talk any sense into herself, she searched out the staircase that likely led up to the private chambers. She stared up into the stairwell, the light far away as it flickered at the upper landing. She leaned against the cold stone that surrounded the staircase's opening, wondering about the person who lived up there.

Voices again surprised her and she stealthily darted up the stairs. For whatever reason, the household staff's schedule ran early tonight. And she had no other way to go but up. The light above got brighter and, as she completed the climb, she found herself in a hallway heading toward the balcony that was attached to the master's bedchambers.

The candlelight almost blinded her after creeping in the shadows for so long and she blinked to adjust her eyes. The two large glass doors that led out to the balcony were left open and the inner curtains of the bedchambers were still drawn to the sides. This late she had assumed they'd be closed and the occupant asleep, but with everything open, that meant someone was still awake.

Instinctively, she darted into the balcony's curtains and snuggled into their pleats. They ran the length of the balcony, but were bunched up enough to hide in because they were still partially opened to the view of the courtyard below. Once she felt safe, she peeked out and noticed someone standing at the other end. Her stomach dropped when she realized she wasn't alone. Now she was unsure of her next move. She might have to wait until he decided to retire before she could escape. She rolled her eyes, berating herself. She would have been halfway home had she ignored her childish curiosity.

Then her stomach flopped when she recognized who was nearby, even with his back turned to her. She hid within a few horse lengths of the man she hated daily. Her first thought was how easy it would be to bolt across the balcony and slit his throat. After all, no one knew she was there. He was alone. And he was the enemy. His quick death would end his disastrous reign.

Then reality set in.

If it were found that she, a Sedoran, killed the King of the Grenan Kingdom, it would mean the slaughter of her people in response. As much as killing him would satisfy her anger, the repercussions stopped her.

With her immediate bloodlust squelched, Sreana watched the King as he turned toward her, oblivious to her presence. He was dressed in the puffy sleeved shirt all royals wore, with slacks and boots. The only thing missing was the thick, decorative cloak. Surprisingly, he wore no crown or any other jewelry that she could see. His long auburn hair was held back by a thick leather tie. His beard ran the length of his face and seemed uneven as if he had let it grow freely. A staff rested next to him, against the railing, with a brass top and mahogany length.

As he leaned heavily against the balcony railing, flanked by the heavy curtains that warded off unwanted weather and harsh sunlight, she could see his facial expression. Just in profile, it was... gloomy. She found herself wondering again what kind of man he was.

When her people found out the Sedoran Royal Family had made a deal with the Carmanic Empire that allowed the invasion to occur, rumors spread that the Carmanic generals slaughtered the Royal Family to ensure that the Sedoran people would resign themselves to their victorious new masters. But her people refused to cower and, with the help of the Grenan forces, drove out the maniacs. With no Royal Family to lead, the Grenan King had agreed to stay and promised to help Sedora rebuild. However, in the last three years, all they saw was Grenan Castle Guards take what they wanted and the King nowhere to be found. Now finding him in his luxurious suite, she knew he reaped the illicit benefits happily.

When he moved again, this time strolling to the middle of the balcony... the Grenan King limped. An injury? How could he be injured, royalty never fought. Maybe it had been an accident? No matter how it came to be, she wondered if it held him back. Could he let a small limp affect his ability to care for the country his Kingdom occupied? He hid away and allowed the Sedorans to suffer because he was... embarrassed? Was that it? Could he not leave this castle at least once and travel around the countryside to see what Grenan greed did to her people? Was he that prideful? His humanity suddenly became reality.

He exhaled, a concerned sound, and in turn, Sreana sighed, frustrated.

"Who's there?" the King demanded, glancing around him.

Sreana stiffened, not realizing she had been that loud. She waited, tensing as his eyes passed over the curtains she used as a shield. As she hesitated, his shoulders slumped.

"I know someone is there. Come out."

She grimaced, then without anything else to lose, she presented herself to the King. He appeared shocked as she approached, either not expecting his quarry to give up so easily or not expecting someone so well-armed. She cocked her head in a cynical mockery of respect.

He stammered, puzzled. "You are neither servant or guard. Who are you? What are you doing here?"

"I'm no one, Your Majesty." Then, after looking him up and down with distaste, "I just wanted to see what kind of man you were," she lied, slightly. Her intention wasn't to be caught alone with the Grenan King, but she wouldn't let him know that. And while she was there, she might as well make the most of it.

"Why?"

"I was curious."

The lack of straight answers angered him. "I should call my guard."

Sreana drew her sword and whipped it up under his chin. The edge barely touched his flesh. "You would regret it."

He hooked his chin over the blade. "As would you," he countered, defiantly staring her down.

"Call them then," she challenged, with a nonchalant shrug. "Might be fun."

"You'd die tonight?"

"I'd rather die fighting than be taken down like a deer."

"You are foolish then."

"We just met and you think you know me?" She lowered her sword to her side before she seriously considered using it as her patience dwindled. "I am not as foolish as a king who refuses to listen to the cries of the people he promised to help."

"The Sedoran people have not cried out."

"Oh, yes, they have. You have done nothing but ignore them."

"You speak lies."

"Come now, I know you have heard stories about the transgressions against you. I'm sure your Castle Guard whine constantly about it. Those actions are not out of boredom or spite. I have seen the damage out beyond these walls. I know what is going on. Unlike you."

Realization spread across his face and he gasped. "You are the rebel."

"Why would the rebel endanger himself in this way?"

"But you know my traitor? Can you relay a message to him?"

She leaned against the railing, gauging him. "Speak then."

"Tell whoever your leader is that, in light of your words, I will go out into the townships and see what is truly occurring. If I see any injustices, I will do my part to remedy them. However, if I do not see these supposed injustices, I will up the reward for his arrest."

She raised an eyebrow. "A futile effort but do what makes you feel better." Then she nodded, standing up straight again. "I will do my best to pass on your message, Your Majesty."

The King looked into her eyes and she could see the determination in his. Then he grabbed her empty hand and kissed the back of it in thanks. She didn't realize how close they were and she chided herself for letting her guard down. She tried to snatch it back, not offended just surprised, but he held onto it. Annoyed, she smacked him on the thigh with the fuller of her sword. He released her hand, smiling at her reaction, an expression that changed him in that moment. He wasn't some tired old man or hateful god. That smile made him…

From the darkened hallways, a low voice echoed, "Who's that with the King?"

She froze, not knowing which doorway it came from.

"Don't worry, I'll protect you," he tried to assure her.

Yet the instant response from the guards contradicted him. "Look, she's a sword! She's trying to kill the King!"

"Get her!" someone else commanded.

"Arrest her!" another shouted.

She rolled her eyes, before glancing around. Near the end of the long hallway that she had snuck in from, the guards were trying to quickly but cautiously approach. Gauging the timing, she began making her way around the balcony, re-evaluating the situation.

He started to follow her. "What are you doing?" Then he stopped when his limp was noticeable.

"Looking for a way out of here," she responded, scanning the drop off the balcony. If she could find a way down to the pillar underneath...

"The fall would kill you instantly."

She admitted that he had a point; the fall was a steep one. She grabbed the draw rope for the balcony's curtains and tugged, testing its strength. She sheathed her blade, watching as the guards approached. Then she grinned at the King, and with an impish flash in her eyes, she pulled herself up onto the railing then leapt off and swung out.

The rope bounced slightly then tightened. Unfortunately, her weight and the force of her jump caused the curtain rod to snap in half and she dropped down faster than she expected. The broken rod slammed down onto the balcony's railing, then slid away from the King. It only stopped when it tangled up in the finials protruding out of the metal work.

Below, Sreana tried to hang on and suppress her squeal of surprise. Swinging and plummeting dangerously startled her but once her drop stopped, she was able to shimmy down the swaying rope toward the courtyard below. Half-way down, she glanced up to see that the King had rushed to the edge of the railing to watch her. She again flashed her grin then made it to the end of the rope. Unfortunately, she was still pretty high off the ground, but she leapt down to the ground. She landed somewhat awkwardly, then looked back up at the King. Giving a cocky salute, she disappeared into the darkness.

~   ~   ~

At the northeast wall, Pirco and Duncar waited impatiently. Sreana had been gone a long time and now they could hear the guards running and shouting throughout the castle grounds. Suddenly, she slipped through the crevice and darted past them.

"Time to go!" she announced.

Pirco and Duncar jumped to their feet and chased after her.

Once they were far enough away, Duncar handed her a dark cloak. They shrouded themselves before climbing into a tree to hide amongst the massive canopy. Sreana pulled her right ankle toward the limb she was laying along. It throbbed in pain and had started swelling from the fall and running.

Duncar took a swig from his flask, then passed it to Pirco. "What happened?" Duncar whispered over to Sreana.

"The guards caught me talking to the King."

Pirco almost spit out his water. "Talking to the King?"

"He saw your face?!" Duncar demanded, trying to keep his voice low.

"No one'd recognize me. It's not like I'm at the castle every day."

"We're going to need something stronger than water," Pirco admitted, handing the flask to Sreana.

~   ~   ~

After waiting out the Castle Guard's search nearby, the trio finally made it back home. Pirco and Duncar walked with Sreana to the hidden pathway that led to her lea, then they separated. She trudged up the path, her ankle throbbing more with each step. She entered her hovel, hanging up her sword and scabbard, then removed her boots. She grabbed an old shirt that she had tossed onto the dressing table earlier, before shuffling out to the firepit.

She sat on one of the logs, massaging her sore ankle in the faint firelight. She really did land badly. She grabbed the old shirt and ripped it. As the material looped around and around her ankle, she thought of the Grenan King.

She found herself lingering on his face. His dark brown eyes. They were the same color as winter mead. How they looked her up and down. His auburn hair. It was pulled away from his face and held back by a tie. How it curled down his neck in an unruly manner, like a toddler's. His beard. It had little shape, as if he just allowed it to grow on its own volition. How it was subtlety lighter in color. The touch of his hand. It wasn't smooth and dainty like other royals. How strong and weathered it felt, like it worked hard every day. And his lips…

She forced herself to stop, knowing that her thoughts about the King were improper. She tried to blame her fascination on immaturity, but she knew that wasn't the reason. There was something else, something different about him. Something unexpected. She shook her head, restarting her wrapping. Sedoran legends described royalty as the descendants of the gods, who came to these lands to lead the people. She knew from experience that it was just that, legend, but she wondered what Grenans believed.

But the Grenan King was nothing more than a man. A man with a limp. A man who hid away, apparently ashamed of his lameness.

Once she tied it off, she rubbed her jarred ankle before noticing Duncar nearby. The shadows produced by the flames made him look so much older. His graying blonde hair shimmered like the stars. His blue eyes were dark and sad, even though his face radiated frustration. They were about to fight again and her patience was already thin.

"I'm fine," she said, "thanks for asking."

"What do you think you're doing?" Duncar demanded. "Sneaking into the king's chambers? Letting him see your face? Jumping from balconies?"

His terrified tone startled her. "You were fine with me going there. I've done it a dozen times before."

"Because you only steal intel when you do. But speaking with the King…?"

16

She snorted. "Never said I had much intelligence."

"Cousin…"

"Oh, now you claim me?" she inquired and took her turn to glare.

"What is that supposed to mean?"

"You haven't called me family since you found me and Alarn in that bog."

His jaw clenched. "He was as much a brother to me as he was to you, Sreana."

She tried to keep her face blank, but if he could see her reliving that day in her mind, he didn't react. "I know. But ever since he died, we have not been the same." Sreana tightened her knot, then rested her foot back on the ground. "We pretend everything is fine, especially for our friends, but we are not and we haven't been fine for a long time." She gingerly tested her foot, then stood and hobbled over to Duncar. "Tell me, did you save my life – all four times – just for me to watch our people wither away like this?"

The hurt finally manifested on his face. He cupped her face gently with his calloused hands and a caring thumb stroked her cheek. She reached up and grasped his wrists, a heartfelt squeeze on his left one reciprocating that love.

"I saved your life so you could live," he answered.

"Is this the life you wanted me to live? Starving? Thieving? Hiding? None of this existence under Grenan rule is living."

"So why visit the Grenan King?"

Sreana glanced down, avoiding his questioning stare. Duncar dropped his hands and she let go of him as well.

"Curiosity," she replied. "And I would have killed him given a chance."

"Why didn't you?"

"Well, at first, knowing the consequences." Sreana bit her lower lip, then looked back into his eyes. "But I saw something in him tonight. Something I did not expect."

"What was that?"

She attempted to say something at least twice, the words escaping her.

Duncar sighed, impatient.

She shrugged finally. "A man. Not a megalomaniac, not a King divined by the gods. Just a man."

"And what are you going to do with that information? It doesn't change our situation."

"Yet."

"I am not going to like this, am I?"

Sreana smirked and Duncar rolled his eyes.

"You never like any of my ideas," she pointed out, "why start now?"

"Tell me tomorrow, after I had a chance to recuperate from today."

"Fine."

An awkward silence developed.

"How's your wound?" he inquired. "Using the salve every day?"

She groaned, tired of the same questions about her old injury. It always ended up as their go-to conversation when nothing else could be said. "Yes," she lied, "though I don't know why. The scar is no bother and it won't be getting any prettier."

"No, but it staves off any possible infections. You're still healing."

The quiet of the night settled on them again. Sreana searched for some sort of kindness, knowing that they both deserved something like that from each other. "Your father would be proud of the healer you've become."

He scoffed. "Yet you didn't ask me to look at your ankle."

She glanced down at her shabby attempt at a wrap. "I just jarred it. I knew you would order me to wrap it and keep it elevated. See? I listen to what you say, sometimes." She ran out of things to say. Anything that came to mind would probably start another argument she didn't have the energy for. "Good night, Duncar. May the gods keep your nightmares to themselves."

"And may they give you dreams worth dreaming," he responded automatically. Sreana started limping toward her hovel, then stopped when Duncar asked, "Can we ever go back to the way we were? After everything?"

"No," she answered, without hesitation. "War, death, all of that, it changes us and our relationships. The question is, can we survive? After everything?" She glanced over her shoulder at him. "That is an answer I do not have tonight." She ducked her head and entered, leaving Duncar alone outside.

~ ~ ~

Sreana had her foot elevated and her blanket tucked around her comfortably. However, speaking of the day her brother died in that horrible marsh kept her awake...

~ ~ ~

They had starved him, but he refused to let that slow him down. He didn't miss a beat as he fought off guards beside her. They had escaped the fortress as quickly as they could and entered the bog around it, trudging toward the tree line. They were both determined to put as much distance between them and the seized stronghold that had morphed into a horrific Carmanic prison.

She had sloshed ahead of him through the mucky swamp. When she glanced over her shoulder to check on her brother, she did not see the guard jump out of his hiding place. As the Carmanic soldier slit her across the abdomen, another came out of nowhere and skewered her brother. Even though pain enveloped her, at that moment, the agony on her brother's face would haunt her forever.

They both fell backwards.

The soldiers chuckled at their triumph and spit on their victims before leaving them to be claimed by the swamp.

Gasping and trembling, she listened to their departing footfalls. When she felt it was safe enough not to alert the soldiers that she was still alive, she rolled onto her hands and knees, then crawled to her brother.

"Alarn?" she whispered.

"Sreana."

She felt her tears burning her eyes as she grasped his shirt. She held on tight to keep from slipping and drowning in the muck. He placed a bloody, shaking hand on her cheek and gasped heavily.

"We die free," Alarn said, his voice faint but proud.

She coughed, tasting blood before responding, "We die free."

She watched as the life left him. His body went limp, his eyes blind and his hand dropped away. Sreana laid her head on her brother's motionless chest and closed her eyes, waiting to follow him into the afterlife.

Until a voice.

"Sreana? SREANA!"

~   ~   ~

She sighed, pulling her quilt tighter against her chest, but the bed and blanket gave no solace from the memories. Watching the life leave Alarn's eyes. Feeling her life draining from her body. The sensation of her leaving her body, lifting up to the sky. Touching the edge only to be yanked away. That chill still haunted her spine.

And it caused her anger to rise up.

She threw off the blanket and sat up. She left the bed and dressed, unwrapped her ankle and slipped on her boots. She hobbled to the horses and unhitched one of the stallions, not bothering with a saddle or reins, then rode out.

She headed north.

As the lone waxing gibbous moon broke the horizon, she found herself approaching the Temple of Dranar. There were many gods she could have turned to, but maybe just sitting at the feet of the goddess of mercy would relieve some of her burden.

She hitched the stallion and limped inside. The pain from her ankle was miniscule compared to the pain in her heart. The Temple was silent, only her uneven footfalls echoing. The mosaics on the walls told the story of Dranar's birth, her many miracles, and ultimately her martyred death that marked her ascension to god. By some divine intervention, the intricate stories and relics had survived the war. However, Sreana knew that if anyone could keep their sanctuary safe, it was the priests here.

She walked toward the wall of memories, where those who grieved lit candles and incense in remembrance, and used one candle to light the one she picked up. She set it next to the others, letting the flame flicker and sway and brighten.

Sighing, she shuffled away and sat near the feet of the deity's statue.

Her mind strayed from the beauty around her and fell back into the darkness that she had tried to escape. At first, she had harbored anger toward Duncar for resuscitating her. She entered that prison knowing she would not survive. Her only goal was setting Alarn free and if they were to die, they would die together. They would die fighting. They would be worthy of the afterlife promised to all Sedorans.

Her plan failed, all because her cousin revived her. Alarn was too far gone, but Sreana... apparently, she didn't die fast enough even after laying in that bog for days. She knew that wasn't Duncar's fault but...

Her response to everything should have been tears. To cry over her brother, over all the people she had lost. To cry over the fact that she didn't die like she wanted to. She hadn't cried since the night Alarn died at her side. It made her wonder. Like Duncar asked, could anything ever be the same? Would she ever feel anything other than anger and disappointment?

She recognized then that war and death and anger had twisted her into someone she didn't recognize. She glanced up into Dranar's merciful expression. There were no answers to her questions tonight. She started to get up when a voice startled her.

"A face I have not seen for a very long time," a woman mused.

Sreana looked up to see one of the priests approach her.

"Evening, Mirna."

Mirna smiled, her blue eyes sparkling in the candlelight. Her blonde hair was pulled into a ponytail and the curls trickled over her shoulders and down her back. Her pastel green sleeping gown covered almost every inch of her and flowed like an aura. She gracefully sat down next to Sreana, folding her hands and resting them on her knees. They knew each other well, from childhood and the days before the Carmanic invasion and the Grenan occupation. Both of their fathers were fishermen and their mothers businesswomen. Mirna had already pledged herself to the Temple years before the invasion and had wanted Sreana to join her. Sreana instead decided to fight.

"What brings you here, Sreana?"

"Quiet."

"Not evading arrest?"

Sreana chuckled. "Not today."

"I thought for sure you'd have had a hand in one of the recent incidents. Especially since something got burned down."

"I am not here to confess any trespasses."

"You come to the goddess of mercy, usually trespasses are required."

"Required to have, not to share."

"You have not forgotten the teachings."

Sreana shrugged.

"Are you sure you won't rethink your calling?" Mirna inquired.

"You know I would never fit in here. I hold too many grudges. I would be thrown out as soon as I pledged."

Mirna stared into Sreana's face, searching for something. "Why are you really here?"

"Guess I was looking for some respite, but only found a friendly face."

A comfortable silence settled on the two women as they stared at each other. Then Mirna made a disgusted sniffing sound.

"You stink, Sreana."

"I've never smelled good, even when we were kids."

"This is true. Your mother could never understand why you weren't right."

Sreana started laughing. "She had a daughter who wanted to be just like her brother."

Mirna stood, just as gracefully as she sat down, and offered her hand to Sreana. "Come, let me clean you up."

"Why? I'll just leave and get dirty again."

"Yes, but sometimes you need to get rid of the old layers to appreciate the new ones."

Sreana's eyebrow rose up, impressed. "Good one, Mirna."

"Been saving that one just for you. Come."

~   ~   ~

Scrubbed within an inch of her life, Sreana left before sunrise. As she traveled home, the Temple hid her under its shadow as long as it could. By the time the sun peeked over the horizon, she had arrived back in the township. It was still early enough that no one had started stirring yet. The township itself was two long rows of buildings on both sides of a dirt road. But behind them there was a sparse gathering of homes where she and a small group lived, hidden amongst the trees and moss. Unless one knew what they were looking for, they'd miss them. They had learned during the Carmanic invasion how to hide in plain sight. Now it helped them avoid the Grenan Castle Guard when they tried to arrest trouble makers.

She tethered the horse and started toward her home.

The shampoo Mirna had used on her wafted up her nose and smelled like seashells. She became homesick. She missed the smell of the ocean air. The sound of fresh fish coming out of the water. The birds calling down in hopes the fisherman would leave the fish guts on the piers for them to feast on. Memories of her childhood, of home.

However, their natural resources were being depleted by the Grenan occupation. So, here she was, thieving to survive and hiding like an outlaw. Her sacrifice of normalcy was worth it though, when she watched the people in her community enjoy the rewards of her crimes.

She sat on her bed, then flopped back and laid there, listening for the first signs of life. As she waited to hear the others stir, she realized her ankle wasn't throbbing anymore. She sat up and pulled off her boot. Even the swelling had decreased. She snorted. Mirna and her mysterious ways. She knew if she confronted her, Mirna would only tell her that the goddess had taken mercy on her. Just for safe measure, she lifted her shirt. No, her scar was still there. Guess the goddess could only handle a sprain today. She laid back down and closed her eyes. Sleep finally swallowed her into peaceful nothingness.

CHAPTER 3

When she finally made her way out of bed, it was late morning. Her ankle seemed to be in fine form, as if she hadn't jarred it just hours before and she actually felt rested for once. Dranar's mercy was in abundance this time. She whispered her thanks while running reverent fingertips along her book's spine.

Dressed comfortably, she walked out to the edge of her lea, to her little exercise area. She stretched her arms up, holding her staff above her. She bent at the waist, laying her hands and staff onto the ground. She followed through with stretching her arms, neck and legs until she felt limber enough to move.

Then she made her way through her exercises, slowly, to make sure none of her muscles protested. Seeing that she had stretched the sleep kinks out, she picked up to half-speed strikes, sweeps, and balancing of her staff. She let go of her thoughts as she moved, the exercises engrained in every muscle and nerve. But as she stepped and swung, his brown eyes flashed in her mind and she struck the nearby dead tree a little too hard.

She growled, annoyed at her lack of control. She hung her head and huffed, his face in front of her closed eyes. Lost in the moment, she let her thoughts linger. He seemed different. She had felt his honesty and the strength of his will. He was not afraid to show emotions, something that not many could manage, Sreana included. He didn't back down, he even acted defiant while her sword was at his throat. Sedoran royalty would have cowered, even begged or bargained.

He almost dared her.

He reminded her of the Grenan armymen she had fought side by side with during the invasion. Even though it took them a while to get used to Sedoran women fighting alongside them, they were good men, willing to protect and fight for people they barely knew. Together, they took out Carmanic camps, strongholds, and battalions.

When the Grenan King and his ministers stepped in after the Carmanic army had fully retreated, there had been hope that their mutual respect would have remained. But things changed incrementally. First, they took over forts, castles and other property once owned by the Sedoran royals. Next, they began to maintain the law. Even though the local leaders had it well under control at the time, the Grenan occupiers still stepped in. Then they moved in on food and other supplies, stating that it was the payment owed to them for their continued governance and protection. And if the Sedoran people had concerns, they should be taken up with the King.

A King no one saw or had access to.

Until last night.

And after her conversation with him, she wondered how much he really knew about life in Sedora. He said he would look into it. She sighed, unsure why she trusted the word of a man who hid away while others suffered. She questioned if exposing him to their life would make a difference, seeing that it had gone on for so long. But he said…

She shook herself. This childish infatuation was grating on her nerves. He was an occupier, an enemy. No, worse. He was the King of the enemy. How could a smile and a promise make her forget that so easily?

Frustrated, she landed a few good whacks with her staff against the tree. Unable to focus, her shoulders slumped and she walked back to her hovel.

~   ~   ~

Later that day, Sreana sat in one of the tavern's corner booths. The small meal of decent produce felt like such an extravagance. Real food had seemed a distant memory, but with a basement full, the luxury lulled her. She could pretend, for a moment, that life was calm.

She gulped down some mead as Pirco approached her table. Usually, Pirco was a light-hearted man with sarcastic tendencies. However, he seemed to have lost that today, because he looked quite displeased.

"Can you come with me, Sreana?" he requested, softly.

"Of course."

Sreana shoved in the last mouthful of food, laid down her utensils while she chewed, took one more gulp of mead, then headed outside with Pirco. They walked around to the alleyway behind the tavern, to the basement door of Trealle's stockroom. Out of habit, they kept glancing over their shoulders to ensure no one was trailing them. He unlocked the bolt and then gestured for her to head inside. He followed closely, shutting the door and reinitiating the lock. The room was already lit with a few candelabras, which made everything feel slightly tawdry.

Pirco moved to a dry sink, where Trealle's staff would divide food, and grabbed the blanket underneath that was snuggled against the wall. He laid it down on the prep table and unrolled it to show Sreana a sample of the different weapons stolen from the food storage unit. There was a saber, dagger, and shield.

"Do you notice anything odd about these weapons?" he asked, watching her intently.

"Other than the fact they appear to be unused?"

"Nothing else?"

Sreana picked up the saber and glanced over it. "Actually, I do not recognize the style."

"Because it's not Sedoran and it's not Grenan."

His tone made Sreana swallow hard. "Then who made them?"

"Carmanic Empire."

She laid down the blade and wiped her hand on her pants. "All of them?"

"Every single one. Carmanic made, but these are not from the war. They're not leftovers. These were made to order."

"Why the hells would the Grenan occupiers have these? And hide them amongst food?"

"That's what I've been asking myself."

She looked a little closer at the other weapons. At a quick glance, just like her, no one would immediately notice their craftsmanship. The Carmanic influences were disturbingly subtle, like the arch of the handle and the sharpened pommel.

"What made you research this?"

"When we stole them, I knew they weren't the usual design and the metal was all wrong for Grenan forges. And we never had anything this nasty in brute design. So, I uh did something stupid."

Sreana smirked. "That's been going around lately."

"I went back to one of the forts they occupied. Found a Carmanic sword." Pirco unsheathed a different saber that had been laying on another table. "This one's from the invasion."

Her smile faded immediately and she shivered. It showed signs of war, knicks and singe marks. Being so close to the kind of weapon that killed her family and people, one that almost killed her, made her a little nauseous.

"Same metal. Same forging. Just less stylish."

"I don't understand," she stammered. "The Grenan Kingdom has us; they have our lands and our resources. Hells, they have our bodies. What would make them want Carmanic weapons?" She knew whatever color she had drained from her entire body as her blood ran cold. "Either we have an inside job for another invasion," she deduced, "or the King has made a deal with the enemy."

He regarded her for a moment. "How comfortable are you with asking the King?"

She rubbed her face with shaking hands, then folded her arms over her chest to warm herself. "I do not fear the conversation. He should be confronted." Then she scolded herself, knowing that she had been trying to find a reason to go back to the castle. However, she didn't want to find out that the man with eyes like dark winter mead had aligned himself with the butchers who they had chased out just years before. "But I made quite the dramatic exit last time, doubt I can get in again so easily."

"Well, we need to talk to someone who knows what the hells is going on. I don't want to be in the middle of another war. And I sure do not want to be under Carmanic rule."

"Anyone else know of your discovery?"

"And start a lynching of all Grenan occupiers? No. I know better." He grimaced, rolling the weapons back up. "I haven't even told Duncar." He met her eyes again. "I do not like keeping secrets from him."

"I know, me either."

"But you keep some good ones from him."

"May the demigod of deception never fail me in that regard."

"So now what?"

"Honestly, I cannot even fathom why these are needed."

"To quell us? To keep us from causing trouble?"

"That's an awful big swat for such little bugs like us. Prior to our latest adventure, we've only stolen back what was ours."

"And arson only happens when you lose your temper."

She watched him return the weapons to their hiding place and sighed heavily. Then Sreana's eyebrow raised up, a devious expression. "Does that one kitchen drudge still have a crush on you?"

The old Pirco materialized in a wicked smile. "Maybe."

~   ~   ~

With the help of Pirco's smitten kitchen drudge, Sreana entered the castle grounds a few days later under the pretense of a delivery. When the Castle Guard finished their rounds on that side of the building, she slipped out of the kitchen and headed up the hidden back stairs the drudge pointed out. She hadn't used them the last time; they led her directly into the King's bedchamber instead of the balcony. She entered warily, glancing around, from bed to couch to balcony… the King was nowhere in sight.

Through the glass double doors, she noticed that the curtain she had swung from had been taken down. The bent rod itself laid on the ground, twisted and scratched, as if abandoned. The matching curtain that drew from the other side had been pulled to the middle of the balcony, to block the evening's wicked weather from reaching into the bedchambers.

A flicker of lightning and she caught sight of herself in the reflecting glass. She fussed with her hair for a moment, letting it down and shoving the tie in her pocket. She still looked like the thief she was, but at least she smelled better.

That morning, she had taken a dip in the river and even washed her hair, before feeling the storm roll in. She thought she heard a shuffle and darted behind the armoire by the servant's door. Silence returned. Settling into her hiding place, she scolded herself, knowing that her motives to clean up were not just for her. She sighed, unsure how long she'd have to wait.

Suddenly, the King's voice carried down the hallway. "I will not repeat this again. I will visit the Sedoran people. They must see me. And I must see them. It is only fair to find out what conditions we as caretakers have left them in. I have recuperated long enough."

"But sire…" a high-pitched voice tried to argue.

Silence hung there but she could sense the look the King gave his audience. "Arrange it," he ordered, the sternness in his voice surprising even her.

"Yes, my King," another voice placated and she could hear the man's clothes rustle as he bowed.

She listened as the large doors to the balcony closed and latched. She heard a heavy exhalation, which made her raise up on her knees and peek out. He had started disrobing, unaware of her presence. First the large cloak flopped over the back of the high-backed chair. Then the puffy shirt noblemen always wore, tossed into the chair's seat. When he was down to his undershirt and trousers, she realized, embarrassed, that she had turned into a voyeur. She cleared her throat. He startled, grabbing his staff to defend himself. When she stood up, his expression went from fear to surprise to pleased.

"You need to work on your security, Your Majesty," she chided, leaning against the piece of furniture. "They'll let anyone in here."

"But how would I see you again?"

Sreana was slightly taken aback by that. "Am I that amusing?"

"That leap off my balcony was quite entertaining. You left my guards rather baffled." He set down his staff and crossed his arms. "I'm glad you came back. I wanted you to know that I had not forgotten my promise." Then he grimaced in displeasure. "Even though my ministers are being very argumentative about the situation."

"Is the King's order not enough?"

"It is not," he answered, looking at her with eyes dark, "when the King is a mere mien."

Sreana moved in front of the armoire and watched as he wearily sat on the edge of his bed. "You think you have no real power?" she asked, surprised. After all, they were always told to take their concerns up with the King.

"I think I have given much of it up."

She couldn't resist jumping straight in. "Will you need weaponry to regain your control?"

"What does that mean?"

"It means," and she felt her irritation suddenly swelling, "what do you plan to do to regain control of Sedora? If you find me a liar, how do you plan to subdue us?"

27

"Regain control? Subdue?" he demanded, confused. "You must tell me what you are alluding to."

"Have you allied yourself," and Sreana swallowed hard, even as her rage was getting the best of her, "with the Carmanic Empire?"

He stood up quickly, facing her, flushed with anger. A loud clap of thunder shook the air. He didn't shout as she expected, but kept his voice low and dark. "Why the hells would I do that? Why are you here, accusing me without proof, of something my Kingdom swore against ages ago?"

Even though there was some distance between them, his fury almost burned her, making her consider her next words carefully. "We found Carmanic weapons hidden in the Grenan food storage units. Newly forged, unused."

His knees buckled and he sat hard on his bed. "How could that be?" Another round of thunder. He rubbed his face with his hands, speaking almost to himself. "We are never to go back to the days of dealing with devils. We learned the hard way when Sedora made that mistake. We lost too much trying to fight them out of both of our borders throughout the decades. Why would we let them back in?"

"What would you know of the fighting?" Sreana made her way to stand in front of him. The thought of him understanding the true damage of the Carmanic invasion made her seethe further. "You are a king."

"I am also an armyman," he responded, offended by her assumption. "I know what it is like to fight. I've seen people fall in battle. Just like you. Why do you assume that I am so sheltered?"

She scoffed. "Show me your scars and I'll show you mine."

"No, you first."

A flash of lightning indicated her acceptance of his challenge. Hand grasping the bottom of her tunic and the shirt underneath, she lifted them up. He lowered his eyes to see her exposed belly. And the scar that ruined its otherwise perfection. Just looking at it, he could tell it hadn't healed right. It ran diagonally across her torso, from under her left breast, down between her rib cage, across her stomach and pelvis, then disappeared into her slacks on the right side of her body. Parts were flesh colored while others were still dark pink. The bulbous portions indicated various infections at one point or another and the skin overreacted during its healing.

"Carmanic saber," she explained.

He stood, nearly pressed up against her. He unbuckled his belt, loosened the waists of his slacks and undershorts, then let them fall to the ground. He turned slightly, exposing his right leg's exterior. Wordlessly, she examined the damage. A long, thick, scar ran from below his knee and up toward the hip. It was slightly raised, but not as nebulous as hers. There were smaller scars that uniformly intersected with the main one, where the stitches had penetrated. His tunic covered the end of it as it hid his more private parts.

"Carmanic ax," he responded, voice gruff.

She looked into his eyes, both knowing that there was more to their injuries

28

than just the weapon that caused them.

"We are more alike than you'd care to admit," he whispered, not wanting to scare her away. "I know we understand each other because we both bear scars from the same war."

Silence held them there, both half-naked and emotionally vulnerable. And very close to each other. When the irony hit Sreana during another rumble of thunder, a smirk manifested.

"What?" he inquired.

"I just realized I got the King half-naked."

It was his turn to smile. She felt his hand sneak along her waist until it rested on the small of her back. Then he pulled her up against him. She let go of her shirt, one hand on his chest.

He felt the cold point of a dagger subtly pressing against his tunic. Gently, he grasped her wrist, feeling resistance at first, then coaxed that hand up to join the other one. The tip of her dagger tickled his throat, still a warning. Giving her that power, however, let her know she had control of the situation. And even though he wanted to undress them completely and make thorough use of the bed next to them, he knew he made the right decision. He leaned closer, his beard brushing her chin.

"You started it," he retorted.

Sreana's feistiness dissolved, her stomach quivering. She felt a lump lodge in her throat. They were at the perfect angle for more than just a face-to-face flirt. What would he do? As much as she found herself attracted to him, her fears paralyzed her. He could kill her or worse... He must have seen something in her eyes because he didn't move closer.

"Do you believe me?" he asked, softly. "That I've nothing to do with those weapons you found?"

Unable to resurrect her voice, she nodded.

"Good. I want us to be honest with each other. It's the only way we can both help your people." He inhaled, deep, the moving air tickling her cheek and his expanding chest pressing against her hands. "Why did you really come here the other night? No lies."

"To steal information."

"Was that the first time?"

"Sneaking in? No. Seeing you? Yes."

"And when you saw me, what did you want to do?"

"Kill you."

"Do you still wish to kill me?"

She searched those brown eyes of his, questioning her own sanity. "I don't know."

"Good."

"No, no it's not."

Without realizing, her empty hand had touched his face, running its fingers through his beard. With his free hand, Gregor cupped it as it lingered against

29

his cheek. "If we want what is best for Sedora, we must get past some things. One is you wanting to kill me. Two is me wanting you arrested for invading my private chambers. So far, I think we're doing pretty well for unsolicited allies, don't you? Now in the spirit of honesty, with you getting me half-naked, there are other things on my mind right now that would make even your randiest gods blush."

Sreana laughed, nervously.

"But I need you to do something for me."

"What's that, Your Majesty?"

~   ~   ~

He had to let her go. Even if unwillingly. They were being foolish. He knew that. He knew she knew that. However, he couldn't help himself. His thoughts lingered on the memory of her body pressed against his... he wasn't sure what to do with all of these new feelings.

The light pitter patter of rain lulled him. Her pliant body told him one thing, but her eyes said another, which stopped him from any further movements. He only wished that he hadn't seen that fear. He hoped she would be fearless and completely receptive next time.

Gregor stared out over the courtyard, hoping to catch a glimpse of her escaping. He knew she would not be so obvious this time, especially since she had managed to remain undetected while inside. Still the memory of her standing below, giving that cocky salute, had fascinated him for days. Sighing, he headed back into his bedchambers. The servants would come in soon to bathe him and ready him for bed.

After all this time, it had taken a would-be assassin to remind him who he was. Who his people needed him to be. And who her people needed him to be. Now if he could get his ministers to remember who he was, before his injury...

~   ~   ~

The next morning, as Gregor readied for his day, he stared at himself in the reflecting glass. He had let himself go, at least in appearance. He had kept up his exercises, catering them to his injured leg, but his hair and his beard, he looked more like a nomad than a King. He sighed, rubbing his chin. Then he heard the house staff enter to help him dress.

"Can you send for the barber, please?" Gregor asked.

Surprised, they smiled and nodded, before disappearing down the stairs. Then after a brief wait, the barber came in with his shears and razors. They moved a chair to the balcony and Gregor sat down.

"I need a haircut," the King said. "And please clean up my beard."

"Would you prefer clean shaven, Your Majesty?"

The memory of her fingers running through his beard made him smile. "No, just clean it up enough to be presentable."

CHAPTER 4

Sreana laid awake for most of that night. She tossed and turned in her bed, trying to come to terms with her feelings and reality. Their interactions wrapped her in a warmth she couldn't fathom. She had never felt that before, with anyone. However, foolish emotions like that made things messy. She knew he understood that as much as she did; his eyes had told her so.

She also knew that whatever connection they seemed to share made her hopeful. Why did they have that connection? What made him any different than all of the other royals she had met in the past? Was it his humanity? Was it that he was an armyman? Someone who fought not only for his kingdom but hers as well? Someone who also became injured during that time? Someone who understood pain and heartache?

She shook herself. She was making assumptions. Just because he was injured didn't mean it was because he was efficient as an armyman. His colleagues could have been glad for his removal from their ranks. After all, the Sedoran Royal Family only knew how to pick up a blade when it was dinner time.

Yet there was a real request made, despite his attraction.

Be his spy.

Work for the enemy? Was he the enemy? Their people used to be allies. Could they be allies again, even after everything?

She had begged for some time to consider his proposition. His eyes had expressed his disappointment, but he ceded to her appeal. However, when she had tried to leave, he wouldn't release her immediately. She had to give him credit for his honesty, admitting his attraction. But for him to be so straightforward, not to mention the feel of his body against hers, it caused confusion in her and, deep down, she had wished she could have done the same.

There was still that battle inside her… her heart told her one thing, her brain screamed another. Why was she being so childish? However, her fear and anger kept her distrustful, reminding her of the one truth that her heart kept skipping over.

He was a King.

Worse yet, he was the Grenan King. And like all the other royals she had known in the past, he could be all talk and leading her on. After all, royals had few imperatives: have children, have riches, and above all else, have power.

She believed him when he said he had nothing to do with the Carmanic weapons. And yes, he made promises but, as she had learned throughout her life dealing with the Sedoran royals, she feared his follow through. She didn't want to find herself in that trap again, left to pick up after those who were supposed to lead and care for their people, but who did the very opposite.

Once the sun broke over the horizon, she left her bed. As she readied herself for the day, she caught sight of her reflection. Ultimately, it revealed the truth. She had her hovel and her thieving. He had his comfort and servants. They couldn't be any more different. And any requests made by him were truly orders for the subservient. And if she agreed to be his spy, she would be nothing more than a servant.

~   ~   ~

Hiding away in one of the corner booths, Sreana ate a simple breakfast of porridge and fruit. She recited in her head what she would tell him, how she would keep herself out of reach, how she would avoid looking into those dark winter ale eyes. As she chewed absently, she swirled her spoon in her bowl. Her thoughts kept her from noticing Pirco's approach. She only snapped out of it when he sat next down to her.

"How did your visit go?" he asked.

"He denied any knowledge of what you found," she answered softly, after swallowing her mouthful. "He actually was quite upset."

"And you believed his reaction was authentic?"

"I did." She glared at him. "Do you think I'm naïve?"

"Of course not. But you've only just met." She didn't let up her glower, making him shrug nonchalantly hoping it would soften her expression. "I'm just saying that you don't know him well enough yet."

She scoffed, glancing back down at her bowl. "And I won't be getting to know him well enough. He will visit our people and make his decisions based on what he sees."

"Even if his own people put blinders on him?"

"If he can't figure it out by himself, what else can I do?"

"You won't be making this a habit then?"

She shoved another spoonful in her mouth then shook her head, trying to keep her response at a minimum.

However, Pirco recognized her expression and sighed. "What happened?"

"He made a proposition."

Pirco's eyebrows popped up. "Oh?"

"Not that kind," she responded, pausing to reminisce about how close he had been the night before. How comfortable his body felt against hers. She blinked and brought herself back to reality. "He asked me to be his spy. To be his eyes and ears out here and report to him things I believe he should be aware of."

"That is an honor, is it not?"

"No. Such a request feels more like enslavement than partnership. He is a King asking for obedience, but I am not his servant or his subject. I can't think of a worse fate."

"Which means you'll have to go back and turn him down?"

Sreana grimaced, finding herself actually dreading the conversation. However, she couldn't shake the image of him standing on the balcony waiting for her to return. "Probably would be rude to leave him unanswered. You'll have to let me know what I owe you, for your sweet drudge's amenability."

Pirco chuckled. "Fear not, I have a whole list of things."

~   ~   ~

A couple days later, Pirco's lovely drudge helped Sreana sneak back in under the darkness of night. She crept up the servant stairs, but when she entered his chambers, he was nowhere to be seen. She listened, then realized that he was in an adjoining room speaking with two women. Startled, she darted behind the armoire and wondered what she had walked in on. She held her breath as she heard the two women walk through the bedchamber, murmuring to each other. She caught a glimpse of them in the reflecting glass. They had clothing in their hands and smiles on their faces as they exited the chamber, trotting down the same stairs she had come up.

Silence settled.

She heard rustling. She peeked around the armoire to see the King entering the bedchamber. He wore only his undershorts and his hair was still damp. He approached the dressing table, grabbed a brush and ran it through his hair. The auburn curls fought back, making him sigh. Her eyes moved from his head to his back, watching the muscles shift under his skin. Even though he had his limp, it was obvious he kept his body fit. She noticed a scar along his lower back that matched one on the back of his right arm, just above the elbow. Her eyes followed the muscles of his arm back up to his head until she caught him watching her in the reflecting glass. Meeting his eyes, she went pale momentarily then felt the heat in her cheeks.

"I've learned it's not safe to walk around naked in my own bedchambers," he admitted, with a sly smile.

Stepping out from her hiding place, she rolled her eyes. "Fix your security and I wouldn't be able to sneak up on you."

"Then I would never see you again, would I?" he inquired, turning toward her. He leaned against the dressing table, crossing his arms over his chest.

"No, but it may save us from an embarrassing encounter. I would hate to accidentally walk in on… something private."

Puzzled, he stared at her, then realized how long she had been in his room. "The household staff help me bathe and dress, as it is difficult with my leg to manage it all alone."

Her blush deepened, embarrassed by her assumption. She glanced out the doors, clearing her throat nervously. "I see they finally fixed the curtain."

"Took some time to find the replacement parts."

Then she approached until she stood in front of him, but remained out of reach. "And I see you have a few more scars than you had shared. I'm sure Grenan has had its own issues on other borders."

"You're right, this wasn't my first campaign." He looked her up and down, before asking, "Notice anything else?"

She raised one of her eyebrows, curious. When she realized what had changed, she forgot her previous decision to keep her distance. She stepped closer and reached out to trace his chin, her fingertips just barely touching his beard. He grasped her hand, letting it brush along his cheek. As it moved along his face, her thumb encountered his lips. They felt so soft against her callouses.

"Thought it was time to be a little more presentable." His eyebrows furrowed, concerned. "You don't approve?"

"I'll have to get used to it," she responded, trying to pull her hand back.

He kept it firmly in his. "I thought I should look more fashionable. I will be heading out soon to see your people. No matter what, I will keep that promise."

"That's all I ask."

"I assume your return also means a decision about my offer?"

His question snapped her out of whatever spell that had befallen her. "It does," she confirmed, keeping her tone resolute. "And I cannot be your spy, Your Majesty. I am either your enemy or your ally. Nothing more."

He straightened and yanked her arm without warning, causing her to careen into him. "Nothing more?" His other hand crept along her waist until it rested on the small of her back and he held her against him. It also encountered her other hand, the one clutching her dagger's hilt, and he gently caressed it, loosening her grip and allowing their fingers to intertwine. As he pressed her close, he relished her immediate pliancy. "Have I not made my feelings quite clear?" Then delight turned into worry as her softness dissolved into stiffness and there wasn't fear in her eyes.

"You have." Sreana swallowed hard, glancing nervously at the nearby bed. The temptation was too close for her liking. However, she reminded herself that no matter her attraction, there was still one wedge between them. "But I fear I have not made mine clear." She lowered her eyes and backed out of his embrace. "I cannot be a King's courtesan."

35

As he let her go, Gregor stared at her in shock. "I did not ask you to be a courtesan."

"What a man says," and she paused, her face unreadable, "and what he means are not always the same thing."

He regarded her for a few breaths, realizing that whatever happened in her past still weighed heavily on her. He was unsure if it was something that occurred before, during or after the invasion but it colored her view of the world in quite a bleak shade.

"What can I do?" he asked, hesitantly. "To make you want me, unconditionally?"

Sreana scoffed, impressed by his audacity and flattered by his attraction. But that question… it hurt her heart. She raised her eyes to meet his, her expression heartbreaking. "Not be King."

"Does it matter that, when I am with you, I am not a King?"

"No. And it is foolish to think otherwise."

He wanted to ask her why, but whatever they found in each other seemed immediately severed by her answer. "Then I will respect your wishes, my lady," he replied, as his shoulders slumped in disappointment.

Seeing his reaction, she felt herself drowning when the awkward silence settled. "I should go." And with that, she started toward the servant's stairs. "Fix your security."

It took a moment for her words to register. "Will I not see you again?"

She slowed her gait, then responded over her shoulder, "No, Your Majesty, you won't." And with that, she disappeared.

He hobbled to the top of the staircase then stumbled backwards a few steps, grabbing the doorway desperately. She was already gone. As quickly as he could, he made his way to the balcony and looked down, in hopes of one last glance. Just one. So maybe that farewell wouldn't be their last moment.

~   ~   ~

She made it down the stairs and to the end of the hallway before it hit her. She stopped, leaned her forehead against the wall, and let the whimper escaped. It took everything for her not to run back up there and throw herself into his arms. Had he leaned forward, touched her lips with his, she would have caved completely. In a feeble attempt to break herself free of her childish emotions, she rubbed her face. She would not sneak back in, even if he didn't keep his promise. They would never see each other again.

Then noises brought her back to reality. Survival instinct kicked in and she pushed down her foolishness. She slipped into the shadows, listening as the guards plodded past her. She mused how easily it was to find the guards. Stomping down the halls in unison, side by side, two guards always. How could they protect the king if they were so obvious?

Light in her periphery caught her attention. Sreana waited until the guards were far enough away to dart across and she stealthily approached the doorway. Then she pressed herself against the edge of the doorframe, which had glass sidelights with different colors in some sort of design. She peered through a small sliver of clear glass, hoping to avoid detection. Inside was a small office, with a desk, candelabras, and stacks of parchment that varied in sizes.

Standing near the desk, almost hunched over while he searched one pile, was a tall, dark-haired man. He wore the robes of a minister in the Grenan King's cabinet. She could barely see his face at such an odd angle, but his thin nose and square jaw made him a strange looking man. He moved documents around the desk, then pulled one sheet out of the group, folded it, then slipped it into a messenger envelope.

Footsteps sent her down to the edge of the hallway, snuggling into another door frame and its closed door. She remained within hearing distance and from her vantage point, she could see who was approaching.

Striding right past her toward the small office was a soldier. He wasn't in the same regalia that always haunted her nightmares, but he did bear the insignia on his shoulders. A tower surrounded in flames.

The insignia of the Carmanic Empire.

Her stomach twisted and her jaw clenched. Sreana reminded herself to breathe, to be patient. After all, how could she find anything out if she killed every armyman she saw? She bit her lip, hard, as he entered the room.

"You're late," the minister grumbled.

"Your King's demands on your time kept me at bay," the Carmanic soldier replied. "Get him under control or get him out of our way."

"Do not make demands of me. You are insignificant." She heard a rustle of a sleeve and assumed the envelope was handed over during the pause. "Here. What your commander needs to know. Get out."

The Carmanic soldier scoffed, then exited the room and headed back the way he came. The minister extinguished the flames from the candles then left as well, striding past the hidden Sreana without a glance. When the minister was out of sight, she set hers on the Carmanic soldier.

~   ~   ~

The soldier strode out of the castle and across the gravel walkway to his horse. She moved swiftly to catch up to him, mindful of stealth. Whatever he had in that envelope, she needed to know what it said. Before he could mount, Sreana jumped him from behind and slit his throat with her dagger. They tumbled to the ground. When he didn't move again, she grabbed the envelope, ripped off one of his badges, then ran to her exit in the castle wall.

~   ~   ~

Sweating and anxious, Sreana returned to her hovel. She stumbled to a halt when Pirco and Duncar stepped into her path. Both of the men's faces fell pale when they noticed the smears of blood on her.

"What happened?" Pirco demanded, moving closer to look her over.

"None of its mine," she reassured.

Duncar folded his arms across his chest. "Where were you?"

"Where have you been?" she snapped at her cousin.

"Sreana."

"No Duncar, you don't get to chastise me. We've got bigger problems."

She raised her hand, the one holding the letter and the insignia. Pirco grabbed both, then opened the envelope. He unfolded the letter, started reading, then cursed.

"Assassination orders," Pirco said. "Telling the Carmanic soldiers to proceed with killing the King."

"Where did you get that?" Duncar demanded, glaring at Sreana.

"They plan on killing the King," Pirco mumbled.

"Does it say when they plan this assassination?" Duncar asked.

"Just says something about an outing the King will be on."

"Is this the outing you talked him into doing?"

Sreana sighed, frustrated. "Of course it is. What's the best way to expose a weakness? Send someone out into an area they are unfamiliar with." Sreana rubbed her forehead with her fingers and thumb, pinching the skin as if it helped her think. "They kill the King, blame us, and allow the Carmanic Empire to march in and subdue us."

"Did you tell the King?" Pirco asked.

Duncar looked displeased. "Did she do what now?"

"No. I killed the soldier after I left his chambers so I didn't have a chance to warn him. I would have been caught had I gone back up because I kinda left the body in the courtyard."

"Now they'll definitely look for a woman that matches the description of the original trespasser," Duncar complained.

"That sketch looks nothing like me."

"Well, you intercepted the message," Pirco interjected. "Do you think that we've stopped it?"

"No, it feels like something that was planned in advance. This is just a confirmation that the plan was still in place. They'll move ahead without it."

"Are you going back to tell the King?"

She felt her heart quiver, thinking about his disappointment over her farewell. "I don't think I'll be able to get to him in time. He said his outing would be soon. It took your lovely drudge two days to get me back in. And with a body in the courtyard, they will be on the lookout for someone who doesn't fit in."

"Then I guess we need to come up with a plan to save the King."

Sreana smirked, mirthlessly. "In public, no less."

~   ~   ~

As Pirco and Sreana sat next to the firepit, Duncar watched despairingly from a distance. He knew anything they planned would end up with them dead. Either during the rescue or at the gallows. He didn't want to witness her demise considering what they had suffered through after her almost-fatal injury.

He had told Sreana that she had faced death at least three times after he resuscitated her in the swamp. She just never knew how much it tortured Duncar to watch her agonize. He had spent so many nights by her side, wiping the feverish sweat from her brow. He held her hand during nightmarish fits, where she begged for her brother. There were nights where Sreana struggled to breathe, edging towards death once again. At one point, Duncar swore he saw tears. During those horrible nights, he wondered if a slip of too much painkiller would have been a mercy… All it would have taken was a miscount of drops… but then he pondered if she would haunt him for such actions.

He saw the disappointment in her eyes when she woke to find that she had survived the rescue mission. But she never lashed out, she never demanded why he didn't just kill her. When she wasn't unconscious, she lay quietly and didn't show any other emotions. It led to their division. They had been so close.

Until he saved her life.

Now he debated if he could allow her to take off on yet another suicide mission. It wasn't in her blood to give in, he knew that. She picked up her sword, she said, because she couldn't expect anyone else to fight. After she went on her suicide mission for her brother's freedom, Duncar laid down his own sword to fight for her life. He wished Alarn was there to ask what he should do.

"Duncar?" Sreana's voice snapped him out of his thoughts.

"We could really use your help," Pirco added.

"Of course."

~   ~   ~

Later that night, after finalizing their plan, Sreana grabbed the reins of the fastest stallion. Pirco still looked dubious as she handed over her sword, while keeping her dagger sheathed.

"If I don't come back, Mirna either agreed to my plan or… she killed me and buried me somewhere on Temple grounds. Either way, if I'm not with you, stick to the plan."

"Hold the line, you got it."

With that, she rode out. It didn't take long for the Temple to rise up before her. She surprised herself at how hopeful she was as she spurred her horse to his top speed. She dismounted, tethered the horse, then entered. Thankfully, she arrived late enough in the evening that many worshippers had already left. The only people who remained were the priests. Three of them were straightening up and murmuring amongst each other.

"Pardon my interruption, but where can I find Mirna?" Sreana asked the priest closest to the entryway.

"Priest Mirna is in the garden," the red-headed woman answered.

"Thank you."

Sreana walked past the statue of Dranar and headed out a back door that led into the garden. The garden itself doubled as a stronghold, with its towering walls and only one entry point. Cut into the walls were small hearths, where fires provided light throughout. All herbs attributed to Dranar grew here under the watchful eyes of the priests, planted after the invasion to limit the priests' time away and to keep them safe inside the Temple.

Mirna kneeled near a bush of nettles, her back to the doorway. Humming to herself, and probably to Dranar, the priest gathered herbs and blooms, placing them in a medium-sized woven basket. Sreana could make out lavender, cloves, and a colorful array of pansies laying carefully inside.

"It's a little late for gardening, Mirna."

Mirna straightened up. "Never too late to serve our god's will."

When Mirna turned to face Sreana, Mirna's expression was a warning.

"What did I do?"

"Were you at the castle the other night? Swinging from the curtains?"

"Um, why would I be at the castle?"

"Sreana," and Mirna's tone made her cringe, "I know how you are."

Sreana knew they had issues about her warrior side, but she wasn't sure if she had the strength to fight with Mirna, especially knowing what kind of favor she needed from the Temple of Dranar.

"Can we please go somewhere a little more private?"

Still glowering at her friend, Mirna grabbed her basket. She led Sreana to her private bedchamber, which was the furthest down the hall, locking the door behind them. Sreana usually enjoyed Mirna's chamber; it was decorated like their hometown port, with seashells, starfish, netting. Such simple things that reminded them of better times. However, her current visit made the room almost claustrophobic knowing what she was about to tell her childhood friend.

"I was at the castle that night," Sreana admitted, "I've been there a few times, meeting with the King."

Her friend laughed. "You? Meeting with the King? Don't you mean trespassing?"

"Why do you think the Grenan King is taking his tour? He didn't just get bored, Mirna." She sighed, hard. "I know I skirt the truth. A lot. Especially with you because you judge like no other priest I know. But he actually listened to what I had to say."

The glare she received reminded her that she had to tread lightly.

"Is the goddess in a helpful mood tonight?"

"Depends on the ask."

"We found out that the Carmanic Empire has plans to assassinate the Grenan King. Now, if we try to warn them, they will likely ignore our warnings and arrest us on sight."

Mirna scoffed. "Carmanic Empire assassins, here, in Sedora? Nonsense. The Grenan Kingdom helped us evict them and now protects our borders." She paused, apparently recognizing the concern on Sreana's face. "What proof do you have?"

Sreana opened her belt purse, then pulled out the insignia she ripped off the soldier's shirt. Blood still stained the gray parts of the tower.

Mirna didn't move. She didn't take it from Sreana but she also couldn't take her eyes off of it. Mirna would never speak of what happened to the priests when the Carmanic army rampaged through the area. They knew how to hide their relics and treasures, but Sreana knew that not all of the women could hide themselves in time.

"What can I do to help you?" Mirna asked, softly.

Sreana shoved the insignia back into her satchel, then wiped her hand down the leg of her pants as if to rid herself of its stench. "Are the priests going to meet the King during his tour?"

"Yes, of course. Priests from all of the nearby Temples will be there. Even those of the Temples that fell. We'll be taking gifts as well. Why?"

"You'll be close to the King?"

"Of course." Then her tone went dark. "Why, Sreana?"

"I need to get as close to the King as I can for as long as I can."

Mirna's eyes narrowed, her anger burning Sreana's skin. "You want to pretend to be a priest to get near the King? Absolutely not! Why would you want to be that close to the King?"

"What if it was to protect him?"

Mirna laughed, surprised. "Protect him? You?"

"I know it sounds insane. But they are going to kill him. And right now, he's a better ally than the Carmanics. Wouldn't you agree?"

Mirna stood frozen, before shaking her head vehemently. "No, I'm sorry but no. I can't let you defile the Temple by pretending to be something you have refused to honor and accept."

Bitter silence held them tight.

"Then I will find another way," Sreana responded, keeping her tone even.

"Thank you, though, for at least entertaining the idea. I should go."

She unlocked the door and strode out of Mirna's chambers. Mirna didn't waste time slamming it behind her. As Sreana made her way down the halls, another woman walked past her. She was exactly Sreana's size and height, maybe slightly wider...

Sreana glanced around to find they were completely alone, whispered, "Forgive me, Dranar," then spun on her heel and followed the other woman...

CHAPTER 5

The priests from the Temple of Dranar were last in a long line of those paying tribute to the King. Each priest wore the same ceremonial clothing. The full skirt was constructed using several panels, each a different shade of blue. When the priests walked, it looked like they moved through ocean waves. The bodice cinched in the back, with the peacock blue ribbons running down the back mimicking kelp. A voluminous blouse covered it, from neck to waist and from wrist to wrist, in a reflection of their god's piety. Matching slippers covered feet from toe to ankle, while the headdress had intricate beading and a veil that covered the entire head, stopping at the shoulders. The priests braided their hair and wrapped it into a bun on the top of their heads, then secured it with the headdress. Under the veil, they were required to adorn their cheeks, forehead, nose, and eyelids with white, blue or gray paints. Hands and fingers were also painted with blue to represent the tides.

Mirna led her group up to the dais and they curtseyed down to the ground in waves. A well-practiced transfer of weight made their movement flawless as they returned to their feet in rows. Mirna offered the King herb infused wreaths, creams, and a handwritten journal of Dranar's teachings in mercy.

The King thanked her, as he had with the other Temples for the demigods, with a bowed head and a gift as well. However, the gift to Dranar differed from the other Temples because Dranar was a main god. It was a book about Grenan herbs, their healing properties, and how to find them. The priests once again curtseyed, then moved to their appointed section to the left of the dais.

Once the spectacle was over, the King thanked everyone in attendance. Then he walked, slowly to hide his limp, to his carriage. Even though the seat in the carriage was padded, the ride through the townships had been a rough one. The lack of maintenance to the roads made them bounce around and it caused his leg to ache. That was one thing he mentally took note of as something to fix. Once he began to climb the steps, the crowd started to disperse. With the voices and footfalls filling the outdoor amphitheater, it was hard to hear anything else.

Until the thwap of something hitting the carriage. Startled, Gregor glanced over at the noise. A crossbow bolt had embedded itself into the carriage's side. Two more thwaps and he heard the guards next to him crumple. The crowd began to run and scream in fear and confusion. Gregor closed his eyes, knowing the next bolt would find him.

However, instead of a fatal shot, a hard shove made him tumble into his carriage and the door slammed shut. He laid there startled, then tried to sit up. The whip snapped and his carriage lurched forward, causing him to fall backwards. He tried to see out the small windows, but all he saw was deep sea blue scarves rustling from the driver's seat. He heard a woman's voice urge the horses on while tree limbs flashed past and bashed into the carriage. All he could do at that point was hold on.

CHAPTER 6

Sreana had kept close to the King, even as the other priests started to leave. She could feel Mirna's curiosity as to why her follower wasn't following, but Sreana didn't budge. Until a crossbow bolt sung past her ear. She ducked, then stayed crouched as she watched the two guards on either side of the King fall dead. He paused, as if expecting and accepting his death. She jumped back to her feet and charged, shoving him into the carriage and slamming the door behind him. More bolts landed, barely missing her but pinning one of her skirt's panels into the side of the carriage. She ripped the panel off then climbed into the driver's seat. Snapping the reins caused the horses to startle, then leap into a full gallop. She almost toppled out of the seat, but a leg braced against the seat's metal frame kept her secure.

She urged the horses out into the wilderness, following a small path that seemed barely used. She, the horses, and the carriage took abuse from low hanging tree limbs and untamed bushes, but they kept charging forward. Yelling from behind warned her that they were being followed, and unsure if they were friend or foe, Sreana directed the horses down a hidden path to the left and they burst through the shrubbery onto the lesser used road. Then she guided them into a hollow under the massive stone that held up the main road above, the very road she had just abandoned. The carriage and horses barely fit, however since her pursuers hadn't seen her bail off the main road, they continued on and sped above then past her. She collapsed on the seat, her breathing ragged and her heart trying to pound out of her chest.

Knowing they were safe for the moment, she wrapped the reins and climbed down from the driver's seat. Sreana flung the door open to find the King still laying on the floor of the carriage and staring at her in shock.

"Are you injured?" she demanded. When he didn't answer, she asked in a kinder tone, "Are you hurt?"

The shock wore off into surprise as he recognized her voice and those gray eyes. "I am unharmed."

She sighed, relieved. Then from behind her a panicked voice. "You kidnapped the King!"

As she stammered, Duncar and Pirco ran toward her. "No, I rescu…" Sreana's eyes widened. "Oh, oh not good."

They stared at her then glanced, frightened, at the man in the carriage.

Duncar shook her. "What were you thinking?"

"I had to get him out of the line of fire…"

"You're quite far from that now," Pirco responded, making Sreana glower at him.

They heard shouting, still a distance away but getting closer.

Duncar sighed, hard. "We need to get out of here. They'll find him soon."

"So they can kill him in the middle of nowhere?" she demanded. "And conveniently blame us?"

"What are we supposed to do then?"

"We need to write a ransom note," the King suggested. Sreana and her friends looked at him in surprise. "Grenan policy is to follow any directions outlined in a ransom note," he explained. "Tell them not to search for me and to await further instructions. That should buy you some time."

"And then what do we do with you?" Duncar asked.

"He comes with us," Sreana answered.

"WHAT? Have you lost your senses?"

Sreana sighed, glancing between Duncar and the King. "If we leave him here, he dies. If he comes with us, then we can show him the truth. That's why he's out here now, to see what has become of us, not some false pageantry. Who better to show him the truth than us?"

Pirco blew out air so hard his lips sputtered. "We are so dead."

"I will write the note, they will recognize my handwriting and honor it," the King responded, digging for parchment and quill. He located everything he needed, wrote the instructions, and then gave it to Sreana. She in turn stabbed it through one of the bolts next to the carriage's door. Then he finally exited and was surprised that it wasn't just the four of them. Groups of three guarded them on either end of the road that led to the ravine, swords and staffs at the ready.

"Bring the horses," she called out to the others. "It might take them too long to find the carriage and the horses don't deserve to be prey." Two different men walked to the carriage and started unfastening the geldings. She turned back to the King and grimaced at his outfit. "Take your cloak and puffy shirt off. You need to blend in a little better and those will not help." He followed her instructions, tossing the clothing into the carriage. He turned back to find her fighting with her torn blouse. She sighed then asked softly, "Can you ride?"

"I will need assistance up."

"Tell me how."

"If someone already mounted helps pull me up, I can manage my leg over."

Sreana nodded, then mounted her horse. She removed her feet from the stirrups, shifted herself into a leveraged position then offered her his hand. He grabbed it, slipped his foot into the stirrup and used her strength to pull himself up. With enough height he swung his lame leg over the butt of the horse and was able to seat himself behind her in the saddle. She helped slip his foot into the other stirrup then she righted herself. He wrapped his arms around her waist and she tapped her reins against the shoulders of the horse. The stallion started off into a trot, sending them deeper into the wilderness. As they traveled, Gregor found himself lost among the trees. He never knew how thick the woods were, only that the canopy seemed to reach for miles from his castle fortress.

He turned his attention to the woman in front of him. He held her tightly around the stomach, to make sure they didn't slip off the horse, and he felt the muscles in her abdomen. He knew she was a fighter, just by the way she held herself, but the strength in those muscles meant she was much more than just some upstart. She had training and had maintained it. He glanced along the rip in her blouse and saw the toned arm that she must have honed during the war.

In contrast, the beating she took through the forest made her look chaotic. The face paint diminished the fierceness he had gotten used to. Half of the petals from the skirt were missing. The tattered headdress looked more humorous than sacred. The trees they had just ripped through even gashed her cheek, the blood caking the wound quickly.

He hooked his chin over her shoulder. "I don't even know your name," he whispered against her ear.

That smile of hers flashed. "That's not an accident."

"I can't just call you 'my lady.' And I'm sure someone will call your name eventually."

"Sreana."

"Suh-ree-na," he enunciated, smiling pleasantly. "It is good to finally know your name." They rode in silence for a little while, then he asked, "Where are we going?"

"My home."

As they rode up to the main road, there was a fork. Sreana halted their horse, confusing the King. Then one of her friends sidled up, handling a sack.

"Sorry, dear King, but we do have to protect ourselves," her friend said, slipping the sack over his head.

With it secure, Gregor felt the stallion start walking again. "This is rather embarrassing," Gregor complained, his voice muffled.

He heard Sreana chuckle. "You should see it from this side."

~   ~   ~

47

First, he felt the horse halt. Then he blinked against the sunlight as the bag over his head was removed. As his eyes adjusted, he found himself in a small meadow. It was surrounded by ancient trees, abundant foliage, and the sounds of excited birds. Sreana watched him over her shoulder, then she urged the stallion over to a stump, which he used to dismount. Once he was clear, she also dismounted but on the other side, then handed the reins to one of her friends. She continued to watch him, amused, as he looked around in amazement. When his eyes returned to hers, she gestured for him to follow her. She led him directly to her hovel and entered without a word.

Her home was modest. No, it was less than modest. The home was smaller than his private bathing room. As he looked around the small cave-like room, questions ran through his mind.

"This is where you live?"

She glanced around her little hovel, smiling. "It is. Safe, warm, home."

"Is this how everyone lives?"

"No, others live in towns, in actual buildings." She saw his disbelief and shrugged. "But this isn't the worst I've lived in."

His eyes continued to take in everything, then stopped near the bed. "You have two swords?"

"That one is my brother's."

"Will I meet him as well?"

"Not in this life." Then she glanced down, realizing how badly the trees had demolished her stolen outfit. "I need to get out of this ridiculous thing." She stuck her head out and motioned for Pirco, who jogged over from her firepit. As he handed over her sword and scabbard, she requested, "Please keep him company while I change?"

"Of course," Pirco responded. "Dear King, please, we have a fire and dinner has been started."

Gregor waited for Sreana's nod, then followed Pirco. Sreana stripped herself of the priest garb and began to wash off the paint. As she scrubbed, she encountered the gash on her cheek, cleaning it meticulously and putting pressure on it until it stopped bleeding. Then she slipped into her other set of slacks, tunic, and boots. She belted on her sword and scabbard, slipped her dagger back into its sheath, and tied her hair back and up into a crooked bun.

Feeling more like herself, she exhaled. She touched the spine of her prayer book, thanking Dranar for protecting them and again asking for her forgiveness. Then she reunited with her friends and the King outside.

She handed the leftovers of her outfit to Pirco, who promptly tossed the evidence into the roaring fire. Then she moved to the King's side. He reached up and caressed her cheek where the tree limb had scratched her. She smiled, patting his hand reassuringly, then he leaned in.

"I wish to speak with your leader," Gregor murmured into Sreana's ear.

"Remember what I told you on the balcony? I do not have unfettered access to this leader."

"You are good with your phrases, Sreana, but you know what I mean."

"Then you should read through my words and understand that I have no such power to fulfill your request."

They stared at each other, trying to gauge who would break first. Instead, they were interrupted by footfalls. He dropped his hand and Sreana glanced over his shoulder, her eyes widening. He followed her gaze and saw a small group standing at the edge of her little lea. She excused herself then walked over to them and they quietly spoke with her. He could tell she was trying to clarify something, but they appeared unmoved. Her shoulders slumped, then she bowed her head to them and walked back to Gregor.

She smiled with some chagrin. "I tried to explain that you were not here to cause trouble, only to visit me... but my friends are adamant. They wish for you to see the entire community. Not just my corner."

"I would be honored to see your community. It is why I am here, is it not?"

She hesitated, the smile fading. "I don't want them exposed or to have fear."

"I will not expose them," Gregor responded. "That would benefit no one."

"Then come, let me give you the tour."

They departed her little corner, leaving behind the forest and her small lea, and headed down the dirt road. She kept a slow pace, knowing what he had done to keep his limp hidden from the public. They walked around some foliage and before he knew it, they entered a quaint township. Buildings that varied in height and shape lined both sides of the main dirt road. There were small walkways between some of the buildings, leading into alleys and other areas that hid sheds and stables.

Gregor stopped, glancing at the life around them. People walked around on their daily business, women with baskets of laundry or food, men with carts of ore or hay. They chatted with each other, catching up on the daily news or checking in with family members. Children played in the road, kicking balls or throwing them to each other. Two children chased one another around and under the empty hitching post nearby. He looked over at Sreana, who watched him with a smile.

"This is the main township," she informed him. "But there are farms, dairies, and ranches further out that call this their community as well. Come, there's more," she insisted, heading down the road and past homes that were actual buildings, like she had described.

He followed, his heart filling with joy. Before him were the Sedoran people he remembered, who still held that resilient spirit he had seen during the invasion. People walked past, bidding them a good afternoon but none bowed or curtsied. He must have appeared confused because Sreana chuckled.

"They know who you are, but they do not think you should be treated different than anyone else. For today, you're one of us."

"I'm honored."

As they headed further down the road, a door swung open and an exclamation reverberated. Then, a little girl, caked head to toe in mud, came running out and collided with Sreana's legs. She looked up with big brown eyes, surprised, her face surrounded by flashes of muddy blonde hair. Sreana placed her hands on her hips, bemused.

"Sabira! Get back here!" a voice yelled from the house. A woman rushed out of the door, her hair and eyes matching the little girl's.

Sabira tried to escape but Sreana grabbed ahold of her and kneeled. "And where do you think you're going?"

The little girl huffed. "I don't want to take a bath!"

"Oh, Sabira." Her mother's shoulders slumped and she sighed. "I do not know what I will do with her, my lady."

"You sound like my mother when I was her age, Habni," Sreana responded, with a laugh. She turned her attention back to the wiggling child in her grip. "Sabira," and the girl stopped struggling, "sometimes you have to take a bath. After all, how can you appreciate the new layers of dirt if you don't get rid of the old ones?"

The little girl blinked, then grinned. Seeing that she understood, Sreana let her go and she darted back into the house. Habni laughed tiredly, then noticed the mud on Sreana's hand. The exhausted mother handed her the wet towel she had been holding. After wiping her hands clean, Sreana handed it back. There was a splash a few moments later.

Habni stepped back to see inside and shook her head. "Not with your clothes on."

"At least you can get all the washing done, child and laundry."

Habni thanked Sreana before entering the home again. The door closed as the playful banter started between mother and daughter.

Sreana chuckled, looking up at Gregor. He offered his hands and helped her back to her feet. Standing face to face, he didn't let go and his smile indicated more than amusement, which in turn caused a heat in her cheeks. But in his eyes, she could see the conflict between sadness and other feelings. Before he could say something, a voice from across the road interrupted them.

"Sreana?" Trealle called.

She pulled her hands free of his, turning to smile at Trealle.

"They're at it again."

Sreana rolled her eyes, then turned back to Gregor. "I need to handle this. You're welcome to go back, I can have someone escort you."

"I think I am quite enjoying a day in your life."

She shook her head, then motioned him to follow her into the tavern. As they entered, two men stood facing off at the counter. One man was short and skinny, black eyes angry, and graying hair hiding his darker brown locks. The other man was tall and portly, with blue eyes and graying blonde hair, and looked as if he could bounce the other man out of the tavern using the girth of his gut.

"Garol, Pendarn, we meet again," Sreana announced as she approached.

"My lady," both men responded, but they did not take their eyes off of each other.

"Is there a reason why poor Malteri came up again?"

"You have to admit, my lady, she is ugly and terrifies all the children," answered Garol, the tall man.

Pendarn, the short man, trembled in anger. "It is not her fault! She had no say in how she looks."

"First, it is rude to insult his heifer," she chastised Garol. Then she turned to Pendarn, admitting, "Second, I mean is he wrong? That cow is not... normal."

"But she gives the best milk!"

"I agree, Pendarn, her milk is the prize of our community." She turned back to the other man. "Do you disagree, Garol?"

"No, my lady."

"Let's make a deal then. Next time you have a disagreement, insult his attributes, not his cow's? Agreed?"

"Agreed," both men answered, then finally turned away from each other. With the dispute settled, they bowed their heads to Sreana before leaving.

Sreana gestured for Gregor to move toward an empty booth in the far back. He sat down first and scooted, giving her room to sit on the same side. Following them, Trealle smiled and handed Sreana two mugs of mead then mouthed, "Thank you." Sreana bowed her head respectfully, then handed one of the mugs over to Gregor and took a sip from the other.

"I would like to see this nightmare cow."

She chuckled. "She leaves an impression. Maybe next time."

They sat in silence as the noises around them ebbed and flowed. She observed him as he looked around, seeing how her people interacted. At one table, two men worked on a standing puzzle in the shape of a god. Another one was surrounded by three men standing, intently watching the two seated women who had playing cards held close to their chests. Next to them were two women bartering in hushed tones until they came to an agreement. People walked past their table, either nodding at Sreana or completely oblivious. Gregor's expression shifted between amazement and concern.

She smiled, reassuringly, but couldn't resist teasing him a little. "No one here will hurt a captive, I promise."

When he looked at her, his eyes had the same emotions from earlier. "You're the only one holding me captive."

Cheeks warming, she lowered her head, clearing her throat, but found it difficult to respond. She began to stammer, so she lifted her mug to her lips in a vain hope of saving herself.

He cringed when he realized what he had said. "I will try not..." and he stopped, unable to finish his sentence.

Awkward silence as the noise in the tavern filled their ears.

"My lady?"

Sreana looked up in surprise, then grinned. A young couple had stopped at their table, holding hands and smiling. She glanced between the two, then cocked her head and asked suspiciously, "Areama, Adir, what are you up to?"

Adir blushed. "She said yes."

Sreana jumped out of the booth and hugged both of them, all three laughing. "Finally!" she exclaimed.

"You approve?" Areama inquired, looking relieved.

"Of course, why wouldn't I? You two have been driving me crazy this last year. If he didn't ask, I was going to order it."

The couple laughed.

"You'll be there, right?" he asked.

"All I need is the date, time, and Temple," she responded. They promised to deliver an invitation soon, then they bowed their heads in respect before rushing out of the tavern with wide smiles. Sreana sighed happily, slipping back into the booth.

"You lied," Gregor said, softly, before drinking from his mug.

She furrowed her eyebrows, confused.

"You are the leader."

She scoffed. "No, just the peacekeeper."

"I have learned enough about your people to know that Sedorans do not call their peacekeeper 'my lady.' And they do not ask a peacekeeper to approve a marriage. They reserve that for someone of a higher rank, like a leader. Maybe even royalty."

"Believe what you will," she replied, smirking into her mug.

Seeing that she wouldn't take the bait, he sighed. "Should we talk about why you kidnapped me in the first place?"

"Rescued."

"Ransom note," he retorted.

She groused into her mug. She stared at the remaining liquid, seeing him out her peripheral watching her. She set down her cup. "Follow me then."

She slipped out of the booth and he did the same. She led him out of the front door, then around the back of the building into an alley. They walked to the cellar doors and she unlocked one. Swinging it open, she motioned for him to enter and she followed, closing it behind them.

As he carefully made it to the bottom of the steps, he first smelled the dankness of the dirt and stone. However, once he rounded a corner, he saw the different food stored there. On one side, fruits and vegetables, fresh or canned. On the other, meats hanging near a smoking fire or laying in vats of salt. The smoke seeped out of the makeshift flue just enough to stamp down the earthiness of the basement, reminding him of the smokehouses back in Grenan.

"This wouldn't happen to be food from our storage units?"

"We have to eat. Even if it means stealing back what was ours." She turned and grabbed a basket. Inside were small, pock-marked vegetables and over ripened fruit. "This is what we were allowed to keep after the last visit. This is what the meat and grains look like too. Can't feed children with this."

"Including yours?"

She raised her eyebrow. "Subtle. But no, children like Sabira. We expressed our… frustrations, as usual. They responded like they have all the other times. Take it up with the King."

She watched as his eyes narrowed and she could feel the heat of his anger. She stepped back, not sure what he would do. He took a deep breath, which was shaky, but as he exhaled, it steadied. He looked at her and must have seen her caution in her eyes.

"I can't stand being made into a monster."

"Isn't that what we've been demoted to? The Sedorans are monsters, criminals, just a group of homicidal, ungrateful trouble makers."

"Some of you wear that as a badge of honor."

She shrugged nonchalantly. "Yeah, I can't argue with that."

"That is the difference. You have the knowledge and the choice of how to respond to what is being said about you and your people. I have neither. And I refuse to allow it to continue. I can't believe my people would take so callously from those we are here to help."

"Greed is an amazing catalyst for change in someone."

He reached out and cupped her face, making her hands clasp his wrists in response. "I will find a way to fix things. No matter what. It will take work, but I am willing to put in the effort."

The honesty in his eyes rattled her, and his closeness caused other emotions to rise, so she pulled away as gently as possible. When he appeared concerned, she cleared her throat. "This isn't the only reason why I brought you here."

She turned and removed a bundle swathed in a tarp from behind the sink. She set it down, then unwrapped it. She felt Gregor straighten. As the metal winked in the low candle light, the weapons menaced both Sreana and Gregor and she caught the King rubbing his scarred leg.

"Do you know if they've been treated?"

"They have not, we checked. Since Carmanic soldiers don't poison their weapons until right before an attack, whatever they were planning wasn't going to happen immediately." Then she flipped open her purse and handed over the note and military badge. "I took this off of a soldier who was leaving your minister's office. Was there a report of a dead soldier the last night I was there?"

"No, not to me."

"Convenient."

"I waited to see you leave," he admitted, his voice soft. "I didn't hear anything. Are you that… efficient?"

She hated that question, rewrapping the weapons and sliding them back into their hiding place. "You have to be sometimes."

"Do you know who he spoke with?"

"No, I am not familiar with those in the castle. I think he was a minister, but you have quite a few. It's my word against his, though, and he has deniability even if I recognized him."

"This is something I never wanted to see," he replied, his tone hurting her heart. Instinctively, she reached out to touch his hand. He grasped it, appreciating the comforting gesture. "But now that I am aware, I can start rousting the traitors. At least now I know I have them. I will have to negotiate the situation… carefully. Especially after this attempt on my life." He squeezed her hand. "I must ask for your patience as my steps may seem invisible to most but they will be purposeful."

"Patience is not one of my strengths," she responded, honestly. "Neither is blind faith. It will not be easy for me to sit still. And you should know that I will do what I must to protect my people. They have not healed from the first invasion and they cannot weather another one. Either Carmanic or something closer to home."

"And that is why I have to make sure you understand that I take all of this seriously and will not falter in my convictions. I will fix what has happened between our people. If you can understand that and be patient, not commit any crimes that I will have no choice but to punish you or your people for, then I know all Sedorans will give me time."

"I wish I was who you think I am, Your Majesty." They stared at each other, then she finally sighed. "Supper should be close to done. We should head back." She tried to walk away but he didn't move or let go of her hand. She stopped and stared at him, confused.

"What happened that made them look to you?"

"Your Majesty…"

"Tell me."

She chuckled mirthlessly, making her way back to his side. "During the invasion, you had to make life or death decisions. And sometimes those decisions were not popular or smart. Many of those who were in leadership were not afraid to sacrifice lives even if they knew they would lose. I believed sometimes you had to pick your fights carefully so you could not just win battles, but survive them too. It made no sense to die because you could. The more I argued, the more I was ignored by our supposed leaders. But they didn't matter. Those who did listen were my comrades, people who fought by my side every day. We made our own way and survived while the others didn't. It just didn't seem to change after the fighting was over."

"There's more to your story than what happened during the invasion."

"Maybe. But that's all you get tonight."

"Will I have more nights then?"

Sreana looked away, trying to hide her face crumbling.

"You were never coming back, were you?" he asked.

"I only snuck back in that night to turn you down and, since you had no further use for me, why keep endangering my life? And I got the one thing I needed that night. You said you would keep your promise and I could only hope you would."

"And after today?"

"We'll go back to our lives," she answered, choosing her words wisely. "We both have a lot of work ahead of us."

"We do, but we still need to work together. I know you do not think yourself a leader, but it is obvious that each person here does. I also think it's safe to assume that they would follow you into any battle happily. And I believe that this respect and support extends outside this community. Which is why I believe if you can have faith in me, so will they."

"Then remember that my reputation is at stake just as much as yours."

Gregor nodded. "That's fair."

She tried to walk away again, but his grip held her still. Her eyebrow raised, somewhat curious, somewhat annoyed. "What else do you want to ask me?"

"Will you answer?"

"Depends on the question."

"We're surrounded by a beautiful township. Why do you live in such a small space away from the people who you care about? You could live like the rest of your community."

Her wry grin flashed. "You want the honest or the diplomatic answer?"

"Diplomatic first."

"I'd rather live in a hole, if that means others could live in better."

"And the truth?"

"I am a wanted criminal by our Grenan occupiers. Shouldn't I hide?" She chuckled, pulling on his hand. "Come, supper time."

~   ~   ~

When they returned to the lea, Pirco motioned her over. He noticed that they were walking a little too close to each other, and as they approached him, he could see that they were not quite holding hands, just fingertips entwined. As tempted as he was to tease, he watched how they looked at each other and wisely said nothing. They would either realize it and pretend it was a coincidence or they would figure out their attraction and act on it.

"We got confirmation that the Castle Guard has backed off from their hunt, which tells me they found your ransom note," Pirco explained. "They did interrogate the Dranar priests, but that was only briefly, because they received the orders to return to the castle."

Sreana grimaced, knowing there would be consequences for her desecration. But she would have to worry about that later. Her friends brought plates filled with small servings of different Sedoran food. She thanked them and led Gregor over to the makeshift benches near the fire. The others made room for them, allowing them to sit next to each other. He reviewed his dish, smiling curiously, and she chuckled.

"I know it's not your usual Grenan faire, but tonight we dine on roasted beef, with a variety of small vegetables in the gravy, along with mashed potatoes made with garlic and cream."

"It looks wonderful," Gregor responded, before taking a bite of the potatoes. His smile widened as a sound of delight escaped. "It's delicious."

While they ate, her friends shared the day's news. Apparently, the King's kidnapping was the tale of the day, with fantastical theories and grandiose assumptions being made throughout the communities. Sreana felt awkward, knowing none of it was true. The King was at her side because of an impulsive decision, not necessarily a noble one. But the amused look on his face calmed her nerves.

Gregor watched as the men and women talked and ate, switching out places at the firepit to enjoy the company of their leader and her guest. They came from different walks of life and from different regions of Sedora.

He met one pig farmer missing his arm from a munitions attack by the Carmanic Army late in their campaign. A woman moved around with a crutch to support her one good leg, explaining to the King that the other had been removed to save her life from infection because of Carmanic poison. Another man, who was a tanner, walked with a cane and had missing fingers, another victim of the invaders' torture. Next to him was a dairyman who limped, telling Gregor that he had been crushed by a building during another munitions attack.

Even with their wounds, they proved their resilience. They still worked in their chosen profession, even if it meant with help or adjustment. They were a proud people, especially considering what they had survived, and he had missed seeing these amazing spirits since he had gotten injured. However, his own injury seemed miniscule compared to the others around him.

After they finished eating, her friends took their plates and started cleaning up. Sreana felt useless, wishing to help, but didn't want to leave the King alone for anyone to accost. Instead, she explained the reason her firepit existed and why it was important for each community to have communal areas where everyone was welcome at any time.

Then Sabira tugged on her sleeve, and when Sreana acknowledged her, the child crawled into her lap. Sabira's hand rested on Sreana's hilt, playing along the beveled tang, until her eyes grew heavy and she started to fall asleep against Sreana's chest. Habni appeared and picked the child up, thanking her for watching her daughter, then mother and child headed down the road to their home.

While they sat around the fire, the group told stories Gregor had never heard before. They were warm and welcoming, making sure that he was involved in the conversations. However, some came to him with testimonials about treatment they received by their Grenan occupiers. Taking produce, meats, and other items without paying for them. Harassing farmers and merchants when they didn't have anything to give. And families tithed when they had no funds to support even their own households. When each person finished their story, Gregor thanked them and humbly asked their forgiveness for the behavior and for his ignorance. Each person was promised better days ahead.

Sreana listened, hoping privately that he would keep his word to each of her friends. Suddenly, Pirco squeezed himself in between Sreana and another woman, pushing Sreana up against Gregor. Gregor had to move his arm, slipping it behind her and resting his hand next to her on the log. She rolled her eyes and knocked Pirco with a shoulder, but he only laughed.

As the night wore on, the group thinned. Each time someone left, they wished Gregor a good night and disappeared back into town. Eventually the only ones remaining were Sreana, Gregor, Duncar and Pirco. Even though they had room to spread out, as Pirco did when the others had left, Gregor and Sreana did not, almost oblivious to the concept.

As they laughed at another one of Pirco's jokes, Gregor shifted on the log. A hand touched his knee.

"Is it bothering you?" Sreana asked.

"I will be fine," he answered, timidly. "Between the riding and the walking, I have done more in one day than in the last few years." He laid his hand on hers, in reassurance. "But it is a good thing."

Then the King realized that Duncar was staring at him. Not at his face but at his leg. Gregor began to feel self-conscious about the man's attention. Apparently, Sreana caught the moment and leaned toward Duncar. "The healer in you forgets his manners."

Duncar blinked, then bowed his head toward Gregor. "I apologize. I have treated many wounds and I wondered about your limp."

"I wouldn't know where to start," Gregor admitted.

"If you would permit, I could to take a look. We can use Sreana's home for privacy."

Sreana smiled and ran her hand along her stomach. "He might have some good advice for you."

Gregor nodded. "Any advice is welcome."

Both men stood and Duncar led the way to Sreana's hovel. She watched as they disappeared inside, then returned her eyes to the fire. Nearby, she heard Pirco snort. She glared at him as he took a swig of his mead.

He looked over with a smirk. "Not what I expected at all."

"What do you mean?"

He shrugged. "It's like you said, he's just a man. Especially when he looks at you."

She rolled her eyes, taking a sip of her own mead.

"Would it be so bad?" he inquired, his teasing tone goading her. "He's not ugly." That warranted him a darker glare, which made a devilish gleam flash in his eyes.

"He is still a King."

He lowered his voice as he replied, the tease gone, "He is not like any King we knew."

Sreana didn't respond, staring solemnly into her mug.

"Not all men are the same," he added. "I'm proof of that!"

She scoffed, a small smile returning to her face. "That, my friend, is a given."

"Then give him a chance?"

"In the hopes of what, Pirco?"

Pirco started to answer, but they heard Duncar and Gregor speaking as they exited her hovel and they both fell silent. Duncar noticed but wisely said nothing. Gregor returned to Sreana's side, who had stood up to greet the two men.

"Were you able to help, Duncar?" she asked.

Duncar sighed as he sat down. "Some suggestions."

"Which I will share with my healers," Gregor replied. "It is nice to have another opinion."

She turned, handing her mug to Pirco. "We should probably let you get some rest, Your Majesty. You've had a long day but it's too late in the evening to send you home. And I think we are the only ones still awake."

Gregor nodded, after stifling a yawn.

Pirco gathered the others' mugs as well, bowed to her then to the King. "May the gods give you dreams worth dreaming."

"And may the gods keep your nightmares to themselves," Sreana responded.

Pirco headed down the road. Duncar worked on taming the firepit while Sreana led Gregor back to her hovel. Once inside, she fussed with the quilt, then gestured to her humble bed.

"You can sleep in here, you'll be safe. Duncar will watch over you."

"Where will you sleep?"

She moved away and started stoking the fire in her small stove, adding small logs and kindling. "I will sleep elsewhere."

"I don't feel safe with anyone but you."

Her eyebrows raised up. "Even if I still don't know if I want to kill you?"

"Even if, because you have been quite honest about it. But it does seem foolish to want to kill me after you saved me from assassination."

She groused, then sighed. "Please, get comfortable. I will speak with Duncar."

She exited her home, lingering in front of the closed door. She didn't know what to do. Was it wise to sleep next to a man who she found desirable, who had already expressed his attraction to her? But he did promise to respect her wishes...

Duncar saw her thinking and waved her over. "What's wrong?" he asked as she approached.

"He wants me to stay instead."

He glowered toward her hovel. "Do you think he'll be inappropriate?"

"No, of course not. I just..."

"Do you want me to stay nearby?"

She faked a smile, trying to hide her concerns. "If he tries anything I'll break his hand." She patted his arm, in thanks. "Go sleep in your bed."

"May the gods give you dreams worth dreaming."
"And may the gods keep your nightmares to themselves."

~ ~ ~

When she returned, the King was sitting on the bed, only in his undershirt and undershorts. His pants and tunic were neatly folded on the stool next to her table while his boots stood next to it. His hair freed from its restraint, it curled unevenly around his face. She moved to her cedar chest and pulled out her own sleeping clothes. Then she hesitated, realizing he was staring at her.

She smiled, somewhat lopsided. "I can't change while you watch."

He apologized then stood, turned his back to her, and patiently waited. A cool hand on his elbow let him know it was safe to look again. When he turned, she wasn't next to him, but hanging her sword next to the other one. She wore the same type of clothing he did, undershirt and undershorts, however they were thicker and darned in the seams with different colored threads to keep them wearable.

Her hair was down, swaying down to the middle of her back. He wanted to reach out and play with the locks, to twist them through his fingers. He craved to feel her skin against his fingertips, no matter the consequences, not admitting to himself that sleeping near her was probably a bad idea. But he remembered the look on her face that last night at the castle, her stepping out of his embrace and the resentment in her eyes...

She turned back around and frowned, then folded her arms over her chest. "You should lay next to the wall. That way they'd have to go through me to get to you."

He nodded, then climbed into the bed. The mattress wasn't even but it was at least comfortable. And the quilt was thick enough to keep heat trapped. She laid with her back to him, facing the doorway in a protective manner. He sighed then rolled onto his side as well, placing his back against hers. As the night sounds crept through the small window, they both fell asleep.

CHAPTER 7

When he woke up in the middle of the night, they were facing each other, having shifted in their sleep. As he laid there watching her, he tried to untangle his feelings. It hurt his heart that she believed she could only be a courtesan to a King. He wanted more. He yearned for a companion, someone who understood war, wounds, heartbreak, and making difficult decisions. He saw that kindred spirit in her, someone who had survived atrocities but still had the will to lead and protect her people. However, her assumptions about what a companionship with him would be like kept her from seeing him as a man. She had already made it clear that as King, he would be nothing more than some Royal from a foreign land residing in a castle that had belonged to someone else. And he didn't know how to prove to her otherwise.

The moonslight cast ghostly shadows on her face, giving her an ethereal glow. He had never seen her so peaceful. Even while they joyfully spoke and laughed with her friends, there was never a moment of real relaxation for her. He could tell by her rigid spine against his arm. But her sleeping serenity gave away her secrets. She was younger than he thought, maybe even close to his age. Her anger and fear and wounds had matured her rapidly in front of the whole world; they even stole the color from the lock of hair above her left ear. But now, momentarily free of her concerns, she was the young woman who still had so much to offer that world around her. He wondered if he could find a way to permanently relieve those burdens so she could take a step out of the darkness. He recognized his foolishness immediately, thinking it would be he who fixed everything for her.

His gaze wandered along her cheek and down to her lips, which were slightly parted allowing her to exhale. Then he saw the scar on her bottom lip. It looked like a natural impression when one glanced at her but now he realized it wasn't. It was too odd of a mark to be made by a weapon and looked old, like a childhood injury. He smiled as he wondered what mischief led to the blemish and if she would even tell him. The image of her smirking at him in response warmed his heart.

Her eyes blinked open and she noticed his gaze. She furrowed her eyebrows, either in confusion or concern, he wasn't sure. Then she reached out and caressed his cheek. He cupped her hand with his and nuzzled her palm, briefly closing his eyes. Then he ran his lips lightly along her fingers. The sensation of her callouses against his skin felt sacred. He moved their hands to his chest, letting them rest against his heart. He leaned forward but stopped, remembering her wishes.

As if realizing his unspoken hope and his respectful restraint, she met him halfway. Then a soft caress of lips, feather light. It wasn't enough. He wrapped his arms around her and pulled her against him. They kissed again, and again, their desires overriding any previous concerns. He grabbed her leg and rolled onto his back, letting her straddle him. She sat up, which made him sit up too, so he could hold her against him. She draped her arms around his neck and kissed him deeply, their tongues playing. The taste of her, the feel of her, even her lingering fingers in his hair drove him senseless.

Pain broke through his madness. He hissed against her lips, flinching and trying to shift his leg into a less painful position. She recognized the cause of his discomfort, moving to kneel on his other side. She pulled his shirt over his head, rolled it and placed it under his knee while adjusting the position of his leg. When she saw it wasn't enough, she removed her own shirt and added it under his thigh. The adjustment and support relieved the pain, causing him to sigh. He stared at her in amazement, her attentiveness warming his heart.

As she returned to her position on his lap, he appreciated her nudity. He saw that her scar not only ran across her abdomen, but it also cut into her left breast. The lower portion, under the nipple, was missing and what remained was marred with damaged skin. He caressed it, then slid his hands along her body down to her thighs. He lifted, urging her up onto her knees, and she complied. With her bosom at face level, he ran careful lips along the scar. Then he moved to her right breast and, with his patience waning, he greedily sucked. He heard her gasp and a small moan escaped her. He finally released it, sighing against her neck before kissing it. She moved away again, this time causing him concern. It was only for a brief moment, as she took time to remove her undershorts and to help him out of his. Both now completely naked, she straddled him again, with his hands helping to guide her. As she surrounded him, they both exhaled small sounds of delight.

The movement of her hips felt extraordinary. He looked down to watch her sway, moving a hand between them. He wanted to taste her skin, but her breasts were too low, so he moved his mouth again to her neck. With her movements and his massage, she quickened her rhythm until a soft, satisfied sound escaped her. That sound in his ear and the feel of her body reacting, he loved it and he wanted more, but found he could not hold off his own release for much longer. He moved both hands to her hips, holding her against him as he pushed deeper. He let himself get lost in her. Then he heard another moan as she stiffened, rapt in another wave of gratification, as he achieved his own pleasurable ending, his coinciding exclamation muffled against her skin.

Shaken by the intensity, he leaned against her. They held each other for a few moments, their panting the only sound filling the room. When he looked at her, she smiled adoringly, which was contagious. Then he kissed her lovingly.

She moved back to his side, then helped him lay back down. He laid on his back while she laid on her belly, with half of her resting on top of him. She pulled the quilt back up and they covered each other with it. His upper arm was trapped beneath her but he could bend his elbow and caress her hip. She ran her fingers through his beard, cheek to chin, while his other hand lightly rubbed her arm. They stared at each other, speechless, trying to catch their breaths. Their eyes began to fall heavy, their exertion finally driving them back to sleep.

~   ~   ~

When he woke again in the morning, she had disappeared. He reached out to where she had laid and found that her warmth had not yet faded. He sat up, searching the small room for any sign of her. Her clothes, which had been neatly folded on top of his, were missing. There was only one sword on the wall and her boots were gone.

Resigned that her escape meant regret over their union, Gregor began to dress. He gathered his clothes and turned back toward the bed. He noticed a small patch of moss along the wall. Fragile looking pink flowers dotted the green, several in full bloom. It was an odd place for a plant and he didn't think that it had been there the night before, but shrugged it off as he finished getting dressed. He had his hair pulled back, his pants and tunic on, when there was a knock at the door.

Duncar peeked in. "Time to go."

"Just need to get my boots on," Gregor responded.

He wanted to ask Duncar about Sreana, but again felt the pang of disappointment and decided against it. He sat down on the bed, trying to pull on his boots. Duncar saw he had difficulty with his right boot, so he kneeled in front of him and assisted. Gregor thanked him then followed the other man out into the lea. Two horses waited, one held in place by a young boy, standing near a tree stump that Gregor could use to get up without human assistance.

As he settled himself into the saddle, he couldn't stop from asking, "Will Sreana be joining us?"

Duncar frowned, confused. "It wouldn't be safe. Even though your note stopped them from searching, the Guard has been vocal about your kidnapper being a woman. If we're stopped, I have deniability."

Gregor nodded in understanding, then grimaced as Duncar brandished a bag. Duncar secured it over the King's head, took the reins, and they headed out of the township and toward the castle.

~   ~   ~

After the two men rode out, the boy who held the horse for Gregor ran toward a tree. Leaves rustled and what was once hidden became less secret. First, her boots, then her scabbard, until she was fully exposed. She sat sideways on the large limb, hands on each side to keep her balance, still surrounded by the lush canopy.

"What say you, Mika?" Sreana asked.

"Not me. The King. He asked if you were traveling with them, my lady," Mika answered, "but Duncar told him it wasn't safe since his kidnapper has been reported as a woman. He was disappointed."

"Thank you, Mika." He stood there for a few moments, making her sigh. "Go play, you've done your duty for the day." His smile flashed bright and the boy was gone.

Sreana lingered in the tree until she couldn't see the horses anymore, then she made her way down and returned to her hovel. When she walked in, it felt empty. Dispirited, she sat down hard on her bed. She smelled him suddenly and glanced around, realizing his scent was now in her bedding. Shaken, she pushed herself up to stand but her hand encountered something balled up. She pulled it out from underneath the quilt and found his undershirt. She clutched it to her chest, unsure if her regret stemmed from their union or her cowardice.

She had tried to be strong the whole day. But with every interaction he had with her people. Every touch. Every promise. His respect and his honor won her over. And when she woke to find him looking at her with such adoration, her heart reacted without her permission. Before she knew it, her hand caressed his cheek. The feel of his beard, his lips under her fingertips, his heartbeat... When he moved closer, then stopped himself out of deference, her will faltered.

Next thing she knew they were entangled. And she didn't want to stop. He felt extraordinary. His kisses perfect. He didn't even flinch when he saw her entire torso. He had only seen part of it before, but once she removed her undershirt, he didn't hesitate. He caressed her as if she were whole, while making sure he didn't cause her any discomfort. And the feel of his lips... his mouth... even remembering the sensations made her tremble.

Each move had been understood even though they spoke no words. It was the sheer exhilaration and exhaustion brought upon by their union that finally ended her madness. Then as they laid together, she would have given anything to stay that way with him. The experience startled her mostly because she had never felt that way before.

When she woke at daybreak, she saw him next to her, both in the same position they had fallen asleep in. His heart beat soothingly against her hand, his breathing slow and steady. He looked so peaceful, a small smile still on his lips. She even found herself entertaining the idea of him staying another day. It was only when she realized he would be leaving that the weight of her actions crushed her. He was the Grenan King and she was nothing more than a common criminal from a country his Kingdom occupied. He would never see her as anything more than that and she knew what that meant for her. She couldn't bring herself to face him or the consequences or his expectations. And fear had driven her away.

She hated herself for surrendering to her feelings, knowing that it was all fleeting. But what would her regret feel like had she just rolled over and made herself go back to sleep? It seemed no matter her decision, surrender or evasion, she would hate herself all the same.

And now he was gone.

She had already made her decision known about not seeing him, and even after their union, her mind hadn't changed. They would never see each other again. Their moments together, from their conversations to the physical, were over. She buried her face in his shirt and sighed, but it sounded more like a sob.

Behind her, the little pink flowers wilted and the moss vanished into dust.

~ ~ ~

Duncar took him as far as the river, where Gregor could ride, bag free, over the bridge and enter the surrounding grounds of the castle. He set the gelding at a trot, trying to rehearse his story. He knew the Guard, the ministers, and the household staff would be grilling him the moment he rode up. Even though he was King, he still had to answer to those around him. And those back home in Grenan.

As Gregor rode alone to the castle gates, the Castle Guard rushed to him. They led him to the staircase at the front door, then helped him dismount. He reassured them he was not hurt, all the while trying to hide the pain in his hip and leg from riding. He was able to make it upstairs to his bedchambers where the healers were waiting, breathless from running up the stairs ahead of him. He sat down in the overstuffed chair next to the fireplace and sighed. The healers hovered over him, checking him for injuries.

"I am fine," he responded sternly to their nagging. "But it is evident that I need to figure out how to walk better. I cannot be among the people if I cannot keep up with them."

The head healer, Genj, blinked in surprise. This was the first time the King appeared willing to get back on his feet since his injury. "There are stretches and exercises that may help with some of your issues."

"Good. I have a few ideas as well. Put together a plan and bring it to me tomorrow. But right now, I need to rest."

As everyone shuffled out of his room, Gregor sighed again. Then someone cleared their throat. He looked up and saw Marga standing by the servant's stairway.

"Would you like me to draw you a hot bath, Your Majesty?"

"That would be greatly appreciated, thank you."

She bowed her head then moved to the bathing room. He listened to her run the water and fuss with the linens and soaps. The noises were easy to block out as his mind flashed back to Sreana. Every time their eyes connected. Every touch. Every kiss. He wished that each memory comforted him but he only found his heart shattering. He was so lost in his thoughts, he didn't realize that Marga had been trying to get his attention.

He stood and entered the room, letting Marga help him out of his clothes. She tactfully maneuvered him into the bath, the hot water stinging his flesh. With him settled in, she excused herself but promised to be back once he needed her. He thanked her, then let the silence settle around him.

He scooped up some hot water and splashed his face. Water dripping down made the only sound in the large room. He blinked away droplets, while others danced along his facial hair as they tried to escape its maze. They felt like her fingers playing in his beard. He squeezed his eyes shut, that memory making his chest ache.

As he sat there in the bath reflecting on Sreana's face, he sighed, miserable. As much as he had wanted her, he made himself be patient. Each kiss tore at his resolve, but he had to let her guide them and took all of his cues from her. She undressed them, took care with his old injury, and shared with him an experience he would never forget. He had been smitten with her since she held her sword to his throat, but he completely fell for her in those intimate moments.

Confusion and hurt engulfed him. Her beautiful gray eyes seemed to light up as they kissed and caressed. And afterwards, she looked as amazed as he felt. And her smile, it was one he had never seen on her face before. How could she be disgusted by their union?

He knew he was assuming that based on his wounded pride. If it wasn't disgust, then what was it? And would he ever know?

She already cut off all ties before. He naively thought their union meant she was persuaded by his words, that they needed to work together, which meant that they would see each other again. However, after her disappearance from her bed, it seemed their union turned into more of a farewell than any words spoken.

"Why, Sreana?" he asked softly, tears streaming down his cheeks. That plea was heavy with so many unrequited questions.

CHAPTER 8

Sreana was quieter than usual after the King left. She still led her community, making sure that the food was distributed fairly and giving guidance regarding travel and household repairs. However, she stopped walking the roads and visiting the businesses and farms. She became even more withdrawn when she received the notice of banishment, as well as the return of her horse and clothes, from the Temple of Dranar. She confined herself to her lea after that, drowning privately in her torment.

And as nothing seemed to change immediately, she had a hard time hiding for long. Restlessness throughout her community and others raised concern and it was her job to reassure her people that patience was key. Reluctantly, she traveled to other townships and held meetings with her own community to reassure them her faith wasn't misguided. As difficult as it was to ease their apprehension, she found the strength and finesse to persuade them to give the King the time he asked for, all the while faking her smile and participation in each conversation…

But both Pirco and Duncar noticed. They didn't want to say anything to upset her more, so they worked with her as always and tried to take some weight off of her shoulders.

CHAPTER 9

It wasn't long after his kidnapping that Gregor had a visit from his general. Gregor waited for the man at the main doors, watching the older gentleman ride up on a well-groomed, well-trained horse. He guided the gelding to the stairs and Gregor could tell that his general regarded him with some annoyance. Then General Kasar halted the horse and dismounted. He marched up the stairs to the King and stood at attention.

"General," Gregor greeted the other man, his tone formal.

"Your Majesty," Kasar responded, bowing respectfully.

Then they both burst into laughter and heartily hugged.

"It is so good to see you again, Gregor."

"It has been too long, my friend. Come, we have much to catch up on."

Chatting mindlessly about the weather and the grounds, they walked into the castle and made their way upstairs to Gregor's chambers. A table with a pair of chairs had been placed on the balcony, with plates and glasses, perfect for a private luncheon. They sat while the household staff served the food, then waited until they were alone before Gregor caught Kasar up on the situation. They ate as Gregor spoke but, eventually, Kasar stopped and sat in disbelief.

"What do you mean you let yourself be kidnapped?" Kasar demanded.

Gregor chuckled. "Well once she got ahold of the reins, I didn't have much of a choice. But when we finally stopped and realized she had basically kidnapped me, I did suggest the ransom note."

Kasar shook his head, speechless.

"But I was shown things I didn't want to see, was told things I didn't want to hear. Mistreatment and disrespect of the people we promised to care for."

"And you're sure it wasn't a trick? You even admit to being biased."

"When I got back, I asked for an accounting of all our funds going in and out of the castle. I was told all of the books had been sent to the Queen for an audit. But I made sure to check with Vehla first and she confirmed nothing had been received in months. So, after some shouting, the books were produced. A minister's assistant was found to have siphoned money that was meant to purchase supplies and he had conspired with some guards to bully instead of pay. He died by suicide that morning and these supposed accomplices were nowhere to be found."

"Convenient."

"Yes, it was. I have a lot of work to do, but now I do not know who to trust."

"I could assign a couple of my trusted lieutenants and their men here. Especially after the assassination attempt and kidnapping, I have an opportunity to work around your sister's wishes."

Gregor grimaced.

"I promise I will not disparage your..." then a sly smile stretched across his face, the general asked, "What is she? Is she your paramour?"

Gregor lowered his eyes to his cup, but didn't hide his solemn expression.

"Ah, she's your heartbreaker." Kasar regarded him for several breaths, realizing the King's true feelings. "After all this time? As long as I've known you, you have never shown any kind of fancy for anyone. You barely raised an eyebrow at that woman you were engaged to before coming here."

"We both know why that engagement was arranged. It wasn't about my happiness. It was about keeping me home and off the battlefield."

Kasar grunted agreement. "Yet this woman sneaks into your chambers, threatens you, kidnaps you for a day only to leave you a miserable fool, and you are completely taken by her."

"She's... complicated."

"Sedoran women usually are," Kasar agreed, leaning back. "Fought beside quite a few during the war. Fighters, lovers, healers, daughters, mothers, sisters... They carry many labels and yet those labels never seemed to be fully accurate." Kasar smiled, remembering his own interactions, then it faded. "There was one, her group fought beside her brother's often because of the areas they covered. When she fought, she was fascinating to watch, even a little terrifying." He stared at Gregor for a moment. "You said your heartbreaker had survived a substantial wound?"

"Yes, but I do not know the story behind it. After talking to her though, I know she fought like the rest of us."

"And yet, even after she breaks your heart, you will follow through with your promises to her?"

"It is not my promise to her. What she and I had, that is personal. And personal issues are just that, personal. It doesn't change my duty to the people that we both have come to respect. Grenan had promised to care for Sedora after everything its people had survived. The King of Grenan will follow through with those promises as they have not been fulfilled."

"To do so, you will need people you can trust. If I assign men here, then you can message your sister without worry of interception. And they can work as your agents among the Sedorans without interference."

Gregor hesitated.

"I will also instruct them not to apprehend any visitors of a certain description, just in case."

"That would be greatly appreciated."

"Good, they are camped just outside the walls awaiting their assignment."

Gregor chuckled. "You are definitely efficient, my friend."

"We should go out and speak with them, so they can understand what is required of them."

"Agreed. Lead the way."

They walked out of the castle, along the gravel pathway, toward the gates. The Castle Guard appeared annoyed when Gregor waved them off, but considering his company was the general of the elite Grenan army, they were not needed.

Just outside the gate, tents lined up along the castle's outer wall and the armymen were speaking softly, honing swords or tending to wardrobe. When one man caught sight of the King and General, he made the noise that all armymen recognized. Each jumped to their feet or straightened quickly, saluting the approaching men. Gregor chuckled, feeling somewhat nostalgic as he remembered his days among the ranks.

Kasar shouted the order to stand at ease and the men followed it immediately. Gregor looked over each man's face, recognizing all of them as they had fought by his side against the Carmanic invaders. Most were with him when he was injured. He knew he could trust them, a feeling he hadn't had with the Castle Guard or the ministers.

"General Kasar has assigned you all here to help me with a very complicated situation. I have found out that harms have been committed by the Grenan Kingdom against the citizens of Sedora. It will take a lot of work to unravel this mess, which means I will need to count on you for more than just military duties. It's going to be tedious, stressful, and honestly, heartbreaking."

"Your Majesty," one lieutenant piped up. "We have fought beside the Sedoran people. We know who they are and they have our respect. If healing our wounds means being your messenger, I will happily do so. And I believe my colleagues concur."

The armymen, twelve in all, nodded and murmured agreement.

Gregor smiled, sighing. "Thank you, Rana, everyone."

"Where do you want us to start?" another lieutenant, Ranthel, asked.

"Inventory. I have been informed that we have taken food and other supplies that may have been in excess of what we need. I am aware some of it was shipped to Grenan, but I need to know what we have here and what we'll need so we can reach out appropriately to the Sedoran communities. We will need to move quickly and under the noses of a few here in the castle."

Next to Rana, the remaining lieutenant, Wenth nodded. "We will work with the household staff and compile the appropriate reports."

"And have them find some quarters for you all. I know we love our tents," which made the men smirk, "but this current arrangement will not be feasible for the work ahead of us. There is plenty of unused space that can be utilized." The men nodded. "Thank you, again. This is important work that should have been done years ago."

CHAPTER 10

Late one evening, a fortnight after the King's kidnapping, Duncar slipped out of the township. He rode for several miles until the Temple of Dranar rose up before him. He hitched his horse, entered the Temple, and respectfully bowed to the goddess. When he straightened, he saw Mirna glaring at him from the altar. He sighed, but patiently waited for her to speak. She apparently noticed his hesitation and made him wait a little longer than usual by tidying up. Making him suffer just enough in the silence to satisfy her, she finally approached him, her eyes narrowed in anger.

"And what brings you to the Temple of Dranar?" Mirna inquired, tone menacing.

"May we speak in private?"

"Fine." She started down the hallway that led to the priests' private chambers. She opened the door to hers and stomped in, letting him catch up to her and close the door behind them. She spun around, her anger radiating off of her. "Did she send you?"

"Of course not. She expected the notice of banishment and she won't fight it."

"Then why are you here?"

"Because I wanted to make sure you were unharmed."

"We are," she answered, folding her arms over her chest. "The Grenan guards came and demanded to know if the kidnapper was one of us. The only saving grace I had was the rope burns on my young priest's wrists. Did you know that Sreana tied her up and tossed her into an armoire? Stole her clothes and face paint? Did she not think about the consequences of her actions? Or the trauma we still suffer and how easily it rears its ugly head? It took some of the women days to come out of their rooms after the Grenan guards showed up."

"She doesn't think things all the way through. Never has. She gets an idea and can't see past it." Then he crossed the room and cupped her face in his

71

calloused hands. "How are you?"

She sighed, hard. "Angry. Hurt." Then she closed her eyes briefly. "Is that all you wanted to know?"

Duncar wrapped his arms around her, hugging her tightly. "Have I told you that I thank Dranar every day for not demanding her priests to take a vow of celibacy?"

She scoffed, disgusted.

"You know I don't come here just for the medicinal herbs," he whispered into her ear. He leaned back enough to watch a small smile finally break through her anger. He kissed her, feeling her melt into him. "May I stay tonight?" he asked, softly. "If only to hold you?"

"I would like that," she answered, pulling away from him.

She began to disrobe and Duncar paused to watch. It never got old. As she shed her layers, the long-sleeved blouse and slacks that covered almost every inch of her, her beauty was amplified. She was gorgeous, her hourglass figure his favorite sight. She glanced over at him and blushed, then rolled her eyes at him.

He chuckled, then started to remove his clothes. He caught her watching him this time and posed in jest. She finally giggled, which sounded like ocean waves, and it reminded him of home. Even after everything they lost, all the steps they had to take away from their previous life, Mirna was his home.

They settled in, with Duncar laying on his back and Mirna cuddled up against him.

"I'm glad you are safe," he admitted. "I was worried."

"And I am glad you are safe, too. I don't know what I would've done had you been caught." She laid her head on his shoulder. "It was so chaotic that day I didn't see everything that had happened. Did she really save the King's life?"

"Yes, surprisingly." Then he frowned. "And there's more, but she won't talk about it."

"You don't think he did something…?" and she paused, afraid of finishing that sentence.

"No, nothing like that. If he had, she would have ended him without a second thought. I don't know how to explain it. There was some kind of connection between them the whole day. I've heard a lot of comments since about how he could touch her without repercussion. Pirco even caught them holding hands. But the next morning, there was obvious regret. She asked me to take him back then disappeared. Even the King was quiet on the way back to the castle. She won't talk about it, not to me or Pirco."

"And the only place she would run to is the one place she's not allowed. But if she won't tell you or Pirco, I doubt she would tell me. She could never admit to a mistake."

"That is true." He fell silent, then shook his head. "She took a huge chance with him. I don't know why. All she would say was she saw something in him, something different. Time will tell if she misplaced her trust in him."

"Be patient, she'll talk eventually."

He sighed. "I hope so, because she won't be able to figure it out herself."

The two lovers snuggled closer together, letting the quiet night pull them under into a blissful sleep.

CHAPTER 11

"Your Majesty, you cannot push yourself so hard," the healer chided as he helped the King into his chair. Even though he had a slight build, he was able to handle Gregor without straining. "You can do more damage than good if your body is not ready to meet the demands of your mind." Then the tall, lanky man sighed. He furrowed his bushy eyebrows, which not only made his forehead wrinkle, but also parts of his bald head. "Your gait has improved significantly since we started a month ago, why the impatience?"

Gregor grimaced. "Have you ever been in love, Genj?"

The healer smiled. "Of course."

"And what did you do for that person?"

"I made him my husband."

"You would do anything for him?"

Genj chuckled. "I wish I could say within reason, but love makes you unreasonable at best."

"Then you'd understand that if I found someone, that I would want to do what it took to be the partner she deserves if I ever saw her again?"

"Are you in love, Your Majesty?"

Gregor sighed. "I've been asking myself that often. If I am, I fear it is one-sided." He thought of Sreana's smiling face, as they held each other in her bed. "But I do hope that I am wrong."

Genj regarded the King silently for a few moments. "If you trust me, Your Majesty, I will do everything I can to ensure that you are capable of walking as well as any other physical activity you wish to manage. But you have to follow my instructions precisely and understand that certain things may be out of the question."

"Understood. And I trust you."

Then the healer smiled, a little slyly. "And I will happily answer any other questions you may have, Your Majesty."

"I do sound a bit naive, don't I?"

"Has it not been a while since you've had a companion? I think you're permitted."

~　　　~　　　~

The Temple had been burned down by the Carmanic Empire during the first days of the invasion. The only part remaining was a large wall and arching doorway. Areama's and Adir's friends decorated it with garlands of flowers such as purple coneflower and white yarrow, as well as silver ribbons, keys and amethyst crystals. Mismatched chairs lined up nearby, ready for an audience.

Those in attendance were dressed in their finest, even though they still looked quite modest, with bracelets of lavender, keys, and bells adorning everyone's wrists. As they moved, the bells rang, bringing another level of life to the Temple's remains. Offering urns were placed along the length of the wall, with small fires burning to light the evening ceremony. Each guest had a small pouch that they dropped into the flames before sitting down, an offering to Sera, the god of hearth and home, whose Temple lay in ruin.

Sreana smiled sadly at her surroundings but felt some happiness that no matter how little was left of the Temple, the surviving devotees lovingly cobbled together a gathering place for worship in the tattered remains. She took her silver pouch of yarrow, flour, sugar, and ashes from her firepit and tossed it gently into one urn before taking her seat in the back. The others had started settling in, conversations quieting at the order of the priest.

As the couple made their way to the priest who awaited them, sounds of awe and joy followed them. The bride wore her handmade dress while the groom donned his finest outfit. The ceremony started once they stood hand in hand near the wall, the fires lighting them warmly. Vows were spoken in strong, loving tones while the priest wrapped silver ribbons with bells and keys tied at the ends around the couple's clasped hands.

Even though she thrilled at the couple's matrimony, Sreana felt her heart quiver. She had promised herself that she would keep certain memories pushed back, but they were stronger than her will. His eyes, his voice, the warmth of his hand holding hers. Berating herself, she pinched her thigh, the sting keeping her tears at bay.

Then cheering snapped her out of her thoughts. The ceremony turned into celebration as the couple held up their bound hands. Then the audience moved their chairs and made way for tables. The tables of different shapes and sizes were spread out to allow the revelers to mill around them while the chairs were pushed under them. One long table was placed by the archway and various dishes were carried in with pride. All of their friends came together for a meal and conversation, embracing each other and the newly joined couple. Before she could head out, Areama caught sight of Sreana and rushed to her. Sreana

75

laughed and hugged her, congratulating her.

"Are you leaving?" Areama asked, disappointed.

"Unfortunately. But I am glad to have been able to make the ceremony."

"Thank you, my lady."

"Please, I am honored that you invited me."

After searching the crowd for his new bride, Adir found them embracing and joined them. "No, not for that." Areama leaned back, tears running down her cheeks. "If it weren't for you taking me in and giving me a home and hope, I don't know where I'd be or if I would have ever met Adir."

"Same here," Adir chimed in, his voice thick with emotion. "You saved us separately and gave us the chance to find each other."

"I didn't want to cry, you two," Sreana fussed, wiping her cheeks.

"But it's true," he continued. "And we will never forget it."

"We are all Sedorans," Sreana replied, cupping each of their faces. "No matter the fiefdom we hail from, no matter the family name we carry." She sighed, patting their cheeks gently like her mother used to do to her. "Now go, celebrate! I will see you two soon."

The pair hugged her and headed off into the crowd. She watched for a few moments, that pain resurfacing. She knew she would never have what Areama and Adir had. And she had no reason to hold onto any feelings for Gregor. No matter her bluster, her faith in him was wavering. With a sigh, she mounted her stallion and headed back to her township.

CHAPTER 12

Days after the wedding, the leader of a neighboring community came looking for help early one morning. His face was bruised from the impact of a fist and he shook in fear as Garol led him to Sreana. She helped guide him to her firepit, asking Pirco for water and Duncar for salve for his face.

While Duncar treated his injuries, Dener trembled as he recounted the incident from the night before. Unfamiliar men roaming the streets, attacking people, trying to assault women, and setting things on fire in an attempt to burn down the township… anything to rattle the citizens with no explanation for the aggression. And they threatened to come back that following night.

"I do not know what to do," Dener said, sighing. "All of my citizens are elderly, except for their children who are there as caretakers. We are not fighters, we have no way to protect ourselves."

"How many men?" Sreana asked.

"Seven."

Sreana chewed her bottom lip, then nodded. "You will need to lock down your township before dark. Close down any businesses, taverns, shops, all of that. Have your people lock themselves safely in their homes and bar any possible entrances. These people need to be funneled down the main street."

Dener looked hopeful. "We can do that."

"Good. I will have a word with these strangers." She glanced over at Pirco. "Can you help Dener back to his township? And take a few others to help with the lockdown?"

Pirco nodded, then helped Dener back to his feet. As they walked down the road, Pirco waved for other men and women to join them.

Duncar waited until they were out of earshot before inquiring, "Who do you think they are?"

"Undesirables paid to cause problems," Sreana responded. "I think we need to make an example out of them, to curb any more bad behavior."

"Are you going alone?"

77

"I will be the one they see, but you and a few others will surround them. We both know there's always one that tries to run."

"Just remember, you can't take any shots to the stomach or chest. You're still healing."

"I am forever healing, cousin," she retorted, then smirked. "That's why I carry a big stick."

~   ~   ~

That night, the township fell dark. No lights. No sound. No movement. Nothing until…

She heard them before she saw them. They were laughing, whooping, catcalling as they rattled doors and pounded on windows. With no response, they moved down the main street. When they rounded the corner, they saw Sreana standing in the middle of the road. Then the group of men started to laugh, along with sharing a few lewd comments about her anatomy. They scoffed when she didn't react. She only stood at attention, her staff at her right side and her left hand behind her back.

One of the men, who was the tallest and bulkier than his comrades, approached her. "The old man sent a woman?" He grabbed her by the chin, as she stood stoic, and laughed in her face.

Without a word, she swiftly brought her left hand around and stabbed her dagger into his forearm. He screamed in pain, then she kicked him away and he tumbled to the ground. The other men glanced down at him then back up at her, startled at first. After sheathing her dagger, she rolled both of her shoulders in unison and clicked her tongue against the roof of her mouth. Then she brought her staff in front of her, at the ready.

The second man, who was average in build and only had hair on the sides of his head above his ears while being completely bald in the middle like a target, rushed at her with a light mace over his head. Instead of blocking the weapon, she ducked away as he swung down and with his balance off, she swept his legs out from under him with her staff. He landed with a dull thump. A strike to the bullseye kept him down.

The third aggressor, who wore a sleeveless shirt to show off his muscular arms, learned from the other's mistake. He didn't rush at her, but challenged her carefully with a swing of his blade. She blocked it easily, cocked her head, and responded with confidence. They bashed weapons, sword against staff, parrying away from the other men. Even though she focused on the trouble maker in front of her, she saw the fourth man, who was short and chubby, moving to attack her from behind. She struck the opponent in front of her in the face with the staff, then smacked him in the chest with the staff's heel making him stumble backwards. She spun around, throwing her dagger into the rotund man's leg. He fell a few horse lengths away, screaming in agony.

Twirling her staff, she returned her attention to the sleeveless man. He was still careening back but after he regained his footing, he lurched forward. She switched her staff to her other hand then swung her fist, landing the blow to his chin. She spun and elbowed him in the gut. Out of pain or surprise, he dropped his sword. Before it could hit the ground, she caught it. Then she kicked him in the groin, sending him into the dirt.

The fifth rabblerouser, based on his stance, had some form of military training. She couldn't wait to see how far he got before flaming out of service. They locked swords, his muscles grossly straining along his naked chest. Disgusted, she rolled her eyes and chose to end their interaction immediately. She pushed him away, bashing his sword with her two weapons. With frightening speed, she beat him back until he tripped over the first man, who still laid on the ground bleeding. He had proven himself a fortnight service man at best.

The sixth man, who was the skinniest of them all, ran for it. Pirco appeared out of the shadows and punched him in the face, knocking the man down to the ground. Pirco looked particularly proud of himself, even though he had to shake the sting out of his hand. He caught Sreana's eye and shrugged as he smirked.

The last aggressor, who was large and flabby but not as tall as the first man, grabbed Sreana from behind while she was distracted by Pirco. She lost her weapons as he picked her up and tossed her onto the ground. Laughing, he stomped over to her and loomed, then bent over to pick her up again. A well-aimed kick to his face knocked him back, stunning him. With another hard kick, she disabled his knee and he crumpled.

She got back to her feet, dusted herself off, and retrieved her weapons. All seven men laid on the ground, either groaning or whimpering in pain. Sreana dislodged her dagger from the leg it was buried in, which made the rotund man scream. Then she walked over to the one who had approached her first, the one she assumed was their leader, resting the heel of her staff against his throat.

"Do not return," she ordered, her voice menacing in its evenness. "Do not even consider revenge. Tell anyone who thinks they can bully and harass, they will receive the same treatment as you did, maybe worse. Do you understand?"

Glaring up at her, still trying to stop his bleeding, all he could do was nod.

"Good. We will help you out of town and you will never show your faces again. If you do come back, I will be waiting for you. And our conversation will be much shorter."

~   ~   ~

From the safe distance of their hiding place in the shadows, Pirco and

Duncar had watched her dominate her foes. It had been years since she had brutalized an enemy. It almost seemed like no time had passed and she had never suffered any injury. Watching her made their days of fighting against the invaders resurface and it was difficult for both men. They remembered their successes, but at the same time, their losses flooded their minds.

After they helped the troublemakers into the township's cart, they watched it ramble down the road. They shared an uneasy silence for several moments after the cart disappeared.

"I forgot how poetic her moves were," Pirco whispered.

Duncar scoffed. "I don't see the poetry."

"Poetry can be deadly... just ask any love sick fool. But admit it, she has always had an elegance to her fighting." Pirco read Duncar's demeanor. "What is it?"

"We both know how hesitant she has been to fight since her injury," Duncar responded, watching Sreana intently. "She does her exercises and practices in private. But this? I hope this doesn't mean she isn't handling her emotions well."

"Still hasn't told you anything about that night?"

"You either?"

They stared at each other, feeling helpless.

"Has she even been back to the castle?" Pirco asked. "I know she hasn't asked for my help getting back in."

"I haven't seen her sneak off. I check every night and I find her home."

A worried silence fell between them.

"Maybe," and Pirco shrugged, "we can use this as a distraction. Keep her busy, instead of letting something else fester. I don't think we need another warrant for arson."

Duncar raised his eyebrows, surprised. "I'll take a diversion any day."

Pirco smiled, mischievously, then walked over to Sreana. She still stood in the middle of the road, having watched the cart full of trouble disappear.

"We need to brawl more often," Pirco said. "You're rusty."

Sreana handed him the sword she pilfered from one of the troublemakers. Once he accepted it, she in turn smacked him in the stomach with her free hand. He grunted in surprise, then chuckled.

"We may need to think about the protection of all townships," Pirco suggested. "As much fun as it is, you alone cannot go to every single one and fight for them. Maybe we should consider training again. Make sure our people are prepared?"

She glanced at the townspeople's relieved faces as they approached to thank her. "We'll have to do so in secret," she answered, under her breath. "Can't have the Grenans thinking we're planning an uprising." Then she met the townspeople to accept their gratitude with a diplomatic smile.

~   ~   ~

Soon after Sreana's handling of the troublemakers, messages trickled in about Grenan armymen making their way through the communities. They asked questions and evaluated the food supplies left for the Sedorans to use. Small changes like that from the castle started affecting the neighboring townships and then eventually all of them, like dominoes.

One day, Sreana, Duncar, and Pirco were sitting at her firepit, discussing exercises and practices that would strengthen their people's fighting abilities when one merchant arrived with a rolled parchment in her hand.

"My lady, different Grenan men came today," Sedra explained, "and instead of taking everything they wanted, they handed me this and said they would return in five days."

"What do you mean, different?" Sreana asked.

"They were armymen, not Castle Guard."

"We had heard they were making the rounds," Duncar replied.

Pirco took the letter from her and read it quickly. "It states that the Grenan Kingdom will begin to fairly trade with the Sedoran merchants."

"I do not understand," Sedra stammered.

"It means that they will now pay you for your goods instead of just taking them."

"Pay? I will be paid?"

Sreana smiled. "Just keep the prices fair, Sedra."

"I don't even know if I remember how, my lady."

Pirco looked past Sedra, noticing a large crowd headed their way. "Looks like they gave the same notices to the farmers."

"We may need to have a meeting," Sreana responded. "Pirco, can you check to see if the farmers and merchants in the other townships got the same notices?"

"Of course."

Sreana patted Sedra on her shoulder. "Come, let's go talk to our friends."

~   ~   ~

After their town meeting, the farmers, fishermen, and other merchants left with an agreement about how they would charge and how often they would sell to the Grenan buyers. It took a few good arguments, because there had been calls to overcharge or to cut off the Grenans completely. Sreana used her finesse to get everyone on the same page, taking them late into the night, but it ended with a successful arrangement.

Exhausted, she sat in her usual booth at Trealle's, staring into a mug. The dark shade of the winter mead reminded her of Gregor's eyes. Talking about him during the meeting took its toll. His smiling face flashed through her mind and it hit her hard. She sighed, rubbing her face with both hands. Then she felt someone sit down next to her. Peeking through her fingers, she saw Pirco next to her, thoughtfully staring at his own mug.

"He kept his word," he said.

She dropped her hands onto the table, but stayed quiet, unsure how her words would sound even if she knew what to say.

"I'm trying to compliment you," he complained. "Your mad plan worked."

She scoffed. "You know me, eternal pessimist. Don't know if this is just temporary."

"Do you want to talk about it?"

"About what?"

Pirco stared at her, realizing she still wanted to keep her secret. He hated it, not knowing what happened between her and the King. He knew it wasn't improper or he would have helped bury the body. Whatever had happened, she still didn't want to talk about it and he had to come up with a different response.

"What to do if it is temporary."

"Stealing back what belongs to us and destroying property worked before." She shrugged, then sighed. "I'm too tired to think that far tonight. Those negotiations took a lot out of me." She moved to slide out of the booth, making Pirco stand to let her out. "Good night, Pirco."

"Good night, Sreana."

She walked tiredly to her hovel. The firepit had burned out and only the moons lit the way. She slipped in and began her nightly routine. She took off her belt and hung up her sword next to her brother's. She laid her dagger next to her pillow, then started to undress. As she stripped, she folded her clothes neatly on the stool. Her hand lingered, remembering how he had folded his and laid them there too. Other memories tried to flood her mind but she pushed them away.

She walked over to the wash bowl. Pirco was right. Her plan worked. Showing the King their lives had made a difference. And his current actions would make sure nothing would be the same.

So why couldn't she celebrate?

Splashing water on her face to remove any dirt, she stared at herself in the reflecting glass. The fact that Gregor kept his word even after their night together mystified her. But she assumed the worse, that their union was convenient, that he only used her for pleasure, and he considered it payment. She choked up, trying to fight back her humiliation. She could never confess to anyone the price she paid.

Sighing, she slipped into her undershorts and the shirt Gregor had left behind. She had gotten used to sleeping in it after she foolishly tried it on one night. It still smelled like him, even after being washed a few times in the river with the rest of her clothes.

She crawled into bed, facing the wall. She could still see him lying there, with that affectionate expression on his face that broke down her last defense. Her heart warmed at that image of him. Then her mind wandered further, remembering the feel of his lips on hers, his breath against her neck, the sound he made at the end... Some nights she could lie to herself and cherish those moments they shared.

Most nights, however, she hated herself.

She wrapped her quilt tightly around her, angry at herself and at her heart. That night, all she had to do was roll over and go back to sleep. She would have regretted that too but at least her memories wouldn't be filled with such intimate moments. Instead, she surrendered to her childish feelings for someone who could never reciprocate them. She sighed loudly and growled a curse. She flopped on her back, staring solemnly at the ceiling. She knew no matter how tired she was, sleep would elude her. And she had nowhere safe to run, to escape her self-inflicted misery.

CHAPTER 13

Things kept looking up. Within the three months after his kidnapping, King Gregor was regularly out of the castle and among the Sedoran people. He visited with them, having conversations with them, showing his willingness to help out where he could. He listened to concerns and stories, building relationships slowly but happily. He made sure supplies were available and equipment was fixed as needed. And soon, the Sedorans started to respect him. Even though some resentment lingered, they saw how willing he was to make amends and soon they started forgiving past transgressions.

One day, after leaving one of his meetings, Gregor traveled back to the castle through one nameless township. He glanced over the faces, trying to meet the eyes of as many people as he could. Behind one small group stood three individuals with thick cloaks. The hoods hid most of their faces, but he recognized Duncar immediately as the other man stared straight at the carriage. Startled, he looked over to the person next to Duncar and caught a swift flash of gray eyes. He lost her in the crowd and knew she had turned away. It took everything in him not to command the carriage to stop. But he forced himself to keep greeting those who lined the road, faking the smile while he yearned to see those gray eyes again.

~   ~   ~

After everyone else had retired for the night, Duncar watched Sreana as she sulked alone at her firepit. He wasn't sure exactly what had transpired between her and the King and, for the last three months, she refused to even acknowledge that anything had happened. But the look on her face when she saw Gregor pass by and her gloomy expression as she stared at the fire... now he knew it involved her heart. He sighed, loudly, causing her to glance up in surprise.

"I am still using the salve," she said, voice soft, "promise."

"That's not why I'm here."

She frowned. "I don't have the energy to fight tonight, Duncar. Whatever I did, I apologize."

"Go to him."

Her eyes widened and he swore he saw a tear well up. "I can't."

"Why not?"

"Because I am a foolish child," she replied, then growled a curse at herself.

"What happened between you two?" When she didn't answer, he made his way to sit next to her. He regarded her for a few moments as she poked the fire with a small stick and avoided his gaze. Then he chuckled in disbelief, a scenario crossing his mind that he hadn't even considered before. "You got naked."

The blush that colored her face deepened with guilt and something else.

"Was it that awful?" he asked, incredulously.

"No, it was…" she stammered, then whispered, "quite the opposite."

"And here I thought you vowed celibacy after Canor."

"Actually, not until the invasion."

He glared at her for a moment. "You took a lover after Canor?"

"Of course not," she responded, faking offense, then smiled cleverly. "I took two."

Her cousin scoffed, shaking his head. After a brief moment of silence, he said, "You never told me what happened with him."

"You really want the full slate of confessions tonight, don't you?"

"It's obvious that whatever happened with Canor has affected your decisions with Gregor."

She tossed her stick straight into the flames. "I found out I was pregnant right after Canor and I announced our engagement. We were elated. He had big plans for his child. But, about a month later, I don't know why, but I…" and she rubbed her hands hard on her legs, biting her lip. "Pirco found me on the floor. I was bleeding. He got Momma and your Papa to help me. And when they confirmed that I had lost the baby, Pirco retrieved Canor, who uh, told me that I was unfit to be a duke's wife since I could not carry a child." She shrugged, sadly. "It was bad enough losing the baby but… that's why I hid away under Dranar's roof after we ended. It was actually your Papa who told me to go and stay with Mirna. Pirco made sure I got to the Temple safely."

"They never said a word. Any of them."

"I don't think they knew how I'd react if everyone knew. When I came back home, Momma said I would make my own decision on who knew and who didn't. Thankfully we hadn't announced the pregnancy, so I didn't have that constant reminder because of someone asking how it was faring. The only thing Momma ensured was that everyone knew that the dissolution of our engagement was due to incompatibility." She hugged herself and exhaled hard. "I grieved more for the baby than Canor, to be honest. Mirna didn't understand of course but some of the women there did. It was the first time I seriously considered the priesthood. I could just hide away forever." She squeezed her eyes shut. "Are they unharmed? Mirna and the others?"

"They are, even though the Grenan guards marching up to their doors demanding answers did not help those still healing from the invasion. Give them time. Give Mirna time."

"No, I told you, I refuse to fight the banishment. I deserve it. But it does make it hard to apologize."

He wrapped his arm around her shoulders, pulling her into a hug. "Why didn't you tell me any of this?"

"Because you and Alarn would have ripped Canor to shreds. It took everything in Pirco, Momma, and Uncle not to. We didn't even tell Papa because of what he would have done. But the consequences were not worth it. He was not worth it."

"Do you think what happened then makes you unworthy of anyone's love?"

"That I do not know. All I know is that Canor saw me unfit and unclean, but he was truly the monster." She rested her head on his shoulder and closed her eyes for a few moments. "That wasn't even the worst of it. A few months later his uncle offered to take care of me since Canor refused."

"At what price?"

"Keeping his bed warm. After all, what could be better than a King's courtesan who couldn't have children?" She sighed, sitting up straight again. "It doesn't matter, fate dealt with all of them."

Her cousin turned to her, cupping her face and making her look at him. "Do you think Gregor will expect the same thing? For you only to be his courtesan?"

"Why wouldn't he? What a prize for the Grenan King, his very own Sedoran whore."

He could see how much saying that hurt her, especially when she choked on that last word. He sat in shock, knowing that her reaction meant that she honestly cared about the King. And she believed that it wasn't reciprocated.

"Go to him. Find out for sure. I'd rather you be miserable knowing that was true than you dwelling on all of those dreadful scenarios that your mind creates."

"He's supposed to be the enemy."

"Is he? If that were the case, we'd all be dead. But we're not. And look at all that he has done since he left here. That has to tell you something about his character."

She sighed, frustrated, and pulled away. "But I left him before he woke up. I didn't even bid him farewell."

"I think he'll forgive you."

"How would you know?"

"Because I saw his face," he responded, with a mirthless chuckle. "And that was the face of a man who'd give anything to see you again."

~   ~   ~

It took her a few nights to work up the courage. She slipped through the wound in the castle's walls and jogged around the building then down the hallways until she found herself tiptoeing up the servant's stairs. She walked softly into his chambers, finding his boots sitting near the doorway to the balcony and the heavy cloak lying tiredly over the chair next to the dressing table.

She located him outside, leaning against the railing of the balcony. He wore what was left of his everyday clothes, an embroidered tunic and tan slacks. He stared out into the night, as if waiting for something to happen. Then he rubbed his face with one hand, a heavy sigh escaping. He looked weary, even dejected. Her heart thumped hard in her chest and she wondered immediately if she had made a mistake coming here. But after seeing him pass by in his carriage, his brown eyes finding hers even in a crowd…

"You still haven't fixed your security," she admonished, trying to keep her tone light.

Gregor spun around, in surprise. "Then how would I see you again?"

She tried to say something else but her voice failed her. Seeing him again, knowing their union had changed things between them, she wasn't sure what else to say.

He seemed just as speechless, staring at her with such wounded eyes. Suddenly, as if remembering himself, Gregor clasped his hands behind his back. "And the reason for your visit, my lady?"

Sreana recognized his tone. She had heard him use it before on his ministers, it was the one he used when conducting business. She bowed her head respectfully for a moment, mostly to hide her reaction. Her visit was the mistake she feared. But Duncar was right, at least she knew for sure. He wanted nothing to do with her and now she could move on and forget him.

At the moment, however, she had to figure out how to exit gracefully. As tempting as jumping off the balcony again was, it wasn't the smoothest option. She felt her diplomacy taking over even as her heart shattered at his coldness. She straightened, but kept her eyes to the ground, like any good commoner would, as she answered him. "We thought it appropriate to thank you in person for all that you have done for, not just our community, but our Kingdom. The changes have been positive, as have the reactions." She bowed her head again. "Thank you for allowing us an audience to express our gratitude. We wish you a good evening. Farewell, Your Majesty." Then she turned on her heel and started to leave.

His tone immediately melted into heartbreaking as he called her name. She stopped, squeezing her eyes shut for a moment. She wanted to run, to escape the humiliation, but his voice tore at her heart. She took a deep breath, cautiously turning back around. Their eyes met and she could see that even he didn't know what to do. Hesitantly, he approached her. As if tied by a string, she walked back toward him. They met halfway, within reaching distance but not touching, their eyes remaining locked.

"Was our union so awful?" he asked.

She shook her head, dismayed. "You know that it wasn't."

"Do I? To wake up alone is not a compliment."

She glanced away, unable to meet his eyes any longer. "I'm... I don't know... I turned you down just days before," she whispered, her voice shaking. "But when I woke up and saw the way you were looking at me... Sounds so silly, to think you looked at me as if you cared about..." She rolled her eyes and stammered, "And then I feared I had made a mistake. I feared your reaction and... expectations." Sreana faltered for a moment, before adding, "That you would cage me for your own satisfaction. And parade me as your prize, your very own Sedoran courtesan."

A heavy silence hung over them for a moment.

"I could never cage you, Sreana. You showed me who you are and I know that is not what you want." Then he chuckled, amusement cracking through the seriousness. "And I could never expect you to be a courtesan either, since you do not follow commands, especially those from some foreign King."

She scoffed, then a shaky laugh followed. He ran his hand along her waist and placed it on the small of her back. Then he pulled her against him when she didn't move away. She wrapped her arms around his torso as both of his hugged her tightly. He leaned forward, the look in his eyes the same as that night, and rested his forehead against hers.

"You did not read me wrong, Sreana. I do care about you. Why else would I write a ransom note so you could kidnap me?" She smiled bashfully and he searched her eyes, seeing her affection glimmer. "What did you see when you opened your eyes that night?"

"I saw you."

"The King?"

She raised an eyebrow. "No, the man."

"You did see past my title then? Can you admit that you surrendered to the feelings you had for me, the man you've gotten to know?"

Words failing her, she only nodded.

"Good. I think we can agree that surrender isn't a weakness. After all, I surrendered the moment we met."

"What do you expect of me?" she inquired, her voice faint.

"I want you, of course, with me at every moment but that is not who you are and not how we will be happy. We both have responsibilities and, like you said, we have a lot of work to do. However, I think we have to come to terms with the fact that we are different people, depending on the situation. I am a King and you are a Leader, who are working together to heal the harms committed these last few years. But we are also a man and a woman, who find each other irresistible."

She laughed at that.

"If we can accept that, then I believe we can make this work. All I can hope is that we, the woman and man, are willing to make time for each other and continue to explore this connection we have." Then he smiled, mischievously. "Do we have time tonight to do more exploring?"

~   ~   ~

Her boots laid in front of his. Her belt and weapons rested on his cloak. Their clothes were scattered along the floor, from the double doors that led from the balcony all the way to the bed. Some pillows littered the other side of the room while several blankets were crumpled off the end of the bed.

Naked and exhausted, they laid in his bed, the only remaining blanket covering them. He was on his back and propped up by the few surviving pillows, his arm wrapped around her shoulders. His hand held her to him, while she cuddled up to him, resting her head on his chest. Their free hands played gently against each other, until he pulled hers up to his lips. He kissed each finger tenderly, making her smile. She looked up at him and saw him grinning as well.

"I've missed you," he whispered, holding her hand to his chest so she could feel his heartbeat.

That rhythm was divine. It had soothed her to sleep that first night and now it beat in a way that reminded her they were both alive. "I missed you, too." She shifted in her position, as if trying to get closer, and watched his chest rise and fall with each breath. "And I am sorry. For not seeing you off that morning."

He kissed her forehead, a content sigh dancing along her hair. "Promise you will wish me farewell every time from now on."

"I promise." Then she added, hesitantly, "You left your shirt behind."

"Ah, I knew something was missing. Did you burn it?"

She propped herself up on her arm, furrowing her eyebrows. "Why would I do that?"

"In a moment of annoyance with me?"

She laughed, shaking her head. "More annoyed with myself than you. No, I…" She blushed. "I sleep in it."

He raised his eyebrows as he demanded, "And how do you think about me when you wear it?" The deep shade of red that colored her face told him everything he needed to know, which inflated his ego a bit. "But not every night, I hope? Can't live up to that."

They stared at each other for a moment then both burst into giggles. Content silence fell as they stared at each other.

"I noticed that you were able to um move better," she said, slyly.

"You didn't think I would just sit around these last three months? Thanks to Duncar's suggestions and, along with my healers' ideas, Genj and I created a routine to help with flexibility and to help me walk better. The main goal was to walk among the people without pain or limp. I will admit, there was one other goal."

"And what goal was that?"

"You, in my arms, satisfied."

She rested her chin on his shoulder as she looked at him. "Did you really hope all this time to see me again?"

"As foolish as it seemed, yes. I kept thinking about that night and seeing your face. I just didn't... I couldn't believe you hated our union or that you had no affection for me." He took a deep breath. "I did have my doubts, like I imagined everything or you faked your feelings to get what you wanted."

"I had similar doubts. Did I fool myself into believing you cared? Was our union my payment to you for helping my people?"

The distress that flashed in his eyes hurt her heart. "I told you, no matter what, I would help them."

"I know you did, but doubts tend to warp perceptions."

"They do. That's why I knew I could only focus on the next steps. I would keep my promises, all the while dreaming about the what ifs. This, right now, was my what if. Us, together, as companions. I knew, if I had another chance, I wanted to be a fair lover. To participate and tend to your needs. I didn't want you to do all the work. But I knew I couldn't be here if I couldn't move."

"If I remember correctly," and her sultry chuckle warmed him, "you participated the whole time that night."

"What about my participation this time?"

"I'd have to say, hmmm… satisfactory?" she teased as she furrowed her eyebrows which made him squeeze her against him and playfully growl at her. "It was extraordinary."

"Hm, goal achieved."

She reached up and ran her fingers through his beard, smiling impishly. "I must send Genj a thank you note."

He laughed. "He would appreciate that, considering I am a difficult patient. But, in turn, I'd ask you to share my thanks to Duncar."

"Happily." Then she laid her head back down on his chest, listening to his heartbeat. She felt her eyes grow heavy and knew falling asleep would be a mistake. "It's quite late. I should go."

"Don't go, please, I've missed you."

"I don't want to go either, but even I can't sneak back out in daylight."

"I will give you permission to be on the grounds."

Sreana stammered for a moment, then took a deep breath. "I don't know if that's a good idea."

"Why? It would give you the option to come here anytime, not sneaking in when you think my guards are distracted."

"Who else will test their work?" she quipped, but she saw how serious he was which made her glance away. "I... I need to think about that."

"Then think about it. We have time." He ran his hand through her hair, then touched her cheek with gentle fingertips, bringing her gaze back up to his. "But I want to see you as often as possible."

Her eyebrow raised up. "How often?"

"You want the honest or the diplomatic answer?"

"Well, I know the truth," she responded, her sensuous tone stirring something in him that he had never felt before.

"Then the diplomatic answer would be... At least once a week?"

"I think I can make that work."

"Good." He paused, tucking her hair behind her ear. "I do have another request."

She scowled at him, drolly. "You're very demanding."

"Yes, well I have to get it all in while I've got your undivided attention. I want us to learn more about each other every time we have our visits. I want our companionship to be without secrets."

"I have a hard time admitting things. You may have to have more patience than you're used to exercising."

"That, Sreana, is a given."

She scoffed in response, which made him chuckle. She teasingly slapped his shoulder after she sat up. And with that, she slipped out of his embrace and started gathering her clothes. She grabbed her undershorts, and with a mischievous grin, tossed them at him. They landed on his face, making him laugh as he grasped them.

"Now you have something to remember me by," she teased, making it clear that he was not going get his shirt back.

"Fair's fair."

He sat up and watched as she hid her beauty under her clothing, first her shirts then her pants. She walked back over to the bed, boots and sword in hand, and leaned over to kiss him. He grabbed her into his arms and she fell into his lap, while her boots banged onto the floor. He captured her lips again, sharing a long passionate kiss. They fell over, lost in the embrace, until she started giggling.

"I have to go!" she mumbled against his lips.

One more fervent kiss. "Farewell, Sreana. Come back to me soon."

"Farewell, Gregor. I will see you in a week."

Feeling reassured by that promise, he let her go and watched as she scooped up her boots and headed toward the stairs. "Maybe one day," he called after her, "you won't have to run away so quickly."

Sreana spun on her heel to walk backwards and she smirked. "Where's the fun in that?" She turned away again and disappeared into the shadows.

Smiling, he collapsed onto his back, holding her undershorts against his heart. He took a deep, happy breath and found his eyes growing heavy.

~   ~   ~

A very perplexed voice woke him. "Your Majesty?"

When he opened his eyes, he blinked against the sunlight in surprise, finding that Marga had opened the curtains. She stood at his bedside, taking in the chaos around his chambers. He moved his arm, then noticed something was still in his hand. He lifted it up and found that he still held Sreana's undershorts against his chest. Then a sound burst from him that hadn't been heard by the household staff in months.

Marga stared in utter confusion as the King laid, laughing, in his disheveled bed.

~   ~   ~

That morning, Duncar and Pirco walked quickly toward the firepit. Sreana sat on one of the logs, tending to a small fire. They could see her in profile and both stopped. She was... smiling. Pirco tapped Duncar on the arm, a relieved chuckle escaping him. Duncar gestured for him to hold off celebrating. They crossed the distance, sitting down on either side of her with hopeful expressions.

She glanced at the two men, enjoying their tempered excitement.

"Did you see him?" Pirco asked finally when she didn't speak first.

She flashed impish eyes at him, her grin widening. "I did."

Pirco laughed, hugging her shoulders. Duncar smiled as well, the relief on his face evident. She giggled at their reactions, her heart warming.

"And this will be a habit?" Duncar inquired.

"We are exploring our connection," she responded, which made both men chuckle.

"I'm glad you went to him and found out," Duncar admitted, "because I could not stand to see you miserable."

"The entire township couldn't stand it," Pirco added.

"Gregor asked me to extend his thanks for your suggestions."

Duncar's eyebrows rose up. "Oh? Well, please tell him I was happy to help."

"Did those suggestions make the night... more enjoyable?" Pirco demanded.

She rolled her eyes at her friend, which made him sigh whimsically. "He wants us to meet at least once a week. I'll have to count on you both to keep an eye on things while I'm away."

"That's an easy task."

"And he mentioned giving me permission to be on the grounds. You know, so I can stay longer, visit whenever I wish."

Pirco cringed, groaning. "With your warrants?"

"Exactly my concern too."

"You'll figure it out," Duncar replied.

"Maybe he can come visit you here," Pirco suggested.

Sreana started to retort, then caught herself stammering.

"I think they might want to take things slowly?" Duncar responded, concerned by her hesitation.

"Slowly, yes," she agreed. "And privately. I don't know who will react badly if they find out about us. For now, we want to get to know each other better before making any announcements." She stared at the fire solemnly. "It's going to be hard to tell him a lot of things."

"I don't doubt that considering how long it took you to tell me about Canor."

Pirco leaned to the side, staring at his two friends. "You finally told Duncar?"

"I had to wrestle it out of her."

"All of it?"

She nodded.

"Will you tell Gregor then?" Pirco asked, cautiously.

"I'll have to, eventually. It might change things…" She shrugged slightly, making Pirco squeeze her shoulders. "But he's already seen my physical scars and didn't flinch so…" She scoffed, poking the fire again. "I didn't realize that would mean so much to me."

"You've had faith in him so far," Duncar replied. "And it's been rewarded."

Silence.

"Wait, does this mean if you two marry we'll have to call you Your Majesty?" Pirco demanded.

Sreana started to laugh. "You can start now if you'd like."

CHAPTER 14

She kept her promise, returning to him exactly a week to the day. She snuck into the bedchambers via the servant's stairs and heard voices in the bathroom. Realizing he was not alone, she hid behind the armoire. While she waited for the household staff to leave, she sat down and quietly removed her boots. She rolled to her knees and unbelted her sword, but kept her weapon in hand. As the two women left, their voices rose then lowered in volume based on proximity. Once the door closed behind them, she glanced around the armoire. After a few moments, Gregor exited, wearing only his undershorts, and he stood at the dressing table. As he reached for his brush, he noticed her in the reflecting glass. His suggestive smile made her grin foolishly.

She left her hiding place, setting her boots down next to the foot of the bed while slipping the sword and scabbard into one of them. When she got close enough, he turned and grabbed her. She wrapped her arms around his neck, pressing suggestively against him. They started kissing passionately, his hands slipping under the hems of her shirts to lift them over her head.

A voice floated through the door from the servant's staircase. "Apologies, Your Majesty."

Sreana instinctively darted toward some sort of hiding place. She knew she would be seen heading back behind the armoire, so instead, she dove onto the bed and slid off the other side.

Marga returned, shaking her head. "I forgot your laundry. I apparently have too much on my mind tonight." She walked into the bathroom, gathered up his clothes, then started to exit. "Again, apologies."

"It's fine, Marga. Good night."

"Good night, Your Majesty."

Once the door closed again and the woman's footsteps receded, Sreana peeked over the bed to see Gregor leaning back against the dressing table, one hand covering part of his face, trying to muffle his laughter. She stood, sighing, and walked around the bed. His amusement was contagious, making her giggle, too.

"Impressive reaction," he complimented.

"Plenty of practice, I guess."

He grabbed her again into his arms, then turned them around until he had her trapped against the dressing table.

"What would happen if we were caught?" she wondered.

"We would no longer be a secret," he admitted, removing her shirts then working on her pants, "and we'd have some explaining to do."

"Well, we need to be careful who catches us then," she replied. "Don't want to announce too quickly."

As her pants hit the floor, his undershorts followed.

~ ~ ~

They laid in bed later that night, wrapped up in blankets and each other. They faced one another and shared the same pillow, staying close enough to kiss without having to move too much. Her hand played along his beard as his hand traced along her spine.

"Where should we start?" she asked.

"Why not where it started… can you talk more about your scar?"

"Can you?"

"With you, yes."

Sreana took a deep breath. "My brother was one of a handful of fighters that were captured by the Carmanic army near the end. It made no sense why they took them, other than revenge, because they had already signed the contract to withdraw. It took a few days to figure out where they held him, but once there was confirmation, I took off to rescue him. I got in without being seen, found his cell, but he was the only one still alive. We were caught leaving, so we fought our way out. We thought we were in the clear, you know, already halfway through the bog, but we didn't see the soldiers. One slashed me and one stabbed him. We both fell. I watched my brother die and waited for my turn."

"But you survived."

"I laid there for a few days. Duncar and a couple of others came to find us when they realized I was gone. He said that Alarn laid next to me, bloated with white eyes. When he picked me up, he said that I didn't look like that. I didn't look dead, just asleep. But he didn't think I could have survived that long. So, as he carried me to the cart, to wrap me in funerary, I moved. None of them could believe it. They got me back home and Duncar did everything he knew to keep me alive. The poison and infection were everywhere. He said that I had almost died three times on his watch."

She pulled away from him slightly, pushing the blanket down and angling her body to show the scarring. The light from the fireplace danced along her skin, shadows filling in where her ribs dipped like valleys and where her scar sunk in and twisted like ravines. He hadn't noticed the smaller scars that hid amongst the large misshapen one. She touched each scar as she listed the surgeries.

"It took cutting out one kidney, pieces of my skin, some fat, a part of my liver and breast to stop the infection and initiate real healing." He gently ran his fingers along her skin, eventually entwining his fingers with hers. "It was two years of setbacks, surgeries and exercises. Duncar always thought I'd be mad about the disfiguration. He didn't expect how angry I was about surviving."

"Die fighting and you have a place of honor in the afterlife?"

She sighed, her eyes staring off into the distance. "I knew we weren't going to survive the escape, that's why I had to go alone. Alarn told me the only reason why he was still alive in that cell was because he knew I was on my way and we could die together, free. We earned it after all of the battles we fought. When I woke up, I couldn't accept it. I just wanted to be there, with the rest of my family. I still have no answers as to why Death didn't take me too." She closed her eyes and took a few breaths, then cleared her throat. "Your turn."

"We were campaigning against the Carmanic army. They had made it toward the Grenan/Sedora border and we knew if they crossed that mountain pass, they could fortify it and cut off our supply route. That would have been the death knell of our campaign. So, we rode out to push them back. Unfortunately, they knew the terrain better than us and set up a perfect ambush: trap us in the mountain pass, then rain arrows and bolts from above."

"They were good at ambushes. Learned that the hard way."

"We did too. It was at the last breath we realized how dangerous it was to enter the pass and started to look for another way through. When they saw our hesitation, they attacked. They were mostly on foot while we were still on horseback. I killed several Carmanic soldiers, however it was one maniac with an ax who took me out."

He released her hand and pushed the blanket further down, exposing his entire right side. He ran his finger along the scar as he described the attack.

"He landed that ax right into my hip and dragged it down until it hooked in my knee."

She traced the wound as well with her fingertips, until their hands encountered each other again.

"I reacted by beheading him, but the damage was done. A few of my men helped me to the fallback position, while the rest had renewed anger toward our enemy. It did not take long after I was wounded for the entire Carmanic regiment to fall dead. We stayed there for a few days to treat the wounded, myself included, as best as we could with what little we had while setting up a permanent outpost to protect that pass." He brought their hands up between them, staring at their entwined fingers. "By the time we returned, we were able to neutralize the poisons, but my wound was infected and I fell into a bad fever.

Thankfully the healers here were able to battle the infection and bring me around, but the damage to the muscle was… permanent. My fighting days were done." He glanced around, blinking away what appeared to be tears. "It killed me to think that I would not be fighting side by side with my men. I had always done so, as my life was no more important than theirs, and I could not see myself ordering men into battle without being willing to fight, too. My men reassured me that they knew that I would be there with them if I could and that my orders were still respected."

"Why did you stay?"

"Originally, I told my sister that it was best I stayed as commander since I could still work, I just couldn't fight. My men would still follow my orders, even injured and away from battle, and that couldn't be dismissed. It would have also taken too long to get someone else familiar with the situation." He met her eyes, taking a deep breath. "And traveling home seemed so ridiculous when there were Carmanic soldiers everywhere. Vehla also thought that in light of the royal family's slaughter that I should stay to help rebuild. Even amongst the sadness and carnage, the Sedoran people… they were kind to us and they fought harder than any armyman in my ranks."

"But shouldn't the King of Grenan be home, ruling even while healing?"

"Ah, you do not know our politics, do you?"

She shook her head.

"My father was not a traditional man. Anytime he could make a minister cry was a good day for him. He made my sister and I co-rulers. So, she is Queen and I am King. Her husband, and my wife if I were to marry, are considered Consorts only. When we heard about the invasion here, we both knew that if they could take Sedora, Grenan was next. We agreed that she and her husband would care for Grenan while I led the campaign here in Sedora. She has full control over the government side: ministers, Castle Guard, among many other responsibilities. I have full control of the military side: border concerns, diplomacy, among other things. So, my country is ruled well by my sister while I tried to rule here. Thanks to you, I learned that being among the people again is the only way to coexist."

"You're welcome."

Gregor started to laugh heartily. "Thank you, indeed." Then he stared at her, the smile fading. "Did you think about my offer? Being an invited guest?"

"I did and… you may have to rescind some warrants first."

He growled playfully, making her giggle, then rolled them until he was on top. "So, you were the thorn in my side!"

"Got your attention, did I not?"

He kissed her, running his hand down her neck to her breast then along her thigh. She wrapped her legs around his waist, invitingly, and he eagerly accepted. It didn't take them long to satisfy each other. He ended up collapsing on top of her as they lost themselves in their pleasure. She kissed his temple, feeling his breath rush across her neck. When he finally lifted his head, they smiled at each other.

She blinked at him, innocently. "Am I still a thorn?"

"You are a salve."

She blushed.

"But at least now I know why things ramped up in the last year."

"And why is that?" she inquired, curious.

"You finally got to join in on the fun."

She rolled her eyes. "I should go."

"Not yet." She smiled up at him as he leaned in to kiss her. A realization crossed his face, making him groan in annoyance then he rolled off of her and onto his back. "I don't know how I'm going to get your warrants rescinded without my ministers losing their minds."

"I actually have an idea about that."

"This should be interesting."

"In the hope of starting fresh with the Sedoran people, the King of Grenan has decided to rescind any warrants for nonviolent crimes that were committed out of desperation."

His eyebrow rose up. "That's actually not bad."

"And since none of my offenses were violent," she shrugged, "you don't just clear me, but others as well and none are the wiser."

"Destruction of property isn't violent?"

"Hm well, I don't remember personally lighting the fires."

Gregor chuckled. "You lit at least one." Then he rolled back on top of her. They stared at each other. "I never thought I would find someone like you."

"Me neither. I guess we had to be open to finding someone from another Kingdom?" She lifted her head enough to kiss him. "I truly need to go now. I will be back in a week."

~   ~   ~

That morning, Gregor made his way unannounced to the Captain of the Castle Guard's office. Gregor couldn't remember his name and relied on calling him Captain to save face, even though he couldn't stand being in the same room with him for too long.

The man startled as the King entered. He had been eating, with his feet up, when Gregor swung the door open. He jumped to his feet, dropped his pastry onto the desk, and stood at attention.

"Captain, I want all of the open warrants for any Sedoran citizen."

"Your Majesty?" the captain asked, shocked.

"Must I repeat myself?"

The captain cleared his throat, then pulled a large book, which was at least two hands' width tall from the bookcase behind him, and set it on his desk.

"Is this all of them?"

"For the last month, Your Majesty."

Gregor's jaw locked. "How many more of these books exist?"

"Several, Your Majesty. The Sedoran people have been blatant in their disregard for our laws."

"Bring all of the books to the large gathering room immediately."

And before the captain could utter a response, Gregor left the office.

~   ~   ~

Gregor watched in horror as books upon books were delivered and piled along the edge of the meeting table. Then he spent his days painstakingly going through each book. His attention was so rapt that he didn't realize a week had passed. He didn't even notice Sreana hiding in his room after his bath, as he stood at his dressing table and stared down at the wooden top.

"What's wrong?" she asked, startling him.

"I'm sorry, I didn't see you."

"Your mind is elsewhere." She crossed the room, and when he turned around, she cupped his face with her hands. His dour expression worried her. "Gregor?"

He slipped on a robe. "I need to show you something," then led her downstairs.

An armyman, with an insignia of Lieutenant, stood at attention by a door. He looked impressive in his pressed moldavite green uniform, shined black leather boots that reached halfway up his calves, and sheathed military-issue sword. He had short cropped black hair and dark mahogany skin, hinting that he came from another region of Grenan than his lighter skinned King. Taller than Sreana but not quite towering over Gregor, he kept his face stoic and appeared intimidating from a distance.

When he saw Gregor approaching, he bowed his head. "Your Majesty, I thought you were done for the evening?" Then he glanced at Sreana and she noticed his amber eyes. "My lady. My colleagues will be annoyed that we missed your entrance. Again."

"We'll only be a few moments, thank you, Rana."

They entered, letting Rana close the door behind them. Sreana looked around and saw disassembled books and piles of parchment.

"What is this?" she asked.

"All outstanding warrants for Sedoran citizens."

Sreana walked along the large gathering table, realizing that even she never knew how many truly existed. "Grenan law has never been fair to us."

"Maybe you can explain something to me. All these warrants, but no one in jail?"

"You fought by our side. You know our abilities to hide when necessary. Our townships are quite deserted during certain times of the week."

"Now I can understand why you hated me so."

"Gregor…"

"No, Sreana, you don't understand. I signed all of these. I didn't read them, I didn't confirm why these were written up. I trusted the Guard when they said that these were heinous crimes, but they are as simple as a four-year-old crying in the face of a guard. Another one is for a grandfather who couldn't lift a basket because of his arthritis. The Castle Guard deemed that as an affront instead of treating him with sympathy."

"At least you can fix this. Rescind the unfair ones and give my people a chance."

"It's going to take me a while."

"I can help for a bit, tonight, if you want me to?"

~   ~   ~

Split between townships, the less heinous or fickle warrants were piled at one end of the table, while those considered more serious were piled at the other. And in that more serious pile Sreana pulled a rather large group and set it to the side.

"What are those?" Gregor asked.

Sreana chuckled, patting the pile affectionately. "These would be the ones I can attribute to me."

"Now the truth comes out." He sighed, walking over to her side of the table. "I knew yours wouldn't be the easiest to write off."

"Well remember, you are rescinding those considered to be out of desperation too, not just the frivolous ones." She hugged him as he got close. "You look exhausted. Let's get you to bed."

He grabbed her pile, making her furrow her eyebrows. "An interesting read for later."

She rolled her eyes, then she pushed him toward the door flippantly. They exited, meeting Rana again in the hallway.

"Thank you, Rana, for keeping this room undisturbed."

"Gladly, Your Majesty. My lady."

"I'll never get used to that," she chided.

Rana looked confused. "What's that, my lady?"

"You know I'm here."

"Yes, well, King's orders are to allow you free reign. But I can only hope one day you can show us how you get by us so we can better protect His Majesty."

One of her eyebrows rose up. "Maybe one day, Lieutenant."

The smile that crept across Rana's face let her know he accepted her challenge.

And with that, Sreana and Gregor headed back up to his bedchamber. When they entered, Gregor moved to the desk that sat near the fireplace. He laid the pile of warrants down, but didn't look at her. He hadn't really said much all evening and when he did, any levity or civility felt forced. She started to unbuckle her belt when he cleared his throat roughly.

"It is quite late. You should go."

She started to joke that it was usually her saying that, but she saw his expression. She stopped herself and re-buckled her belt as subtly as possible. "You're right. You've had a long day and you should get some rest." She walked over to him and kissed his cheek as he stared at the fire. "Farewell, Gregor."

She had witnessed his anger and his frustration, but as she watched him, she saw it change to resentment and remorse. She grabbed her boots and, after she regarded him for a few more moments, left him with his thoughts. Time would tell if any of those emotions would be focused on her.

~ ~ ~

Before leaving, Sreana made her way back downstairs where Lieutenant Rana stood guard. She approached cautiously and when he caught sight of her, he glanced over at her in surprise. She stood in front of him, holding her boots behind her back and keeping enough distance between them that he could not grab her.

"I uh wanted to ask, even though I have no right, but…"

"I saw it too," he interrupted once she began to stammer. "I have served with His Majesty for many years and I am familiar with his moods. And the King is quite affected by this. I will keep an eye on him."

"Thank you, Lieutenant Rana."

~ ~ ~

A few days later, and after some coordination, Gregor called the captain to the large gathering room. The warrants were organized by township along the long edge of the table, minus Sreana's pile, and the King stood at the head, flanked by two of his lieutenants. The captain walked in, stood at attention, and waited for the King to speak.

"It has taken me an enormous amount of time to go through all of these warrants. This is beyond reason. There was a warrant for a four-year-old. A four-year-old." Gregor didn't see any empathy on the captain's face. "You made the people we are here to help sound like savages. They are good people, hardworking and proud." Chilled silence. "There is now a moratorium on warrants, until I can straighten this mess out."

"Your Majesty," the captain responded, almost too arrogantly. "I must remind you that you have no control over the Castle Guard. We are not your armymen, you cannot order us around. We answer only to the Queen."

Gregor's eyes narrowed and without a word, Rana stepped around the King to hand over a parchment sealed with the Queen's mark. "Yes, you do answer only to the Queen," Gregor conceded. "And she has some strong opinions about your behavior. She expects you to arrive expeditiously."

CHAPTER 15

Pirco strode into her lea, fixing his pants and tunic. He knew he was late and she would thrash him for it because last time, she was pacing around, impatient for him to relieve her so she could run off to the castle. However, when he approached, she was sitting, poking the fire with a small stick. Confused, he rounded the fallen log.

"Aren't you heading out?" Pirco inquired, sitting down next to her.

"Not tonight."

She could feel him counting the days in his head, then he frowned. "What happened?"

"Nothing."

He furrowed his eyebrows, confused.

"I mean it, nothing. No word about the warrants, or anything. There has been no news or gossip from the castle. I do not take that silence as a good sign."

"Why?"

"Because last time I was there, after we dug through the books of warrants, I gave him an entire pile that were mine."

He groaned. "Sreana, why?"

"He wanted honesty. He wanted no secrets. So, now he knows what a prolific criminal I am." Frowning, she stabbed at the fire. "I do not take his silence as good news."

"Why did you do that? You know how Grenans look at law breakers, that's why they were so adamant to make us all criminals. That way they could treat us so poorly."

"If he cannot accept those facts about me, then he will not accept other parts of me. Is it not best to be honest now and end it before it got more complicated?"

"I hate that you are so noble."

"Oh no, this is completely selfish. If anyone could break my heart... I don't

103

know if I could survive that. But I... I accept his decision. We're incompatible and I can deal with that, because I understand the reasons behind his decision."

"You two will be the death of me."

Sreana chuckled, mirthlessly, then grimaced. "Don't say anything to Duncar."

"No fear of that. I want nothing to do with that argument."

She fixed his collar. "You should go home, I know your bed is not empty. I'm here if anyone needs me."

"You'll be fine?"

She nodded. Pirco knocked her shoulder with his, making her smile, then stood and left. She watched until he disappeared, then returned her eyes to her dwindling fire. She would let it die out on its own then retire to her hovel.

She dwelled again on Gregor's face, like she had done all day, staring at that pile of her warrants. She knew it would be easy for him to ignore the others, they were all frivolous even though they were damaging, but hers... He could probably forgive hers just like the others, at least in writing. But what would he think of her, knowing the list of her crimes? The Grenan Kingdom saw criminals as the lowest of creatures which made it easier for the Castle Guard to charge her and her people so they could disrespect them daily, starve them, and expect them to lay down and die.

She would wait. It had only been a fortnight since they talked about warrants and she assumed that following morning was when he had requested them. A fortnight of nothing but crimes had to be daunting.

He had already asked her for patience. Even though it was against her character, she knew for the betterment of her people she had to find a way to respect his wishes.

~   ~   ~

A few days after her missed visit, Duncar sat at the dead firepit honing his sword, while Sreana bashed her staff against poor Pirco's as he fended off her quick strikes. They stopped battling when Habni and Garol rushed into her lea, one looking worried while the other incredulous.

"My lady, the Grenan armymen are here," Habni whispered. "They refuse to speak with anyone but the leader of the community."

Pirco frowned. "A trap? Castle Guard dressed as armymen?"

"No, these are the same men who talked to us about buying goods," Garol answered.

Curious and with staff in hand, Sreana followed Habni and Garol back into the township, where three men in Grenan army uniforms waited. Duncar and Pirco hung back, keeping their eyes and ears open, gripping their swords firmly. As she entered the road and approached the Grenans, a smile crept onto the lieutenant's face. She stopped in her tracks, causing her friends to tense. She sighed, realizing that her location was no longer a secret, then made her way to stand in front of the men.

"Good morning, my lady," Rana greeted, his smile widening.

"Good morning, Lieutenant Rana, what brings you to our little community?"

Rana pulled out a rolled parchment, secured with the King's mark. "The King wanted to make sure each of the community leaders were informed personally of his decision to rescind all warrants against the Sedoran people." Sreana grasped the parchment, but Rana did not release it. "My lady, he wants to ensure that you understand, all of the warrants."

"Thank you, Lieutenant, I understand."

With that, he released the document and bowed. The two armymen behind him also bowed, in unison.

"He sent you on purpose, didn't he?"

"Of course, my lady. Why not send a friendly face with good news?" Then he leaned forward and whispered, "Will you visit soon?" He regarded her for a moment, noticing her hesitation. "You won't tell me when so I can tell the King?"

"I won't tell you when because that would just make it easier for you to catch me," she retorted, finally smiling.

Rana chuckled, then bowed again. "My lady. Have a wonderful day."

She watched as the armymen turned around to leave. Pirco and Duncar then flanked her, keeping the Grenan men in their sights.

Then Pirco whispered in her ear, "Do we need to take them out?"

"No, I think my secret is safe. Gregor trusts him."

"Do you?" Duncar inquired.

"Aren't you the ones who keep telling me to have faith?"

"So? You'll go tonight?" Pirco asked.

Sreana glanced down, fiddling with the parchment in her hands.

"I'll take tonight's shift," Duncar said to Pirco, not waiting for her answer.

"And I'll share the announcement," Pirco responded, grabbing the parchment from her and walking toward their friends that had gathered behind them.

Sreana sighed, then noticed Duncar glaring down the road. She followed his eyes and saw that Rana had paused, staring back at them. By the path of the Grenan's gaze, she knew that he wasn't interested in her.

"What is he looking at?" Duncar wondered, hand grasping his hilt again.

She chuckled. "Not me."

Confused, Duncar looked at her but she had started walking toward their friends. He glanced back at the Grenan armyman, who also had turned away and was almost out of sight. Knowing that they were a safe distance away, Duncar followed his cousin.

~   ~   ~

As Rana updated him on the distribution of his announcement, Gregor sat solemnly in the overstuffed resting chair next to the fire. When he told Gregor that he spoke with Sreana, the King looked up at him in surprise.

"I do apologize, Your Majesty, she would not say when…"

"… because I didn't want to make his job easier," a voice interrupted from behind.

Rana turned to see Sreana standing in the balcony's doorway. Her eyes were focused on the King, not him. He turned back to Gregor and bowed. "Good night, Your Majesty."

"Good night, Rana, and thank you."

Rana then bowed to Sreana. "Good night, my lady." Rana exited down the servant stairs, closing the door behind him.

She stared at the door for a moment, not moving. "Your men made sure the news got out to everyone about the warrants being rescinded."

"I wish I had gotten through them all sooner. One day was too long to leave them hanging over your people's heads." He didn't get up, but regarded her sadly. "I also noticed that no further crimes were committed during my review. Thank you for exercising your patience."

"It wasn't easy, but you had asked for it and I had to honor that request."

Silence.

"You missed a visit."

"I knew you were busy," she answered, guardedly crossing the room until she stood in front of him. "I didn't want to be a distraction."

"I had hoped that you were prone to exaggeration. But you were telling the truth." The tears that trailed down his face shattered her heart. "I cannot apologize enough for the misery I caused you and your people. You all suffered, because of me and my ignorance."

Hearing him say that made her choke back her own tears. She stepped in closer and pulled him into a hug. She felt his arms wrap around her and he rested his head against her chest. "Gregor, we both know harms have been inflicted. We also know why they happened. And when one thing happened it led to retaliation and so forth. This will help stop that vicious cycle." She ran her hand through his hair, as it wildly swirled against her face. "Thank you. Thank you for giving my people their freedom. Thank you for taking away the fear they have lived with. Now they can start truly healing." They held each other for a few moments, his deep sigh releasing his grief. That precious moment warmed her and broke her at the same time. But she knew she had to let him go. She kissed his forehead and started to slip out of his arms. "Knowing they have their lives back gives me peace and I can walk away."

"Walk away?" He paused and hung his head. "I can understand if you don't…" and he leaned back, letting her go.

"I don't what?"

"After seeing all of those warrants, how could you want me?"

She scoffed, surprised. "How could you still want me?"

He looked at her, puzzled. She walked over to the desk, where her warrants laid and she could tell they had been rifled through. A few had been set aside, while the others were stacked into separate messy piles. She gestured helplessly, her fingers dancing along the edges of the papers.

"Do you think this ends us?" he asked, moving to her side. "You telling me the truth?"

"Doesn't it? You read my warrants, you know what I've done. Mostly out of desperation. And I'll admit, some out of sheer spite. How can you still want me? Knowing that the woman you took into your bed is nothing more than a prolific criminal per your laws? It was one of the reasons why I ran from you that morning. You're a King and I'm… by your own laws I'm not even a person. Just something to exterminate."

"Sreana, you made it quite clear that our laws were not yours. And why you did what you did and that none of your actions were ever violent. What I read backs up everything you told me, freely. You were honest from the start." He cupped her face with both of his hands, making her grasp his wrists. "Why would knowing the actual acts change how I feel about you?"

The look in his eyes made her realize that her doubts had been unfounded. She grabbed him by the shoulders and turned them around. He stared at her, concerned, until she untied his robe and pushed it off of him, pulled down his undershorts, and knocked him down onto the couch nearby…

~   ~   ~

Exhausted, they laid naked and panting on the couch. He was on his back, one of his legs bent at the knee and its foot resting on the floor. She straddled him, with her head on his chest and arms along each side of his torso. Holding her close with one arm, he kissed the top of her head, as he ran his other hand along her shoulder blades.

"Does this mean you won't be walking away?" he asked, once he caught his breath.

She lifted her head and, as she looked at him, rested her chin on his chest. "Only if you don't want me to."

"Don't walk away," he whispered, running his hand up her back, around her neck, and to her cheek.

She raised herself up and kissed him. As she did so, he grabbed his robe that laid nearby and wrapped his arms around her, then rolled them onto their sides. He trapped her against the back of the couch, keeping them skin on skin while the robe covered them. Leaning his forehead against hers, their breathing fell into unison. She had closed her eyes and he memorized the peaceful expression that washed over her face. Then he closed his, letting the night protect them and the fire warm them. After a few moments, she took a deep breath, making him open his eyes to find her staring at him.

"Why would you believe that I'd give you up so easily?" he inquired.

"When you sent me away the other night, how you… you didn't wish me farewell… I didn't think I'd be welcomed back."

"I sent you away because I knew I wasn't good company that night. I found myself losing patience while working on the warrants and I didn't want to snap at you or be inappropriate. And yet… when I finally got out of my dreadful fog, I realized I was cruel to you and that wasn't my intention. Forgive me?"

"I am laying here, naked, with you. I think it's safe to say you're forgiven."

Gregor sighed, in relief, then kissed her tenderly. "Rana told me you went straight to him after I sent you away. You asked him to keep an eye on me?"

"That's what I get for not telling him that was a private request."

"He still would have told me." Gregor tried to hide his amusement at her annoyed scoff. "He doesn't answer to you, remember?"

"I wasn't angry, Gregor. Hurt, yes, but I understood. I forced you to see a truth that was devastating. And when I gave you a pile of my crimes, I knew the man in you could not prevail over the King. You could never look at me the same way. I… I had accepted our fate, that we were done. I accepted that and knew I would always hold you dear to my heart even if you couldn't stand to look at me. Then you sent Rana to find me."

"He volunteered."

"He knows where I live."

"But I will not let him tell me."

She furrowed her eyebrows in confusion.

"Too many ears and too many enemies. My sister gave the Captain of the Guard quite a ringing when he reported back to her in Grenan. None of the Guard are thrilled with me and we need to be careful."

"What does that mean for my people?"

"The Castle Guard will only do that, guard the castle. No more law enforcement, no more supply runs. Queen's orders. And no more warrants, even if the crime is heinous. The law is back in your hands. You and the other leaders can manage fine without us. Rana and his men will continue to be my representatives, my eyes and ears, and offer any help your people need."

"Meaning less occupation and more collaboration?"

"Yes, the way it should have been since the beginning. Vehla agreed when I told her I needed to take back control of the relationship between Grenan and Sedora."

"Did you tell her about me?"

"I did. I thought it best she knew why I believed my handling of the situation made sense. Which means the ministers are also displeased, as they thought they and the Guard had it managed." He grumbled a curse, regretful. "I wish I had known sooner. So much was done in my name."

"Gregor, you are righting the wrongs. Just like you've been doing these last few months. If you weren't, I wouldn't be here. We wouldn't be together like this."

He kissed her, running his hand down her back. Enjoying the shape of her body, he held her even tighter against him. He rested his forehead against hers once more, staring into those beautiful gray eyes.

"I'm glad you weren't angry. It was hard to tell."

"You'll be able to tell when I'm angry. Something will be on fire."

"I'll remember that. But don't think that my reading all of your warrants exempts you from telling me about yourself."

She groaned a sound of complaint. "Do I at least get a reprieve tonight?"

"After that enthusiastic union? You get a reprieve, just for tonight. But you are required to tell me someday how you could escape on a sheep."

She burst into giggles, which was contagious. When their laughter settled, she admitted in a matter-of-fact tone, "They are fast little buggers, that's for sure," which caused them to fall into laughter again.

"If I did not know you already, I would disbelieve every word and recommend that the Castle Guards have their eyes checked for defects."

"Nothing I did surprised you?"

"No, I was surprised, actually impressed, but only you could succeed with some of those escapes. After all, you did swing off my balcony and survive."

He kissed her again, this time allowing their tongues to play. Then he moved his lips to her neck, until his mouth decided to wander lower. His devoted attention to her breasts made her moan softly. She lost herself in the sensations until his beard tickled her, breaking the spell. She ran her hand through his hair, then tugged as she sighed in disappointment.

"Speaking of escaping, I should go."

He grumbled a complaint against her skin, making her chuckle.

"I'll come back soon."

He raised up again and kissed her passionately. "You don't have to go. The warrants are rescinded." He still wouldn't release her, pressing her against the back of the couch. She felt his hand slip between her legs, just above the knees, and it started to slide toward other private areas. She squeezed her thighs together, stopping his hand halfway. She felt him grouse against her neck.

"No, but we are not prepared to announce yet, are we?"

Another disapproving noise escaped him then he looked into her eyes. "Don't stay away for so long this time."

"I don't plan to," she responded, kissing him lightly. "I will see you in a week."

"Promise?"

She kissed him again, suggestively, making him grip her thigh. "You have my word. I will be here, with you, naked, in a week. And your hand?" And she squeezed her leg muscles again. "It can finish its journey."

CHAPTER 16

The week had passed quickly. Sreana sat in her usual booth, eating breakfast, her mind running through a list of tasks as she made her way through her porridge. She had quite a few things to do before heading to the castle. Her stomach quivered, a good feeling, knowing her nights with Gregor were becoming her favorite. However, as the voices around her ebbed and flowed throughout the room, one particular conversation behind her caught her attention.

"I was up at the castle a few days ago," one man mentioned, after noisily chewing his food. "Those maids are a gossipy bunch. They kept talking about how that King of theirs hasn't been acting normal. He laughs for no reason. They catch him staring off and it takes them a few calls to get his attention."

"Sounds like he's gone mad," another man responded, his tone shocked.

"They also said on certain days, they catch him preening and that very next morning, his room is a mess, clothes everywhere, furniture moved around."

Sreana felt the color drain from her face.

Another man scoffed. "He's probably having fun with a drudge."

"They had decided it wasn't someone inside the castle," the first man replied. "Maids think he's got a visitor. A nice little whore."

Suddenly, "Watch your language, Trynur," Trealle's voice chided. "You know better." The man and his friends apologized while Trealle refilled their drinks. "It's his business, not yours," Trealle added. "Just like your business isn't anyone else's. We don't talk about how easily you offer yourself to anyone sitting near you at the bar on your free days after you make your deliveries."

The other men at the table burst into laughter while Trynur groused at Trealle. In her booth, Sreana almost inhaled her mead. She tried to hide her coughing as Trealle walked by, who grinned with pride at her handling of the gossiper.

~   ~   ~

She had spent the rest of the day trying to figure out how to tell him that they were not so secretive in their dalliances. However, after Sreana snuck in that night, any speech she had rehearsed evaporated when she found Gregor lounging in his bed, completely nude.

He watched her slip through the door with an amused smile. Then he beckoned for her to join him, and as she approached the bed, he slid to the edge and sat there. She became breathless as he loosened her boots, first the left next the right, then held her hands to help her step out of them. He casually removed her belt and sword, slipping the scabbard into one of the boots and slid them to the foot of the bed. He started on her clothing, first her pants and undershorts, then pulled her into his lap to slip her shirts over her head. With them both naked, he rolled them onto the bed.

They laid together afterwards, him on his back with his arm around her shoulders and her laying against his side, using his shoulder as a pillow. It seemed whenever they were together, nothing else mattered. But there was something on each of their minds and the silence tested their patience on who would speak first.

Gregor sighed. "You're quiet tonight."

"Am I?"

He grumbled a confirmation.

"Well, I wasn't quiet earlier."

He laughed, squeezing her shoulders. "You know what I mean."

"How did the household staff get things done so early?"

"I told them I wasn't feeling well and wanted to retire early. Surprising how quickly I felt better upon your arrival." He kissed her forehead, his breath lingering along her hair. "It was for the best really. My patience was rather frail today." She could feel him thinking. "I've realized that once a week isn't enough," he admitted. She stiffened in surprise, making him add immediately, "That wasn't meant to pressure you. I just want to be honest."

She sat up, leaned back on one arm and stared down at him. "We're being talked about."

"What? Wait. How?" Gregor propped himself up on his arm, furrowing his eyebrows in confusion. "No one's seen you, except Rana, and I know he hasn't said anything."

"That we know of."

He groused at that.

"I was in the tavern this morning and overheard someone talking about some suspicious behavior in the castle. The household staff are talking which is being overheard by deliverymen and from what I could gather, we apparently leave evidence."

"Like what?"

111

"The first night," and she grimaced, "your entire bedchamber."

"We did make a mess of it, didn't we?"

"Why didn't you pick things up?"

He raised himself up a little more to nuzzle and kiss her neck, making her inhale deeply. "Because you wore me out so, I fell asleep the moment you left."

"And then the second time… well, the poor dressing table."

Gregor chuckled. "Poor dressing table indeed." He rested his chin against her shoulder. "They did ask me that morning what had happened because when they walked in, everything was still on the floor and there were handprints on the glass."

"What did you say?"

"I tripped and landed against it in the dark."

She rolled her eyes.

"I know, it was a terrible explanation. I panicked. My answer worried the household staff so much, especially when they found the leg broken, that they had Genj come and check me. I had to admit to him what really happened."

"Your healer knows about us?"

"I had to tell him or I would have been under careful watch day and night. He already knew I had met you but didn't know you had started visiting. He was quite proud to know his regimen had worked. He just asked that we make sure the only thing we break is furniture and not each other."

She groused at that. "But I didn't think we left much evidence the last time."

"Marga was surprised to find me naked and asleep on the couch."

She glowered at him. "I left you in your robe."

"Barely."

He finally sat all the way up, shoulder to shoulder with her. He wrapped his arm around her, pressing her against him, and they both sighed.

"If we do not want to announce," and she met his eyes, "then we'd better start hiding the evidence of my visits."

"We should be a little more respectful, shouldn't we?"

"I think it's fair to say we've been a bit rude to your household. And it'll help with the rumors. Especially because those in my community will start putting pieces together."

"Good thing I was already naked when you arrived tonight." He massaged her hip gently. "Who knows about us?"

"Pirco and Duncar. I'm sure they've told their loves, but they are all trustworthy. Who else have you told?"

"There are only a few here who know about you. Genj, Rana, and of course, the other men that General Kasar assigned here after you kidnapped me…"

"That's more than just a few, Gregor. And what is the point of giving me permission if half your household already expects me?"

"You know being an invited visitor has more meaning than just saving my men's egos?"

She shrugged, noncommittedly. "I do, that's why it's hard to accept right now. We're still getting used to seeing each other. We're still getting to know each other. If this doesn't work out, then we can end it privately." He frowned and she caressed his cheek. "I don't like that thought either, but we have to be realistic. It's only fair to us and our people. We are very different and we've already had a few rough patches. And if I am seen by those who are not already privy, then we are not a secret anymore and nothing will be private."

"It has been amusing to see the frustration in my men. They have yet to see you sneak in. And they've been watching."

Sreana rolled her eyes. "I haven't even been trying anymore. I really didn't think I was that good."

"You are that good. Their pride is getting quite wounded."

"Sounds like I need to keep sneaking in, so they can keep practicing."

"I would like to see you walk in the door rather than hiding behind the armoire."

"That gives me the upper hand though. You can't get away with anything."

That made him laugh heartily.

"I heard something else today," she hinted.

"What was that?"

"They said you preen for me?"

He stammered in surprise. "I don't know if I'd say... I may manage my beard a bit..."

She started to giggle, running her fingers through his beard.

"I guess I'll save time not taking a few extra steps..."

"What! No, I like that you preen for me. Maybe just do it with no one around?"

"I'll try. So, what, you don't do anything for me?" he demanded.

"It may be your fault that I bathe more often now. With soap even." Her smile turned sly. "Maybe if we get the rumors under control, I will visit more often?"

"A reward? Hm, you know I could just order them to stop gossiping."

She scowled at him, the disapproving look making him laugh again.

"No cheating allowed?"

"You know it would only make it worse."

"True. We'll manage our enthusiasm better and end the gossip." Silence settled and he started kissing her neck. "Do we have any enthusiasm left this evening?" he whispered in her ear.

She leaned away from him, face blank. Then she tackled him back onto the bed.

CHAPTER 17

The following weeks found the gossip of the King's madness dwindle quickly. Sreana and Gregor hid their romps by straightening up his chambers and by avoiding damage to any other furniture. It did not temper their passion for each other, but with the gossip dying down, the visits occurred more often.

Mingled with their unions were stories, preferences, and even business. She listened as he told stories about growing up in Grenan and his days in the ranks of the army. He described the different campaigns, from horrifying weather to amusing interactions with locals. He enjoyed her tales of raiding and harassing the Castle Guard. She even told him about the sheep incident. They made sure to use their time together as wisely as possible, but every night she snuck in, pleasure was first and foremost on their minds.

One night, they sat up against the headboard, pillows cushioning their backs, as they cuddled. He had his arm wrapped around her shoulders, while she rested her head on his. Her leg laid over his, their hips touching. The blanket covered them up to their torsos to ward off the chill that snuck in as the fire dwindled. Their hands played against each other, fingers entwining, caressing, and dancing.

She sighed, nuzzling his cheek and closing her eyes. "I will have to skip our next visit."

"Why?"

"This week we celebrate the rebirth of Dranar as a god." She paused, trying to avoid admitting her banishment to him. "It's the first time we'll be able to truly celebrate and to give thanks. It's important that we all do so. We have a lot to be thankful for this year."

"Come the next night then."

Sreana chuckled. "You have no idea how well Sedorans celebrate."

"Can I ask a favor?"

"Of course."

"Give thanks for me? For us finding each other."

She leaned back enough to meet his eyes. "Already on my list."

"I will miss you that night."

"I will miss you too, but you will be in my thoughts."

"And you in mine."

~   ~   ~

Those who volunteered to stay back readied their stations the afternoon of the celebration, while those making the pilgrimage to Dranar's Temple started to head out. Joyful voices floated throughout the township as excitement for the special festivities lightened moods and minds.

Preparing to protect the emptying township, Sreana set up her station with water and snacks. Smiling, she reached into her pocket and fiddled with the small offering she had gathered to burn in her firepit when she was relieved sometime before dawn, to give thanks for all the good that finally came to her and her people. Especially crossing paths with Gregor.

Pirco approached with Duncar, both looking dejected. She had spent most of the morning reassuring her community that staying back was an honor, knowing that it meant others could go. Duncar and Pirco hadn't argued with that, but the looks on their faces now made her realize they regretted her exclusion from the festivities.

"It won't be the same without you," Pirco admitted, as he reminisced about the prior years.

"But it will still be lovely," she replied. "I want you both to enjoy yourselves."

Duncar groused. "I should stay…"

"No, Mirna is expecting you. She's expecting both of you. So are the others. Go, celebrate. Give thanks. I will hold the line with our friends here and we will celebrate in our own way."

~   ~   ~

After she was relieved from her post at the end of her uneventful shift, Sreana walked to her lea and tossed her offering into the fire that still burned. She whispered her prayers of thanks, incorporating Gregor's request as well, then entered her hovel. After undressing and cleaning up, she slipped into her undershorts and Gregor's undershirt.

Sreana curled up in bed as she heard the revelers' noisy return. The joyous sounds made her smile. She closed her eyes and sighed, pulling her quilt over her shoulder. Then she heard her door open. She opened her eyes and lifted her head, to find Pirco clumsily sneaking into her hovel. He tried unsuccessfully to close the door quietly, then made his way to her bed.

"What are you doing?" she demanded.

"I can't remember where I live."

Sreana chuckled. "How are you that drunk?"

"Very."

That made no sense, but she didn't bother asking any further questions. Pirco sat on the edge of her bed, managed to free himself of his boots, scabbard, and every piece of clothing, and left it all on the floor. She lifted her quilt up so he could crawl in but he laid along the edge. Shaking her head, she scooted back and wrapped her arms around him to pull him further onto the mattress, then covered them both with her quilt. With his back to her, he grasped her arms and made her hold him. Then she heard snoring.

A few moments later, her door opened again. This time Duncar stumbled in, looking as drunk as Pirco. She watched as he inelegantly stripped down to his undershorts, then climbed over them to lay against the wall. He slid under the quilt and pressed his back to hers. Snoring followed. She rolled her eyes, then fell asleep between the two people she loved most.

~   ~   ~

It wasn't until lunchtime when all three finally woke up. The two men groaned in pain as the sunlight poured into her hovel. She laughed at them, pushing Pirco off the bed and climbing out from beneath Duncar's weight after he had rolled back onto her while they slept. She slipped on a tunic, even though she wasn't sure whose it was, and headed out to the firepit. She came back inside with three steaming mugs, some food, and a pitcher of water. Both men sat miserably on the edge of her bed as she handed each a mug, then set the pitcher and food down on her small table. She sat in the chair and started eating while they nursed their mugs.

"I am incredibly jealous," she complained. "You two had more fun than is allowed without me."

Both men stayed quiet, guilt and regret darkening their eyes.

"What happened?"

"You go first," Duncar ordered Pirco.

Pirco groaned, annoyed. "There was a bit of a revolt over your absence."

"What kind of revolt?" she demanded.

"The jahlas knew about your banishment, because of our connection to them. That didn't stop them from being quite sour about the situation and they made it obvious that they didn't want to be there knowing that you had been punished. But to make things worse, no one told the eahzals."

"Oh no."

"Every nymph in that Temple almost walked or swam out. It took every trick I had to keep them there. I finally told them that you decided staying back was more important to you than fighting the banishment, because it meant more of our friends could celebrate, including them. That seemed to do the trick. Once I got them calmed down, the priests were able to get the celebration started and I made sure certain members of the two groups drank enough to keep everyone mellow."

"Then why were you so drunk, Duncar?"

Duncar groused. "Mirna and I had a massive row. We're over."

"Duncar..."

"No, it really is over. She... our row was over her refusal to commit to me. Either by marriage or pledge. She said she would only take one pledge in her life and it wasn't to me."

She stared at Duncar and Pirco, frowning. "I send you two to celebrate all the good things that have happened in the last few months and you're either drinking to keep the peace or drinking to bury your heartbreak." Neither man responded. Sreana sighed, crossing the room, sitting between them and taking each by the hand. "I am sorry you both had a terrible night. And I am sorry I could not be there to help."

"I'm just glad you didn't lock your door," Pirco responded, making all three laugh.

"I guess I have some meetings to make, nymphs to appease?"

"No, they love you. That's why they were going to riot."

"Still, I need to make sure that doesn't happen or even have a chance of happening again. I need to make sure no factions are battling while we try to keep our peace with Grenan."

Pirco rolled his eyes. "You hate diplomacy."

"And yet, it is very much a part of my life. You two rest, I'll go talk to Jya."

~   ~   ~

Sreana gave Duncar a few days to adjust to the idea that he and Mirna were over. She didn't know if she believed that it was, but by the way he sulked around her lea, she knew he did. They took lunch around her firepit, discussing any business he needed to be aware of while covering for her that night. As he nodded and mumbled that he understood, she rolled her eyes.

"You want to talk about it?"

"About what?"

Sreana scoffed. "You are definitely a Rathfeather. You cannot deal with your emotions any better than I can." She watched as he stabbed the vegetable on his plate with a little too much vigor. "You have loved Mirna ever since you saw her in her pram when Auntie parked yours next to it. Duncar, talk to me."

"What is there to say? She doesn't love me. She never has."

"No, that's not true. I know she loved you, at one time." She chewed a bite of food, then sighed. "She has changed just as much as we have because of her own experiences during the invasion. Ever since then, she has immersed herself in the Temple. She even stopped coming here to visit us. I thought it was just to help her deal with everything but now I think she wants to hide forever. I... I understand that feeling. Hopefully, someday, she will find out how useless that is."

He moved his remaining food around his plate, trying to fight back his tears. "I thought we'd be at least parents by now. Before the invasion, we talked about having a trawler full. We'd raise them close to the Temple and teach them both sides of our lives, fishing and religion. But when she told me she would never pledge herself, she said she had never wanted children and she had lied to keep me happy. And now, after everything, why bring children into this world to suffer?" The tears started to run down his cheeks and Sreana wrapped her arm around his shoulders. "If she can't see me as a part of her life, if we don't have the same goals, why keep hanging on? And why didn't she just end it sooner? Why lead me on like that?"

"I don't know the answer to that. She never talked to me about these doubts and changes. I only fear that she will regret what she said to you and not know how to fix things."

"If she does, it will be too late for an apology. I can't trust her ever again." He sighed, a heavy exhalation that deflated his entire body. "I will never trust another. I will never love again."

She scoffed, which made him glare at his cousin. "I said the same thing after Canor. Never again. It wasn't worth it." Then she squeezed his shoulders. "Don't tempt the Fates, cousin, they like a challenge." She stared at him for a moment. "Do you need me to stay home tonight?"

"No, go see Gregor. I will wait here and be thankfully distracted by whatever comes my way. Do you mind if I stay here tonight? I feel too much laying in my bed knowing she won't share it with me ever again."

"Stay, I don't mind." She hugged him again then let him go as she returned to eating. "Do me a favor though?"

"What's that?"

"Don't slobber on my pillow like Pirco does?"

He furrowed his eyebrows, as if offended, then finally laughed at the image of Pirco passed out, drooling in her bed.

"Do me a favor as well?" he asked.

"What's that?"

"Try not to forget that I'm there when you come back."

Sreana chuckled, taking a swig of water. "No promises."

~ ~ ~

Later that night, Sreana hid behind the armoire while the household staff finished up with Gregor. She sat on the floor with her knees against her chest, already barefoot and disarmed. But during the rare moment alone, she felt her heart break for her cousin. The things Mirna said to Duncar were the right things to say to drive him away, but she didn't know if her friend really meant those words. With her banishment, Sreana would probably never know. She didn't know how to fix things with him and Mirna but she also wondered if it was worth it.

"Sreana?"

She startled, a fist at the ready. Gregor peeked around the armoire, his eyebrows furrowed in worry. She sighed, standing up and kissing him in apology.

"What's wrong?"

"Nothing."

He pulled her into a hug. "You are a bad liar."

She wrapped her arms around his torso and groused into his chest. "I just have something on my mind. I'm sorry."

"Come to bed. You can tell me about it."

He released her, except for her hand, and pulled her over to the bed. He undressed her, then himself while she climbed into bed. They laid next to each other, face to face, and he wrapped her up in the blanket while keeping them skin on skin.

"Tell me what happened."

"Remember that celebration I told you about? Everything that could go wrong did. There was a bit of diplomatic incident that could have turned very bad if Pirco hadn't kept his wits about him."

He looked at her oddly. "You were there to handle it, weren't you?"

"We never leave our townships empty. We always have some who stay back. Because this was such a big celebration, I wanted as many of my people to go to the Temple so I stayed back to watch over things. And because I wasn't there, there were some hurt feelings. Which caused me to have quite a few meetings with the upset factions to make sure peace would be maintained."

"Was it an issue between communities?"

"You could say that."

"Sreana, secrets?"

"It's just very hard to explain," she responded, kissing him in another apology. "When I figure out how to describe it, I promise to explain it."

"What else happened? It's obvious a tiff between factions wouldn't keep you from paying attention to your surroundings."

She frowned. "I'm worried about Duncar. He has loved Mirna all of his life and they've always had falling outs about this and that. They know how to fight, but they also knew how to resolve their issues. But this time, I really do think it's over. And I don't know how to fix it."

119

"If you don't know how, then it sounds like it can't be fixed."

"I hate that. I'm supposed to fix things. It's my job."

"Your devotion to your friends is immeasurable."

Sreana blinked, realizing Gregor didn't know. "He's more than that. He's my cousin."

"And now your relationship makes a lot of more sense," Gregor admitted, with a laugh. "I always saw you, him and Pirco more as siblings than friends. But Duncar being your cousin, it explains a lot." He caressed her cheek. "If you can't fix things, what can you do?"

She shrugged, moving the blanket up and down. "I think the only thing I can do is keep him busy. And not rub my happiness in his face."

"That sounds very noble."

"It's completely selfish. I can't stand seeing him miserable. He's been through just as much as the rest of us. I truly thought he and Mirna would make it official." She glanced away, hiding the tears that threatened. "Not many relationships survived the invasion. Actually, I think Duncar and Mirna were the last. They outlasted all of the others, just to suffer the same fate."

"Does their ending dampen your faith in us?" he asked hesitantly.

"No, my inspiration has always been my parents, how much they loved each other and the things they weathered together. They are my guides." She grimaced, rubbing her face roughly. "I'm sorry. This isn't how I planned tonight."

"Why because we're not sweaty? We're together, that's what matters. Even though our unions are one of my favorite activities, we're more than bodies, Sreana."

She smiled, sadly. "Thank you for listening."

"Always."

She kissed him, then moved to straddle him. He must have sensed something in her kiss because he stopped her and mumbled her name against her lips. She leaned back, eyebrows furrowed in confusion.

"I am content with just holding you tonight."

Her face crumbled, the pain she felt over her cousin's heartbreak darkening her eyes. Gregor pulled her into a hug, letting her hide her face in the nook of his neck. She sniffled, then released a heavy sigh. They spent the rest of their evening holding each other, Gregor kissing her forehead periodically and running fingertips along her hair.

CHAPTER 18

A few nights later, she returned and she could hear Gregor's voice in the bathing room as well as Marga's. She darted behind the armoire, removing her boots and belt, then waited. She heard Marga wishing Gregor a good night as she departed. He exited the bathing room and headed toward the bed. He rearranged the pillows and turned to find her watching him. He held out his hands, beckoning her to him.

Once she was close enough, he hugged her and kissed her forehead. Then he helped her undress and led her to the bed. They sat up against the headboard, pillows piled behind them and he had his arm around her shoulder while she rested her head against his.

"What shall we talk about tonight?" she inquired, softly.

"Your last visit made me realize there is something we need to talk about." Gregor sighed, hard, then admitted, "I have never married. But I was engaged before I came here." He ran a hand through his hair. "She was pleasant enough, but it wasn't love. She was a choice made by matchmakers in the court. There were ulterior motives to the arrangement as I had very little interest in her or in marriage. Then when we heard of the invasion, her response was to let you all deal with it. Sedora had made the mistake and should suffer the consequences. That ended our engagement quite quickly. Prior to that, I had a couple of lovers but nothing serious. I have not had a relationship since the end of my engagement. Honestly, I've not been interested in anyone. Until you."

Sreana hesitated in responding, fearful of his reaction to her story. Noticing her reluctance, he cupped her face with his hand, making her look at him. The honesty and care in his eyes told her the truth was the only thing he wanted to hear.

"I had been engaged as well, years before the invasion," she replied. "We were as close to a love match as you could find, or so I thought. We had already announced our engagement when I found out I was pregnant. But I miscarried soon after and he decided that I was not duchess material. So, he broke the engagement off immediately and a few months later, he had married some younger girl." She saw anger flare up in his eyes and she braced for his words.

"Where is he now?"

"Dead."

"Good. Or I would do the deed myself."

She stared at him, confused.

"That was not a man, but a coward. To leave a woman because of something that's not her fault."

"That's not how he saw it."

"Most men don't. My sister has had a difficult time bearing children. It is a hard thing to endure, but she has four brash boys for all her trouble. She was the strongest woman I knew for surviving such heartache." He kissed her forehead, making her sigh in relief. "That was until I met you." He pulled her into a hug and he knew she was holding something back. "There's more, isn't there?"

She swallowed, hard. "The King called for me not long after and told me how disappointed he was in his nephew for not taking care of me. He said he would happily take over the responsibility..."

"... if you became his courtesan. There is a reason why no one mourns that family." Gregor growled a curse in annoyance. "And then you have some pretentious royal ass like me trying to bed you."

"You didn't know."

"I should have known better, just with everything that happened during the invasion. But I couldn't help it, when you showed yourself that night... I had never met someone like you. I was smitten."

"I held my sword to your throat."

"Yes and jumped off my balcony. It was all quite attractive."

She rolled her eyes. "You are a unique man."

"If I wasn't, you would not be here."

"That is very true. Thankfully we could work it out. And you did get me in bed, eventually."

"And I am completely humbled by your consent." He grimaced. "We never talked about... the consequences of our unions. Genj has helped me take precautions now but I was not prepared our first night."

His consideration regarding the matter made her heart warm. "We have our ways, if we're not ready for children. It became a habit during the invasion that I never broke." She held her breath, fearing again his regret, but made herself speak. "I don't even know if I can have children now."

"Have you seen healers?"

"A few, but no answers. The last one I saw before the invasion said I would find out if and when. But after everything," and she stammered, "I don't expect any children."

"Good thing my sister has four smart children. Grenan will be taken care of."

"Aren't children one of your main goals as royalty?"

Gregor scoffed. "Again, my father was not traditional. That was never a main goal. And after my failed engagement and my own injury, I never thought love or children would be in my future anyway. I'll take you over the other any day." He kissed the top of her head and gave her a reassuring squeeze. "How old were you?"

"Um, we courted when I was sixteen, he wasn't much older. Engaged at seventeen, and within a few months after my seventeenth, no longer engaged. Seems like a lifetime ago, since the invasion occurred, what, four years later? I don't even know how long it's been since."

"The Carmanic invasion happened almost three years ago now." Then she felt him thinking. "We are not that different in age."

"You look older," she admitted. "Must be the beard."

They laughed, then silence settled.

"Was there anyone else after that?" he asked.

"I fooled around for a short time, but never fell in love again. I... didn't want to."

There was a brief pause, then he sighed, dramatically. "Now you tell me."

"What?"

"I wasn't prepared for this to be just fun."

She furrowed her eyebrows, confused, then realized what he meant. "Something could change that. If the right person..."

"Ah the right person?"

"I'll let you know when I find him."

He made an offended sound, which made her laugh. She lifted her head, making him shift his body to look down at her. She caressed his cheek and kissed him tenderly, which made him smile. They snuggled again, letting the silence settle.

"So, this duke, is your community part of what would have been his fiefdom?"

"My community is what's left of it," she answered. "It had stretched from the seaside up to the mountain pass you spoke of defending. Do you remember seeing a large manor up that way? That was his residence. When we finally could settle, we also took in survivors from a neighboring fiefdom, whose townships were decimated by the Carmanic army."

"You are taking care of his people even after what he did?"

"I always have, because they are my people as well. I was a citizen of his fiefdom when he courted me. I later found out it was his mother who chose me, saying that I looked like a strong baby maker. I was also known among the communities because of my parents, so I was good for the Royal family's poor public relations." She shook her head. "From what I heard, the Carmanic soldiers castrated the men of the Royal Family when they found them. A sign that the Royal line had been ended."

"They did not only mutilate the men," Gregor responded, softly.

"You found them?"

He nodded. "We received a request for rescue. We rode out to their location to gather them up and bring them back to one of the nearby forts we had secured. When we arrived, we were ambushed. We knew it was a possibility, so we were prepared for the fight. But after we took down that horde, we found the mutilated remains of men, women, and children. There wasn't much left, but different organs were strung up like a party banner."

She scoffed. "If I had married him... I would have been one of those bodies."

"Fate thought you worthy of more."

"Or Death really doesn't want to deal with me," she retorted.

The sound of his laughter rumbling through his chest made her smile. They fell quiet again, his arms tightening around her. She sighed against his chest, making him nuzzle her head.

"Your experiences explain a few things. Why you are always ready to run. Why you think you're not good enough for me. That family made you believe you would never be good enough for anyone."

"I don't know why I let them get to me like that. I know I'm better than what they decided I was. I made sure I did everything they couldn't and helped my people the way they should have. I guess when the fighting started, I didn't think beyond that purpose, because I never expected to survive. These doubts only festered and meeting you, someone I could possibly feel something for, seemed to bring them up."

"Have I changed your mind yet? That you are good enough?"

"Every night together, when you touch me as if nothing is missing... that definitely has helped change my opinion about some things."

"Good. Now my job is to remind you every day that I don't deserve you."

She lifted her head enough to kiss him, then laid her head on his chest. His heart beat against her cheek in that rhythm she loved. She closed her eyes, letting his comforting embrace lull her.

CHAPTER 19

A soft voice roused him. "Your Majesty?"

He stirred, blinking against the morning light then he felt movement next to him. Sreana still laid in his arms, both nestled under the blanket. Her back was against his chest, with his arms around her and her hands hooked over his forearms. Their legs were entangled and his face had been buried in her hair. He smiled as he glanced over his shoulder at Marga. His movement made Sreana inhale deeply, then she froze. She must have realized it was morning and that she was still in his bed. He squeezed her reassuringly.

"Can you give us a few moments, Marga?" he asked.

She smiled and bowed her head. "I will come back when breakfast is ready." Before she exited, she disappeared into the bathing room and he could hear rustling. She returned with two robes still folded in her hands and laid them at the foot of the bed. Then she left, closing the door behind her.

"Oh gods, its morning," a complaint whined from underneath the blanket.

He kissed the back of Sreana's neck. "Good morning."

She pulled down the blanket, blinking against the sunlight. "I should have left already."

"Is it so bad to wake up with me for once?"

"No, but my friends will wonder where I'm at."

He chuckled at that. "Will they really?"

She scoffed, covering her face with her hand. He kissed her ear, then made his way down her neck, while his arms pulled her closer against him. "They're going to walk in on us."

"They won't come back until breakfast is ready," he answered, shifting his hips.

"Well then, we'd better be quick."

~   ~   ~

She would have preferred just getting dressed, but Gregor convinced her to try the robe on since Marga had kindly retrieved one for her. She fussed with it, not used to a swath of material. She was either dressed in her usual attire or naked, there was never an in-between. Gregor chuckled as he properly wrapped it around her and showed her how it tied to the side. Once he got her situated, he put his own robe on, then leaned in for a kiss. They were interrupted by the household staff, who brought in food and coffee. They placed everything on the small table outside on the balcony, smiled foolishly at the two lovers, and exited giggling.

Glancing at each other and blushing, Sreana and Gregor walked out to the table and moved their chairs and dishes closer before sitting down. Gregor glanced over at the bowl in front of Sreana and frowned, confused as to why she had such a simple breakfast compared to his. She had a bowl of porridge that sat in the middle of a plate, which held different fruits diced into pieces along the edges. Compared to his bacon, toast, and fruit, it looked almost an insult. However, she appeared flattered.

"What is it?" he inquired.

"I didn't think your kitchen would know what I ate for breakfast," she answered, sprinkling the pieces of fruit into the bowl. She mixed the fruit into the porridge, then lifted a spoonful. She blew on it as it steamed up, until she felt it was cool enough. Her smile widened once she took a bite. She caught Gregor staring at her, making her blush. She chewed and swallowed hastily, demanding, "What?"

"Nothing, just appreciating our morning together. The first of many I hope?"

She reached out and touched his cheek, her fingers running through his beard. He grabbed her hand and kissed the palm. She leaned in and they shared a tender embrace. His dark ale brown eyes searched hers for a moment.

"Can we do this again? Waking up together. Having a proper good morning?"

She chuckled. "I liked it, too. But there are consequences to us being found. We will no longer be a secret after today. Are we ready for that?"

"I am. Are you?"

"Do I have a choice?"

"No," he answered. "And you cannot avoid me giving you permission to be on the grounds now."

"Next step taken, I guess."

They enjoyed the rest of their breakfast in pleasant silence, their hands clasping and fingers entwining, until it was time for her to dress and leave. He dressed as well, tunic and slacks, then led her down the stairs.

"Come back tonight."

"I have responsibilities, you know."

"I know this. Doesn't mean I can't ask." Gregor walked with her to the door, grabbing her hand and pausing at the threshold. "Come back tonight for dinner."

"Night after tomorrow."

"Come to dinner night after tomorrow."

"I will."

Then he lifted her hand and he kissed it lovingly. "Farewell, my lady."

"Farewell, Your Majesty. I will see you the night after tomorrow."

"Just remember, come to the door."

She scoffed and slapped his shoulder, making him chuckle. She slipped her other hand out of his, trotted down the stairs, and headed down the gravel walkway to the main gate.

"My lady?"

Sreana stopped, startled to find the woman from earlier, Marga, waiting at the gate. Her dark brown eyes seemed to sparkle and her light blonde hair wound up in a bun. She was younger and shorter than Sreana, with a stout build. She wore a beige blouse and skirt, which seemed to be the uniform for the household staff.

"I wanted to let you know that I cannot keep a secret. That I cannot promise not to share that our King has found a companion," she rambled, excitedly. "It's just that, since he arrived here in Sedora, he had not found anyone. Even though he had plenty of options here in the castle. He has never... been inappropriate. But for him to find someone who is Sedoran..." The other woman blushed deeply when Sreana's eyebrow rose up in curiosity. "I recognize your leather wears as Sedoran design and not something we Grenan citizens would wear. What I mean to say is that well, it means a lot to us that our King is happy."

Sreana smiled. "Can I make a request?"

"Of course, my lady."

"When you say that you met the King's companion, please make sure that all who hear it know it is a love match."

"Try and stop me," she responded, then giggled. "I am happy to hear that, honestly."

"Thank you, Marga. Good day."

~   ~   ~

As she arrived in her lea, some of her friends were finishing up their breakfast chores. She felt herself blushing, hoping no one would realize she had been out all night. Habni glanced up and smiled, then handed her a mug of coffee. Sreana thanked her, heading to her hovel. As she opened the door, she found Pirco passed out in her bed. She sighed, feeling guilty. Usually, she came home before he dozed off, but she had left him waiting and apparently drove him to her bed instead of his own.

She closed the door, kneeled by the bed, and let the smell of the coffee waft under his nose. He groaned and inhaled deeply, then opened his eyes. When he realized that she was home and had coffee, he grumbled a complaint. She chuckled, handing him the mug after he sat up.

"I am sorry. I didn't mean to fall asleep."

"You fell asleep? In the arms of your lover?" he inquired, a sly smile creeping across his face. "How did that feel?"

"Amazing…" she whispered, blushing. "Until we got caught."

Pirco started to laugh.

"It is not funny," she groused, sitting next to him on the bed. "We are no longer a secret."

"It was bound to happen, Sreana. I thought it'd be sooner when all the rumors of his madness were spreading. But you two started covering your tracks, which only prolonged the inevitable."

"I know, but will we be accepted? A Grenan and a Sedoran? A King and a commoner?"

"There is nothing common about you, Sreana." Pirco took a sip of his coffee, grimacing at the heat and bitterness. "And do you really care? Accepted or not, you two will continue your visits and your collaboration to help our people."

"He wants to have dinner."

"An actual social engagement?"

"We've had breakfast, I guess dinner is next?"

"You really don't remember how any of this works?"

"I really don't. Seems like a lifetime ago."

He watched as her thoughts darkened her eyes.

"What is it?"

"I've never actually slept, you know snoring and drooling, with anyone, other than you and Duncar."

"What about Canor?"

She lowered her eyes. "The latest I ever stayed was dinner. I only spent time with him during the day, we fooled around while his parents were distracted and we never fell asleep. Now that I look back, I think I was only one of a few he bedded. He used me as the public companion, to keep our people loyal to the royal family." Then she inhaled, deeply. "My other lovers were flings, and quite secret, so there wasn't much cuddling afterwards."

"Not all of them were secret." He smirked when she glowered at him. "There was some pretty obvious pining for you."

She rolled her eyes.

"Does it feel wrong to sleep, drooling and snoring, with Gregor?"

"No, it feels… marvelous."

"You're smart, you'll figure it out. You two have made it this far. Enjoy his company. In private and public."

"You're right. I'll join him for dinner and I'll try not to stay all night again."

Pirco snorted. "You will stay all night. You will wake up naked with that lovely man as often as you want and I will know better than to wait up for you." Then his sly smile crept across his face again. "Good luck persuading Duncar."

CHAPTER 20

Sreana found herself nervous thinking about spending time with Gregor, now that they had been caught together. She didn't know if she had to act differently as a guest of the Grenan King. Sneaking in made things simple, she had no one to impress, and no one to offend. She also didn't have to worry about what she wore or when to show up, because her clothes never stayed on long and he was always waiting for her no matter what time she arrived.

But there was one thing she did want to bring with her for their first official dinner. She walked into Trealle's tavern, finding the older woman back in the kitchen working on a stew she would deliver to Sreana's lea that evening. Sreana peeked in baskets and bowls, mostly just out of curiosity but also searching for a specific item. When she noticed Trealle giving her the annoyed side-glower, Sreana sheepishly made her way to the cook's side.

"And what are you looking for, my lady?" Trealle inquired.

"Do you have any of those treats I like?"

"You mean the treats that you like to steal off the plate when you stop by?"

Sreana smirked. "Well, I take one as payment since I stole the ingredients."

"Are you taking them to the castle?"

Sreana furrowed her eyebrows, as she handed over the salt to Trealle's waiting hand.

"There are rumors, you know."

"That was fast," she muttered to herself, then asked Trealle, "Good or bad rumors?"

"Salacious."

"What?" Sreana squeaked.

Trealle's tone sounded more teasing than judging. "My lady found in the embrace of the Grenan King?"

"Didn't think she'd go that much into detail."

"Were you the reason for the rumors about his madness?"

Sreana couldn't stop the mischievous smile spreading across her face, making Trealle shake her head.

"I knew it. I saw the way you two looked at each other, like a pair of fools. I couldn't tell anyone that I suspected it was you. You made it clear you were trying to hide it, even if you failed terribly at it in the beginning. Honestly, beyond the rumors, it was obvious to me because you were bathing more than I had ever seen you bathe in your entire life."

"Is that why you defended us when Trynur tried spreading gossip?"

The other woman shrugged nonchalantly and passed the salt back, then held out her hand for another spice. Sreana grabbed the black pepper and delivered it. "But now that your secret is out, what I hear is that some fear you are in his sway, while others believe you have him under your spell. I wonder which is true."

"Both, I would say."

Trealle's smile widened. "So, it is true. My lady has found love?" Sreana felt her cheeks warm, which made Trealle chuckle. "Finally." She sprinkled the pepper and began to stir the pot filled with vegetables. "When do you need these treats?"

"Tomorrow, for dinner."

"Oh, a social engagement even?" Trealle handed back the pepper and Sreana returned it to its slot. "Garol's love made a new soap that smells heavenly."

"Is that a hint?"

"Well, it is a special event, is it not? You should smell good and look good."

"Am I not presentable?" Sreana demanded, glancing down at her clothing.

Trealle sighed, shaking her head. "You could do with a new shirt or two. Your patches have patches. We finally have material and leathers because the Castle Guard isn't thieving it from us. Go visit Madni, she should have something she can alter for you. Maybe something with color."

"It's more important that our friends use that material."

"You are a Leader and the Grenan King's lover," the older woman chided. "I think we can allow you some new clothes. Get a new shirt and I'll have your treats for you."

~   ~   ~

Sreana stared at the front gate, frowning. Two guards stood there, one on each side, and her instinct told her to knock them down. She took a deep breath instead. Gregor wouldn't know how to explain why his guest thrashed his guards for just standing there. Another deep breath and she ordered her feet to move. She strode up to the gate, glancing between each guard, then stopped when the one to her left held up his hand.

"Your business?"

Sreana's eyes narrowed. "King Gregor is expecting me."

131

The two guards looked at each other, then settled unkind eyes on her. "You'll have to be more specific," the other guard replied.

Before Sreana could rethink thrashing the two men, a voice from behind them startled the guards.

"You are aware of the King's orders," Rana responded, marching up to the gate. "She is an invited guest, no questions."

She bowed her head in respect. "Good evening, Lieutenant Rana."

Rana returned the gesture, his small smile signaling that he was impressed with her manners. "Welcome, my lady. Please, follow me." He glared at the two guards as she walked past the gate's threshold. Then, keeping a safe distance, she followed him up to the doors of the castle.

There, backlit by the torches glowing in the hallway, Gregor waited patiently. He grasped her hand when she made it to his side and kissed it.

"Welcome, my lady," he greeted her, his sly smile giving his thoughts away.

"Good evening, Your Majesty."

Then he guided her down the hallway, up the stairs that led to the balcony, where a table and two chairs were placed. Plates, silverware, and glasses were set in front of each chair. And the chairs were set close together, so Sreana and Gregor would sit shoulder to shoulder, as they had at breakfast.

Finally alone, Gregor grabbed her into his arms and kissed her. She giggled against his lips when he wouldn't let go, which made him kiss her even more ardently.

"That color looks amazing on you," he said.

"Thank you. I was told it was time for some new clothing. I didn't think teal would be so lovely as a blouse."

"I'll make sure to remove it carefully later." Then he glanced at her hand, which held a small cloth bag. "And what's this?"

"Well, I thought it only fair that I bring dessert since you would be catering the dinner."

"I guess we should eat then."

When Gregor released her and approached the table, he frowned. She followed and glanced over the table, unsure what concerned him. She set down her cloth bag near the left placement, then squeezed his hand.

"What's wrong?" she asked.

"I feel terrible. I invite you to dinner and I have nothing on the table."

"Were they supposed to have it ready?"

"Yes, upon your arrival."

Sreana furrowed her eyebrows. "Then something's wrong."

She rushed down the servant's stairs, Gregor close behind, and they descended into the kitchen. There they found the cook alone, sitting on the floor and cradling her arm. Stew had spilled all over the floor and cabinets, while the large pot laid nearby on its side. Sreana tiptoed through the mess to reach the cook, kneeling next to her.

"I don't know what happened," the cook murmured, tears from the pain running down her cheeks. Her damp clothes clung to her curves while her brunette hair clung to her streaked face.

"Looks like the handle broke off," Gregor answered, picking up the pot and placing it on top of the preparation table.

The cook's green eyes widened and she tried to get to her feet. "Your Majesty!"

Sreana grabbed her shoulders, shushing her. Then she looked at the burn on the cook's arm. "What's your name?"

"Gwena."

"Gwena, you have quite the scald. We need to have the healer take a look."

"I'll send for Genj," Gregor responded, heading back into the hallway.

"No, I must finish…"

"You are not doing anything but staying still," Sreana instructed.

Gwena sniffled. "I am sorry, my lady."

"No apologies necessary. You've done nothing wrong."

From behind her, she heard the shuffle of feet and looked up to see the healer entering, bag over his shoulder. She switched sides so he could look at the burn while she held Gwena's other hand. The healer, who Gregor introduced as Genj, dabbed it clean, slathered on some ointment that made Gwena whimper, then started to wrap it. All the while Sreana held her hand, whispering reassurances and asking questions to keep the other woman distracted. Once he was done, they both helped her to her feet and Genj walked Gwena down the hall to her chambers.

Sreana finally realized that Gregor had watched her the entire time. She blushed at the expression on his face. "What?"

"You are good with people."

"The wounds were extensive during the invasion and we had to find ways to help and cope." She cleared her throat. "Oh, this place is a mess."

"I should call for the drudge."

"Why? The poor drudge has to start his day before sunrise. No, we should be able to make it right." She started searching through cabinets for supplies. She opened and closed, opened and closed until she found the mop and a bucket. She handed the bucket over to Gregor. "Here, fill it with water."

It didn't take them long to get the kitchen floor mopped, the counters cleaned, and the offending pot banished to the garbage. They looked around, proud of their work, but stomachs started to grumble.

"I cannot cook," Gregor admitted.

"Neither can I," she responded. "There has to be something we can figure out."

She foraged through the cold storage and found slices of meat. With that, bread, and a few vegetables, they whipped up their own meal. They sat down on the bench next to hearth, Sreana straddling it while Gregor sat with his back to the heat and their plate between them. They ate, talked, and laughed, proud of their endeavors.

"How did you know something was wrong?" he asked, after swallowing his bite of a carrot.

"Your household is precise in their adherence to a schedule."

"Are they?" He looked at her, suspiciously. "How many times have you snuck into the castle?"

She laughed. "How many times did you have an incident?"

His eyebrows raised in surprise, then he told himself that he shouldn't really be astonished. They ate again in silence until he sighed.

"This was definitely not my plan for the evening," he lamented.

She shrugged. "Like you have said before, we are more than bodies. And we still got to spend the evening together. We also figured out how to work together in an awkward situation. I would say that is better than some plan."

He smiled adoringly at her, then leaned over to kiss her.

"Your Majesty?"

Gregor and Sreana glanced at the door, seeing Marga staring at them in disbelief.

"They had said you came down, but didn't say why," Marga explained.

"Long story, Marga," the King responded, with some chagrin.

"Oh. Did you wish me to draw you a bath before bed?"

Gregor looked back at Sreana, his eyes flashing with mischief. "I'd say we earned it after cleaning up the kitchen."

~   ~   ~

Marga assisted Gregor out of his clothing while the tub filled. Once it had enough water, she turned off the tap and helped Gregor into the steaming, soapy liquid. Sreana sat nearby, unlacing her boots first then unbuckling her belt. Marga turned to her, with a kind but dutiful expression on her face.

"May I assist you now?" Marga asked.

Sreana hesitated, then smiled shyly. "Thank you, Marga, but I can manage."

Marga appeared perplexed, looking toward Gregor. When he nodded, she bowed her head to Sreana, then to Gregor, and exited the bathing room. Once they were alone, Sreana finished undressing and joined Gregor. The tub itself fit them perfectly as they sat side by side. He wrapped his arm around her shoulder, making her lean her head against his.

"I didn't think you modest," he commented.

Sreana shrugged. "My body can rattle the faint of heart. I didn't want to startle her."

"That was very thoughtful," he replied, pulling her in for a kiss. "Even though she is familiar with my wound, I forget that the household staff are fairly protected from things like war."

"I hope I did not offend her."

"I doubt offended. Confused maybe."

"I will have to explain to her that I am…" and she took a moment to think, "I am very independent."

Gregor chuckled. "I think that will explain a lot. They are accustomed to being dutiful to me and not used to someone who does everything for themselves."

"Sounds like I am going to confound them every visit."

"Hm well, at least I won't be alone in my confusion."

That made her laugh.

"I should leave before breakfast though," she said.

"Why?"

"Because Gwena will not be able to manage the kitchen until she heals. The drudge, as lovely as he is, has limited knowledge of what to do. I do not think it's fair to expect him to know what to do that isn't the normal every morning routine."

Gregor stared at her in disbelief, then he kissed her ardently. "You honor my people with your thoughtfulness."

"You said I was good with people," Sreana responded, her voice soft. "I think my parents made sure I understood that no matter the walk of life someone comes from, they deserve respect and you should take the time to learn about their lives. The more you understand about others, the better person you become."

"I have so much to learn then."

Sreana smiled up at him. "Not as much as you think. I see how you treat my people and how you speak with those around you. I never met a King who thanks the people around him like you do. Our royal family didn't even know the names of their staff let alone even looked at them." She grimaced, lowering her eyes. "I was admonished one day for thanking the drudge who cleared the lunch table." Then she raised her eyes up to his, her face lit up with a devilish smile. "I continued to thank the staff, every chance I got."

"Again, there is a reason why no one mourns that family."

"No and we never will."

He pulled her into a hug, the water sloshing slightly at the movement. She nuzzled her face into the crook of his neck, sighing contently.

"I wanted to ask, how is Duncar?"

"It's been tough, but so is he. I found a few projects to keep him busy, but he made it clear he knew what I was doing. Then he went about working on the projects."

Gregor chuckled. "Definitely your cousin."

She groused loudly, which made him laugh harder and hug her tighter. "So how long do you bathe?"

"How long? Sreana, we can stay as long as we want."

She lifted her head, eyebrows furrowed in confusion.

"Do you ever just relax in a bath?"

"No, a bath is to clean up and then you move onto the next task in your day."

Gregor laughed, in surprise. "And sometimes a bath is to unwind, after a long day or a stressful one. You really don't know how to relax, do you?"

She shrugged, almost dislodging his arm.

"Then I guess there is something I can teach you, for once," he said, readjusting his arm and nudging her head back onto his shoulder.

She settled into his embrace, his free hand finding hers and their fingers playing against each other while water dripped down their hands and back into the bath. The comfortable silence held them until they heard Marga return. Gregor asked her to leave the robes and towels on the small stool next to the tub, then requested something to drink to enjoy with the treats Sreana brought. She smiled and nodded, heading back out quickly. Gregor got out of the bath first, drying off and wrapping himself up in his robe. Then he held out his hands for Sreana, who used his strength to stand up and step out of the tub. He patted her dry and wrapped her up in her own robe, tucking it in the right places and tying it closed.

When Marga returned they had already settled at the table and she served each a glass of milk. Sreana offered her one of the sweets, startling the woman, but she accepted. Both Gregor and Marga bit into the fluffed mousse treat that Trealle made and both agreed that it was amazing. Then Gregor took Sreana by the hand and led her toward the couch. Seeing the couple was ready to retire, Marga wished them a good night and first closed the door to the balcony then to the stairway when she left.

His smile changed from pleasant to sly. He grabbed Sreana into his arms, pressing her close. "Finally, I have you alone with no interruptions."

"What will we do with all that time?"

He chuckled and, lifting her up into his arms, carried her to the bed.

~ ~ ~

The next morning, Sreana woke up before daybreak. She opened her eyes, feeling them protest, as she heard Gregor softly snoring next to her ear. She laid on her back while he was on his side, still holding her tightly. She had her hands hooked over his arm, her forehead leaning against his chin. She inhaled deeply, careful not to disturb him. When he didn't react, she moved her head enough to look at his face. That small smile said it all. It reminded her of their first morning together. He had looked so pleased, as if their time together had satisfied more than the physical body.

If she hadn't promised to always wish him farewell, Sreana would have left him sleeping. The content expression on his face made her feel guilty about disturbing him. But like she had told him, she didn't need to be a burden on the household staff. She kissed him firmly, rousing him enough to return the embrace. She pulled away and he opened his eyes. His smile grew as he realized who woke him so lovingly. More kisses followed and eventually he rolled on top of her. He kneeled over her for a moment to adjust her hips then moved back into position as she wrapped her legs around his waist. They both made delighted sounds when their bodies connected. They took their time, rapt in the pleasure they shared, until they were both satisfied. He stared down at her in wonder, then they laughed together, giddy with gratification.

"Good morning," he whispered.

"Good morning indeed."

"Is it awful that I want that kind of greeting every morning?"

Sreana giggled, a sultry sound that drove him crazy. "Definitely not a bad way to wake up."

"You have to go now, don't you?"

"It is the right thing to do. Next time, I will stay for breakfast, I promise."

"When? When will you visit again?" he demanded.

"Let's give the kitchen at least three days? I think that's fair enough time to prepare for a guest. Maybe Gwena will be up to ordering others around."

Hearing the number of days, he actually pouted.

"I could always just sneak in and leave before Marga catches me?"

"You don't realize how beautiful you looked walking up that pathway, do you?"

"Flattery will not change my mind."

He chuckled. "I had to try. I can't help it. I finally found you and now I get to announce that I found you."

"I will be back in a few days. This is no different than when we were trying to keep it secret."

"Fine, I will wait impatiently for you to return."

Her sly smile stirred his desire for her. "It'll be worth the wait, I promise."

~   ~   ~

When Marga entered to open the curtains and wake them, she found Sreana and Gregor already dressing. She appeared shocked, but only greeted them. Gregor left for a moment, entering the bathing room, while Sreana finished lacing her boots. Marga finished her routine then waited at the balcony door for her instructions.

"Marga?" Sreana called to her, making the other woman glance over. Fully dressed now, boots and belt included, she stood and approached Marga. "I wanted to apologize for last night."

"What for, my lady?"

"I understand that it is your duty to care for the King, but I, well, I am used to doing things myself. I have been called, sometimes unkindly, too independent. But I didn't mean to be disrespectful to you or the great service you provide so diligently to Gregor."

Marga stammered, then blushed deeply. "I appreciate that, my lady. I was just confused, but your explanation has cleared that up."

"I'm glad," Sreana responded. "I was concerned that I might have offended you."

"There was no offense, I promise. I will respect your independence, my lady, but you may need to be patient. I know I will try to help you without meaning to offend you."

Sreana chuckled. "As long as we are willing to be patient and willing to learn from each other."

"Indeed, my lady."

"And now I must apologize for leaving so early. I hope the kitchen hasn't started breakfast?"

"No, my lady. The drudge wasn't sure where to start so I told him I'd check in with the King first."

"Thank you, Marga, for being so thoughtful," Gregor responded as he reentered the bedchambers. "Please let the kitchen know I will only require something simple for breakfast and our lady will not be staying."

"I will do so now, Your Majesty."

As Marga left, Gregor offered his hand to Sreana. "Come, I shall walk you out."

"First, can we check on Gwena?"

"Of course."

Sreana and Gregor headed down to the household staff's quarters and they ran into Genj in the hallway.

"Good morning, Genj. How is Gwena?" Gregor inquired.

"Doing well. She will heal quite well thanks to the timely treatment. She rests again. I am sorry she will not be able to provide breakfast."

"That is not the worry, Genj. We just wanted to make sure she did not suffer any setbacks overnight."

"If it were not for your quick thinking, Your Majesty, she would be in worse shape."

"Not mine," Gregor responded, squeezing Sreana's hand and smiling.

"I should get going," Sreana said, nodding her head respectfully. "Good day, Genj."

"Good day, my lady. Your Majesty."

~   ~   ~

As Sreana made her way out of the gates and down the road, the hairs on her neck rose up. When she glanced over her shoulder, she didn't see anyone, however instinct told her she was being followed. She rolled her eyes, veered off the road, and headed into the trees. Hidden by the foliage, she quickened her pace then darted past a large tree's trunk. Behind it hung her cloak, which she had left there out of precaution the evening before. After covering herself swiftly, she climbed up the tree.

The old, massive hornbeam housed a jahla named Jinjia, who materialized underneath the canopy. Sreana gestured to her to be quiet, then laid along the large limb and completely covered her body with her cloak. Within a few breaths, a Castle Guard rode past, glancing around for his prey. He halted his horse, appearing quite confused. Cursing, he turned his horse around and headed back to the castle. When he was out of sight, Sreana sat up, straddling the limb.

Jinjia shook her head, annoyed. "They are not very smart, are they?"

"No, not very smart. But it is concerning that they are still aggressive." She sighed, hard, then started to shimmy down the tree. "Thank you, Jinjia, for the protection."

"Always, my friend. You protect us, we protect you."

CHAPTER 21

Three nights later, Sreana strode up to the castle. This time however she didn't stop at the gates. She breezed by the resentful guards and made her way to the castle's entrance. There, Gregor awaited her. They greeted each other as irreverently as the last time, then he led her up to his chambers. With the door closed behind them, Gregor grabbed her into his arms and trapped her against the front of the armoire. They shared passionate kisses while hands wandered.

"Three days," he complained between kisses. "I waited three days for this."

She giggled, wrapping her leg around his waist to pull him in closer. "Told you it'd be worth the wait."

"I want to break this armoire."

She reached up and grabbed ahold of the large finial, positioning herself better. "I'm up for that challenge."

He growled playfully as he showered her with more kisses, his hands working her belt loose.

Suddenly, the door to the servant stairs swung open and Marga walked in. When she saw that they weren't by the table, she turned to find them inappropriately pressed against the armoire. Her face turned a deep red when she comprehended what she had walked in on.

"Oh! Your Maj... my lady... I am so sorry!"

Sreana dropped her arms, which made them land onto his. Gregor groused, mortified, resting his forehead against the wooden door. Sreana started to laugh, hiding her face against his shoulder.

"We apologize, Marga," Sreana responded, after clearing her throat. "I think we'll have to make some adjustments to our..." And she flashed an impish smile at Gregor, "greetings."

An annoyed sound escaped him and he finally looked at her. For the first time since they had met, his face was red with embarrassment.

Marga stammered, finally averting her eyes. "We didn't know if we should serve a snack or something since it's too late for dinner."

"Are you hungry?" he asked, stepping away and letting Sreana stand on her own.

"No, I am not, thank you. Is Gwena back in the kitchen? I would like to see her."

"And she you, my lady," Marga replied.

"Let's head down to the kitchen then," Gregor agreed.

Still smiling with embarrassment, they straightened their clothing and Sreana refastened her belt. They followed Marga down to the kitchen, where they could hear Gwena fussing at the drudge. Their entrance caught her eye and she squeaked then ran over to hug Sreana. Sreana hadn't expected it and was knocked back a couple of steps by the impact. Grinning, Sreana wrapped her arms around the other's shoulders and patted them.

"It is good to see you again, Gwena," Sreana responded, seeing that the other woman was not letting go. "How is your hand?"

Suddenly, Gwena recognized her error and released Sreana, then she stepped back and lowered her eyes. "Oh, um yes, it is very good. Thank you, my lady. Genj says it is healing very well."

"I am glad to hear that."

"Will you be dining with His Majesty?"

"No, I knew I'd arrive late so I ate before heading here. Thank you, though."

"She will be joining me for breakfast, though," Gregor added, making the staff giggle and clear their throats.

Then Sreana reached out and touched Gwena's chin, making her look up. "I am very glad you are healing well."

The cook blushed and smiled. Seeing that Gwena knew that no offense was taken by her hug, Sreana winked at her in jest. She clasped Gregor's hand and they started back to his chambers after wishing the staff a good night.

~   ~   ~

The next morning, Sreana kept her promise and stayed for breakfast. They sat on the balcony this time, enjoying the morning's mild weather. He snuck a bite of her porridge, surprised at the heartiness of something so simple, and in response, she stole a slice of bacon.

"Before I forget again, I was followed the other day, after I left the castle grounds."

Gregor's demeanor changed. "How far?"

"Only to the tree line. I was able to lose him there quite easily."

"Do you know which guard?"

"No, I couldn't see his face from my hiding place. He also wore plain clothes, not his uniform, but all Castle Guard have a certain way they ride a horse."

"If you feel unsafe..."

She squeezed his hand, seeing his worry. "I will be just as careful as when I was sneaking in. I expected this."

"But if something changes?"

"You'll be the first to know."

He raised her hand to his lips, kissing the back of fingers, before returning to his breakfast. She knew he wasn't completely reassured, but he also knew she could take care of herself.

~   ~   ~

Sreana's visits stayed consistent, as did her shadow. Each time, she slipped on her cloak and hid in Jinjia's tree. Then during her next visit, she tried to figure out which guard followed her. Unfortunately, there were several that fit his description. She knew she had nothing to accuse them of, seeing they could dismiss her claims as paranoia or say the guard was following different orders. She knew all she could do was take her precautions.

However, one morning, her patience finally expired. She made her way behind a tree and waited for the guard to ride past. He sighed, annoyed, then dismounted. Looking for some trace of her, he walked around, like he always did. When he turned on his heel, a fist met his face. He staggered back from the impact and fell to the ground. But as he glanced around, his assailant was nowhere to be found.

The next time Sreana visited, she saw the bruise around his eye and pointed him out to Gregor. "That one."

Gregor waved his hand and the stalker was rushed away by Lieutenant Wenth and a few of his men. After that identification, no one followed Sreana out of the castle grounds. She still took her precautions, just in case, but found the Castle Guard avoiding any actions that would be deemed against the King's orders.

CHAPTER 22

As time moved along, the visits started to feel natural. Eating dinner, spending the night, and waking to share breakfast, among other things, seemed to fit perfectly. With Pirco and Duncar keeping an eye on things, and knowing that very few incidents occurred during her absence, Sreana was able to relax more.

One night, as they ate dinner together, they made small talk about apprenticeships because two of Gregor's nephews were deciding theirs. He had mentioned that one had been considering following in his uncle's footsteps by entering the army, while the other was still unsure. This prompted Gregor to ask what she would have been doing professionally had the invasion never occurred.

She chuckled, before answering, "Well, if others had their way, I'd be a priest."

"Wait. Priest?" he demanded, surprised.

"Why do you think I knew how to look and act when I rescued you?"

"Kidnapped."

She rolled her eyes.

"Tell me."

"My friend and I were recruited to study under the Dranar priests when we were pretty young. She stayed, I... had a hard time being demure, abased, and merciful. Over the years, they continued to offer me a place. However, marrying a duke would have been a boon, financially and in status, which outweighed the priesthood. The only time I actually took the offer seriously was after the dissolution of my engagement." She toyed with her food for a moment, then shrugged. "But my parents were showing signs of ill health and my brother was learning his trade on long haul trawlers. One day, my father hurt himself and couldn't check his nets, so I took over. At that point, I thought it would be best to stay home and help with the business. Until... I had to fight." She hesitated, making Gregor reach out and grasp her hand. She smiled sadly, admitting, "I think after my desecration the invitations to join Dranar's ranks will finally stop."

"What penance did you have to pay for your theft and deception?"

"Banishment," she answered, softly.

His eyebrows furrowed in concern. "Permanent?"

"Undetermined."

"I could…"

"No," she responded quickly, then squeezed his hand in apology for her tone. "This is one of those things that a Grenan King cannot fix."

"I'm sorry."

"Don't be. I made the decision, fully knowing the consequences."

"Is that the real reason why you did not go to that celebration?"

"I would have stayed back either way. Like I said, it was important for as many of my friends to go because of the type of celebration it was."

They sat in silence, then he asked, "Do you only know about Dranar?"

"Oh no, they taught us about the others as well."

"Fancy a walk?"

She furrowed her eyebrows, confused. They finished their meal quickly, then Gregor handed her a candelabra from their table while grabbing one himself. Then he led her by the hand down the main hallway. They walked further into the castle, far from his bedchambers and to the back of the building. The small doorway hidden among the bricks was deceiving as the room they entered opened up into a huge space.

Sreana moved her light around, taking it all in. Furniture remained hidden under large swaths of material but the legs of chairs, tables, and a bed peeked out from underneath. Along the walls, mosaics dedicated to the gods of mercy, hearth, and sorrow. Near the fireplace, a small altar still stood with wilted and dried offerings covered in dust and left fragile by time.

"This was definitely a woman's room," she murmured. "Men do not make offerings to Dranar, Hendar, and Sera." She ran her fingers over one image of the three women surrounding an empty crib. She choked up, surprised at how hard that image struck her. She felt a hand on her shoulder and smiled sadly at Gregor. "She had the same heartbreak." She sighed, laying her hand on his. "I wonder if this was the home of the King's cousin? She was kind and so was her husband. They were always lovely to me when they visited. She died not long after my engagement ended. She never had any children."

They heard someone clear their throat and turned, to find some of the servants huddled in the doorway. "We saw the light," one woman said, apologetically.

Gregor waved them in. "Come. We were admiring the art."

Four women stepped into the room, holding their own candles, shyly keeping their distance.

"These lovely ladies found this room," Gregor said. "It had been walled up. Probably when the lady of the house died. But some of the bricks had fallen which caught their attention." He glanced over the mosaics thoughtfully. "I know Dranar, but the other goddesses don't sound familiar."

"Hendar and Sera were the prominent gods in the southern fiefdoms. Their Temples were completely abandoned once the invasion started. That region was hit first and hit hard and not many survived. There are a few who still worship, but not in the same numbers. The Temple of Dranar stands as a testament of the priests there. If it wasn't for their strength and tenacity, that Temple would have been abandoned as well."

"Maybe a rebirth of the gods will follow the rebuilding of Sedora?" Gregor wondered.

"Maybe. It depends on the people's faith."

"Um, how many gods do you worship?" a small voice from the servants asked.

Sreana smiled. "We have twenty main gods. But there are at least a hundred total when you add the demigods." The look of shock on the servants' faces, as well as Gregor's, made her chuckle. "Imagine having to learn all of them. We start very young reciting their names and their responsibilities." She glanced over each face, then realized she didn't know about their beliefs. "How many gods do you have?"

"Depends on the religion," Gregor answered. "We have several in Grenan."

Sreana's eyebrows rose. "Oh, I didn't know that."

"I just noticed that there are some mythical creatures represented here."

Sreana looked at the relief he pointed out. "Saehwas are the messengers of gods like Hendar and Sera. Eahzals are the messengers of Dranar, among a few others."

"Now knowing the story of this room, I am not sure what we should do with it."

"For her soul to rest, I think it would be best to wall it back up. Keep her grief locked away so it doesn't weigh on her in the afterlife." She touched the relief again, her fingers lingering on the crib. "Before you do, I'd like to leave an offering."

"Of course."

~   ~   ~

Sreana hadn't made this type of trek in ages, her days of offerings over the moment the invasion started. She made her way deep into the woods, in search of certain herbs and flowers. Even though she thought she remembered the different meanings of each, she had to retrieve her book of Dranar's teachings and study the list again before heading out. Herbs like hypericum and milky oats were easily recognizable by their blooms, but grew in very few leas in the area. The same was true for the gladiolus flowers she needed.

She hiked further and further in, until the mountain pass came into view in the west. She stopped for a moment, recalling Gregor's story about how he was injured. She knew that if she traversed the pass and headed just a little to the west, she would find the compound where Alarn had died. To the east, Canor's old residence. She sighed, knowing that even though so much time had passed, the people were still healing. Places like the mountain pass would always remind them how deep their wounds ran.

She made herself walk again, heading east instead. Once she passed through two very large, ancient chestnut oak trees, she stepped into the well-hidden but massive lea. The flowers were in full bloom, from dragon flowers to snow drops to heathers, from blues to pinks to yellows. She stepped lightly, trying not to trample the beautiful blooms, letting the tall grasses tap her legs and kiss her fingertips. Any grass that had wilted or flowers that had started fading away shivered and resurrected at her touch. She bit her lip, feeling the flowers caress her hands.

Sacred places like this brought out even her deepest secrets.

In her periphery, she saw a flash of yellow and recognized the hypericum peeking through the blades of grass. She skillfully made her way over to them, kneeling down and picking the flowers, all the while whispering her thanks. When she felt she had enough, she glanced around and caught sight of the milky oats nearby. It didn't take her long to harvest the right amount for her offering.

It felt too fast.

She regretted having to leave. She couldn't remember the last time she took the time to just stop. She sat down and inhaled the various perfumes. The song of the lea was reassuring and odd at the same time. The birds twittered and flitted around her, while the sounds of bugs and frogs that inhabited the nearby pond echoed through the grasses. Hidden within all the other sounds, the faintest caught her attention. It sounded like a voice, wispy and melodic. As she sat and listened harder, the sound became words and her breath caught in her throat.

"Priest," the voice whispered.

"No, I left that path a long time ago," she answered softly.

"Then why are you here gathering?"

"Offerings are a right of all believers."

Sreana looked over at the figure standing just outside the lea, between the two ancestral trees. No features were visible, but the shape was definitely female. Sreana stayed seated, waiting for the other to make her move. The stranger circled the lea, still among the trees. When she was closest to Sreana, she stepped forward. Long, oak-colored twigs encircled her shoulders and torso, hiding much of her anatomy like long hair. She glided along the grass, her pale skin and eyes mesmerizing.

"Elemental."

Sreana scoffed. "No, I am not."

"You are one of us. All of us. None of us. You must accept that."

"You can't offer that title to a killer."

"No, but we can to our protector. You kept us safe when men from another land came to annihilate us. You kept us safe when the rulers here tried to use us and destroy our home. Now? There has been a change in the forests," the jahla admitted, her eyes locked on Sreana's. "Those men who carelessly ripped away trees and life no longer trample through here."

"I'm glad to hear that. There has been a lot of hard work being done to better life for all of those who live in the borders of Sedora."

"We know that is because of you. My sisters say you have been working with the Grenan King."

"He is a good man, Jayna."

"Then we are happy and relieved." With that the jahla floated back to the tree line and disappeared in a gust that rattled every leaf.

With a deep, regretful sigh, Sreana stood up and left the serenity of the lea and headed back to her township.

~   ~   ~

The next evening, just as the sun started setting, Sreana entered the abandoned room, her offerings wrapped in a blanket of blue and yellow. She walked over to the relief of the gods surrounding the empty crib and knelt down, the last rays of sun filtering through the doorway. She unfurled the blanket, which let the offerings tumble along its length. She straightened them out, the herbs to the left, the cooled embers of her hearth in the middle, and the flowers to the right.

"We place these offerings for the gods Sera, Dranar and Hendar. Please take these blessings and our prayers to our sister in her afterlife. May she now be free of the pain and sadness that she suffered in this life."

Sreana lowered herself into a pose of abasement, staying there for several breaths, then rose back to her feet and exited the room. Gregor and most of the household staff were in the hallway, watching breathlessly through the doorway at the simple ceremony. When she crossed the threshold, Gregor held out his hand and she gratefully clasped it. Then the masons moved forward and resealed the doorway. Whispers trickled down the hallway, prayers to other gods that Sreana didn't recognize. Then, one by one, from the cook Gwena, to the cleaning staff, and even the masons who laid the bricks, each bowed their heads and thanked Sreana for letting them be part of the ceremony. Then they all departed, leaving Gregor and Sreana alone. He waited until she smiled, then they both headed back up to his bedchambers.

CHAPTER 23

As Sreana walked up, she saw Pirco standing in his doorway, in a tender embrace with another man. She slowed her pace, trying to give them enough time for their farewells. The man stepped away and into the street, then waited as a woman approached Pirco from inside and they too shared a passionate embrace. All three smiled at each other, then the man and woman clasped hands and walked away. Pirco noticed Sreana dallying on the walkway and blushed.

"Why don't you just announce and be done with it?" she teased, approaching him. "Keep them honest?"

He chuckled, but his amusement faded fast. "Not everyone accepts our ways."

Sreana leaned against his doorway, folding her arms. "If they're not Sedoran, no they don't. But luckily, we are Sedoran." She stared at him for a moment then smirked. "Anyone comes at you, I will happily show them every edge of my staff."

He smiled and grabbed her into a hug. "We've already taken our pledges, that's enough for us." Then he whispered in her ear, "Dini's pregnant."

Sreana stiffened and leaned back, her smile ecstatic.

"It's Darner's, but... we'd be a family."

"Then be a family, Pirco. After everything we've been through, have we not learned that we must make the best of everything this life is willing to offer us?"

"Hm, like you and the King?"

She scoffed. "Do not use us as an example. You know I am not a good influence."

They both started to laugh.

"I'd have to move to their farm."

"Cows and horses and pigs," she responded, wrinkling her nose. "Right back to childhood."

He groaned in annoyance, making her laugh. "What does the day hold for us? Must be something important if you couldn't wait for me in your lea."

148

"I've a meeting with one of our fishermen at Trealle's. Something is worrying the whole lot of them but they wanted to speak in person. I could use your perspective. Come, let's find out what is concerning them."

~   ~   ~

The morning held a chill that heralded autumn. A slight breeze carried the scent of the ocean like a tease from Trealle's kitchen, filling Sreana's heart with joy. After inhaling deeply and savoring it, she headed down the dock to a small fishing boat. It was only big enough to hold about five people, while the rest was devoted to nets, storage, and tools of the trade.

Waiting at the end of the dock was a man about her age, his vocation aging his face with windburn and wrinkles. He was bundled up in a knit sweater and pair of double thick slacks, waterproofed boots and a bulky jacket with multiple pockets. His pecan brown hair was hidden by the knit cap that covered his head and the tips of his ears. His matching full beard also made him look older than he was, which was one reason to wear it besides protecting him from the cruel ocean winds.

"There she is, Sreana Rathfeather, the rabble rouser."

She stopped walking, feigning shock. "Me?"

"Kidnapping the Grenan King," Trehan responded, folding his arms over his chest, "thieving his horses."

"I refuse to confirm or deny the horses part."

The fisherman laughed heartily, reaching out for a hug. They embraced, just long enough for him to clap her on the back. "It is good to see you. Just wish for a better reason."

"Me too. I will try to make time to visit more."

"You say that every time," he chided, before looking her up and down. "It is going to be odd for a woman to be standing around on our deck."

"Standing around?" she demanded, offended. "I plan on showing your lads how things are properly done."

Trehan chuckled, then gestured for her to follow him. As they climbed onto the boat, a boy waited for them patiently. He hadn't hit double digits in age yet, but he stood at attention and saluted them proudly.

"This is Migan. He did the drawings."

She bowed her head to the boy. "Migan, thank you for your amazing renderings. The details you provided made it imperative for me to come see with my own eyes. May I keep them to show others?"

Migan smiled shyly and nodded, then disappeared below deck.

"One of the children you adopted?" she asked.

"Youngest of the five. All good kids, ready to take on the world."

"You're a big-hearted lout, Trehan."

With a shrug, he turned away. "Ready to head out?" Trehan called out to his men.

They answered, "Aye!"

With that, the seiner left the dock and headed out toward the entrance to the bay. The bay was surrounded by mountains until the north section, where it had collapsed into the water, creating the port. However, the ocean hid a secret. The opening only existed because the volcano underneath the water had crumbled. Its caldera was visible from above on a good day, but anyone unaware of it could run onto any protrusions, or worse, hit a heat vent that could melt any material made by man.

They anchored in a good spot and dragged their nets, pulling up different types of fish that flipped and flopped on the deck. The splashing and smell made Sreana think of her father, who took her and her brother out as often as he could to teach them the trade. The shouts from Trehan were no different than what her father had expected. Mixed with the orders, she could hear the memory of her mother chastising her for being covered in kelp and beach sand. Her brother and Duncar laughing and shouting insults as they pretended to sword fight with tree limbs. And her aunt telling Duncar to stop chasing Mirna and his frustrated complaints that she wouldn't stay still long enough to let him kiss her.

That joy slowly turned to an ache.

Even though there were so many happy memories from her childhood that rose up, there was also the pain of her losses that seemed to outweigh it all. Their parents' bodies burning on the remaining boats after the brutal slaughter of their community. The farm animals and beasts of burden left to rot in the fields – the ones they didn't burn to ash. Their homes and businesses destroyed beyond repair. The survivors abandoning the beaches to hide in the surrounding forests. Living in fear and moving from place to place to either stay ahead of the Carmanic horde or in the hunt of it.

She had to choke back emotion, but when she saw Trehan's men proudly watching her, a true daughter of the craft, her heart lightened a little.

Once the nets had all been cleared, she made her way down below and used Trehan's magnifying scope to scan the ocean for the reason she had joined them. Just past the caldera, in unclaimed ocean, there were three unfamiliar full-rigged ships. She stared at the masts, the sails, and the figureheads. They were not Grenan, or Carmanic, and definitely not Sedoran. She could see movement, just ants on a hill from her vantage point, so she couldn't make out gender let alone nationality. She heard footsteps and saw Trehan approach out of her periphery. He stood next to her, while staring out the other porthole.

"So, they just sit out there?" she asked.

"Aye. They made sure to anchor far enough out that even a swell won't land them into our waters."

"They don't look local." She sighed, dropping the scope. "No colors, no flags. But the masts and sails remind me of the Yvesian navy."

"What are those fools doing on this side of the sea?"

"My guess? They're a distraction for what is sneaking up behind us."

"You think those maniacs are coming for us again?"

"That is not a rumor I need running around," she responded, sternly.

Trehan exhaled, then nodded. "Me and my lads will hold our tongues."

"And the other boats?"

"If you ask it, it will be followed. Once we dock, I'll share your wishes."

"Thank you."

"But for today, our work here is done…"

"Like I said, when you're done, I'm done. I have seen enough. And no need to make them suspicious. Let's go home."

Trehan headed back up, then she heard him call her name. She trotted up the steps back to the deck, and saw all of the men gazing over the side of the boat. She peeked over the side too and saw a flash of a shadow. It flitted under the boat then swished back out until a face stared up at her from underneath the crest.

"She must have sensed me when I touched the water," Sreana muttered to herself, then called out, "Trehan, do you have something for cover?"

"Yes, a moment." Trehan strode into the main cabin then returned with a thick wool quilt. "Here. Men, avert your eyes."

Sreana stretched her arms out with the blanket, an invitation to the creature in the water. Splashing could be heard as the creature jumped up onto the side of the boat. Then she stood on her fin lined legs in front of Sreana, who wrapped the material around her. She cuddled into Sreana's embrace, smiling up at her. The eahzal had long, black seaweed for hair, black eyes, and a green tinge to her skin that helped her blend in with the water's waves. Her dorsal and pectoral fins laid flat under the blanket, but Sreana could feel them, along with the scales that protected her body. The gills along her throat shut, holding down her operculum. This allowed for air to enter through her nose, letting her breath like a person. Short and slight, the top of her head barely reached Sreana's shoulder and the quilt engulfed her.

"Trehan, hold off on heading back?"

"Yes, my lady."

"Thank you. Come," she told the visitor, "this way."

Sreana led the woman into the lower cabin, where she had watched the intruder's ships, to talk in private. The woman stayed close to her, her icy breath dancing along Sreana's exposed skin.

"You know about the boats?"

The woman nodded.

"Stay away from them."

The eahzal glowered, her anger at being ordered not to do something vibrating off of her.

"Please. They are from another land, they do not know about you and your kind. And I am afraid that, either out of fear or curiosity, that they will hurt you."

The water nymph's demeanor changed, as if recognizing the concern in Sreana's voice. After hesitating for a few breaths, the eahzal nodded as if realizing she was right. Then a flash in her eyes warned Sreana that she really took the order as a suggestion.

"I will only agree to an altercation if they pass into the bay. The moment they cross the caldera," and Sreana sighed, "you and your people can sink them without hesitation."

The devilish smile that lit up the eahzal's face sent chills down Sreana's back. They had a tentative peace with the eahzals, a relationship that took longer to build than that with the jahlas, but Sreana had always worked with both groups to keep all Sedorans safe. Eahzals' destructive side always seemed to come out when they felt slighted. Sreana tried to be soft in her strictness, but there were times she didn't expect their full cooperation.

"We should get you back into the water."

Sreana started to guide the petite creature toward the stairs, but she cuddled up against Sreana again. She smiled, a different impishness in it, and Sreana chuckled.

"I am flattered, but you know things like this never work out," Sreana responded, watching the nymph's shoulders lower. "But thank you, you have made me feel very special."

The eahzal giggled, then darted up the stairs. Sreana followed quickly, just in time to watch the blanket land on the deck and the eahzal's sleek body enter the water with a clean dive. She watched as the eahzal's shape disappeared into the depths, then sighed in relief. She glanced over at Trehan and nodded, who in turn started shouting orders to return to the docks.

~   ~   ~

She waited until they had already eaten dinner and the staff had cleared the table. Once alone, she removed sheets of parchment from her satchel and laid them out on his desk. Gregor stared at Migan's renderings, his eyes dark with concern. "There's three?"

"Sitting out in neutral waters. They haven't moved for days, so the fishermen began to worry and reached out. So yesterday, I went out to see with my own eyes. I saw three massive ships with no reason to be out there. They are full-rigged, readily armed, but no flags or colors."

"They don't look like Carmanic and we both know they are not Grenan or Sedoran."

"I think they're Yvesian."

Gregor turned and leaned back on the desk. "Instigators from another continent?"

"We know the High North Kingdom keeps the others in line, but even countries like Yves and Ariela like to test the rules. They are like children trying to outsmart their mother."

"Queen Elissabeth will not tolerate the test."

"How long would it take to send her a message?"

"Directly from here? Quite a while. But I will draft something and ensure it gets sent from my sister. She has the vehicles to hasten the message. It'll be worth it to just get under our stalker's skin." His tone hinted at something more than strategy. There was real worry. Sreana walked around to stand in front of Gregor. He wrapped his arms around her waist as she draped her arms along his shoulders. "Here I thought getting Sedora back to its former glory was going to be the hardest part. This? This is more than I expected."

"I know. Maybe that's the reason for the attention. We were not a threat while weak, but now?"

"I don't like waiting for the enemy to make their move. If it cannot be seen, then it is a surprise, and that is never good."

"I think…" and she inhaled for strength, "it's time that you meet with all the community leaders."

"I agree, this information is too disconcerting to keep to ourselves. Can you set it up?"

"Of course. However, we may have to deceive the others." When she hesitated, Gregor squeezed her reassuringly. "It may cause issues. Not all of them trust you."

"I am completely aware that I only speak with proxies and not the actual leaders in some of the communities. Take whatever steps you believe are necessary."

CHAPTER 24

She had tried to clean up and make herself look proper. She wore walnut brown leather riding pants, a short sleeve undershirt with a new, maroon tunic over it. Her short leather gauntlets only held her sleeves at the wrist, while her boots were strapped all the way up to her knees. Her belt slipped comfortably through the loops of her pants, holding her sword, dagger, and purse. She had her hair pulled back and up into her usual crooked bun.

Sreana glowered at her reflection, then sighed in annoyance. "I am not a leader," she complained.

"You are our leader," Duncar responded, stepping up behind her and meeting her glare via the glass.

"I don't look like one."

"You're right," Pirco agreed, leaning against her door. "You look more like a thief."

She rolled her eyes, then turned to Pirco. "That's what I am."

"Just remember not to start another fight with Terga," Duncar reminded her, as he tugged on her shirt along the shoulders. "It doesn't look good drawing swords during a conversation."

"But it is so much fun to embarrass him," she retorted.

"Sreana…"

"I know, I know. Be a leader. But I'm not."

Pirco scoffed. "Who tells us what to do every day? Who runs to help someone at a moment's notice? Who helps distribute food weekly and makes sure supplies are available to our community?"

Sreana lowered her eyes.

"So, if you do the job, you're stuck with the title," Pirco continued. "You're bossy, and therefore, the leader."

She looked at herself again in the reflecting glass, this time feeling insecure. "I don't belong there."

"Yes, you do." Duncar sighed, grabbing her by the shoulders. "You are our

154

voice, our grace and guiding light. And Gregor needs you there. Dressed or naked, you're his only true ally among the community leaders."

"You're right. If anything, I am there to support the agreement made between Sedora and Grenan. Each leader is bringing a second, which one of you…"

Both Pirco and Duncar responded, "NO."

"I can't take anyone else. Both of you know what's at stake and are just as much an ally to Gregor as me."

Both men huddled together and argued over how the other would be the better choice. Then Pirco sighed and added, "And if she stabs Terga again, between the two of us, you're the only one who can make a decent tourniquet."

She shrugged. "He has a point."

"Yes, but if I'm not there, you might not be tempted," Duncar retorted.

She groused.

"Fine, I'll go," Duncar finally conceded, then smiled slyly. "Pirco can stay and deal with the situation in the stables."

"Oh well played," Pirco complained.

~   ~   ~

Trealle's tavern appeared heavily guarded by the number of armed people loitering nearby. In preparation for the evening, the mismatched tables were pushed together to form one large gathering table, with the chairs lined up along the sides. The curtains were drawn and the storm shutters closed, blocking any voyeurism. And the doors were locked and guarded, to ensure no one could just walk in.

Inside, it bustled with over a dozen people. Gathered were the leaders of the various communities, along with their seconds, who were there as backup representatives, to assist with note-taking as well as arguments. The leaders would sit, while the seconds stood at their right elbows. The head of the table however had no chair, as the speaker would stand instead.

Ever the dutiful host, Sreana assisted Trealle with mugs of mead, her back to the room. Suddenly, the other woman's eyes widened.

"If it isn't Sreana Rathfeather," a voice boomed.

Sreana cringed at the sound of Terga's voice. She turned, forcing a pleasant smile. He was a large man, dark skin and eyes, with broad shoulders and stout legs. Sreana had to tilt her head back to meet his dark mahogany eyes, since her head barely reached his collarbone.

"Terga, I'm glad you agreed to this meeting."

"Well, your message made it sound important. Are we expecting a happy announcement between you and the Grenan King today?"

She rolled her eyes. "That would not be a good enough reason for all of us to meet in person."

"This better be worth it, Rathfeather." Then he turned away and stomped over to his seat.

After setting mugs at each chair, the leaders began to take their places. Leaders like Terga and Dener sat near the head since their communities were the largest and smallest respectively, while a leader like Sreana usually sat near the end. However, since she had called the meeting, she took her place at the head. Duncar was to her right, strategically placed between her and Terga. After everyone settled in, Sreana straightened and folded her hands behind her back.

"Thank you, everyone, for agreeing to meet tonight. We have had some eventful months, but the aggressions toward Sedora haven't calmed. Recently, it was brought to my attention that unknown vessels had been seen outside our port, just past the caldera. But that is only the latest incident." Sreana sighed, lowering her head for a moment. "Seeing that border issues are not my responsibility, I think it's best if someone else explained the situation."

She stepped to her left and Gregor slid out of the booth nearby and took her place at the head of the table. Some of the leaders gasped in surprise, others cursed in anger. Terga stood and grasped the hilt of his sword, but Duncar swiftly clasped his hand and stared him down.

"That is unnecessary," Duncar warned, "and you know it."

Sreana glanced around the table, her dark eyes meeting those of each man and woman seated around it. "Give him a chance to speak."

"He is an occupier," Sella retorted, after locking eyes with Sreana. "Has sharing his bed truly blinded you to that?"

Sreana scoffed. "Do not judge our companionship as you are not invited to join it." Sella stiffened and avoided eye contact. "I have not forgotten our past with Grenan. But I have been working side by side with King Gregor, trying to build a better Sedora. Have any of you?" She glanced around the table again and found that no one could meet her eyes. "You hide and send proxies to complain but what have you done? You speak harshly of our companionship, but tell me, has nothing gotten better, for any of you?"

Silence.

"Grenan and Sedora face a common foe, again, and if we do not work together, we will fall together. Animosity and stubbornness will not only lead to that fall but make us just as guilty as the Sedoran royals that left us to die."

"I think it is fair to hear him out," Dener's usually soft voice rang out.

Terga huffed, wrenching himself free of Duncar's hold. Then he sat down, causing all eyes to finally shift back to Gregor.

"I'm afraid Sreana is correct," Gregor said. "Our common enemy, who we once faced together on the battlefield, is making plans for another invasion." Everyone around the table murmured to each other in disbelief. "Smuggled Carmanic weapons were the first sign, then foreign naval ships holding near the port entrance. Not to mention the attempt on my life. I have been working on finding out who the traitors are in my own household, but I am afraid there may be more within your communities. Caution and suspicion are unfortunate, however I believe it is necessary to roust those who do our countries harm. We can only do that with a united front and the sharing of resources."

His words held some sway, keeping the leaders in the tavern for further discussions. The rest of the evening was spent with Gregor, Sreana and Duncar fielding questions and arguing over details on how the Sedoran communities could protect themselves. Some wanted to stay independent, and make their decisions without interference, but Sreana reminded them that mindset had hindered them during the original invasion.

Eventually, the other leaders agreed to deliberate within their own communities and come back to the table with ideas. They started filing out after a few hours, some returning home while others accepted the offer of food and mead in Sreana's lea.

As the room emptied, Gregor sighed, reaching for her hand. "We presented our case, all we can do now is wait."

"That's the hardest part for someone who has no patience."

He chuckled, pulling her to his side.

"As far as the Castle Guard and ministers are concerned, I am with my men at the border and will not return until tomorrow afternoon."

"Oh? Trealle has some wonderful rooms upstairs."

He growled playfully at her, making her laugh.

"Come. Our friends are probably waiting for us at my firepit."

Sreana was right. The fire lit up the entire lea. As they greeted her friends and spoke jovially about daily life, Sreana and Gregor made sure they didn't give away the concerns that brought everyone together. They finally made it to the firepit, sitting on one of the logs. He wrapped his arm around her waist and held her close, as they sipped from their mugs.

"Were you offended by what they said about us?" he asked against her ear.

Sreana smirked. "I expected a lot worse, to be honest."

"It took everything for me not to laugh when you said that no one was being invited into our companionship. The looks on their faces…"

"What can I say? I don't want to share."

With a chuckle, he kissed her. They sat in comfortable silence until Gregor tried to stifle his yawn.

"It's been a long day, hasn't it?" she inquired.

"Diplomacy can be draining."

She ran her hand along his cheek, then glanced around to see that the crowd had dwindled quickly. Not many were left, mostly her friends and a few other leaders. Duncar was speaking quietly with Terga's second, a man named Griezen, which reassured her immediately. She knew if anyone could get Terga to listen it was Griezen and in turn, Duncar was the best advocate to sway Griezen.

"Then let's retire for the night. No one will be offended. But before we do, there is someone else you need to meet." They stood and she led him to the tree line. "Jya? Do you still want to meet the King?"

From behind the tree, Jya appeared. She glanced between Gregor and Sreana before she respectfully bowed her head to Gregor. Jya smiled shyly then it faded into a worried frown.

Gregor stood in shock. His eyes glanced over the nymph several times, as if trying to discern if she was real. He tried to say something but nothing came out. Sreana reached out and grabbed Jya's hand, then Gregor's. They both looked at her and she squeezed their hands, reassuringly.

"Jya, this is King Gregor from the Grenan Kingdom. Gregor, this is Jya, our jahla friend."

"It is an honor to meet you, Jya," Gregor finally said, after clearing his throat.

"It is our honor, Your Majesty," Jya responded. To Gregor, her soft voice was reminiscent of leaves rustling. Sreana translated for him, who bowed his head in respect.

"She wanted to meet you this time, since we announced our companionship." Sreana reached over and hugged Jya with one arm. "Good night, my friend. May the gods keep your nightmares to themselves."

"And may they give you dreams worth dreaming," she replied automatically then let go of Sreana and disappeared behind her tree.

Gregor followed, walking completely around the tree but not finding the jahla. Sreana tried to hide her laughter, however she failed and grabbed his hand again. Sreana led him to her hovel, letting him enter first then closing the door behind them. He stood next to her little table, turning slowly and leaning against it. Gregor still appeared intrigued and astonished.

"That is a big secret."

"And difficult to explain," she responded, sheepishly.

"Try."

"Others call them nymphs, but that is a generalized term." She stammered, then sighed. "The jahlas serve as our connection to each other."

"That's how you can communicate without sending someone out to another township?"

"Yes. We can tell one jahla and it is shared immediately with all of them."

"How many are there?"

"Their population is in the hundreds," she answered, folding her hands in front of her. "They took heavy losses in the beginning of the invasion, but are thriving again. Most live throughout the forests around us, living their lives just as we do. Per our treaty, they assign each township a jahla, who resides in a tree nearby and communicates to the others to help us stay in touch and warn each other of any dangers. It is mutually beneficial because what is a danger to us is a danger to them. So this way, we are always keeping each other safe. We've had this arrangement for generations with the jahlas. The eahzals? Not as long."

"How many types of nymphs exist?"

"There is one tied to each element in nature. Jahlas are earth nymphs, eahzals are water nymphs. There are also the saehwa, halha, and aetha. They represent fire, air, and the celestial respectively. But our treaties are only with the jahla and eahzal." She hesitated, her fingers twisting against each other as she tried to find the right words. "Not everyone can speak to them. Only some of us can talk with jahlas or eahzals depending on our Talent. And then there are even fewer who can speak with all of them."

He stared at her for a moment, realizing why her nerves were so rattled. "Are you one of the special few?"

"I am, yes. My Papa and uncle could only speak with eahzals, which made sense because they were fishermen. Some of our fishermen now have the same Talent. Pirco and a few others here can speak with the jahlas. I am the only one in several townships that can communicate with both types of nymphs."

"I've heard rumors of Sedoran magic, but…"

"Magic?" she inquired, eyebrows furrowing. "We don't use that word."

"Then what do you call it?"

"The nymphs call those like me Elementals, as we can connect with all elements in nature. It is not magic, it is natural."

"You don't tell many people about what you can do?"

She sighed, her eyes darkening with memory. "No, it is not something I like to tell others. Our Royal Family thought people like me were crazy. So, we never shared our friends or our Talents with the Grenan armymen when they fought with us because we did not know how they would react. But most of my people know what I can do, because it's hard to hide it when you're trying to survive."

Gregor closed the distance between them, grasping her hands, finding them sweaty. "Why were you afraid to tell me?"

"Because it is not your way and I would be considered, well you say magic, but not a person. I was called several unflattering things when I was younger."

"Like you said before, we are different people and still learning about each other. Thank you for sharing this part of you."

"I hope you understand that this is a secret that we cannot share with your ranks. Considering the animosity between our people and those villains who still hide, it could be used against us."

He stared straight into her eyes. "Even though it will take me a while to absorb all of this, your secret is safe with me."

She kissed him heartily. "Thank you." She took a deep, relieved breath. "We should get some sleep."

She walked over to the bed, turning down the quilt and trying to puff up her pillow. When she straightened, he wrapped his arms around her waist and she leaned back against his chest.

"I can't help but think about our first night together," he admitted, nuzzling her hair.

"I'm sure there are parts you wish to change?"

He let her go, sat down, then pulled her onto his lap. They kissed, a long passionate embrace until she pulled away. "Be here when I wake up," he replied, "that's the only part I'd want different."

Then, without another word, he rolled her into the bed. Afterwards, they laid side by side, their legs entangled, their arms wrapped tightly around each other. Once they finally caught their breaths, they shared an ardent and lingering kiss.

"Is it awful that I've missed your bed?"

She chuckled. "My lumpy bed? Why would you miss it?"

"We had our first union here, for one. And it was here, for the first time, that I slept well." The look in his eyes told her that he was not being flippant. "I still had nightmares, especially about the day I was injured."

"I'm sorry, Gregor," she whispered, frowning while she caressed his cheek.

"For what?"

"For not making this the safe place it should have been for the both of us."

"It always has been my safe place. When we are apart and I feel lost, all I have to do is close my eyes and remember the moments we had here. If I needed that reminder that I could be a man and not some useless figurehead, my mind always brought up the memory of us together that night. Did you think of us, here, when you needed somewhere safe to hide?"

"Only when I could lie to myself that it was acceptable to care about you."

"No more lies?"

"No more lies."

"Good, because if not, then telling you how much I love you would be quite awkward."

She kissed him. "Finally."

"Why didn't you say something first?"

"A Sedoran woman does not pledge herself to another so easily."

Confusion crossed his face as he furrowed his brow. "Pledge?"

She blushed, running fingers through his beard. "In the old days, when we found someone we intended to be devoted to, we made a pledge to each other."

"So, you've taken this pledge before? When you were engaged?"

"No. The Royal family had deemed it ignoble."

"But some still take this pledge?"

"A few but not everyone remembers the old ways."

"Would you? Now?"

"Hm, I don't know. At my age, monogamy just isn't very alluring."

His playful growl made her giggle. She stared into his eyes and felt her heart flutter. She would take the pledge happily, knowing that they truly loved each other, but she hesitated. She didn't want to put him in a situation of not returning the words. However, as she recognized the love in his eyes, she couldn't stop them from escaping her lips.

"Gregor, I pledge to you my faithful heart and undying love."

Those words were said in a strong but loving tone. He stared at her, in awe, speechless. He could only respond by kissing her passionately. When their lips separated, she raised an eyebrow.

"It doesn't count if you don't say it back," she chided, with a smirk.

"Say it again."

She obliged.

"Sreana, I pledge to you my faithful heart and undying love."

Her smile said it all, then she crinkled her forehead. "How do your…"

"I love you," he answered immediately. She stared up at him in surprise and he blushed. "I know, it's simple. But it's what we say."

She pulled him in for another kiss.

"It doesn't count if you don't say it back," he retorted against her lips.

She rolled her eyes then, again with a sure tone, responded, "I love you."

More ardent kisses were shared before their physical satisfaction and emotional happiness drew them into sleep.

CHAPTER 25

That morning, they laid entangled, hiding under the quilt. A loud playful knock on her door roused them out of a deep sleep. Then the door opened, with Pirco announcing, "Good morning!"

With the sound of Pirco's entrance, Sreana groaned unhappily and Gregor chuckled at her. Sreana reached blindly behind her, causing the quilt to move and expose their heads.

"What are you doing?" Gregor asked.

"Trying to reach my boot so I can throw it at him."

Gregor grabbed her arm, laughing, then pulled her hand to his lips. "Good morning."

"Good morning," she responded, looking up at him, and they kissed.

They heard Pirco make a happy sound and the door creak as he leaned against it heavily. "If I hadn't pledged my heart already, I would jump right in there with the two of you," Pirco admitted, sighing whimsically.

"Get out," she ordered, burying her face into Gregor's neck.

"Our friends wish to know if you will be joining us for our exercises?" Pirco inquired.

She sighed. "In a moment. Get out." She heard the door close and felt Gregor's lips press against her forehead. "There's something else I haven't told you."

She felt Gregor lean back, making her look at him again. "Something else? We promised no secrets."

"This was necessary, too, I promise."

She pulled away and got out of bed, then started to dress. He followed, both getting decent before they walked out of her hovel. Her lea was filled with men and women of different ages, all armed, practicing fighting moves. Some had staffs, others swords, a few with daggers. They moved in slow motion at first, then they started to pick up speed with each round.

"You've been training?" Gregor asked, after a small gasp.

"We had some trouble a while ago, so we thought it'd be best to knock the dust off. But it seems we are preparing for more than just paid rabble rousers."

"Why not say something?"

"Well, we started right after your kidnapping and we didn't want you to think we were mounting a true uprising."

Gregor glanced over the group. "It could look like that, couldn't it?"

"And when we reunited, I didn't want the wrong ears to hear about it if I told you."

"Sreana!" Pirco called out. "Want to fight?"

"I left my sword in my hovel."

"Go get it!"

She rolled her eyes and waved him off. "I don't even have my boots on."

"Never stopped you before."

Then she noticed Gregor's expression. "What?"

"I've never seen you fight," Gregor pointed out.

She frowned. "You would think differently of me."

"No more secrets?" Gregor whispered, squeezing her hand.

Duncar appeared wordlessly on her other side, offering her the hilt to her sword. Sreana sighed, then stepped away from Gregor. She unsheathed her sword, which made Pirco grin. Everyone, including Gregor and Duncar, began to form a circle around them. She stretched her arms, using her sword as a weight, then cracked her neck and indicated her readiness. She tuned out the audience and focused on her friend. Pirco made the first move, striking her sword with his and causing them to parry. Sreana blocked each aggressive move then answered it with her own. She saw his weakness and she bashed his sword until she could lock hilts and push him back. After an impressive spin on her toes, she used the fuller of her blade to smack him in the ass. He yelped, jumping back and rubbing the insulted cheek.

She chuckled. "You always keep your..."

"Left side open," they said together.

Pirco glared at her. "You're holding back."

"Always." She shook her shoulders loose. "You really want me to show off?"

"Absolutely."

Accepting the challenge, she rolled both of her shoulders in unison then she clicked her tongue against the roof of her mouth.

"Duncar?" Sreana called out, winking at her friend as she switched her sword from her right to her left hand. "Make sure you have plenty of salve ready."

Pirco laughed, more worried than amused. Then she attacked. She bashed his sword hard and fast, using her speed to drive him back, which pushed the crowd backwards. When she realized he was preoccupied with what she was doing with her sword, she dropped down and, with her leg, swept his out from under him. He landed with a dull thump and another yelp, his sword clattering away. She stood over him, with the tip of her blade under his chin. He sighed, waving his hands in surrender. Pleased, she sheathed her sword. She reached out and he grabbed her hand, letting her help him back to his feet. Sheepishly, she glanced around, catching the awe on their audience's faces. Applause erupted as Sreana and Pirco grasped arms. She walked back to Gregor who appeared impressed.

"That is skill I have never seen," Gregor admitted. "I do not know if I am impressed, scared, or even more smitten. I think all three at the moment."

She laughed at him in disbelief, then shook her head. "You are a unique man."

Gregor pulled her against him, and with a sly smile, kissed her. She melted against him, until they heard whispers and giggles. They broke their embrace and glanced around to see those in the lea staring at them. Then they heard Pirco's lusty laugh, making them blush.

"You should see her with a staff," Duncar said, walking up behind them. "The sword is just a toy compared to that."

"My lady?" a young voice asked from her other side.

Sreana turned to find three teenaged boys staring at her, bashfully. "Yes, my friends?"

"How can you fight with your weaker hand?" asked the boy who got her attention.

Pirco chuckled, rubbing his hip as he joined them. "She doesn't have a weak hand."

"Practice mostly," she answered, ignoring Pirco. "And necessity. I dislocated my right shoulder after a particularly nasty fight with some Carmanic soldiers. I had to improvise while I healed."

"Because she would not stay still while she healed," Duncar chided.

Sreana scoffed. "Had too much to do."

The boys thanked her, then headed back into the group to practice.

"Is it hard to admit that you're a fighter?" Gregor asked softly.

"It's hard to admit that I am…" and she took a deep breath, "that I am a killer."

"Never unnecessarily," Duncar responded quickly.

"No, and never for pleasure," she agreed.

Gregor must have recognized the look on her face because he diverted the conversation. "Are practices like this occurring throughout the Kingdom?"

"Yes, each community has their own."

"With Sreana providing the lessons," Pirco added.

She grimaced, then she shook herself. "We should see what Trealle has for breakfast."

"If you don't mind," Gregor said, stopping her from walking away. "I think I would like to try your training."

"Come, dear King," Pirco waved. "I'll show you the steps."

CHAPTER 26

Within days of their meeting, their fishermen confirmed that the ships disappeared from the nearby neutral waters. Their absence over the last month relieved Sreana, even though she knew that didn't mean the other menace wasn't still stalking them. The other community leaders finally agreed to keep up heightened security just in case and to check in daily with each other through their jahlas. She impressed on everyone that they needed to keep their eyes on both horizons.

Sreana ate breakfast at Trealle's, enjoying a little privacy in her booth. Each of her visits with Gregor always started with updates at dinner, making sure they were on the same page. Then they would shed their clothes, and daily responsibilities, to enjoy their companionship behind closed doors. However, that did not stop gossip about the King and the Leader and their obvious love for each other.

As she felt the blush warm her cheeks, Duncar sat down next to her, exhaling dramatically. Chewing her toast, she gave a side-glower. She knew he had something on his mind that she wouldn't like, and it had been festering for a few days now, but she patiently waited for him to speak.

"You know that I am glad you and Gregor found each other..." then he began to stammer. "The farmers have been asking for you." Duncar frowned. "Because they've been asking about things I have no knowledge of. Their questions are important and complex and they can tell by the fear on my face that I don't know what to say and that I don't want to say something wrong."

"We do have a big planting season coming, don't we?"

"And I do not know the difference between a plowing field and a tillable field. Ask me when to net for Red Fish, or what herb helps with food poisoning, I can do that... But this is beyond my knowledge. And Pirco is just as baffled. He's been great with the animals, which to slaughter and when to make certain dairy foods, and all that, but even he has his limits."

"You two have done an amazing job picking up my slack, but you're right,

I've slacked off too much." She chewed another bite of toast, shrugging. "I'll spend more time home now, to get our crops ready as well as any other matters."

"Don't stop seeing him."

"I won't. We will just back off a little bit. It's good for a relationship, right? Distance makes for a better reunion?"

"It would just be easier if he came here," her cousin admitted.

Sreana laughed, mirthlessly. "It would, wouldn't it? But we do not trust the Castle Guard not to invite themselves to harass us and his lieutenants are terrified to let him out of their sights. I still don't know how he managed the last visit."

Duncar stole a grape, popping it quicky into his mouth. "I don't even know how you know all of this."

"Canor's father. When we were courting, I spent a lot of time at Canor's side, so I heard a lot of conversations. Papa always told us to listen." Duncar murmured something in agreement. "The farmers and ranchers would come to his residence often to ask for advice and direction. After his father died, Canor was expected to step up but he was completely inept and his mother was just as useless. Our friends would leave confused and frustrated. So, I uh started asking questions when I came back into town. I ended up learning more about what it took to have a good season and what it took to keep the meats and milk available. Then we started meeting before they would travel to speak with Canor, coming up with a plan and then it was up to the farmers and ranchers to persuade him into believing it was his idea. We never told anyone."

"So that's where you disappeared to every week? Hiding away, plotting how to manipulate your former lover?"

She shrugged, nonchalantly. "When my engagement ended, I knew they were afraid I would turn them away. After I came back home, knowing how incompetent Canor was, I couldn't. Our people needed someone to help and guide, which he couldn't do. I guess it was fortunate that my time away was not during a critical time for the crops." She scoffed, her shoulders slumping slightly. "And ever since, they never stopped asking my advice when issues arise."

"I remember they were even knocking on your door when you were sick. They were trying to figure out what to do since the Carmanic army had withdrawn and we had settled here."

"Didn't you learn anything during that time?"

"It was too much for me then as it is now."

"I don't even remember the early days, you had me quite drugged."

"Yeah, I had to keep you still. But I had to back off the pain relief so you could think straight and talk coherently. The first time they visited you, they looked quite worried, because of how you responded. You told them to plant the chickens." That made her laugh. "And the farmers weren't the only ones to visit. It was hard to keep you on a schedule. They didn't understand how bad it was. Even when you got so bad that I thought I'd lose you, they never knew."

"Hiding the truth sometimes is kinder."

Duncar chuckled, mirthlessly. "Not bad for some fishmongers' children."

"You know Papa and Uncle were more than just some fishmongers. And they taught us both that our paths had nothing to do with where you came from, but where you were willing to go."

"And you're more than just a daughter, fighter, and leader, Sreana. Does Gregor know everything?"

"I told him about our connections to the jahlas and my... Talents. There are still some things I haven't admitted, decisions and such, but we're still getting to know each other. I will tell him, eventually. Just have to find the right time. But right now, I have to figure out how to tell him we won't be seeing each other as often."

~   ~   ~

The next night, as they awaited dinner, Sreana broke the news. As she explained the necessity for her absence, his demeanor darkened. His shoulders slumped and he sat back, deflated, in his chair.

"What does that mean for us?" he asked.

"We won't see each other as often. Maybe return to the once a week we had agreed on in the beginning, until my responsibilities lessen and I have more free time. But this will also help with some of the resentment that seems to be popping up throughout the communities. Fears of favoritism and all that."

"Have they not reaped the same benefits as your community?"

"They have, but jealousy makes people think odd things. There were some comments that slipped out during our gathering after the leaders' meeting. Pirco reported them the next day."

"I've gotten used to falling asleep with you in my arms," Gregor responded, frowning. "I expect many sleepless nights now."

She left her chair, walking around the table slowly. Then she straddled him, wrapping her arms around his neck as he reluctantly embraced her. "Subtle way to make me feel guilty."

"I know I'm being selfish but..."

"I will not stop visiting. And you will still sleep well every night knowing that I will return to your arms." Then her eyebrow rose up as she whispered, "I promise the next time I visit I will do that one thing..."

He growled at her playfully, making her laugh.

"We both can agree it'll be worth the wait," she added.

"Agreed," he finally conceded, pulling her in for an ardent kiss.

Then a knock on the servant's door interrupted them, making them part and greet Marga as she brought in dinner.

~ ~ ~

She heard rustling in the room and opened her eyes to find Marga quietly opening the curtains and doors to the balcony. Sreana inhaled deeply, feeling Gregor breathing against her neck. When Marga turned around, she smiled when she saw that Sreana was awake.

"Good morning, Marga."

"Good morning, my lady." Marga moved into the bathing room and returned with two folded robes, laying them nearby on the couch. "I will return soon with breakfast."

"Thank you."

As Marga left, she felt Gregor stretch his legs and sigh as he woke.

"Good morning."

He grunted and buried his face in her hair. She chuckled. Usually, she was the grumpy one. He didn't move again, even as Marga brought in wonderfully smelling food and coffee. Sreana thanked her again before she left.

"Gregor?"

"I refuse."

She laughed in surprise. "Refuse what?"

"I refuse to say good morning, I refuse to make it a good morning. If I do not take those steps, then you will not eat breakfast and leave me alone for a week."

She rolled her eyes, seeing that he wasn't going to budge from their position. She wiggled one arm between them, her hand encountering his thigh. Then she brushed it against a very private part, making him inhale sharply.

"I demand my good morning," she responded, impishly.

His voice gruff in her ear questioned, "Oh you demand it?" as his hand returned the favor, making her squeal with laughter.

CHAPTER 27

Even though the day had been long and physically exhausting, she couldn't sleep. She tossed and turned, then sighed hard. She chided herself that she had put on a brave face for Gregor, telling him they would be fine apart, yet she couldn't get comfortable knowing it was one of the nights that they usually spent together. She missed the feel of his arms around her and weight against her back. She wrapped her quilt around her shoulders in hopes to feign his embrace but it failed as a surrogate.

She rolled her eyes and left her bed. After dressing and slipping on her beat-up sandals, she exited her hovel, staff in hand, and decided to take a stroll along the fields. She felt great pride in the work they were doing, preparing for crops that, for once, would be theirs alone. No one would come and take the best, no one would involve themselves in their delivery or sharing of benefits. Her heart filled with joy when she likened it to the Sedora before the invasion, before the occupation. The Sedora of old that cultivated and strengthened itself and its citizens.

She found herself far out of the main township, along the fences that surrounded Garol's farm. The moonslight cast uniform shadows along the rows of plowed soil. She wandered toward the large oak tree that grew up between the fence and road, leaning against the trunk. The bugs calling to each other and the wind rustling the grasses made her sigh contently. If she remembered correctly, corn would be seeded in this area while smaller vegetables would be planted closer to his residence. As she glanced around the fields, her reverie was interrupted by rushed footfalls. No one else should have been awake this late so she flattened herself against the tree trunk. She saw three men walking towards her as quickly and quietly as possible. When they were close enough, the moonslight showed her enough to confirm she did not know these men.

She wanted to attack immediately but when she saw that one of them was carrying a heavy bucket by its rope handle, she decided to wait. They moved closer to the plowed field, then set the bucket down at the edge. Seeing her opportunity, she grabbed the bucket and dashed away, causing the men to gasp and curse and give chase. When she got far enough down the road, which placed her in shouting distance of the township, she dropped the bucket then spun on her heel to face her pursuers. Staff at the ready, she planted her feet firmly in a defensive stance. They halted in front of her, then started to circle her.

Even though Sreana knew she could take these three men down, she didn't know if there were others nearby. She would have to get her people's attention somehow, but most were sound asleep. There was only one sound that would rouse the entire township.

She screamed.

The trespassers staggered backwards, surprised by the strength and volume. Then they all heard faraway voices and startled shouts, which made the strangers start to run away from her. Sreana didn't hesitate. She chased after them, holding her staff horizontally, and with a leap, smashed her staff and body into their backs. They crashed forward, with Sreana landing on one of them, her staff clattering a few feet away. She turned him over and delivered a punch, knocking him out. Rolling away, she grabbed her staff, slamming the heel against the face of the other man who was able to get back to his feet. He spun from the force and fell, a lump of unconscious flesh. The last man laid helplessly on the ground, raising his hands in surrender. She pressed the end of her staff against his throat, making him gasp in pain.

More footfalls approached and she glanced over her shoulder to confirm it was friend not foe. Duncar, Pirco, and several others arrived, half-dressed, barely awake, with weapons drawn and lanterns lighting the area. Sreana ordered them to search the township for any other strangers, fearing the commotion could have alerted them. The trespassers were secured immediately, even the two who were unconscious, while Sreana turned her attention to the bucket. She kneeled next to it and looked inside. Thanks to Duncar's torchlight, she could see that the bucket was caked in large, sticky crystals. She cautiously sniffed then flinched at the pungent smell.

"What is it?" Duncar asked, standing behind her.

"Some sort of natron-based poison," she answered. "To dry out the seeds and any roots, making the crop die. And make the ground infertile."

"They want to starve us," Duncar mumbled.

"Pirco, send word to everyone to check their fields."

He darted off, while Sreana examined the substance warily.

"Starve us, starve our herds," Sreana whispered. "Starve our Grenan friends." She watched as the poisoners were taken back to the township, then she stood and wiped her hands on her pants as if to wipe away her disgust. "Come, let's find out if anyone else was hit."

~   ~   ~

170

The sun hadn't started to rise yet, only shedding its halo of predawn light on the horizon. A galloping horse heading toward the castle's closed gates startled the Castle Guard. They wouldn't let the person in, until Rana, barely dressed in his pants and nothing else, arrived and recognized the rider. He ordered them to open the gates and, even before they could be widened fully, the visitor spurred the horse on and sped past. The rider made it to the main doors, dismounted, then brushed past the guards and other armymen. Up the stairs and across the balcony, the rider found the King sitting at his table, awake and staring out over the forest's canopy. When he saw the visitor, he jumped to his feet.

"Sreana? What's wrong?"

"We were attacked."

"What?"

"Three men were caught poisoning our fields, trying to destroy crops and soil. I stopped them before they could poison our plowed fields, but they succeeded in dousing a neighboring township's crops."

"Where are these men now?"

"Since they perpetrated the full crime on our neighbors, their leader has the right to punish them. We tried interrogating them before handing them over, but they wouldn't speak."

Then she watched as Gregor looked her over, eyebrows furrowing. "Were you hurt?"

"No, I'm unharmed. The only ones injured in the altercation were the poisoners."

He sighed, leaning against the table for a moment. "No doubt they were hired by our traitor or by the Carmanic Empire." Gregor frowned. "Had you kept your usual visits, you wouldn't have been there to catch them."

"I'm sure they were counting on me being distracted. I surprised them."

"Any crops you can't salvage?"

"A few. We had alfalfa and hay already started for the animals. Those were hit first and effectively destroyed. Because we hadn't planted yet, and we interrupted their distribution of the poison, we were able to save our soil. Thankfully, no other communities had been hit." She pursed her lips, tight, frustrated. "We had focused our security on the townships, but now we'll have to start planning stronger measures to protect the crops."

He stood straight up, as if something caught his eye, and grabbed her right hand. "Come, let me look at your face." He pulled her inside and toward the bathing room.

"My face?"

Have you not seen yourself?"

She glanced in the dressing table's looking glass and saw a figure of gray gravel dust. She allowed him to guide her into the bathing room, where he wet a hand cloth and wiped her face. She sputtered as he ran over her lips, making him chuckle, then she hissed when he wiped her cheek.

"You have quite the abrasion on your cheek. I should call for Genj."

"I'm sure Duncar will slather me with something when I get back."

He kissed her gently, then dabbed her cheek. "I'm glad you are safe. I am glad your people are safe."

"We are safe for now. But if they're willing to starve us, they are willing to starve you as well."

"I will speak with Kasar regarding our security measures, since we're just as much a target as you. Our collaboration is no secret, not since you kidnapped me."

She chuckled, mirthlessly. "No, it was no longer a secret after I got caught in your bed."

Then they heard someone clear their throat. They glanced through the doorway, to see Rana and Genj standing in the main bedchambers.

"I saw your injury, my lady, so I asked our Healer Genj to check it."

"It is just a scratch," she chided.

"It will make me feel better," Gregor responded, tossing the dirty hand cloth into the hamper near the bathtub.

"I find myself outnumbered. Please, Healer Genj, prove to everyone that I am fine."

"I will be gentle, my lady," Genj replied, moving past Rana and meeting Sreana halfway. He cupped her chin and moved her head, glancing along her cheek with midnight blue eyes. "I think you have gravel rash, easy to treat."

"Gravel rash only? I expected worse with all the worry."

"How did it happen?"

"I tackled three men as they tried to run away."

She watched as Genj, Rana, and even Gregor stop what they were doing and stare at her. Then she saw Rana glance at Gregor with a raised eyebrow, while Gregor just laughed.

"May I suggest that you not tackle anyone for few days?" Genj inquired. "Allow your cheek to heal?"

"You can suggest, but I cannot promise," she answered with a smirk.

Genj shook his head, rummaging through his satchel and pulling out a jar. He unscrewed the lid, dabbed his two longest fingers inside, then returned to Sreana's side and lathered on the salve. She hissed again, the sting taking her by surprise. He apologized, as he worked it into the wound until he was satisfied, then returned the lidded jar back into this bag. When he turned back to her, something caught his eye and he grabbed her left wrist.

"Your hand, my lady."

Confused, she looked down and saw that her fingers were a deep red, as if they were blistering after being exposed to a high heat.

"Sreana, what happened?" Gregor asked, worried.

"They must have gotten some of the poison on the bucket's handle."

"What kind of poison?" Genj demanded.

"Smelled like natron, that's all I could determine."

Genj examined her hand thoroughly then sighed. "I would treat it as a burn, but it is unlike any I have ever seen."

"I will have my healer look at it when I get home," she replied, pulling her hand free gently. "He understands poisons well. And he has dealt with most of my injuries and understands my sensitivities."

Genj bowed his head. "That is a wise idea, my lady."

"Thank you for tending to my cheek, I will try not to aggravate it further." Then she turned to Gregor. "I need to head back. I will return in a few days and let you know if we've learned anything."

Gregor kissed her, lovingly. "Make sure your healer looks at your hand."

"I don't think I could stop him."

"I will walk you out, my lady," Rana offered. When she looked over at him, he had found a shirt to slip on when he searched for Genj.

"Thank you, Rana."

~   ~   ~

Sreana kept her promise. When she returned home, she had Duncar examine her hand. They hid away in his home to make sure no one saw the extent of her injury. At first, she thought it just looked awful but the blisters had grown and multiplied during her ride back from the castle. She didn't feel the pain until he touched the skin. She cursed at Duncar, which was something he was used to, then he shook his head.

"I agree with the Grenan healer, it looks and acts like a burn. I will treat it as such, along with our usual antidotes. We must keep a good eye on it, we know how effective the Carmanic Empire is with their poisons. Against human and plant alike."

"Will you have to wrap it?"

"Yes, to stave off infections and because you're a bad patient who will continue to use it otherwise. Why?"

She frowned, looking down at the blisters. "I do not like worrying our friends."

"We will tell them you injured it in the fight. That way they won't worry."

"Thank you."

"I still do not know what we should do with the poison. We can't just throw it away."

"I'll ask the jahlas. They dealt with several varieties of poisons during the invasion."

"No, when I'm done, you should get some rest. I know you didn't get any sleep last night and now it's past lunch. Before you argue, we have plenty of sentries watching every horse length of our community; you are not needed.

You will also more than likely be dragged along the entire countryside dealing with the consequences of the attack during the next few weeks, so you should rest now while you can. I'll ask Pirco to speak with Jya on your behalf."

After a long, dirty look at her cousin, she finally conceded. Duncar took her hand again, cleaning it first then slathered on a heavy cream, which made her language even more foul. He ignored her, then wrapped it with a cotton bandage. After checking her cheek again, he humphed approval. He helped her out of her boots, since she couldn't use both of her hands, and ordered her again to get some sleep. He left to speak with Pirco, while she undressed and cuddled up on his couch. He was right, she was exhausted, and sleep took her quickly.

CHAPTER 28

Sitting near the dwindling late morning fire in her lea, Sreana nursed her second mug of coffee. She was exhausted. Between her shifts guarding their township and surrounding properties, coordinating with the other leaders about the next steps for crops, and attending the trial of the poisoners, sleep was a luxury. She had promised Gregor that she would return tonight with an update, but she felt she would face more questions than she had answers for. She took another sip of her bitter brew, hoping it would get her through the afternoon.

Footfalls caught her attention and she turned to see Pirco approaching. He sat down somewhat hard on the log, looking perplexed.

"Terga just sent a very confused message. He said that the Grenan armymen just delivered bales of hay and alfalfa for him to distribute."

Sreana scoffed, but her heart warmed. However, she knew that the help might not be appreciated by a stubborn clout like Terga. "Just tell him you're welcome."

Pirco looked at her oddly. "Do you know where it came from?"

"I do. But he doesn't need to know."

Her friend's face changed from puzzled to pleased. "Give Gregor a kiss for me."

~   ~   ~

Sreana rode up to the gates, her stallion trotting past the guards and carrying her to the stairs. Gregor stood, impatiently awaiting her arrival. She dismounted, giving the reins to the nearby handler, then jogged up the steps. He started to reach for her hand, but saw the bandage, so he reached for the other instead. He kissed it before leading her up to his chambers.

When they entered, he turned and touched her elbow, making her raise her arm so he could see her wrapped hand. "Is it healing well?"

"Duncar is taking good care of it. I think it looks worse than it really is, but he is insistent that we bandage it so I don't agitate it. We told our friends that I injured it in the fight."

He shook his head. "We've talked before about you fighting during the invasion, but you seem to still be fighting."

"You never stop fighting, not when others still harbor animosity toward you and your people."

"You believe they are outsiders."

"They were not familiar to any of us."

"Do they continue to refuse to talk?"

"They refused even up until they were executed."

Gregor frowned, then nodded. "Their crime was egregious."

"It was, since the intention was to kill us off slowly. I didn't know at the time I spoke with you, but they had severely injured one of the townspeople who was on guard when they were poisoning the fields."

"Will their victim heal?"

"Yes, but he will need more time than I."

He pulled her into his arms, holding her close. "I am glad it wasn't worse."

"We were fortunate."

Gregor's eyes darkened, which made her wrap her arms around his neck.

"But right now, I believe I owe you a thank you."

He furrowed his eyebrows in confusion, then she kissed him heartily. He returned in the embrace, his arms tightening around her. When she finally pulled away, he stammered, breathlessly.

"How did I earn that?"

"Weren't you the one that initiated the shipment of supplies to our communities?"

He grinned, proudly. "We are collaborators, aren't we? We should help our friends when they need it. Vehla made sure to expedite the delivery to ensure there was no gap in your process." He squeezed her gently, sighing. "You can't stay tonight, can you?"

"Not while we're still on alert. Every person counts, every leader is in constant contact. Everyone knows I'm here updating you."

"Please let your people know that we have heightened our patrols on the border as well. Kasar has his men searching for any holes in the perimeter that our poisoners could have slipped through, including the parts of the border where our countries meet."

"I will relay that to the others."

"Thank you. I do not want the others thinking we are ignoring the situation."

"Words aren't as useful as actions."

"Agreed." He leaned his forehead against hers. "Can't you stay a little while?"

"I can stay until sunset. Then I need to head back to cover my shift."

"Then, come, sit with me until then."

They cuddled up on the couch, watching the wind move the forest's canopy in the distance. With her head on his shoulder, she gently laid her bandaged hand over his heart. He kissed her forehead and frowned when she didn't respond.

"Sreana?" he inquired softly.

She mumbled something then sighed. He smiled when he realized that she had dozed off. He would let her rest until sunset.

CHAPTER 29

Weeks passed without any new attacks or developments in who planned the poisoning. The Sedorans stayed vigilant, making the necessary adjustments to their daily activities. Sreana dedicated two nights a week to stay with Gregor and she visited every other day at lunchtime to keep him updated with any news.

Gregor made sure to visit the communities often as well, speaking with those who represented the townships. He listened to their concerns while sharing his own, as well as the steps his people were taking to catch any new trespassers as quickly as possible. He even made a few stops at Sreana's township, meeting with her and the farmers that were targeted. Lieutenant Rana was with him most of the time, but sometimes Ranthel or Wenth accompanied him instead.

One morning, Sreana honed her sword at the quiet firepit, something that focused her mind and calmed her nerves. She looked up as footfalls announced someone's arrival. Her eyes widened when the skirt's panels of varying blues swirled around the visitor's legs. The priest, a young lady she didn't recognize, approached wordlessly. She stopped at Sreana's side, her eyes looking down at the ground. Sreana stood and stepped over the log, facing the demure girl. The priest handed over a sealed parchment, curtseyed to the ground and rose up in that well-practiced move, then turned and left.

Pirco stopped on the pathway, watching as the priest strode past him and disappeared. He looked back toward Sreana who had already started reading the announcement. He walked up to her, trying to read her expression.

"What is it?"

Sreana started to read the notice out loud. "Dranar has made it clear that she misses her devotee greatly. She has rescinded your banishment and hopes you will return to her Temple knowing her unending mercy and loving forgiveness."

"That's good, right?" Pirco asked. "You can start visiting the Temple again?"

She didn't answer immediately. She fiddled with the announcement, then started to fold it delicately. "These last few months, I have... I've had time to reflect on a lot of things. I have found myself moving farther and farther away from Dranar. And even with her teachings being in my life for so long, it is obvious that I never belonged to her."

"Why would you say that?"

"It is hard to be a devotee of mercy when you are an agent of Death."

"Sreana…"

"It's true. When I started training at the Temple, the head priest admitted not knowing if I would ever really fit in. But because of who my parents were and the fiefdom I lived in, my invitation to the Temple was required. I guess it looked bad every time I turned them down, but they didn't have a choice. And as much as I tried to follow Dranar's tenets, I didn't understand mercy from her point of view. Fighting, protecting people, killing quickly and making sure no one suffered at my hand, that is the only definition of mercy I can understand. I know who I am, what I am, now more than ever. I don't belong to any Temple as I do not subscribe to one vein of teaching."

Pirco wrapped his arm around her shoulders, squeezing her gently. "I'm sorry."

"For what? Banishment was best, Dranar knew that. She didn't lift my banishment for me though. She did it for our people. And to make sure we don't have another incident when the next celebration happens in a few months. We can be thankful for her decision." Then Sreana rolled her eyes, groaning. "Now I have to make a thank you gift."

CHAPTER 30

Kasar, along with Rana, were off dealing with border assignments and Sreana wasn't planning on visiting that night, so Gregor decided to accept the invitation to join his men for drinks around the bonfire they built outside the castle walls. It was a rare moment, where Gregor could enjoy the camaraderie of the men who fought at his side for years. They joked and laughed, drank and told stories, like they used to during campaigns when they had a brief moment to relax.

One armyman with black hair and eyes named Perrie grimaced, after gulping a large amount of mead. "So, you think our collaboration will continue to be this smooth?"

"Why wouldn't it?" Gregor inquired.

"Well, you have to be careful with these Sedorans."

"What do you mean?"

"Well... There are stories about monsters that live in these forests. Fairies, goblins, or whatever. Suck men into tree trunks. Milo here heard some stories."

Milo sniffed before taking a swig of his mead. "You know those knots, they look like faces? They are, they're the faces of their victims petrified. You think you hear an owl screech? Nah, men to their doom. Forests full of banshees and sirens. And they say some of the Sedorans can control them, order them around like their own army. All them Sedorans gotta do is talk to them trees."

Another armyman, Gherdan, interjected, "I heard chatter from other armymen about one person who told them monsters to kill the Carmanic soldiers and, within the hour, dozens were dead."

"Have you heard the stories about the Sedoran women?" Milo queried. "That they're the ones that talk to trees, able to bespell men into doing their will through magic? Pretend to love them, use them, then kill them. Don't trust no Sedoran widow or broken-hearted woman, they do it to their own men. I mean, I can't speak to your lady, Your Majesty, but..."

"But did you ever see any of this with your own eyes?" Gregor demanded, incredulous.

Perrie scoffed. "Nah, they knew how to keep their secrets from everyone. Only a few got to see, don't think any of them are alive now, though."

"Sounds fantastical. After all, if they could destroy regiments with these creatures' help, why didn't they fell the whole forest onto their heads and be done with it? Sounds like stories to scare misbehaving children and keep lovers from straying." Gregor sipped at his mead. "Obviously didn't scare the Carmanic Empire."

"But what if they ain't?" Gherdan asked. "What'll stop them from doing that stuff to us if they get unhappy again? Like if you and your pretty get sideways and end your relationship?"

"Why didn't they do it when they were unhappy before?"

"I dunno. Maybe their queen tree talker was hurt or sick? Or maybe she's biding her time? Can't guess what's on others' minds, can we? Even if we are allies, thinking we can trust them? They might have other ideas."

Gregor frowned, hiding it behind the mug as he took a drink. The mood changed suddenly, when Mihin pulled out his mandolin and began singing songs of old Grenan heroes. The other men joined in, the different singing styles clashing in a joyful way. However, it failed to lighten Gregor's thoughts.

~   ~   ~

The stories from his armymen weighed heavily on Gregor's mind all morning. He had a hard time reconciling those tales and, knowing what Sreana could do, and that creatures like the tree nymph were real. He struggled with the idea that his own people believed that the Sedorans used magic to get their way. And there were those who thought Gregor might even be under some spell.

Grenans believed magic and spells were ill willed. Gregor remembered the lessons all Grenan children learned. Witches, monsters, magic. Dangerous creatures with malicious intentions. However, he was always told that they didn't exist, not anymore.

She had initiated the conversation though. She told him about the nymphs and what she could do, at least what she willingly confided... but she tended to withhold things. He wondered if there was more to her abilities. More to her magic. And what would she and her kind be willing to do?

His thoughts ran all day... until she arrived for dinner.

Their conversation was typical, ranging from things that transpired in the communities to what new mischief little Sabira created.

"I think she might be like me," Sreana admitted, her voice low.

"One of your kind?"

"Kind?" she asked, confused. "I don't think of us as a kind. I think she might have my Talent." Sreana stared at Gregor, finding the conversation suddenly uncomfortable due to the look on his face. "Is there something on your mind?"

"I've been told things about you."

Her eyebrow rose up. "Sounds like they have not been good tales."

"I don't want to believe them."

"And yet you fear they may be true."

"In time of war, desperation changes people." He watched her, his eyes dark. "They say your friends in the woods are malicious. That any treaty you have with them allows you to use them in a malevolent manner. And that... those who can talk to them are just as dangerous. That your kind can manipulate men as you do nymphs."

She tapped her fork against her plate. "Someone has had fantastical dreams."

"Did you use your magic against the invaders?"

Her eyes focused on his face while she contemplated her response. "When the invasion began," she responded, setting down the utensil, "the Royal Family ordered questionable behavior that their generals happily executed. They even came up with plans that included the nymphs. We refused to pass on those plans. The jahlas and eahzals agreed they would only respond if attacked, not the other way around. We did not make them do anything against the enemy and they only took actions they felt were necessary. It was the only way to keep them safe and, if they were out of sight, then they were not targets. We are not monsters."

"I didn't say..."

"No but obviously your people think so."

"I don't know how to defend you if..."

"Defend me? If someone has issues with my kind," and the way she said it made it sound like an insult, "they can take it up with me."

"I can't have you thrashing my armymen to the point they cannot perform their duties. I need all of my men at the ready."

"Your armymen are spreading these rumors? They should know better if they fought beside us. Like I told you, we didn't parade our friends around, we didn't tell your people our secrets because we had to protect the nymphs too. They are Sedorans, the same as me. You keep using that word that we don't. It sounds like magic is something your people fear, which unfairly vilifies mine."

"I know we both have been maligned by all sides. But you have to be more honest with me. And I cannot have you ordering your... friends..."

"That's not how any of this works. If it were, I would have told you."

"Would you? Like you've said before, you have a hard time admitting things. I don't want to require you to follow Grenan law again. But I will do what I must to keep my people safe, just like you. You will not use your friends to attack my people."

Sreana's eyes narrowed at that, as it sounded like a command. "Are you my companion or are you my King?"

Gregor hesitated, the question apparently rattling him.

"Maybe we've spent so much time together in your world that you cannot see mine as clearly as I thought. I should go."

She stood and grabbed for her boots, but Marga interrupted them when she entered to check on them. She saw Sreana standing by the couch, so she turned to clear the table. She paused, noticing that Sreana hadn't finished and looked at her with concern.

"I'm sorry, Marga, my appetite isn't like it should be. Please share with Gwena my regrets."

Marga smiled and nodded, returning to her task. Gregor and Sreana stayed silent until she was done. She exited with a good night, then closed the servant's door behind her.

"I should have approached this better," Gregor admitted, regret coloring his tone. "I've waited all this time to sleep with you in my arms and I... Please stay. I'd rather you sleep with your back to me in anger than for you to leave and make no promises to return."

She didn't look at him, but he could feel her thinking. Slowly, she started to undress, but kept her undershirt and undershorts on when she climbed into bed. He removed his own clothes and joined her, as she turned her back to him. He sighed, laying on his back with his arms above his head. A few breaths passed in bitter silence. Then she rolled over and snuggled up against his side. He wrapped his arm around her and kissed her forehead. Silence settled and they fell asleep.

~   ~   ~

In the middle of the night, Sreana stirred. Gregor snored softly next to her, his arm having gone limp and she was able to sit up without disturbing him. She stared down at him, the tales he shared running through her mind. She knew some were true, she admitted that to him, but she wasn't sure if he believed her. However, the stories that had been created to scare caused rage to fester. That was the reason why she hesitated to tell him. And now those lies had infiltrated their companionship. And his reaction to them... The threat of Grenan law, that he believed he could order her like she was nothing more than...

The King finally prevailed over the man.

She thought she would feel differently when she woke, but she didn't. She would break her promise tonight. She couldn't stay and have him try to fix things in the morning; if that was even a possibility. It wouldn't be an honest attempt in her eyes. He would again look at her with those doubts in the back of his mind.

She felt an ache in her chest when it hit her that they could truly be broken. She reached out and touched his cheek, running her fingertips along his beard. She stopped when he shifted in his sleep with a content sigh. She waited until he settled back into a deeper sleep then slipped out of the bed and got dressed. He remained undisturbed by her movements, even as she leaned over and kissed his forehead, whispering her farewell. She choked up for a moment, feeling like it was her final one.

Then she turned and softly descended the servant's staircase.

As she walked toward the front doors, her thoughts distracted her and she didn't recognize the running steps coming up behind her. When the sound registered, she reacted last minute by spinning around and swinging her fist. She contacted cheek, knocking her assailant back a few steps, then she was grabbed from behind. Her enemy dragged her into a side room and the one she hit followed, closing the door behind them. She struggled but her captor wouldn't loosen his grip. She buckled her knees, tipping them forward, then pushed up with her legs. They jerked back and up, which allowed her to run up the other man's chest and kick him in the face. The motion caused her and her captor to stumble backward, making him lose his grip. She drove an elbow into his stomach as she landed on him. She rolled, jumped to her feet, and unsheathed her sword.

Another man had been waiting in the room, but now he stood a few steps away looking fairly stunned. Smiling, she rolled both of her shoulders in unison, clicked her tongue, then gestured for him to take his chance. Hesitantly, he drew his sword and advanced. As they circled each other, she waited until he made the first move. Then he swung his sword. The angle was weak and Sreana took advantage. She parried hard and fast, barely letting her opponent breathe, till he lost his grip on his sword and it clattered uselessly onto the floor. His eyes widened. Her patience gone, she kicked him in the stomach, pushing him back and making him trip and fall over his unconscious colleagues.

She glanced over the three men, confirming they were no longer a threat, then strode over to the door. She swung it open to find four crossbows aimed straight at her chest. Her shoulders slumped and she regretfully surrendered.

One guard grabbed her sword out of her hand, while another searched her for other weapons and found her dagger. They secured her hands with metal restraints and escorted her down a long, unfamiliar hallway. A group of men dressed as ministers met them halfway, their leader appearing quite angry.

"You were supposed to kill her."

The guard who held her restraints glared at the minister. "You didn't tell us she was a fighter. She injured three of my men without flinching."

Sreana refrained from reacting, keeping her expression stoic, and stayed silent.

"You are a rather impressive piece. The King chose his whore well," the minister sneered. "With you out of the way, we can finally return to what worked before your interference." Then he glanced at the guard. "Keep her jailed until you can dispose of her."

They pushed her to walk, taking her to the deepest level of the castle. As the large doors opened, she saw the cells that were housed within and she could tell they were not original to the structure. Freed of her restraints, she was shoved into one. The door slammed shut and one guard locked it using the keys attached to his belt. Then they placed her weapons on one table, next to the torture implements that laid on it, which was too far for her to reach.

"We'll be back for you soon, pretty," the guard threatened with a dark chuckle.

As soon as they were gone, Sreana started looking for a way out. However, she wasn't left alone long enough. The disgusting guard returned, with a friend, and they entered the cell. She backed away but the cage was too small. The taller guard grabbed her arm then spun her around. A firm grasp around her torso and one hand wrapped in her hair made it hard to move. The other guard, who had promised bad things before, stood in front of her.

"You're not so tough without your weapons, are ya?" The guard smiled at her like a predator. "But I do love how women fight so hard as if it'd change the outcome."

"Amazing how Grenan guards sound just like Carmanic murderers," she responded, still struggling against the guard who held her. The one in front of her delivered a closed fist blow to her face and for a moment she saw stars.

"What is going on here?" a new voice boomed from behind her assaulter. One of the Castle Guard lieutenants stood in the doorway, glaring at the two men in her cage.

"She was misbehaving, sir. We decided to straighten her out."

"Any misbehavior must be reported to me, your lieutenant, to decide discipline. Get out of there."

Annoyed, the guard didn't let her go. Instead, he flung her against the wall. It happened so quickly, she didn't have time to brace herself and cheek contacted brick. With a proud grunt, he stomped out and the other guard scoffed, then exited as well. The lieutenant locked the door, looked her over as she laid crumpled on the floor, then ordered the two men to follow him.

~   ~   ~

Dawn had to be coming soon. Cradling her face, Sreana investigated every inch of her cell, trying to figure out how to escape. She made her way around her entire cell, trying hinges, the lock, even the welding. Nothing showed weakness. She sat in the corner, back flat against the bricks, frustrated.

There had to be a way out.

Suddenly, the dungeon's door opened and the predatory guard had returned. He leaned up against the bars, rubbing himself inappropriately against the metal.

"Good enough for the King, quite sufficient enough for me."

"Weren't you ordered to leave me alone?"

"He doesn't know what's best." He looked her over, tilting his head to the side to check her out at another angle. "When my lieutenant retires to bed, you and I will pick up where we left off."

"Will your friend be joining us?"

The guard scoffed. "No, don't like to share. Anyway, I think I can handle you just fine on my own."

Sreana stood then leaned closer to the bars, making his lecherous smile widen. Suddenly, she shoved a dagger straight into his abdomen. Shock washed over the guard's face, then she twisted it and blood started trickling out of his mouth. "Your friend really should have checked his weapons after an altercation with a Sedoran woman." She snatched the keys and dislodged the dagger, watching him crumple into a lump of dead flesh.

Free of her cage, she stepped over the dead vermin. She belted her sword and slipped her dagger back into its sheath. She drew her sword, swinging her arm to ensure the cruel restraint practices the guards enforced hadn't affected her mobility. She snuck out of the dungeon, creeping through hallways and stairwells. She knew she couldn't make it back to Gregor's bedchambers because she could hear the guards stomping up and down the hallways. And with the Castle Guard potentially aware of her escape, she instead headed toward her secret exit.

On her way out, she passed by an office where the group of ministers were talking about their plans. Her hand tightened on her hilt and for a brief moment, she thought of how easy it would be to slaughter them. They were not trained to fight. Easy kills. But her conscience reminded her how easy she would be pointed to as the perpetrator. And the repercussions against her people would be swift and fatal.

She backed away from the door, then darted down the hallway. She trotted down the darkened paths that led her out through the castle's walls.

~ ~ ~

She made her way back home, her cheek throbbing. It was the only thing she could feel, as the rest of her had become numb. She entered her lea, where Duncar had started to squelch the firepit. She caught his attention and apparently there was still enough light for him to see the swelling in her face.

"What the hells happened? Sreana? Where were you? And what did I tell you about getting hurt?" Duncar demanded.

"Don't worry, he only got one lucky shot," Sreana responded darkly, trudging past her cousin.

Before she slipped into her hovel, he noticed blood on her sleeve. Duncar followed her, finding her standing in the middle of the small room and trembling. "Sreana?"

"Please leave," she whispered, her voice cracking.

He grabbed her by the shoulders and turned her around. For the first since Alarn's death, tears streamed down her face.

"What happened?" he asked as he checked her face then the rest of her.

She shook her head. "I was leaving… I don't know. The one who ordered my arrest was dressed like a minister. I think he was the same one who helped with the assassination attempt. But the guards… They arrested me."

"Did they do anything else to you?"

"No, just the blow to my face."

"Promise?"

"The lieutenant interrupted them. When the bastard who hit me came back, I killed him with his friend's dagger and got the keys so I could escape."

"Where's the weapon now?"

"Down the river with the keys."

"We have to tell Gregor."

"I can never go back to the castle."

Duncar stopped his check of her, thinking. "Gregor still does his tours through the townships. We'll get a message to him that way."

"I can't get close to the carriage."

"You're not the only one he knows."

"I killed a guard," she snapped. "Gregor will have to sign my death warrant."

"You were protecting yourself. He will understand that."

"He…" and she swallowed hard, "… may not care."

He stared at her, confused. "Why?"

"I may have broken a promise."

"Is that why you're home early?"

More tears poured down her cheeks, making her cousin pull her into a hug. "We did not part on good terms. It's my fault. I've ruined… I've endangered *everyone*…"

"He still needs to know, Sreana," Duncar responded, his heart breaking for her as she sobbed. "What happened affects not just the two of you, but all of us. You both know that. We'll figure it out. Come, we'll hide you out in my home for now. And let's get some ice for your face."

CHAPTER 31

When he woke, she was gone.
   No good morning, no farewell.
   Her warmth completely gone.
   He felt his heart shatter.

CHAPTER 32

Within a day, word spread that the Grenan Castle Guard had a warrant out for Sreana, in connection with the murder of a guard. Each township was shown a copy but never given one to keep. When the Castle Guard arrived in her township, Sreana slipped on her camouflage cloak and climbed up into Jya's tree. The limbs warped around her, allowing her to blend in perfectly, and no one approached her until it was safe. Pirco retrieved her and, along with Duncar, hid in her hovel to discuss her options.

"The warrant advertised alive or dead," Pirco warned.

"Which means the Guard is determined to kill me on sight," she responded.

Duncar frowned. "I think we can all agree that you should avoid entering the township."

"Especially knowing they'll be back in a few days to rattle us again," Sreana replied, rubbing her face roughly with shaking hands. "Gregor knows this is my township, they will no doubt focus on it."

"Doesn't feel that focused," Duncar admitted. "The other leaders are complaining about their numerous unannounced arrivals and unwelcomed questions."

"And if Gregor sent them, why they didn't come to the lea?" Pirco asked. "They seemed oblivious to it."

Their deductions didn't persuade her.

"How is everyone handling the situation?" she inquired.

"Took everything in our friends not to stab them with pitchforks and daggers," Pirco answered, grimacing. "They hate the Guard for everything they've done and this is just another reason to kill them and bury the bodies."

"They should be aware that murder doesn't stop them," Duncar responded. "We have to be careful with all interactions, reactions, and who deals with them. It's best that when they come here, they are directed to me. That way I can keep the answers the same each time and frees up Pirco to communicate with Jya to keep our other communities on the same page."

"I'll tell the others to do the same thing, to use the same proxy each time."

She sighed. "Just remember if they aren't afraid to come after me, nothing will stop them from arresting anyone they think is complicit."

"Agreed," Duncar replied. "We will keep the sentries in place that we've been using since the crop poisoning so they can't sneak up on us."

~   ~   ~

For the next few days, Sreana stayed sheltered in her hovel. They kept the fire squelched and canceled all gatherings. The first few days found her curled up in bed, her heartache evident. Then restlessness settled in and even though she tried to hide it from her friends, Duncar knew that leaving his cousin alone with her imagination was never a good idea. One day, they snuck her into Trealle's to eat and socialize, trying to impress upon her that her community was behind her completely.

Those who entered the tavern all made their way to Sreana, to either clasp her shoulder, hug her, or share words of encouragement. It reminded her of the old days, after a food raid or some other crime she committed to help her people and a new warrant was posted throughout the area. Everyone would share their love and appreciation for the danger she put herself in for them. They were doing the same thing now, showing support in her darkest moment, even though they only knew the half of it.

After lunch time, Sreana stood behind Trealle, mind elsewhere. Then Garol rushed in and whispered, "Guard!" Sreana ducked under the bar, with Trealle immediately securing nearby crates and barrels to cover her. Sreana could see above her through the slits between the wood and she held her breath when she heard the Castle Guard enter. She couldn't understand the exact words as well as she had hoped, but by the tone, Sreana could tell the Guard demanded information about their quarry. Trealle kept her tone pleasant, until Duncar entered.

Her cousin, his tone harsh and voice loud, demanded why they were harassing them again, when they had already told them everything they knew. Duncar dismissed them, adding to his bluster, "If the King doesn't believe your reports, then tell him to come talk to me directly. He knows where to find me."

The Castle Guard cursed Duncar, storming out of the tavern. Sreana could hear someone follow them out the door, then an all-clear whistle several breaths later. Trealle pulled out some of the crates, helping Sreana crawl out from underneath. Sreana smiled her thanks, then sighed hard.

"That was close," Trealle murmured.

"Too close," Sreana agreed.

"They blew through on horses before anyone had a chance to react," Garol explained, apologetically, making Sreana grasp his arm in reassurance.

Duncar didn't like the look on his cousin's face. "What are you going to do?"

"The only safe thing I can do," Sreana replied before slipping on her cloak and headed back to her lea.

Ducking into her hovel, she searched out her satchel then started to pack. She had her blanket and clean underclothes stuffed inside when she heard Duncar and Pirco enter, a concerned gasp from her friend and a frustrated sigh from her cousin.

"Sreana, where are you going?" Pirco demanded.

"Away. It's not safe for me to stay and it's not safe for our people for me to be here. They will continue to show up unannounced until I make a mistake. And I can't let the others bear the burden of the consequences."

"We'll go with you."

"Your loyalty makes you foolish," she snapped, making the two men glower at her. "The consequences of being caught with me would be fatal. And those who love you would never forgive me. No, you stay here." Then her tone melted into sincerity. "Stay here, in my stead, and protect our people. Make the decisions you know I would make and stand up for those who I would stand up for. And make sure Gregor knows what really happened. You're my only hope to get a message to him."

"And what about you?" Duncar asked.

"I will go further into the forest, follow the old hunting trails. I know there are a few hunting cabins I can shelter in."

"Go to Mirna, stay at the Temple instead."

"They can't suffer another scandal if I get caught there. No, I can't endanger them again." She glanced between her two friends and shrugged. "I'll come back when I think it's safe. We'll stay in contact through Jya and the other jahlas." Her brave face faltered. "It will be just like old times, right?"

"You'll be alone this time," Pirco responded. "We won't be with you."

Her courage finally faded. "Alone or together, we will hold the line."

"Just remember, Sreana," Duncar said. "If you find yourself staring down a Grenan guard, do not kill him. You can claim self-defense at the castle, but as a fugitive? Gregor won't be able to forgive a pile of bodies."

She nodded, realizing Duncar was right.

Her cousin grabbed her into his arms, whispering, "And please, be careful. You're all I have left."

After he released her, Pirco hugged her too.

With a satchel of supplies and her cloak around her shoulders, she started toward the door. "Hold the line."

As she exited, she found Trealle and Garol waiting. Trealle grabbed her satchel, stuffing a sizable bag inside. Then Garol handed over another bag, which Sreana found held different types of jerky. She smiled her appreciation, grasping their shoulders in thanks before walking to the tree line. She had one more thing to do before leaving.

Sreana approached one tree and called, "Jya?" The jahla peeked around the tree trunk. "Men will be hunting me. Tell the others not to hurt them. Do you understand? They must remain unharmed."

The nymph glowered. "They hunt our friend? No, we will protect you."

"The only way to protect me is not to hurt them. Please, do not hurt them."

Jya nodded, reluctantly.

And with that, Sreana disappeared into the thick forest that stretched out behind her lea.

CHAPTER 33

The sun had started to settle in the west as dinnertime came around. Rana found the King standing on his balcony, staring out across the empty courtyard, and saw the hurt and confusion on his face. "Still no visitor, Your Majesty?"

"It's not like her." Gregor grimaced, trying to quell his anger at himself for their argument. "She's never been away this long since I had to scour through all of those warrants. I admit, our last conversation was... complicated. But I cannot see her not coming back to have the last word though."

"Do you think something's happened to her?"

Gregor nodded, solemnly. "Have you been told why the three guards appeared to have been thrashed to an inch of their lives?"

"Nothing more than a drunken brawl."

Rana and Gregor shared a look of doubt.

"We will look into it, Your Majesty."

"Thank you, Rana."

CHAPTER 34

Sreana hadn't gotten too far into the forest when she heard their stomps. She balled up against the tree, her cloak blending her into the mossy stumps nearby. They moved past her, completely unaware how close she was to their path. She was thankful again that there were only a few Grenan who knew how the Sedorans survived during the invasion.

As one guard walked close to her, it took everything in her to stay still. Instinct ordered her to kill, to take the dagger that she gripped in her hand and drive it into his jugular. She was adept at that, incapacitate and kill quickly without much sound. But Duncar's words kept her still. He had been right, massacring a legion of Castle Guard would be impossible to explain, even if they deserved such retribution. She took a quick breath as another guard approached, then that man too walked right past her without noticing anything amiss. Once they were out of hearing range, she exhaled and moved in the opposite direction as stealthily as possible.

~   ~   ~

It took her most of the day, but she finally found the hunting shack. If someone didn't know it was there, they wouldn't ever notice it. Hidden behind thick foliage, it was located far enough from roads and walking paths. It had been abandoned for years, probably last used weeks before the invasion. She inspected it closely before entering, ears still open for anyone approaching.

The logs were stacked evenly on top of each other, with chinking filling the spaces between. The window's glass had been shattered into a spiderweb by a fallen limb that still rested against it. Hinges creaking from age, the crooked door scraped along the dirt floor. Thankfully, the thatched roof appeared to be in good shape, no holes or tears. She could prop the cot against the door to stop any surprise entries, while the window next to it would help her keep an ear out.

It would do for shelter.

It started to drizzle again, tickling her face and hair. It would be a cool rainy night and the shelter was appreciated. And she knew the Castle Guard wouldn't spend time out in the woods on a rainy night so she could count on getting some sleep. Instead of flipping up her hood, she entered the cabin, pushed the noisy door closed, and checked for critters. It was truly deserted, not even a mouse or squirrel nest.

She set her satchel down, then began to settle in. She tapped the old cot with her foot but it didn't rock or fall apart. She huddled up against the door, eating some of the jerky Garol had given her. She sighed, hoping her people were safe, that none of the Castle Guard tried to hurt them for information. She wondered about the Temple priests as well, because it was well known that they would protect their followers. She never told Gregor that she had been forgiven but that wouldn't matter to the Guard. Duncar had sent someone to warn Mirna, but still… And Pirco, with the help of Jya, had spread the word to the other communities. She knew no matter how much some of the other Sedorans hated her, they hated the Castle Guard more.

But what would they think about Gregor?

She squeezed her eyes shut and swallowed hard to keep the sob from escaping. He had to have signed the warrant, because he had to abide by his laws. Lover or not, pledged or not, the law meant more to him than her. He made that clear when he threatened her with reinstating Grenan law. She felt her stomach rebel when she thought of a proclamation because of her actions. The image of him signing the warrant and proclamation, dutiful and determined, flashed through her mind and she couldn't stop the next sob.

With her heart and dreams in tatters, she began to wonder what her future would be like. If she stayed in Sedora or if she escaped to another Kingdom, her life would never be the same. She would never be safe and never truly live again. Wanted for murder, the man she loved leading the hunt… maybe surrendering and hanging would be a kinder fate than surviving on the run. And it would make things easier on everyone…

Then Duncar's words repeated again in her head. All he had left. He was right, they were the only members of their family left. Everyone else was gone. But could he deal with a fugitive cousin if it only made his life harder?

Noises outside interrupted her thoughts and she reached for her sword. Then she heard leaves rustling, limbs creaking. She peeked through the crack in the door and saw flashes of blonde oak and gray hornbeam bark. She popped the door open and saw a handful of jahlas moving around the shack. They were manipulating the trees around them, twisting limbs and canopies to hide the shack even further from sight. They also touched the sides of the building, urging moss to grow and vines to climb, making it look just like another boulder in the forest.

One jahla turned and smiled at her. "We protect our friends," Jayna announced, as she ran another hand along the northside of the shack.

"You shouldn't be here," Sreana responded, wiping her face with her sleeve. "I don't know what those men would do to you if they saw you."

The jahla's eyebrow rose up. "They did not see nor will they see us. Just like they will not see you or this building."

As the canopy grew heavier around them, what little sunlight peeked through the clouds began to fade. She felt like she was in her hovel, which made her choke up again.

"Our friends the eahzals and halhas will continue to bring rain and cold winds. We know the men do not like it. Go inside, rest. We will protect our friend just like our friend has protected us all this time."

Seeing that she wasn't going to be able to talk them out of helping her, Sreana nodded and ducked back inside. The fortification the jahlas provided made it not just darker but cooler. She shivered, unpacking her blanket and pillow, making her bed in the old cot. Thankfully it held her weight well and she didn't fall through. Still chilled, she tried to bundle the blanket around her. Exhaustion finally slipped her into a sleep that wasn't very deep but she let it take her, knowing that her body needed to rest.

CHAPTER 35

Sweat trickling along her lower back woke her. She was warm. No, hot. She hadn't started a fire to ensure the smoke wouldn't be seen. Confused, Sreana opened her eyes. Within reach glimmered a bright light. Startled, she sat up and almost tipped the cot over.

The stranger sat on the floor near the middle of the room, her crossed legs resembling the cooled embers of campfire wood. The crackled and cooled skin reached up to her abdomen, then it changed into flames. The outer layer burned bright yellow, with hot orange flashes bursting through intermittently. As her eyes adjusted to the light emanating from her visitor, Sreana was able to make out eyes and mouth; they shone as a deep maroon. The tip of the flame moved like hair floating in water and a gaseous blue beat rhythmically in the middle of the torso as if it was the heart.

The saehwa blinked, then smiled kindly at Sreana. "Rest, Elemental," the nymph whispered. "Our sisters keep you safe, we keep you warm."

Relieved that the visitor was friendly, Sreana smiled and nodded, then laid back down and drifted back off to sleep.

~   ~   ~

When she woke in the morning, the saehwa still sat watching over her. She blinked against the nymph's glow, still thinking it was a dream.

"Good morning, our friend," the saehwa whispered, her flame wavering as she adjusted her posture.

"Good morning, my friend," Sreana replied, softly. "Thank you for keeping me warm all night."

The nymph bowed her head. "It was our honor. We will come back tonight to do the same."

"Thank you. Wait, before you go. What is your name?"

The saehwa flickered brighter, as if surprised by the recognition of her individuality. "Reshepha."

"Thank you, again, Reshepha. See you tonight."

As the saehwa flickered into oblivion, Sreana laid in the cot for a moment. Her heart leapt in surprise. No, surprise was an understatement. She sighed, sitting up. Unable put her feelings into words, she readied herself for her day.

~   ~   ~

Sreana took breakfast inside, nibbling on the rations that Trealle had shoved into her bag. Some bread, cheese, and dried meats were divided and wrapped so carefully that she didn't know how Trealle had them ready so quickly. But the love she felt with each wrapped portion helped her breathe through her pain.

Jayna materialized and sat next to her on the floor, staring intently as she ate. "We know what has happened, why those awful men hunt you. Jya told us everything."

"I have made terrible decisions that have brought fear and danger upon my people and yours. I am so sorry."

"If you believe you had made a mistake, you need only to learn from it," Jayna replied, matter of fact. "It is the only way to learn what works and what doesn't. But understand, your decisions have affected all of us, for the better. If you didn't try with the Grenan King, we wouldn't have flourished. If you didn't protect yourself, we wouldn't be safe. You can fix the things that went wrong, once all of this is settled."

Sreana grimaced. "I wish I had your faith."

"You have given us that faith."

Silence.

"Eat. Rest. We will keep an eye out for those men. They already turned back because of the weather this morning. We will continue to make it miserable for them. In the evening, you can forage and walk."

Sreana thanked Jayna, who left her to the quiet of her cocoon. The mention of Gregor made the pain in her chest worse. The order and the threat still stung. She knew they were over, but did he? Or did he think he owned her? She bristled at that. Owned, like she was just another object. That's how the Sedoran Royal Family saw her, something to own until she was no longer useful. Did all of his thoughtfulness and words and affection truly hide the fact that he was just like them?

Then a chill ran through her. Gregor had succeeded in caging her after all. He molded her to his life, how he wanted their companionship to be, all the while pretending to accept her for who she was. It proved what she feared he would always be.

A King.

Even if she returned and Gregor offered peace, she would make sure he knew that their companionship was over immediately. If his betrayal was still unknown to the masses, she would never admit it to the others. She would take the necessary steps to keep the peace and to keep her humiliation private. That is, if she could return. She sighed, resigning herself to consider other plans. But deep down, she hoped she could go back home.

~   ~   ~

Sreana finally got a break from her hideout after sunset. She walked through the trees, the faint glow of the moons seeping through the forest's canopy to light her path. As she searched out some fresh fruit to go with her provisions, the light got brighter further in. She stopped and looked up, to see a swirl of glitter above her. It lowered and surrounded her, then incrementally took shape before her. She knew as the shimmering points of light solidified into a female shape that an aetha had graced her with their presence. When Sreana smiled at her, the aetha brightened with pride. However, she didn't keep her shape long, dripping back into the galaxy of lights and rising back up above Sreana.

Whispering thanks up to her guide, Sreana started walking again until she found an apricot tree. She dropped her satchel and started to remove her sword so she could climb up, but before she could unfasten her belt, a gust whooshed and rattled the trees above her. Suddenly, something soft hit her head. When she heard the others falling, Sreana had to protect herself as several apricots rained down. Once the thumping stopped, she glanced around, seeing at least a dozen apricots laying around her feet. Then from behind the tree she heard a mortified gasp.

Sreana saw a misty cloud snaking around the trunk. Just like the aetha, the halha floated to the ground and took on a humanlike shape. But her eyes were wide with horror after unintentionally pelting Sreana with fruit.

"I am so sorry!" the halha whispered, before whimpering in dismay.

"Do not apologize, I am unharmed." Sreana chuckled, then bowed. "Thank you, I did not look forward to climbing this tree in the dark."

By the halha's body language, if she could, the nymph would be blushing. And just as she appeared, the nymph disintegrated into her cloudy mist and disappeared into the night.

Still trying to wrap her head around the fact all of the nymphs were helping her, Sreana gathered as many apricots she could fit in her satchel before returning to the cabin.

~   ~   ~

The next morning, she woke to a weight against her back. She opened her eyes to see Reshepha flickering nearby. The saehwa smiled, then nodded good morning. Confused, Sreana glanced over her shoulder to find the aetha who had ventured with her glowing softly behind her. The aetha smiled too, then disintegrated into stardust before swirling out the broken window and into the sky.

"You were having a nightmare," Reshepha explained. "Setarah thought she could comfort you. It worked, so she stayed all night."

"Oh, I will have to thank her. And I apologize for disturbing you."

"It was no disturbance. Have a good day, our friend."

"Thank you. Again."

Reshepha bowed her head then extinguished her flame.

Sreana exhaled, her heart wrenching. A nightmare. She hadn't had one in months. Not since... she huffed, making herself sit up. She knew the subject of her nightmare, something she thought she had dealt with ages ago. However, with the hunt to find her, it reminded her of another who thrilled in pursuing her.

During the invasion, there had been a Carmanic general who had fixated on her. No, he was obsessed. Their first altercation found him overtaking her, grabbing her up like a toy, and carrying her away from her friends and family. Her brother had lodged a dagger into the back of his knee, but it didn't faze him. It took a quick thinking jahla who dropped a large limb on his back to loosen his grip enough for her to slip out of it. She fell to the ground, pulled free the dagger and ran until she could hide up in the treetops with the rest of her people. She had a bruise around her waist for weeks after that.

Every time they met, he would grumble with pleasure and ask if his gods believed he was finally worthy of his prize. That's all she was to him, a prize to possess. To torture. She thanked her gods that his always deemed him unworthy and gave her the ability to escape each time. During their last altercation, Pirco had set a fire in their munitions, which blew the two factions apart several horse lengths. The general hadn't regained consciousness by the time she had recovered. But she knew if anyone else could survive that blast, it would have been him.

Another hard exhalation and she made herself stand up and stretch. She was thankful the aetha cuddled with her to calm her, it was something she must have seen during the invasion. The Sedoran fighters always slept in groups of two or three. The Grenans had called them dogs because they moved, ate, and slept in packs. Since Alarn had his own group to lead, he wasn't there for her, but Duncar and Pirco were, snuggling up with her every time. Without their comforting presence, their backs against her while she laid in the middle, one always awake while the other two slept, she knew the actions of the Castle

Guards instigated her night terrors and she was left to face them on her own.

She corrected herself. She wasn't alone. The nymphs were there, protecting her, helping her, and caring for her. She found reassurance in that. After all, their treaties were only with the jahlas and eahzals. The others showing that they were willing to take the risk in helping her made her wonder if there could be more between them… She let that thought drift to the back of her mind as she started her day.

~   ~   ~

Sreana took her lunch inside, her heart always warming at the care put into every wrapped meal. While she ate, a beam of light caught her attention when it settled on her face. Apparently, some of the chinking had fallen out. She knew it had to have happened recently because the jahlas had covered all noticeable holes with vegetation.

Childish curiosity got the best of her. Hesitantly, she reached out and lightly tapped her fingers along the logs. Nothing happened. She rolled her eyes, not knowing what she had expected. She nibbled on her jerky, glaring at the hole. Frowning, she tried again, this time focusing her full intention on the hole. Slowly, green fuzzy material started to grow, reaching up and out of the hole until sunlight no longer seeped through. Before she withdrew her hand, small yellow flowers bloomed and quivered under her fingertips.

"So, my eyes did not deceive me in the meadow," an astonished voice whispered. Jayna walked over to her and sat crossed legged beside her. "You still have the touch."

"Didn't know if I could still control it after all this time. I honestly thought what happened in the meadow was a fluke."

"Sedora recognizes you, will always see you for who you really are. Our Elemental."

Sreana took another bite of jerky to avoid responding.

"What made you try after all this time?"

"All of you. I haven't had issues understanding any of you. Which made me wonder if I could still do certain things."

"We could always tell when it was you," Jayna admitted, folding her hands in her lap. "Did anyone ever realize that we jahlas weren't the only ones shifting limbs and growing leaves to protect your warriors?"

"Only Alarn. He caught me doing it one day, early on in the fighting. He grabbed me afterwards and started asking questions in private. He didn't know, our parents never told him, because he was too busy learning his own craft to worry about what his little sister was. And when I told him everything, he swore he'd never tell anyone. Not even our cousin."

"Do they know now?" Jayna asked.

Sreana's lip trembled. "No." She stared down at her hands, feeling the sensation of her little trick lingering, almost as if begging her to do it again. "It was hard enough to break through the fear of the Talented. Dismantling all those years of misunderstanding. We're finally at a point where no one blinks an eye." She rubbed her hands along her thighs, trying to snuff out the tingling. "To show anyone what someone like me can do...? No, it's probably safer to keep it secret for now. I had already misplaced my trust telling Gregor about you. About me. The Grenans fear us. Fear my kind." That word tasted bitter. "They will never understand and this will make them fear us more. We cannot afford that, not with the enemy still lurking at our borders."

Jayna nodded, solemnly. "Then we will keep your secrets until it is safe. You will decide when the time is right, as you have always done. You always keep us safe." Then the nymph rose up and disappeared into the shadows.

~   ~   ~

Sreana started settling into a routine. She would stay close to the cabin all day, trying her hand at different plants and trees to see how much she remembered. Then she ventured out at night when the nymphs gave her the all clear. The aetha would join her, providing a faint glow to ensure that Sreana didn't trip or get lost. She thanked the nymph for her company each time, which made the aetha, Setarah, glow brighter with pride, before she floated back into the night sky. And when Sreana returned, the saehwa Reshepha waited for her, spreading warmth and light throughout the small cabin as they spoke before Sreana retired for the night.

As Sreana climbed into her cot to settle in for the night, after a walk through the forest gathering berries, the saehwa spoke up.

"We are pleased to have spent time with you, Elemental. We have not invested much interest in your people, only working through our sisters. They always told us that our safety hinged on your instructions. Talking with you, getting to know you better... We have been thinking that we should be like our sisters."

"What do you mean?"

"These agreements you have, they seem beneficial and fair. Would you think it good for our kind, as well as the aethas and halhas, to have the same arrangements?"

Sreana laid there in shock. None of the other nymphs had ever seemed interested in a treaty before. But Reshepha opened the door for negotiations.

"I think it would be beneficial," Sreana admitted. "And an honor."

"Good. May we discuss this in the morning? We know you wish to rest. We would have our leaders meet with you here."

"That would be wonderful, Reshepha."

CHAPTER 36

It was late in the afternoon when Rana entered the tavern, glancing around for a recognizable face. A man in the back booth looked familiar, he had stood behind Sreana when Rana gave her the news about the warrants. He walked over to the table, which caused the other man to stand and rest a hand on his sword.

"What happened?" Rana demanded, surprised by the other man's reaction.

"You tell me."

"Our lady has not been seen for over a fortnight and the King is worried." The color drained from the other man's face. "He doesn't know?"

"Know what?"

"Come, you need to speak with Duncar."

~   ~   ~

The carriage slowly ambled along the road as Gregor sat inside, lost in thought. He noticed how his visits had become much shorter than usual. He also saw how the leaders regarded him suspiciously. They kept their answers short and appeared expectant of a different conversation. Even though he was frustrated by the changes in the interactions, he thanked them for their time but didn't push them. He could only assume that she had told them what had transpired and he was again the villain.

He told the driver to continue on to the castle, not wanting to stop in Sreana's township. As they traveled through, a small group of people gathered on the side of the road. Gregor straightened his back, so he could see out the window better. Gregor recognized Sabira as a man held the little girl up to the carriage window. She offered a flower with a parchment wrapped around it, held in place by a ribbon. Gregor grabbed it and thanked Sabira, then held the flower close to his chest. As the carriage left the township, he glanced down at the flower and saw writing on the inside of the parchment. He untied the ribbon and read the message before reaching the castle.

Rana met Gregor at the carriage, his face reflecting the same rage Gregor felt brewing in him. "We know what happened."

"I do too," Gregor replied, handing over the note. "Gather everyone and send for Kasar."

"He's already on his way, Your Majesty."

~   ~   ~

All of the ministers and the Castle Guard were summoned to the large gathering room without knowing why. Grenan armymen lined the room, standing at attention. The King stood at the head of the massive table, the fury on his face startling everyone as they entered. Once everyone was accounted for, they bowed in unison then awaited his announcement.

"I have very few expectations. Very few requirements. However, the incompetence in this castle has underdelivered on each one." Gregor's anger shook everyone in the room. "What happened more than a fortnight ago on these very grounds?"

One of the Guard's lieutenants stepped forward. "During our shift, we were informed by your ministers to apprehend the woman sneaking around the castle as she was reported to be an assassin. As we have been instructed by the Queen herself, our job is to protect the castle. Therefore, we made the arrest immediately upon locating her."

"What do you mean you arrested her?" the King demanded, his fists clenching.

The lieutenant and his men glanced at each other. "Sir, we extend our apologies for letting her escape."

"You…" Gregor paused, then took a deep breath, "arrested my permitted visitor and did not think to discuss it with me?"

Silence.

"Did anything happen to her while in your custody?"

The lieutenant cleared his throat, clearly worried. "One guard attempted to harm her, but I stopped him. When we learned that she had escaped, we found him dead."

"Is there a warrant out for her now?"

The Captain of the Castle Guard stepped forward, making his man step back in line. "Of course, Your Majesty, she committed murder."

"From the sounds of it," the King snapped, "she was defending herself. Would you not do so if you were trapped and threatened as she was?"

No response.

"And you have executed a warrant without my permission or signature?" He placed his hands flat on the table, leaning heavily on it. "I tell you what warrants to act upon, not you, Captain, or the ministers. You will pack up and return to Grenan where the Queen will determine your fate."

The captain bowed, then stepped back in line with the other guards.

The King then straightened and turned angered eyes to the ministers.

One of the lower ministers scoffed. "Your Majesty, she is nothing more than…"

"Think about how you will finish that sentence. Carefully."

The minister did not finish his sentence.

"You have failed not only the Kingdom of Sedora but Grenan as well. We came here to help but instead you spent years pissing away resources and goodwill. You will also pack up and return to Grenan, where the Queen will decide your fate."

Jamos coughed. "Your Majesty…"

"Get. OUT."

~   ~   ~

It took two days for the Castle Guard and ministers to organize, pack, and leave the castle and the other various estates they had resided in over the years. With the castle empty of vipers, at least he had hoped, Gregor stood watch while Kasar stood beside him.

"Make sure they leave Sedora completely," Gregor ordered. "We know what they've planned in the past and can only guess what could be planned for the future."

"Of course, Gregor."

The King sighed. "I should have demanded that you stayed in charge, Kasar."

The other man shrugged. "The Queen was adamant that you had the same lifestyle here that you would have in Grenan. Castle Guard, ministers… anything but the military life you were accustomed to."

"But what was the cost?"

"You've made great strides with the Sedoran people. They were fine with our men working as your agents. They will hopefully be unfazed by the change from Castle Guard to military regiment. And hopefully, your heartbreaker will continue to be your advocate."

Gregor hesitated, then replied, "I do not know if she still has faith in me, let alone come back, not after everything."

"Rana knows where she lives…"

"I have to wait for her to come to me. I can't force her."

Kasar gave him an annoyed side-glower but decided not to push him. "Did

205

the household staff put together the rations?"

"Probably, why?"

Kasar chuckled darkly.

"Why?" Gregor demanded.

"The Castle Guard and some of the ministers are having a very miserable trip back home."

CHAPTER 37

Sreana stood within her tree cocoon, staring out into the darkening forest. She awaited the go ahead from the nymphs to forage for the night. But Jayna approached her, smiling with excitement. "We have heard from Jya. She says it is safe. You can go home."

Sreana didn't respond, wrapping her arms around her torso. The more time she spent in solitude, she found it harder to muster the excitement to return. After all, what did she have to return to?

The sun was setting later and later with the change in seasons. She thought about the crops they would need to reap and which ones they would use to replenish the soil's nutrients. However, every time she worried about something like that, she knew immediately who would step in. She warmed with pride, but chilled quickly with the feeling of uselessness. She lowered her eyes to the ground, wondering if her leadership even made a difference. Her people knew what to do. They didn't need her around barking orders.

"What is wrong?" the nymph asked, her smile fading fast.

"I don't know if I should go back," Sreana admitted, her soft voice cracking under her emotions. "Maybe it's best I just stay away."

Jayna frowned, her voice stern as she responded, "You are too important to your people and to mine, Elemental. You connect us, protect us, and keep us from doing regretful things. If you run away, who will take your place? Who will teach the children who share your gift? Who will lead? No one, because they do not know what to do. And we will fall apart. Our treaties will fall apart. And Sedora will fall apart." Seeing her words didn't appear to hold any sway, she changed tact, "Sreana."

Hearing the jahla say her name so gently startled Sreana, making her look up.

"Everyone else has let us down, from the Talented to the Royal Family. You never have. When the duke started courting you, we were torn because we knew what they thought of us but we also knew you would be the voice to protect us. We never anticipated how your voice would save us from more than ignorance. It advocates so much for us and our sisters, especially if they choose to enter an agreement with your people like we did. We cannot lose your voice now."

Sreana stayed silent for a few breaths, then nodded. "You're right, I have to honor my responsibilities. That's all I have left to me."

"What about your King?"

"I am quite sure he is lost to me now." Sreana dropped her arms to her sides. "But I honored my responsibilities before him and will honor them after him just the same. Thank you, Jayna, for the safety and the message and the reminder of who I am. Please share my thanks with all of your sisters. I have been honored by your protection, thoughtfulness, and attentiveness."

"You are special to us just as you are special to the others," Jayna reaffirmed, taking Sreana's hands in hers. The jahla's bark felt softer than it looked, warm and pliable. "We would do the same again no matter the situation."

~   ~   ~

Duncar impatiently paced the length of her lea, frustrated that she wasn't back yet. The message was relayed to Jya hours ago. None of the hiding places were that far away.

Where was she?

It was almost midnight when a rustle announced an arrival. He turned to see Sreana walking out of the forest. Jya appeared out of nowhere and accosted her with a hug and kiss on the cheek. Sreana hugged her back with one arm, since the other held her satchel, and they whispered to each other. Then Jya, relieved that Sreana was safe and home, disappeared back into her tree. Freed of the jahla's embrace, she looked toward the dwindling fire and saw Duncar.

As she approached him, he could tell she was exhausted. When she got close enough, he grabbed her into his arms. "Welcome home."

"The jahlas said it was safe."

"We got the message to Gregor. Pirco and I both spoke to that one armyman named Rana. Gregor knew something was wrong and sent his own man to find out what happened. It's been confirmed that Gregor has rescinded the warrant. You're safe."

"He is unharmed, correct?"

"Rana confirmed no harm came to Gregor during your absence."

Sreana only nodded.

"You should go to…"

She sighed and stepped out of his embrace. "Please, I just want a hot bath and a good night's sleep in my own bed. I haven't smelled this bad all year."

"Trealle said you could use one of her baths."

"Hm a bath with soap even, I'm spoiled."

"Will you go to Gregor? He's worried about you."

Sreana shot a dark glare at her cousin. "I will go to him when I'm ready." With that, she walked to her hovel and started settling back in.

~   ~   ~

Early the next morning, Duncar approached Sreana's hovel. He could hear her voice and stopped at the door. She wasn't speaking words, only mournful sounds that shattered his heart. She hadn't had nightmares in months.

He knew he had to take matters into his own hands.

CHAPTER 38

Two days after the warrant was rescinded, a man rode up to the gate but was barred from entering. Kasar walked out to meet him, with two soldiers flanking him. "What's your business?" the stoic general demanded.

"I wish to speak to the King," the rider responded.

"You will have to be more specific in regards to your intentions."

"Tell him Duncar is here on his cousin's behalf."

Kasar glanced over his shoulder and nodded to one of the men. The soldier reentered the castle and after several breaths, returned to Kasar in a sprint. He whispered in Kasar's ear, making the general's eyebrow rise.

"Follow us, then," Kasar invited, turning on his heel and leading Duncar into the courtyard.

Once they reached the stairway, Duncar dismounted and walked up to Gregor, who waited just inside. They grasped arms in greeting, but only respectful smiles were shared.

"Please follow me," Gregor said. "So we can talk privately."

Gregor led Duncar to a small greeting room, followed by Rana. Rana opened the door for them, then followed them in and closed it behind him. Gregor stood a few lengths away, rather formally, as if he didn't know what to expect. But Duncar could see the concern in the King's eyes.

"She's unharmed," Duncar reassured. "She worried about you, though."

Gregor shook his head in amazement. "Worried about me?"

"She was afraid of what they would do without her constant presence."

"Whatever they had planned, they did not act on it before I sent them back to Grenan."

Duncar glanced out the window at the men in military uniform. "Explains the difference."

"Trusted men who have fought next to me against many enemies."

The healer nodded, then solemnly admitted, "She does not know I'm here."

The King raised an eyebrow.

"Fancy a ride?"

Gregor hesitated, his last conversation with her echoing in his head. "No, I will wait for her to come to me."

"She won't," Duncar answered, frowning.

Gregor leaned back against the table, as if all of his energy had been drained. "It's true then, they finally succeeded."

Rana stepped forward. "Your Majesty, let me…"

"No, I will respect her wishes."

"Sometimes you have to face the bull," Duncar responded.

"I have. Twice. Both times she left without saying farewell. I think I know well enough now the limits of her forgiveness."

"Are you foolish enough to love my cousin?"

"Duncar…"

"If you two do not love each other, if this has just been some fun, then I will leave."

"They love each other," Rana answered, making his King glare at him. "They have said the words many times in front of the household staff and myself."

A realization washed over Duncar's face. "Are you telling me," and he stared Gregor down, "that Sreana pledged herself to you?"

"We…" Gregor stammered, "both took our pledges."

"She will never look at another."

Rana scoffed. "Neither will he."

"Then get on a horse and go to her. For three months, you two were too proud to admit how you felt and it was impossible to watch. I do not know what is going through her mind now, but she has been left to her own devices again and she is despondent."

"So is he," Rana admitted. "Your Majesty, I know it is not my place as your soldier. But as someone who has seen you and our lady together often, I cannot remain silent when I know where your heart lies. And when I know where her heart lies."

Gregor sighed, reluctantly. "You're both right. Lead the way."

"Good," then Duncar grew even more serious, "but there are some other things you need to know."

~   ~   ~

Gregor dismounted just outside the firepit area. Sreana was nowhere to be seen, but Duncar insisted she was there. The other man had warned him, however, that after being hunted, he didn't know how she would react to seeing Gregor, especially when she expressed hesitation about returning to him. He didn't care though. The closer he got to the township, the more he wanted to see her and for her to see him. He needed to tell her his side. He tied his horse to a nearby hitch then heard her door open. After shutting it, she started walking toward the road, eyes down. Then she saw movement and looked up. She stumbled to a stop, her eyes widening in surprise.

"How…?" she stammered.

"Duncar. And Rana." Gregor crossed the distance between them, cupping her face with his hands. She looked exhausted, the dark circles under her eyes and her drawn expression hurting his heart. He moved her face to the side, to see the bruise still discoloring her cheek. "Duncar said you were injured."

"Just got a little roughed up." Then she tried to back away, out of his hands, avoiding his eyes. "You didn't have to come all this way. My friends told me that the warrant had been rescinded."

He secured his hold on her again, making her look up into his eyes. "I know but I had to tell you in person. I never signed it and therefore it was executed illegally. Do you hear me? I did not sign it. I did not know it even existed. Even if you banish me, if this is the last time I ever see you, I needed to tell you myself that I did not order the warrant."

The strength in his tone was something she had never heard before. For a moment her heart warmed at the conviction in his voice and the fact that he was determined to tell her himself. She nodded, her voice failing her.

"At least some good came out of this," he continued. "It gave me the perfect opportunity to send the ministers and the Guard back to Grenan where my sister will happily deal with their insubordination." Then he chuckled, mirthlessly. "I think the household staff had them packed up even before I was done shouting. Once the whole lot were all gone, they started asking when our lady would be back."

"I've missed them, too," she whispered, her voice cracking.

He wrapped his arms around her, holding her close. She resisted at first, confused about his willingness to touch her. After what had been said… but when he didn't let go, she slipped her arms around his torso, the relief melting her into him. Even after everything, his warmth, his strength, his words, even his smell meant so much to her. For a moment, she could pretend that she was safe. She sighed into his shoulder.

Then they felt something impact their legs. They looked down to see little Sabira hugging them. They laughed at her as she giggled, hearing other voices grow louder. They raised their eyes toward the road and saw a large crowd gathering. Sreana glanced over each face and knew that her duty was to reassure her people. Her conversation with Gregor would have to wait until a more private time.

"Will you stay?" she asked, softly.

"I hoped you would have me."

He kissed her, for all to see. Relieved laughter and cheers rippled through the crowd as they watched their famous couple confirm that all was well.

~   ~   ~

The bonfire roared to life and food began to be prepared. A sense of normalcy and calm settled throughout the lea. Gregor stayed at Sreana's side as much as possible, keeping her hand clasped in his. He spent most of the afternoon reassuring the townspeople about the changes being made immediately, with the ministers and Castle Guard being banished back to Grenan. Rana also worked the crowd, with Duncar at his side, confirming again and again that those who trespassed against Sreana would be held accountable.

As evening arrived, Gregor ate while sitting between Rana and Sreana. He kept her in sight even as she spoke to those who came to share their relief and joy at her return. She smiled and thanked them, until something caught her eye, and she jumped to her feet.

Sreana set down her mug then strode toward the tables where their buffet of food had been laid out. Gregor watched as she approached a visibly upset Habni, grabbing the young mother into a hug. Sreana leaned back after a few moments and they spoke quite intensely. Then they stopped and watched as a giggling Sabira ran around the trees. The toddler chased after the jahla, who happily played with the girl. Sreana cupped Habni's face and said something, her expression serious but kind, and Habni appeared reassured.

He didn't need to know the conversation. Gregor again felt the weight of his actions pressing on his chest.

CHAPTER 39

As the fire began to die down, the crowd started to dissipate. Sreana and Gregor wished everyone good night as they passed by, then they retired to her hovel. Duncar and Rana stood near the pit, having watched them all evening with cautious optimism. Duncar squelched the remaining embers, then Rana sighed hard.

"We should get combat pay dealing with those two."

Duncar chuckled. "You get paid? Lucky." Then he tapped Rana's arm. "Come. I've a couch you can sleep on."

They headed down the dirt road to the row of houses and entered Duncar's home. The fire was already flickering and warming the living area. There were only a few pieces of furniture adorning it; a small couch that sat in front of the fireplace at an angle, and a chair and breakfast table near the window. Another door led into the bedroom, where a decent sized bed could be seen.

"I've never been in a Sedoran home," Rana commented.

"Well, this is not an average home," Duncar admitted. "It is not the one to judge my people on."

Rana chuckled. "It is nice, nevertheless."

"I will get you a pillow and blanket. Please, make yourself comfortable."

"Thank you."

Duncar exited the room and a few moments later reemerged with a pillow, a blanket, and a sheet to cover the couch. Rana had taken off his belt and sword, as well as his boots, and set them against the left side of the mantel. His heavy army jacket hung on the back of the chair, while his uniform tunic was neatly folded in its seat. He stood in front of the fire, toes touching the hearth, admiring the flames in his undershirt and uniform pants.

The Grenan was fit, his army exercises admirably forming the muscles in his arms and chest. Noticeable scars broke up his dark coloring, one along his bicep, another ran down the right side of his neck until it disappeared under his shirt. His dark hair was short as required, with small bursts of highlights from sun exposure decorating the top, and his face had been clean shaven but short stubble had grown during the day.

Duncar caught himself staring. He cleared his throat and hastily made his way to the couch. "Again, it's not much," he said, as he covered the couch with the sheet and laid the pillow and blanket down the cushions. "But you're closer to the King than if you stayed at Trealle's."

"Duncar, this is fine. I appreciate you bringing me into your home."

Duncar was so focused on making the couch comfortable that he didn't see Rana move closer. He didn't even realize how close he was until he caressed Duncar's forearm. Duncar glanced up in surprise, the look on Rana's face appreciative and affectionate. When Duncar straightened, the armyman stepped closer still, until their faces were a mere breath apart. Rana's amber eyes were beautiful, especially with the devilish glint flashing in them. Then Rana leaned in, a soft and tender kiss shared. Duncar stood, frozen in surprise, by how gentle the kiss was and by the fact it felt sincere. Duncar stepped back however, eyes on the ground.

"I'm flattered."

"But?"

Duncar's mind ran with reasons and excuses, but ended up blurting out, "It's been a long day. Good night, Rana."

"Good night, Duncar. Sleep well."

Duncar awkwardly nodded then darted into his bedroom.

~   ~   ~

They entered her hovel without speaking. Sreana unbelted her sword and hung it up, her hand briefly brushing her brother's, then she turned toward Gregor. She knew what she had to say, but he must have recognized the look on her face.

"I don't want to fight," he begged, keeping his voice low. "Not tonight. Not in our safe place. I just want to hold you and be thankful that you are home."

Before she could respond, he grabbed her into his arms and kissed her. She gave in immediately, unable to deny his request. No matter how conflicted her brain was, the determination in his embrace let her heart pretend. They helped the other out of their clothes before tackling each other onto the bed.

Afterwards, they laid on their sides, facing each other. She had forgotten how wonderful he felt, his warmth and strength reassuring her. As she listened to the sounds outside, she remembered their other nights together, when they lost themselves in each other. It confirmed that she still loved the man who currently shared her bed. But outside of it...

She stopped her train of thought. He was right. Tonight wasn't the time to fight. She was home, she was safe, and that was something to rejoice. She cuddled up closer to him, nuzzling his neck while he held her tight and let sleep take her.

~   ~   ~

Duncar caught himself tossing and turning, thinking about the man in his living area, who was probably sleeping soundly while Duncar struggled with his regret. He would've given anything to feel that affection offered by Rana. However, since the end of his relationship with Mirna, he swore to himself that he would live his life alone and miserable. After all, that was what one was supposed to do when one ripped out their heart and left it on the floor of their true love's bedroom.

Right?

He found himself slipping out of bed. He walked softly to the doorway, to peek in on Rana one more time before he resigned himself back to his bed and his life of loneliness. However, he found Rana still awake. The Grenan armyman laid on the couch, with his pillow propped up against the arm, while he had one of his arms folded back and behind his head for more incline. His body ran the length, one bare foot dangling off, barely touching the floor. He caught movement out of the corner of his eye and saw Duncar leaning against the doorframe.

Duncar frowned. "I am sorry."

"For what?" Rana inquired.

"For earlier. I am a mess. And it wouldn't be fair to you…"

"You thought my intentions were noble?" the armyman asked, sitting up. "I am sorry if you read me wrong. I assure you my expectations were not honorable."

"Then what were they?"

"Convenient. I thought we'd be compatible considering how well we have worked together and I thought we had enjoyed each other's company throughout the day. But I apologize if I broke a boundary."

"No, it's… like I said, it's flattering."

Rana looked Duncar over, then with a sly smile, stood and approached him. "But?"

"I wish I could. I ended things with the love of my life and… honestly everything I thought my life would be, well, it isn't. I have nothing to give you. I've wasted away. There's nothing left of me."

"That, my dear Duncar, I doubt." Rana reached out and caressed his cheek, making the other man close his eyes for a moment. "I have found that the broken-hearted are the most passionate. I wish you would let me prove that to you." Silence held them as did their gazes. "But you should know, I am a heartbreaker. And I am an armyman in the Grenan military, I go where my King commands. I could be gone tomorrow." His eyebrows furrowed together. "I just realized this is the longest I have stayed in one place." He moved his hand and cupped the other man's chin. "I admit that I would hate to leave it, knowing what I've found here."

Without a second thought, Duncar landed a kiss on Rana's lips. Rana pulled him into his arms, pressing the healer against him. Soon, what little clothing they wore lined the path to the bed...

~   ~   ~

Gregor was abruptly awakened by movement. He blinked in the darkness, his eyes finally adjusting and he could see Sreana struggling in her sleep. Small noises escaped her, mostly whimpers. He tightened his arms around her and whispered careful placations until she settled down. A deep sigh and incomprehensible muttering signaled the end of her nightmare and she fell silent except for her light snore. He kissed her forehead, his heart breaking for her. He hoped she would confide in him sooner than later.

~   ~   ~

Duncar felt warm lips on his neck and he inhaled deeply, opening his eyes against the predawn light that glimmered through his bedroom's window. Warm hands caressed his chest, then one traveled down to his ass and groped it seductively. Duncar smiled, then he froze, realizing who was still in his bed.

Apparently, Rana felt his reaction and stopped his overture. "Have I overstayed my welcome?"

Duncar glanced over his shoulder, to see Rana frowning. "No, of course not. I apologize. I thought I was dreaming."

Rana's lips turned up into a sultry grin. "I'll take that as a compliment." He kissed Duncar passionately, causing him to roll over so they could hold each other. When Rana pulled away, Duncar stammered then inhaled sharply. "Speechless and breathless? Even better compliments." Then he moved his lips to Duncar's neck again. Rana must have felt Duncar's hesitation and he leaned back to look into his bedmate's eyes.

"I took advantage of you," Duncar admitted, the guilt darkening his eyes.

Rana grinned wryly and shrugged. "I could say I did the same thing."

They stared at each other, Rana waiting for Duncar to speak while Duncar was at a loss for words. Blue eyes searched amber ones, making Duncar's heart flutter in a way it hadn't in a long time.

"Thank you."

Rana groused, rolling his eyes. "Don't thank me. Sounds like I fixed your window."

"Then what should I say?"

"Why use words?"

Duncar cupped his face and pulled him down, kissing him fervently. They lost themselves in the passionate embrace, until they had to catch their breaths. Rana touched Duncar's nose with his own, the armyman's smile warming the healer's heart.

"I don't want this to get out," Duncar whispered.

"Because of who I am?" Rana asked, another frown wrinkling his face.

"What do you mean?"

"I'm Grenan. I know my King and our lady have gotten away with it… but someone like you with someone like me…?"

"No, it's not that at all. I know this is just a tryst, but I don't want others' opinions or teasing to ruin something that I will hold dear to my heart. Call me old fashioned, I guess."

"We do deserve our privacy." He kissed Duncar tenderly in apology. "I'm sorry I assumed the worst." Then he stared into those blue eyes, so different from his cousin's but just as emotive. "But maybe it doesn't have to be a one-time thing?"

"I thought you were a heartbreaker?"

"I am. But I think what I have found here makes me question if breaking your heart is the best I can do. Maybe there's more to us than one night."

"Why the change of mind?"

"Well, you made quite the impression and I quite enjoyed our union. I am hoping we can fit one more in before I have to leave. And seeing that I'm not far from here and I do have free days… If you'll have me?"

Duncar paused, causing Rana concern, then rolled them while planting another passionate kiss on his lips.

~   ~   ~

That morning, Sreana was already awake and dressed when Gregor stirred. She smiled at him, an attempt anyway, and she slipped out the door. Gregor started dressing, then a few moments later, she returned with two mugs of coffee. He took both mugs and set them on her small table. Before she could question him, he grabbed her around the waist and kissed her. When she didn't return the passion, he hesitated kissing her again.

"Good morning," he whispered against her lips.

"Good morning."

"I have to go back today."

"Of course. You don't have your usual amenities here and I'm sure you miss your bed."

He squeezed her gently. "Sreana, I love your lumpy bed, remember?"

She pulled away and picked up the mugs again, handing him one while sipping from the other.

"Kasar is still a little paranoid about me being outside the castle. I think I'm safe until lunch before he sends in the cavalry."

"Pirco already went to fetch Rana."

He watched it for a moment, lips pursed. "Will you come back with me? We've reassured your people but I fear mine need the same."

"I will go back with you. But before you both leave, we should feed you. Trealle brought a pot of porridge to the firepit. It's not much, but it will at least tide you over until Marga can feed you properly."

He grasped her free hand, kissing it. "I am honored she brought breakfast here. Remind me to thank her."

"Come. She should still be out there."

CHAPTER 40

Later that morning, Rana led Gregor and Sreana through the gates, their horses trotting along the gravel path. Awaiting their arrival, the Grenan armymen were lined up ceremoniously close to the entryway. They dismounted at the steps, with someone from the stable taking the two horses by the reins.

"Which one?" she asked.

"He brought up..." Then Gregor appeared worried. "Sreana…"

But she had already crossed the distance between her and the main gossiper. She walked up to him, cocked her head, then landed a blow into his chin. The soldier stumbled backwards and cursed, glaring at her for her audacity. Rana and the other soldiers laughed then reserved themselves after a stern look from Kasar.

"Next time you wish to gossip," she stated, tone harsh, "remember this moment, because you only get one warning." Her eyes moved to Kasar. "I hope he has a long time to think about his behavior while cleaning the stables?"

"The stables? You are too kind, my lady," Kasar responded, his lips trying to twitch up into a smile.

After another disgusted glance at the gossiper, Sreana entered the main hallway, where the household staff all stood off to the side. She caught sight of them, then braced herself as Gwena rushed into her arms. She hugged the cook tight, forcing a grin. The other staff approached, welcoming her back and sharing how much they had missed her.

Kasar watched the scene as he stood by Gregor. "You've a queen, Gregor," the general whispered. "Don't let that one go."

Gregor wisely said nothing as he watched his people embrace Sreana.

~   ~   ~

220

As the day began to dwindle, Sreana and Gregor headed up to his bedchambers. They had spent the entire afternoon with the household staff. There had been a surprise set up in the meeting room, where the staff lined up little snacks for Sreana. She hugged all of them, even the kitchen drudge that hid shyly behind Gwena, and thanked them for their welcome and thoughtfulness. Then Rana, Wenth, and Ranthel snuck in to steal some of the treats, which caused Marga and Gwena to bat at them with wound-up hand towels. Laughter echoed through the castle, a sound that was sorely missed during Sreana's absence.

When they entered the bedchambers, Marga was already there, tidying up and readying the bed, tweaking the linens. She laid out the table settings as well, with the help of another woman named Tsalan, keeping dinner inside. Tsalan stoked the fire and fed it more logs, then exited when Marga thanked her for the help.

"Shall I draw a bath before dinner?" Marga inquired, with a small kind smile.

"I think that would be wonderful, Marga, yes please," Gregor responded, pulling Sreana against him and kissing her when she frowned. "Let me spoil you."

Sreana smiled half-heartedly, then nodded, watching Marga walk into the bathing room. As Marga ran the water and fussed about the linens, Sreana started to undress. Marga told them to go ahead and get in, then she excused herself so she could finish up the dining table settings. Gregor finished helping Sreana out of her clothes and guided her into the water as it steamed around her. She thanked him and he moved to undress himself.

Marga cleared her throat. "Apologies, Your Majesty. But Lieutenant Rana wishes to speak with you."

"Thank you, Marga." Gregor kissed Sreana. "I'll only be a moment."

Gregor stepped out of the bathing room and crossed the bedchambers to Rana, who was holding a parchment with a broken seal.

"I am sorry to interrupt, but I thought you would like to know the Queen sent this message. She thought it imperative that you were informed that Jamos and the other ministers have been stripped of their titles and dismissed from their government positions. The Captain of the Castle Guard has been remanded to house arrest and will go on trial for his abuses of power here in Sedora. Kasar is also moving forward with recalling the gossiping armymen within the next few days to have them dismissed from service."

"Thank you, Rana. My sister's diligence is not only appreciated but inspiring."

"Shall I pass those compliments on?"

"Yes, I think you should."

Rana caught a glimpse of Sreana in the bath. He frowned then returned his attention to his King. "I hope you will share this news with our lady. She may feel safer knowing they can no longer harm her and will atone for their crimes against her."

Gregor nodded, solemnly. "I will. Good night, Rana."

"Good night, Your Majesty."

Once Rana exited, Gregor turned to stare at Sreana through the doorway. She sat in the tub full of steaming water, her head only visible from the lips up. However, her face was cold as stone and he could see her eyes were lifeless. His heart sank. He exhaled, rubbing his face.

"Was our lady harmed?" a voice behind him inquired, the tone low and shaky.

Gregor turned around to find Marga had reappeared, with fresh towels and robes. "Why do you ask that?" When she didn't respond, Gregor whispered, "Marga?"

"It's just…" and she bit her lip, before continuing in a hushed voice, "when she thinks we're not looking, she gets that same look my grandfather would get when he remembered the war against his will. I saw it downstairs, it's the same look she has now. It's the same look you got when you first got hurt." Then the color drained from her face when she saw the pain cross his face. "I'm sorry for speaking out of turn…"

"Don't ever apologize for caring about us. We are fortunate that we have such considerate friends among us." He patted her shoulder. "We have a lot of work ahead of us to remind her that she is safe and welcome here."

"We will do our best, Your Majesty."

He smiled at her confident response, then walked back toward the bathing room. But as he approached, he felt his smile fade as he watched Sreana sitting completely motionless. Before, he knew in his heart that she was slipping away, but at that moment he realized he truly had lost her.

~   ~   ~

They fell asleep without speaking much that night. When he woke a few hours later, he discovered her missing. He found her sitting on the couch, wrapped in her robe, and staring at the fire. Her spiritless expression worried him.

He called out to her, but she didn't move. He left the bed, slipped on his own robe, and sat next to her. He wrapped his arm around her shoulders but her pliancy had completely dissolved.

"I assume that we cannot avoid our fight any longer?" he asked, softly.

She didn't respond, her eyes still focused on the fire.

"You broke your promise to me," he said, his voice low and hurt.

"Why should I have kept mine when you broke yours?"

Bitter silence settled.

"I couldn't stand the way you had looked at me," she continued, still facing away. "Like I had maliciously held back secrets from you to stay in your good graces. Like I was some monster using you. Like I was something… unnatural. I knew you would never look at me like you used to with those stories in your head. And I knew you would look at me that way when we woke in the morning."

"Sreana…"

She pulled away from him, making him withdraw his arm, and she stared at her knees. "The men who told you those tales knew… That me and my friends were not the monsters they made us out to be." Her fingers dug deep into the couch's seat. "But, whatever their motives, they wanted us apart and they succeeded because you gave into doubt."

"I didn't just doubt you. I doubted the men who told me, those who I fought beside time and time again. I doubted myself. I found myself not knowing who to trust again."

She finally met his gaze. "If we cannot trust each other, Gregor, if we so easily lose faith in each other, then this isn't the companionship we had hoped for, is it?"

He didn't know how to respond.

"I can accept what happened to me, because I understand enemies and retribution. Those are as familiar to me as diplomacy and survival. But I cannot accept the possibility of this happening to anyone else. I have to protect my people. I also have to protect the nymphs who you fear. And I have to protect the next generation of what you call my kind. Our enemies are at our doorstep every day and it is my job to keep *all* Sedorans safe. I must honor my responsibilities and I can no longer let myself be distracted. I am a Leader and a protector, that is who I am."

"Companion is not part of who you are?"

"Am I a companion? That's not how you looked at me that night. All you saw was a subject of your Kingdom, someone to order and threaten. It became obvious that night that I have been nothing more than entertainment for you. I know now that you could never appreciate who I am or what my life is truly like. I can tell you all the stories about my life but you will never fully understand. We gave into the fantasy that we were compatible but what happened just confirms that we were foolish in thinking our companionship was acceptable. It's been made clear that I must walk away from you."

She let the words hang there for a moment but neither of them could find a response immediately.

"Did we mislead our people then?" he asked.

She folded her hands, resting them on her knees. "I will never break my pledge to you, Gregor. I will never be with anyone else. But even though I love you, I cannot be with you. After all, you are a King and I'm…" She inhaled, shakily, then continued, "For the sake of our people, we will maintain some normalcy until things settle down and then…" and she shrugged.

"What will our visits consist of from now on?"

"We will still use them to conduct business, to keep up to date on what is being done and what needs to be done. Once I have updated you… You can do with me what you want."

"I will not bed an unwilling partner," he snapped back, his voice dark with anger.

She flinched and lowered her eyes to her hands. "Then I will sneak out afterwards and you can use whatever excuse you wish as to why I am not present for breakfast. Eventually, my visits will become less frequent. Once my absence is expected more than my presence, we will announce publicly that even though we still care deeply about each other, our responsibilities come first and we must focus on those. I know that you will keep Grenan's promise to care for my people and help them as you have done this whole time. But I need to be there for them as well and make sure my foolish entanglements do not negatively affect them. We will continue to work on getting Sedora back on its feet. And then eventually, time will come for you to go home."

"You mean go back to Grenan."

"That is your home, isn't it? You have been gone long enough. I am sure your family and people would celebrate your return."

"There is nothing I can say or do to change your mind?"

"I had enough time to think about this while I…" and she stammered, unable to finish. She took a deep breath and stood. "It is what's best for my people." She removed the robe, showing that she had already put on her undershirt and shorts, then she slipped on her pants and tunic. With a shaking hand, she grabbed her boots and sword. "I need to go. I know there will be some confusion in the other townships about the changes you've made here but I will reassure my people and help them understand that it is for the better. I will return in a week with any updates, Your Majesty."

Gregor sat in shock and felt his heart shatter as she left his bedchambers.

CHAPTER 41

She spent several sleepless nights, alone in her bed. As she fought to get comfortable late one night, Sreana wrapped herself up in her quilt and stared at the ceiling. She hadn't told anyone of the dissolution, leaving that announcement to Gregor. She hated keeping the secret from her friends, but she knew that the appearance that they were still together was the only thing keeping their kingdoms' collaboration moving forward. And if Duncar and Pirco found out, they would only interfere and make things worse.

They would never understand.

She sat up in bed, leaning against the cool rock and stared at the fire that flickered weakly in her stove. It reminded her of the saehwa's glow, haunting but reassuring. She found herself missing their company, the sounds of their voices and the beauty they radiated.

She berated herself quietly. She should have told Gregor her secret in the beginning, like she did her warrants, so they could have ended sooner. Maybe things would be different. She chewed on her lip, her conscience giving her more grief. Because there was one thing she did lie about. She had told Gregor that there were others like her in Sedora, but there were no others that had Talent like hers, not in several generations. The last person she knew of was her great-great grandfather.

When she was young, her father had taught her everything he knew about nymphs. He could speak with eahzals like all of the others in their family that had Talents. But it wasn't until her days at the Temple, when they were sent out to gather offerings, that she realized she was different. She met Jayna in a lea and that was when she found out she could talk to jahlas too. She didn't tell anyone about the encounter until she got home, when she told her parents. Her father's face crumbled with worry and her mother sat speechless. Eahzals were expected due to her father and uncle, but jahlas? And possibly the others? That was the first time she saw such concern in their eyes.

And the first time they suggested that she keep a secret.

When she was growing up, Talents were frightening to those who didn't understand. She had been teased enough as a child about her Talent with eahzals. However, her parents feared worse treatment if anyone found out about her other Talents.

And even though the treaties that were in place had been finalized to ensure everyone's safety, they hadn't stopped the fear. During the invasion however, no one had time to worry over who had Talents. The benefit outweighed everything else. What treaties were scoffed at before by the ignorant became tenets to survival. And those with Talents, like Pirco, Darner and herself, were respected instead of feared.

Until now. Now, Sreana knew that Gregor and his people would continue to fear them. She had imparted warnings to the nymphs and those with Talents to continue to keep their existence a secret to their Grenan allies. The Grenans knew about her, but they didn't need to know about anyone else.

~   ~   ~

The next evening, after everyone started to wind down and head home, Pirco and Sreana sat at the firepit. Pirco had accepted her excuse for not visiting Gregor again so soon, having explained that because she had been gone for so long she wanted to reassure their community that she was back and ready to work on any project in need of help. Even though it was obvious he believed her, he still clung to her side as if protecting her. He refilled her mug with fresh mead, then sat next to her with his elbow touching hers.

Then a sly smirk appeared. "I know you've had a lot going on but I thought I should tell you. Apparently, you are not the only Rathfeather to jump the border."

"What are you talking about?"

"That armyman, Rana, spent the night with Duncar."

"Duncar said he'd let him sleep at his place."

"The farewell was sweet."

Sreana poked at the fire. "Don't tease him, please?"

"I had no intention. As torn as I am because I love Mirna like a sister, Duncar is as much a brother to me as he is to you. I want him happy. After everything, just some happiness. Even if it were just one night."

"Did anyone else see?"

"I doubt it. I just caught a glimpse in the window when I was walking up to retrieve Rana. Then he stepped out and I led him back here. I didn't say a word."

"I will find out if Rana will be a recurring visitor, so we can make adjustments to give Duncar free time."

"Good. I want them to have their privacy and them to enjoy whatever they decide to do." He took a gulp of his mead. "Did you want me to stay tonight?

All Dini does right now is visit the privy and not sleep."

Sreana chuckled. "I'm fine, but thank you." He didn't look pleased by her answer. "What? Is she that terrible right now?"

"No, I..." and he took a deep breath, "Duncar and I have heard you."

Her eyebrows furrowed in puzzlement.

"You've been having nightmares. I thought maybe staying with you would help them stop. Since that's how we got through ours the first time. Together."

"I didn't realize I was still having them."

"When did they start up again?"

She stared at the flames as they danced along the logs and sticks, remembering how Reshepha and Setarah comforted her. "I'll be fine, Pirco. They'll fade like the old ones did." Then she smiled, a small but honest one, and she bumped his shoulder with hers. "I'm home, I'm safe. I have my friends and my family to protect me." She tossed her stick into the fire. "Go be with your loves. You know it's safer to sleep with them than me when I have a nightmare."

Pirco chuckled. "You have never shared a bed with a very pregnant Dini when she cannot get comfortable."

~   ~   ~

The next day, Sreana and Duncar took their lunch in her lea, eating side by side. Duncar hovered around her as much as Pirco, but at least she finally understood why. However, if he had other things on his mind, she didn't want to be a distraction. Before she could interrogate her cousin, he spoke first.

"How are things with you and Gregor?"

She grimaced. "Complicated."

"Do you want to talk about it?"

"Not much to say." She chuckled, trying to fake some humor. "It's just amazing how many emotions one can have in one singular moment."

"Well don't make Rana's and my work futile. It took everything to get you two back in the same room, as it were."

She bit her tongue, staring at her food. "Do you think it's hereditary?"

"What's that?"

"Our attraction to Grenan men."

Duncar choked on his food. He coughed hard several times before he could catch his breath. "Who saw us?"

"Pirco."

Duncar began to stammer excuses.

"Duncar, stop. He says what he saw was sweet."

"I know but..."

"No, no buts. As her friend, I'm annoyed, but as your cousin? I'm thrilled.

I like Rana."

"Me too." He stared at his plate, a shy smile creeping across his face. "It's odd. I told him I couldn't offer him anything. That there was nothing left in me. He was determined to prove me wrong that night."

"I told you not to tempt the fates. Grenan men are quite direct. And always up for a challenge."

Duncar laughed. "Now I know why you fell for Gregor."

"So will we be seeing more of him?"

"He will visit on his next free day."

She forced a grin. "Good, let me know before each visit and I will make sure I will not need you for anything."

CHAPTER 42

Each week, Sreana arrived before dinner. She sat on the other side of the table and ate the meals prepared, out of respect for Gwena and all of her hard work. Once they finished eating, she stayed far enough away from Gregor, usually standing near the balcony door for an easy escape, and only spoke when he asked her a question. When she felt she had stayed long enough, she disappeared through the doorway with little more to say than, "I will be back in a week, Your Majesty, with any updates."

Each visit seemed shorter and shorter. Within a month she started missing visits. And then, eventually, they stopped altogether. Gregor would stay up as long as he could, waiting to see if she would change her mind, but always ended up dozing off on the couch or in his chair. Marga finally insisted that he start sleeping in bed. When the visits stopped, there were mornings where Gregor didn't even bother getting out of bed. But every morning that Sreana was supposed to have breakfast with him, Gregor would request a bowl of porridge which he would eat solemnly.

Rana caught Marga one night standing at the main doors, after helping the King ready for bed. She leaned against the doorframe, staring at the gate. He draped a throw blanket over her shoulders, startling her out of her depressed stupor. He stood by her side, a kind hand still on her shoulder, as he joined her in looking out into the night.

"You will catch your death," he chided, "standing out in this cold weather."

Her face stayed solemn. "We didn't do enough, did we?"

"Oh, Marga, you can't blame yourself."

"Yes, I can. We didn't protect her."

"None of us were prepared for what happened."

Tears glistened in her eyes. "But we didn't do enough, did we? We didn't show her that we loved when she came to visit, that we appreciated how her laugh always lightened up the day. She was always so kind to us, knew all of our names. It had to be us because I can't believe that she... she never loved us."

"She loves our King and she loves us, but I think what happened to her... I think it hurts her more than she is willing to admit. Such horrible things can stain the most precious."

"I wish we had done more than give them food poisoning."

Rana chuckled in surprise. "So that was on purpose? Well, it was the best you could do, considering. But we both know our wise Queen will ensure they are punished to the fullest extent of her power."

"It will not bring our lady back."

"No, it won't." He sighed, resigned to that fact. "Come, we must lock up. If our lady changes her mind, I'm sure she'll find a way in. Let us rest tonight with that hope."

~   ~   ~

One morning, after breakfast, one of the other lieutenants asked for an audience. Ranthel was about the same age as Rana, with amber eyes that were two shades darker, short curly black hair, and similar skin color. Gregor knew both men had grown up in the same town back in Grenan and joined the military at the same time. They moved up the ranks together and worked well throughout the war. Since moving into the castle, that collaboration continued to benefit Grenan and Sedora. However, because Ranthel towered over everyone else in the castle, he was an easy target for short staff who needed something out of an upper cabinet.

"What is on your mind, Ranthel?"

Ranthel appeared grim. "You need to see what we found."

"Lead the way."

Gregor followed Ranthel down several stairways and hallways, realizing that he had never seen this part of the castle. It had to be the lowest level, because of the drainage pipes and lack of windows, but it was also the furthest back. The large hallway they walked down had been hidden behind massive doors that served to protect the inner plumbing.

Then they came to another set of doors. These were newer, not original to the structure. As Ranthel pushed the left one open, Gregor could see they were battlement heavy and took Ranthel some effort. As Gregor entered the room, he froze in the doorway. The room itself was still original to the castle based on the masonry, but had been updated with metal and wood as a prison. A half dozen jail cells lined one wall, while strips of wood lined the other one. Attached to the wood strips were metal restraints, where someone would be held by their wrists and ankles in a standing position. A table running perpendicular to the wall had different restraints laid out along its top, as well as rags, knives, and other implements he could only relate to torture.

"How did you find this?"

"At first, we only wanted to secure the grounds to make sure the dismissed Guard or disgraced ministers didn't have any secret access to the castle. To make sure they couldn't seek revenge. But as we did so, we couldn't figure out where they hid our lady from us. We had made our rounds as usual that night and never saw any evidence of her capture. As you said, she fought back and had escaped from somewhere here in the castle. Now we know they had built a dungeon with prison cells right under our very residence."

Gregor felt his rage rise up. Imagining Sreana, or any Sedoran citizen, imprisoned within those walls caused his anger to explode. He grabbed the table with the revolting tools and shoved it. The table and items flew across the room and crashed into the wall, disbursing the restraints throughout the room. He stared at his work, gasping for air as if he were drowning in the sea.

"If we could burn it down alone," Gregor said, his voice low and harsh, "I would set it afire myself. Dismantle it, all of it. And ask the others to check the other residences where the ministers lived to make sure this was unique."

"Yes, Your Majesty."

"And... we must find out if there were any other victims of this... disgusting place."

"Rana, Wenth and the others are already investigating," Ranthel responded. "We know the Sedorans hid themselves well to avoid arrest, so we have hope that this room saw no other use than holding our lady for a brief time. We have also sent documentation to the Queen to use as evidence against the captain and any others that may need to be held accountable."

Gregor shook in anger. "Are we truly no better than the scourge we banished from their borders?"

"We are better, Your Majesty. Only a select few decided they were not true Grenans."

~   ~   ~

Kasar found Gregor sitting on the balcony, overlooking the empty courtyard, a couple of almost empty pitchers on the table. In his hand, a mug that was filled to the rim with mead. Gregor had a glaze to his eyes, the intoxication slowing him down enough he didn't realize Kasar was present until the general sat down at the table.

"That room was disturbing," Kasar admitted.

"I had never seen anything like that even from the Carmanic Empire. I never expected to see that curated by our own people."

"At least we have confirmation it hadn't been used yet, other than to hold your heartbreaker."

Gregor didn't respond, taking a long swig.

"I've been told that she has stopped visiting."

"Given the circumstances, she decided it was appropriate to end things."

Kasar glared at Gregor, looking quite displeased. "I told you to hold onto her."

"Can't hold onto someone who can't stand you touching them. And before you ask, she said no one violated her." Gregor lifted the mug to his lips and gulped. "If they had, I would have executed them myself. Grenan law be damned." Then he set it down, a little harder than he should have. "I can't imagine reliving that fear as long as she did. Being in that room, then being hunted like an animal."

"What will you do?"

"Continue to keep my promises to the Sedoran people. And when the time is right, return to Grenan."

Kasar glanced away, his stone face breaking for a moment. "I don't think any of us have ever thought about leaving."

"No, none of us have. I know a few who have made Sedora their home and I can't imagine ordering them to leave. But I will negotiate for those who wish to stay. I am prepared to come to the table with my quick exit as the sweetener. I believe that will make them amiable to the others staying. I have already notified Vehla that I plan to return soon and leave you in charge. We will see if my departure lessens the animosity before trying any other negotiations."

"I cannot believe this is what you want."

"No, it's not what I want. I had hoped to make this my home. With her. I had plans to ask her to mm… But that is no longer an option, is it?" Gregor growled a curse. "I wish I had kept my mouth shut that night." He rubbed his face with trembling hands, then dropped them down onto either side of his mug. "I failed her, Kasar. I knew I lost her the night she left, but I think I had hopes that maybe… I had foolishly hoped that seeing all of us, showing her how much we all love her here, it would break through and she would come back to me, but it seems to have made it worse." Gregor sighed, disappointed. "We pretended it wasn't over after we reunited because we wanted to save face and reassure our people that nothing could change our alliance. We have agreed to continue to present a united front, for both of our people, but the companionship is over."

"I am sorry, Gregor," Kasar responded, his usually gruff voice soft. "For both of you."

"Me too, my friend." Silence. "I will also limit my travel outside the castle for now. I can't imagine what her people think of me after everything." Another mouthful of mead. "We knew they were going to come at us. It was inevitable. But I thought it'd be me again, to be honest. I didn't think they'd go after her the way they did. I know they thought her weak, an easier target, and none of those fools realized her fighting skills. But hunting her like that? We were just not prepared for their cruelty."

Gregor reached for the last pitcher, but Kasar moved it away.

"This is not helping."

232

"I had hoped it would numb everything but I still feel it all."

"May I suggest that you retire to your bed, Your Majesty?"

"There's nothing in my bed that I wish to retire to."

Kasar stared at him then shook his head. "Don't make me order you, Gregor. You may be King, and you may be discharged from my ranks, but I am still your General."

Gregor chuckled, mirthlessly. "Yes, General." Then he stood and walked unsteadily into his bedchambers and collapsed, fully clothed, onto his bed.

CHAPTER 43

A few months after the illegal warrant was rescinded, more differences became evident. Everyone that worked with or traveled to the castle confirmed that the Castle Guard and ministers were gone. Armymen and household staff were the only residents, besides the King. However, the King had withdrawn into his castle again. There was a lack of sightings since he was last with Sreana in her township, but at least he kept contact with the community leaders through his armymen who were well-known and trusted.

Her devotion to her friends, her responsibilities, and expectations however never faltered. Sreana was seen more at her township, always available if anyone visited her lea. She still interacted with her people, visiting farms, walking the roads, and eating among them. There wasn't the same devastation in her eyes like before, but they could see the spark was gone. And if she still traveled to the castle, no one could figure out when.

As time moved along, whispers started that the King and the Leader were no longer companions, but no one was willing to confront her about it. After all, everything still appeared well even if they were no longer together.

CHAPTER 44

Even though everyone else seemed to accept the changes in Sreana, Pirco did not. He hated not knowing what was going on and he refused to respect her privacy this time. At dinner one night, as the crowd began to dwindle, Pirco caught Sreana on her way to her hovel.

"Sreana, are you going to the castle tonight?"

Reaching for her door, she shook her head. "No, not tonight."

"You know, I need to know your visitation schedule. Especially with Dini's pregnancy almost to term."

"Don't worry about it," she replied, faking her smile again. "Dini and the baby are more important."

Eyes narrowing with annoyance, Pirco grabbed her arm and pushed her into her hovel. He slammed the door behind them, keeping his tone hushed so they couldn't be overheard.

"You haven't asked me to cover you for over a month. Before that it was random and you didn't stay the night anymore. You stopped asking Duncar to cover for you ages ago, using Rana as an excuse. Now you're using the baby as an excuse not to ask me? What happened?"

Sreana stammered, torn about admitting what happened and protecting her friend from heartbreak. He liked and cared for Gregor too. But he had a right to know, at least to stop any assumptions that ran through his mind. "We're over."

"What?"

"When the Castle Guard hunted me the way they did, I knew it was because of who I was to the King. That didn't bother me; we were aware it would happen sooner or later. But it didn't hit me until I was hiding that they could target anyone. I couldn't take the chance of anything like that happening to someone else. What if they came after you or Duncar or someone else, someone who couldn't survive and fight back?"

"But those men are gone."

235

"They are, but there are others who could pick up where they left off. I just can't take that chance."

He stared at her for a few breaths, realizing she couldn't meet his eyes. "Fine, that is your official statement, now tell me the truth."

She didn't respond.

"There's more to your ending than just protecting us. You love that man more than you can put into words. You pledged yourself to him. You wouldn't even do that for Canor, not that he would have cared, but you were going to marry him. So why did you leave Gregor that night? What could have been so horrible that you can't bring yourself to be with him?"

She wrapped her arms around her torso, as if comforting herself. "Some of his armymen told him stories. About my kind, people like me and you, someone they see as magic. That we are nothing more than monsters. He acted like I had lied to him, out of spite. I could see right then he had stopped trusting me. I think he may have even feared me. I left so I didn't have to see that look in his eyes again. And even though we reunited, we couldn't reconcile. We tried, but when I returned with him to the castle, surrounded by his staff and armymen and the amenities he required, it was obvious that he would never understand. And he would never be able to accept what I am."

The tears streaming down her face as she spoke tore at his heart. Pirco grabbed her into his arms, hugging her.

"I was never meant to be happy, was I?" she demanded, her following sobs breaking his heart. Her knees buckled, making Pirco hold her tighter. He could tell by the wracking sobs that there was more, but he could only hold her.

~   ~   ~

Rana and Duncar sat together on the couch, Duncar nestled under Rana's arm. Duncar rested his head on his lover's chest, both watching the fire dwindle.

"I saw Pirco spirit our lady away."

"I hope she finally told him what happened," Duncar responded. "Everyone's noticed the change in her. It's different from the first time but she hasn't been the same since..."

"Has she said anything to you?"

"Nothing." Duncar sighed, bringing Rana's hand up to kiss it. "How long has it been since she visited the castle?"

"Over a month. The King hasn't said anything." Rana rested his head against Duncar's. "But I saw something I didn't want to, or should have."

"Tell me," Duncar replied when Rana hesitated.

"A statement by the King announcing their amicable ending. It looked like several drafts, but none seemed to please him. I started asking the household staff about any rumors they heard and found out what their argument was about. I don't know how she only hit the armyman once."

Duncar sat up, meeting his lover's eyes. "What was it about?"

"About how different she is, about her magic."

"Magic? She doesn't use magic."

"No, not in the traditional sense but it is the only way we can define it. But the rumors that were shared made her sound like a monster. Or more like, a monster that could control monsters. They told him these things because they believed the Grenan King should not be involved with some Sedoran whore."

The look on Duncar's face broke Rana's heart.

"What happened to the armymen?"

"Sent back to Grenan. They were not part of my regiment. Believe me I would have known sooner and thrashed each one personally. Wenth's recommendation was for them all to be discharged immediately from service. General Kasar agreed." Rana kissed Duncar, reassuring, "I do not believe she is the monster they described."

"No, but Gregor has been convinced she is. And it explains why she refused to go to him."

"I don't know what he thought when he heard the stories and I do not know what words were exchanged between them. All I know is that it was too much for both of them." Rana's expression switched from unhappy to tormented. "I wish I hadn't gone to the border that night. Had I been around, I would've… done something. But now they are lost. The wedge was driven hard enough to shatter them."

Duncar hesitated, wondering if he should admit what he heard. But he knew his lover deserved honesty. "I think the repercussions of that have already leached into the townships."

"What do you mean?"

"Someone used a word I hadn't heard since Sreana brought the leaders together with Gregor." Duncar grimaced. "They are calling you occupiers again."

Rana let Duncar go, leaning his elbows on his knees and covering his face with his hands. "After all of our hard work only to end up back where we started." The long exhalation that escaped the armyman sounded distressed. "That could mean we might have to leave?"

"That I do not know, I am not a part of those conversations. I don't even know if Sreana would tell me, if it's not official. But you should warn Gregor."

"I will. Maybe also suggest not releasing a statement that would give your leaders an even better excuse to expel us."

Duncar wrapped his arms around Rana's shoulders, making Rana return the embrace. "I do not want you to leave."

"Me neither. This is home, not just this land but you. I don't know what I would do if I had to leave you."

"Let's try not to think about what ifs tonight," Duncar responded, touching his nose to Rana's. "That is what tomorrow is for. Tonight, I just want to be the reason you make all of those lovely noises that drive me crazy."

~   ~   ~

That morning, after Rana left Duncar's home, the armyman headed straight to his King's chambers. Gregor was awake, eating his porridge inside due to the rainy weather moving in. Rana stopped at the open door and knocked, waiting for recognition. A wave of a hand permitted him to enter, then he stood near the table.

"What news do you bring, Rana?" Gregor inquired, eyes intent on the other man's face.

"I heard something in the township that bothered me," Rana admitted. "The Sedorans won't say it to our faces but, behind our backs, we are being called occupiers again."

Gregor sighed, frustrated, and dropped his spoon. "I wish I was surprised. Nothing's been right for a while."

"Nothing's been normal since the unauthorized warrant on our lady."

The King sat silently, his face crumbling under the weight of his thoughts. "The trust is broken, isn't it?"

"I fear it is gone."

"Ask Kasar to gather Ranthel and Wenth. We need to find out what everyone has heard and determine what our next steps should be."

"Yes, Your Majesty." Rana started to leave, but the scribbled notes on the desk made him pause. "May I make a request?"

"Of course."

"Do not release your statement about you and our lady."

Gregor's eyes widened. "How...?"

"Your notes are visible, Your Majesty. For the sake of negotiations with the Sedorans, and for those of us who have found happiness among them, it would be detrimental to announce the dissolution of your companionship. It could provide fuel to a fire we want to extinguish."

Gregor nodded, standing and walking to his desk. He gathered his scribbled notes, with the different versions of the announcement, then threw them into the fire.

CHAPTER 45

Sreana entered the Temple, expecting everyone but the overnight priest to have retired for the evening. That priest, Chieron, nodded as she walked past. She approached the statue of Dranar, who gazed mercifully down, then laid a delicate wreath of drift wood, milkweed, ivy, and pansies at the goddess's feet. Closing her eyes, she whispered her prayer of thanks.

"I thought you had forgotten everything," a voice behind her mused.

Sreana bowed to Dranar, then turned to face Mirna. "Offerings are still the right of all believers."

"Are you still a believer?" the priest demanded, skeptical. "I heard you converted to some peculiar Grenan religion to appease your King."

"Ah, you are one of them."

"Them?"

"The ignorant," Sreana snapped back. "Good night, Priest Mirna." And she started to leave, brushing past the other woman.

"Sreana, wait."

Sreana paused, keeping her back to her childhood friend. "You're allowed to still be angry, Mirna. But be angry at me for the right reasons."

"You're right, that was unfair."

Strained silence held them.

"I am glad you brought a gift. Dranar appreciates your recognition of her mercy."

"The offering isn't personal. I do it for our people."

"Diplomacy? You?"

"I've gotten quite good at it," Sreana responded, facing Mirna again. "Especially after the incident at Dranar's rebirth celebration."

Mirna grimaced, folding her hands delicately. "I didn't expect things to go so bad."

"No, I'm sure the head priest didn't either."

Knowing the head priest well, the image of the older woman's face reacting to the fiasco caused both to laugh. It was a brief moment of levity between two friends, but the atmosphere still crackled with tension.

"So, what? You bring this gift to ensure those attending the next celebration understand there are no bitter feelings?"

"That's the plan. I hope you spread the word." Sreana started slowly walking backwards toward the door. "I should go, I wasn't planning on staying very long."

Then Mirna's fierceness faded. "How is Duncar?"

"Do you want the diplomatic answer or the truth?"

"Don't lie to me," Mirna answered, softly.

"He found someone," Sreana responded, pausing her exit. "Well, I should say someone found him. He's content."

The priest glanced away, blinking a little too quickly. "Good, I am glad."

"Did you mean the things you said to him?"

"Not all of it. But I knew it wasn't fair to keep him attached when I knew my calling would always keep me inside these walls."

The leader glanced around the Temple, frowning, before looking back at her childhood friend. "Mirna, I know you gladly seclude yourself here now, but I do hope someday you will see that these walls are not protection, but a prison. And you deserve so much more than this gilded cage."

Another bout of silence.

"Good night, Mirna. May the gods keep your nightmares to themselves."

"And may they give you dreams worth dreaming," the priest whispered, as she watched her friend disappear into the night.

~   ~   ~

While Duncar and Pirco waited for Sreana to return, they sat shoulder to shoulder at the crackling firepit. They had suggested that she send a proxy instead of going herself, not knowing how a return to her former Temple would affect her, but Sreana made it clear that the offering wouldn't mean as much if she didn't deliver it herself. She was right of course, but after the change in her since her return, it was hard for them not to be protective of her. The days of fighting haunted all of them and her continued nightmares fueled the ghosts of theirs.

Listening to the night, from the sounds of people talking drifting up from the township's streets to the birds settling in for bedtime, Duncar sipped from his cup while Pirco stirred the embers.

"Did you talk to Sreana?" Duncar inquired.

"Yeah, we talked."

"Is she going to snap out of it?"

Pirco's eyes narrowed, startling his friend. "Duncar, we can't expect Sreana to bounce back and be herself anymore. She was hunted. Just like during the invasion, always having to look over her shoulder. Knowing that if she was caught, what horrific acts those bastards would happily perpetrate. And we weren't there with her. We weren't there to sleep in shifts, to lay there with our backs against hers. She was by herself. And she was left to believe for days that the man she loved, someone she put all her remaining trust in, the man that she pledged herself to, had signed the paper that sent the hunters after her."

Duncar stammered at the hurt in Pirco's voice but he couldn't form any words.

"Every tragedy has broken pieces of her away, the invasion, her..." and Pirco clenched his fists in anguish. "You weren't there when Canor dismissed her. You didn't see what torment she endured knowing she lost something precious. I had to watch the little girl who used to swim with the eahzals completely against her father's wishes vanish within an afternoon. And now this? I don't know if we'll ever get her back, not to who she used to be."

"I... I'm sorry, I didn't realize..."

"None of us realized how bad it was, because she hides everything away. She pretended everything was fine with Gregor to ease our worries, but she knew there was nothing left of them. I only know her pain because she let me see it firsthand." Pirco blinked back his tears. "Duncar, she doesn't think she's allowed to be happy. That all she has left to her are the responsibilities she has as a leader. After this, and I know she didn't tell me everything, I do not expect her to ever really smile again, or ever get that little diabolical look in her eye... let alone love anyone again. All I know is I have to understand this version of her and remember that I love her like the sister she has always been to me."

Duncar exhaled hard, trying not to completely break down in tears. He didn't know. Even after what Rana had told him, he had hoped it was just a lover's quarrel that time would heal. The anguish in his friend's voice drove home the realization that, once again, she was left without.

"Then we will help her any way we can," Duncar responded, his voice low.

"That is all we can do." Pirco rubbed his face with shaky hands, inhaling deeply. "She'll be back soon, we can't let her know I told you."

"Agreed. Go splash some water on your face, I'll watch for her."

Pirco nodded, standing and walking to Sreana's hovel where water remained in her washbowl.

~   ~   ~

The next morning, Pirco crawled out of her bed and started the fire. He had been adamant about staying the night, claiming exhaustion when Sreana knew he worried over her conversation with Mirna. She gave in, appreciating his body heat during the chilly night. She soon followed him out to the firepit, straddling

241

one of the felled trees.

"What plans today?" he inquired, stirring the embers he ignited.

"I've noticed some of the children gravitating toward Jya."

Pirco's eyebrows rose up. "Talents?"

"I think it's time to test that theory. And once we've got our children figured out, we will need to help the other communities. Would you and Darner be willing to teach those Talented with jahlas and eahzals?"

"Of course. Who else could teach them?"

She grimaced, picking at a splinter and tossing it aside once it was freed.

"Sreana, you can't do it all."

"No, I can't. Especially when Habni thinks her daughter is like me."

He whistled, a sound of surprise. "That's rare. Well, Darner and I will happily help out where we can. Between nappies and feedings of course."

"I appreciate that and I will schedule accordingly. I will also make time to babysit."

He chuckled at that.

She watched her friend for a moment as he warmed his hands. "When I was away, the nymphs helped me," she admitted.

"Why wouldn't the jahlas help?" he asked, absent-mindedly.

"Not just jahlas, Pirco. All of them. The jahlas used the trees to keep me safe. The saehwa stayed with me at night to keep me warm because I couldn't have a fire. The eahzals and halha kept the rain falling and wind blowing, because they knew that the Castle Guard wouldn't search in bad weather. And the aetha, they helped light my way when I gathered food and water at night so I didn't get lost in the dark. I was never alone."

He sat and stared at her, speechless.

"I found myself thanking them constantly, but they always responded by thanking me for always keeping them safe. They all spent time with me, one on one. They would ask me questions about how things worked between us and the jahlas and eahzals. We eventually discussed drawing up treaties."

He stuttered, shook his head and took a deep breath. "That would be phenomenal."

"That's why I need to look into who has Talents. Before we can move forward, they want to see if any of our children have Talents for their kind. If we have that connection, then we can consider building our relationships with the new generation. Connect early, so that whatever we create can last."

"Sreana... we've never had a truly unified Sedora like that. Not even..."

"I know, not even when my great-great grandfather was alive. It's tentative at best, they are nymphs after all. But it's a start."

"What was it like? Talking to all of them?"

Sreana smiled, her cheeks warming with the memories. "Just like this. I didn't have any issues understanding them. They asked so many questions and I didn't hesitate to answer every single one. I think my willingness to address their curiosity made it easier for them to come forward, because there was no fear of disrespect." She fell silent for a moment before adding, "There's something else."

Pirco's eyebrows furrowed.

"Remember that trick I used to do when Mama's flowers would start wilting?"

He nodded.

"That's not the only thing I could do."

"I know."

It was her turn to look confused.

"I'm Talented, I knew when a jahla was nearby and when they weren't. So I watched you one day. I could see you concentrating hard."

"You never said anything."

"We both know how things were back then. It was safest to stay quiet and protect you when you did... your thing."

She scoffed, her heart quivering because he had shielded her as much Alarn had.

"If you move forward with all of this, what does that mean for you?" he asked, knocking his knee against hers. "You are the only one that I know who can talk to all of them."

"I'd have to finally accept that part of me. Accept the abilities I've let waste away. And it would mean making deals. I've been trying to think of how we can help each other and what would benefit them as much as us." Her smile faded and she sighed. "Honestly, it would be a welcome distraction."

"Will you need Duncar and I to step back in to help with our community?"

"I don't know. I'm sure there will be travel required to the other communities when it's time to find out what other children have Talents. We'll have to figure it out as we go along. Hopefully the nymphs will be comfortable enough to meet here and keep me from running everywhere."

Silence settled, then Pirco exhaled hard. "I don't want you to think I betrayed your trust but..."

"I know you confide in them, Pirco, I'm not naïve."

"You're right, I told Dini and Darner about you ending your companionship with Gregor. I had to talk to someone about it. They are heartbroken to hear that, but they brought up something I hadn't thought of and I agreed with their suggestion." He grabbed her hands, confusing her, and looked her straight in the eye. "Join our companionship. We know you'd never share our bed or take any pledges or make any vows or anything like that... but you could move to the farm."

"Pirco, you need all the room you have for all those babies you three are planning."

"After her experience with this one, Dini is rethinking how many she will tolerate carrying."

That made Sreana chuckle.

"You could take one of the rooms. Or there's the small cabin near the barn.

We could update the inside. You'd have your own space. But you would be part of a family. Our family. Be a mother to our children. You don't have to be alone."

"I love all three of you for your offer."

His shoulders slumped. "But?"

"A normal life isn't meant for someone like me. I know you disagree, so do Dini and Darner, and that makes me love you three even more. But this," and she gestured to the lea, "is my home. It is where our people know where to find me. And as a leader, who must be a conduit between our township and the others, it is beneficial that I stay close to the nymphs." She hugged him around his shoulders. "Thank you for the invitation. It truly is an honor because I know what a loving home you three have built. And your babies are my responsibility no matter what they call me or where I live."

He hugged her back, squeezing her tightly. They held each other for a few breaths, then let each other go. They sat shoulder to shoulder, smiling with the affection they felt for each other and his loves.

Quick footfalls made them look up. Duncar approached, carrying a rolled parchment.

"What's wrong?" Sreana demanded, straightening.

"Rana asked me to give this to you."

Pirco grabbed it and read through it quickly. "The Grenan King is asking for a meeting to discuss revisions to the Grenan and Sedoran agreement."

She felt the color drain from her face. She knew eventually this would happen, but the reality of things changing more stole her voice for a moment. Shaking herself, she cleared her throat. "Did all the communities receive the same request?"

"Rana said every leader got one," Duncar confirmed.

"I'll reach out and find out where and when the leaders want to meet," Pirco offered, handing her the parchment before heading over to Jya's tree.

"Sreana? Is there something we should know?" Duncar asked.

"Other than our people calling the Grenans occupiers again?"

Duncar lowered his head, exhaling hard.

"I've heard the same things you have. The warrant, even illegal, caused a lot of damage. I've done what I can…"

"Except explain your absence at the castle," Duncar snapped.

Sreana scoffed. "I'm sure Rana has kept you informed."

"He told me how you just went missing after a few visits."

Pirco returned to the firepit, making Sreana glance up at him. "Dener's community will host in three nights."

Sreana nodded. "Duncar, since you've been my second for all things Grenan, I hope you will continue standing by my side?"

"I will go as your second."

"And I will stay here in your stead," Pirco said.

"Thank you. Until then, I have parents to persuade." With that, she stood and walked back to her hovel.

~   ~   ~

Rana walked onto the balcony with a parchment in hand. The broken seal told Gregor that the armyman had read it first, to ensure the importance of the message, but his expression caused concern. After saluting the general who was taking lunch with the King, he handed the message to Gregor.

"The community leaders have agreed to the meeting," Rana reported. "They have invited you or your favored agent to speak with them."

Kasar grumbled a curse. "I do not feel comfortable sending you out with such rumored animosity. I shall go as your agent."

"No offense, Kasar," Gregor replied, grimacing. "But your gruff attitude will only cause hackles to rise."

"I will go," Rana volunteered. "The people know me. The leaders know me. And I believe I am still trusted."

"Agreed, thank you. Sit. Let us discuss the message I wish for you to convey."

~   ~   ~

In their community, there were seven children that appeared to have some Talent, based on their interactions with Jya. Sreana spoke with each child's parent or guardian, requesting that they allow her to investigate the child's abilities. Each gave their consent and she set up what she called a playdate for the children and the nymphs the day before the meeting with the Grenans.

Sreana gathered the children around the unlit firepit. "Thank you for coming to play today," Sreana said to the children, who all stared up at her with wide eyes. "Before we play, I have to tell you a story. A story of our Kingdom and all those who live within its borders."

She leaned forward, resting her hands on her knees, trying to convey all the details her father had told her, Pirco, Mirna, and Duncar when they were children.

"When the gods created the world, they made a very important decision. They chose variety over everything being the same. So, they created different animals, different plants, and even different types of water. When it came to us, they didn't want just the same hair, same skin, so they made us have different colors. But they knew something was missing. It was our god Finleyn that realized that there was a connection missing between us and the life around us. That's why he created the nymphs and the Talented."

245

She hesitated for a moment, then after a deep breath, she admitted, "But not everyone understands the Talented." Careful to keep her tone even, she warned them, "It isn't hate, just ignorance, jealousy, and misunderstanding. It is your job, as someone with Talents, to be the ambassadors we and the nymphs need. Do you understand?"

All of the children nodded, their serious faces hurting her heart because of her warnings, but she felt pride that they appeared to understand what she meant. Before she introduced the children to the other nymphs, she started with Jya since they already knew her. She had them follow her to the nymph's tree, where Jya greeted them. Some of the children frowned, looking around confused.

"It's fine," Sreana reassured, with a gentle smile. "You won't understand every one of them. We just need to find out who you can understand."

A few told her that even though they didn't understand what she said, they felt drawn to her and described her voice like the rustle of leaves. Even though not everyone understood her, Sabira and another little girl started chatting with her immediately. However, the real test was to see if they could talk to other nymphs.

Sreana had the children return to the quiet firepit and made them wait. Then flames burst up and lit the lea, casting shadows throughout. Gasps and giggles escaped the little ones. Slowly, the flames began to take a human shape. The saehwa, Reshepha, rose to her feet and smiled down at the children who stared at her in awe. Reshepha started to speak softly and Sabira and a little boy responded. To those who could not, they described her voice like the crackles of a fire.

Sreana thanked Reshepha for her visit. The saehwa bowed to Sreana, then to the children, wished them farewell and extinguished her flame. Then the other nymphs appeared in their own way and different children responded to whom they understood. Sreana found herself fascinated by how the children described the voices of the nymphs. She heard words but she never thought about those who didn't understand their language. As Dymlan introduced herself, the eahzal's telepathic voice reminded the children of the waves as they lapped the beach. They surprised Sreana when they said that the halha, Oya, didn't make a sound. They described it as feeling the wind tickling their arms and faces. The children giggled with joy when they listened to the aetha, Setarah, because they said she sounded like chimes jingling in the wind.

To her surprise, each child had Talent.

As the parents and guardians returned, Sreana sat with each separately and explained what their child could do and who would be an appropriate mentor. She informed the parents that the mentor – which would be Pirco, Darner, or herself – would reach out and set up the child's training.

Habni waited until the others left, her face wrinkled in worry. Sreana waved her over, gesturing for her to sit at the firepit while Sabira played again with Jya. She sat close to Sreana, hips almost touching.

"Sabira is like me," Sreana admitted. "The other children are only able to talk to one kind, but she can understand all nymphs."

"I knew it," Habni responded, after a deep breath. "Explains so much."

"It is a big responsibility. And it won't be an easy life, for any of them, seeing that there is still fear from others."

"But you will teach her? Help her?"

"Of course, that's what I'm supposed to do! The other children will learn from those just like them and so will Sabira. But I will rotate her out to other mentors, just to make sure she is well-rounded in her knowledge, patience, and comfort."

Habni's face crumbled and Sreana pulled into her a hug. The young mother sniffled and sighed against Sreana's shoulder. "I wish her father was here."

"Sarehb was a good man. And much better at this than us." Sreana chuckled, making Habni lean back to look her in the eyes. "I will try not to teach her too many bad habits."

Habni laughed, the stress finally washing from her face. "Will I have to keep an eye on both of you?"

"Don't you already?"

Movement pulled them out of their conversation. They glanced over their shoulders to see Jya and Sabira dancing nearby. Their unpretentious joy was contagious.

"She is so much like him," Habni whispered.

"Lucky for us."

"I am sorry, my lady. I do feel like I count on you too much."

"What's the saying about raising children? It takes a township?"

Habni giggled, wiping the tears from her cheeks.

"Don't ever feel guilty about asking me for help or for advice. I didn't flippantly make my vow to her on the day she was born. I meant every word. We are all here to support each other, especially those of us who are missing the people who should be here to help but can't. But I do believe that Sarehb will guide us, because he wouldn't want to miss out on any of this." Sreana patted Habni's shoulder, sighing. "Maybe she is too much like him. Sabira is now up a tree."

Habni blinked then her eyes widened. She spun around to find her daughter sitting high up in Jya's tree. "Oh gods! Sabira, get down from there!" Habni sprung to her feet and ran over to the tree, trying to coax her adventurous daughter down.

Sreana watched with amusement, but covered her smile so as not to encourage the child.

CHAPTER 46

It was late. The moonslight seeped in under the heavy curtains, casting ghostly wisps along the floor and ceiling. The fire crackled intermittently as it started to fade from inattention.

Gregor laid on his back, snoring softly, then rolled onto his side as if uncomfortable. He fidgeted then mumbled, furrowing his eyebrows, until careful hands laid a pillow in front of him. The slight brush of the pillowcase made him reach out and he hugged it as if it were a person. With something in his arms, he settled back down into a deep sleep.

Sreana sat down on the floor next to the bed and watched him for a few moments. She frowned as a tear rolled down her cheek and wiped it away with a shaky hand. It was difficult to see him restless, only to be comforted by holding something. She too had a hard time sleeping, finding herself tossing and turning in her bed, wishing for the comfort of his embrace. That ache in her chest that never seemed to let up, clenched suddenly like a vice. Being so close to him, but not being able to touch him, it rattled her harder than she expected.

She didn't know why she talked herself into sneaking in. She foolishly believed that seeing him would stoke her anger, but it only compounded her heartache. As did knowing that his request to meet with the Sedoran leaders meant he was taking steps to announce his departure soon. Even though it had been her suggestion, one made out of hurt and anger, the thought of never seeing him again became a razor-sharp stabbing in her chest.

She caught herself reaching to caress his cheek and snatched her hand back. What would he do if he saw her? He was still King and she was again just a trespasser. She remembered the first time they met, the King and the criminal, their verbal altercation and her sword at his throat. She never thought such a situation would have led them down the road to love and companionship, and ultimately, heartbreak. With a deep inhalation, she resigned herself to honoring her decisions. They were done and she shouldn't be there.

She raised up onto her feet, then quietly made her way to the servant's door. She popped it open and cringed at the noise, but he didn't stir. She slipped through then started to close it when the hinge creaked slightly. Rolling her eyes, she didn't understand why it had to start making noise now. Staring through the small slit, she held her breath and the door.

Still holding the pillow, Gregor rolled onto his back again. He looked at it groggily, then laid it to the side. He rubbed his face, took a deep breath, then raised up on his arm. He looked around, as if expecting to see someone, but when he realized he was alone, he frowned and laid back down.

She waited a few breaths, letting go of the door and not daring to close it all of the way. She made her way down the steps and escaped from the castle...

CHAPTER 47

Duncar stood as Sreana's second as Rana approached the head of the table. Rana's eyes avoided his lover's, making contact only with the leaders whose decision on their future could make or break them. The different expressions imparted that he had very few allies in the room at the moment. However, he knew if his King had enough faith in him to be his representative, then he believed he could sway these men and women. He inhaled deeply, to settle his nerves, before speaking.

"On behalf of King Gregor and all Grenan citizens who reside within your borders, thank you for giving us audience. We see things have changed. And we are aware of what we are being called." He glanced around the table again, seeing some shift in their seats while others kept their faces blank. "The partnership between Grenan and Sedora has been reduced again to occupation. Our intention was never to return to that. If we are considered as anything other than collaborators, then we believe it is time for a decision. Please know that we will not make this decision ourselves. It must be made by you, the leaders of Sedora's communities." Another test of who would meet his eyes showed that most of the leaders couldn't. "However, if our help is still needed, we are willing and able to stay and be the partners that Sedora needs and wants. We will honor our agreement to help Sedora rise from the ashes of the Carmanic invasion until Sedora decides we are no longer useful."

"Thank you, Lieutenant Rana," Dener responded, "for bringing us the voice of the Grenan people who reside in our borders. You are correct, there has been some animosity toward the Grenans since the Castle Guard overstepped their boundaries and hunted our friend and fellow leader."

All eyes settled on Sreana for a moment, but she kept her face emotionless.

"May I state again that the King and the armymen stationed at the castle had no idea what the Castle Guard and ministers had planned?" Rana asked when Sreana didn't respond. "We also received an update from Queen Vehla before I arrived. The captain was found guilty of the charges against him and he will be executed by the end of the week. The ministers who also conspired to harm our lady will be tried soon and we expect the same conclusion."

"But you cannot guarantee that this won't happen again?" Terga demanded.

Rana hung his head for a moment, then raised those bright amber eyes to meet Terga's. "We cannot control the minds of all who call themselves Grenan. Just as you cannot control the minds of your citizens. However, we can hold them accountable for their actions." Rana held Terga's gaze until the leader looked away.

"Rathfeather, do you have anything to add?" Sella inquired.

Sreana glanced around the table, her gaze landing on Rana. "No, I do not, thank you. I came only as a witness and ask that I be permitted to recuse myself from any decision-making."

Each leader stiffened in surprise, as they had expected her whole-hearted backing, or in some opinions her fervent criticism, of the Grenan King. As they looked at each other, confusion set in, until Dener cleared his throat.

"We honor Sreana's decision. We again thank you, Lieutenant Rana, for speaking in the stead of your King. Do you have anything else to add?"

"We wish to note our concerns about the prior incidents that have endangered Sedora, the ships that threatened your ports and the poisoning of your fields. We fear that these acts are just the beginning of aggression towards the Sedoran people. We do not want to leave our allies without ensuring such actions do not occur again."

Dener nodded. "I believe you have somewhere you can await our decision?"

"I do, yes."

"Good. We will deliberate now in private. We will send a messenger to you when a decision has been reached."

"Thank you." Rana bowed his head in respect, then headed out the door. He dared a glance at Duncar, who was watching him, but exited without a word.

~ ~ ~

Rana lost track of time, but he knew it was the longest wait of his life. It didn't even compare to the waiting he had to endure during campaigns, in raining or snowing conditions, while the enemy made their move.

He couldn't read any of the leaders, or their seconds, while in that room. He hated not knowing. He had never spent this much time in one place, other than when he was growing up. To think he could be banished from Sedora, which truly was bad enough because he had fallen in love with the Kingdom, but knowing that Duncar wouldn't leave with him because his life and family were here... He chewed on his thumbnail, his nerves on end. He hated having such a personal investment in the situation.

Sighing, he dropped his hand and sat back. He stared at the fire Duncar had started before they headed to the neighboring community. Then he glanced around Duncar's home, trying to memorize the little things. The books sitting on the shelves next to the fireplace. The small quilt that laid in the wooden chair next to it, where he had found Duncar reading one night. And on the other side of the fireplace, the small kitchen where his lover would make their meals. He felt tears threaten, which surprised him. He cared about Duncar and the idea of missing those little moments became overwhelming.

He was left to wait.

~   ~   ~

It was late at night, even the moons had already left the night sky. Rana rushed into the King's chambers, not even bothering to knock. He had something in his hand and he looked flushed, as if he had run all the way from the township to the balcony. "Your Majesty, they've made a decision."

Gregor saw the sealed parchment in his lieutenant's hand, his stomach dropping. He hadn't expected an answer so quickly. "Tell me what happened first."

Rana tried to catch his breath. "I spoke on your behalf, expressing the importance of all the facts you asked that I convey. Our lady did not speak and recused herself from the process, citing her relationship with you. Apparently, she had not said anything about ending her companionship with you because her silence confused many. But they respected it." Rana handed over the parchment. "I don't know their decision. They dismissed me while they debated. I was told that the vote was secret, and that only one community leader, Dener, tabulated the votes and wrote the decision down."

Gregor opened the parchment, reading with no hint until a deep sigh and raised eyebrows. "Grenan has been asked to stay."

Forgetting himself, Rana plopped down hard into the chair nearby and covered his face with his hands, making a sound of deep relief.

"They agree that the unknown ships just outside the bay and the attacks on their crops increased their concerns about security. They too fear the aggression from the unknown assailants will escalate if we withdraw back to Grenan. They want their borders to be secure and state that they can only do so with our help. Our continued collaboration is entreated."

"We can stay," Rana whispered.

Gregor stared at him for a moment. "You can stay."

The lieutenant lifted his head, frowning.

"I still plan on returning to Grenan."

"Your Majesty…"

"It is time. But I know that I leave Sedora in good hands. Now go, get some rest. You have had a long day."

Rana raised wearily to his feet, then bowed his head, and left the King's chambers.

CHAPTER 48

Pirco ran into the lea, beaming and crying and panting. "She's here!"

Sreana and Duncar glanced at each other, confused. Then her eyes widened. "The baby? The baby's here?"

Pirco nodded, breathless and speechless. His friends rushed over to him, hugging and laughing with sheer joy.

"A girl?" she asked. "You have a little girl? Have you named her?"

"Dini wants to name her Parni, a name honoring her parents."

"Parni, that is an amazing name."

"Come, you have to meet her."

They rushed back to the farm, excited to meet the new member of their family. Darner sat next to Dini on the bed, as she held a little blanket wrapped bundle. Both had big smiles and tear streaks down their cheeks. They glanced up as Sreana and Duncar entered, waving for them to come closer. They peeked into the blanket to see a sleeping infant, who had a streak of dark hair along the middle of her scalp. Parni was perfection, all toes and fingers accounted for, her nose and lips flawless. As they chatted about the birthing, Sreana checked Pirco's head for bald spots, which made everyone laugh.

"Rana!" Duncar exclaimed suddenly. "He's coming to visit..."

Pirco chuckled. "Go meet him, bring him here."

Duncar apologized then darted out the door. Sreana shook her head as Pirco and Darner excused themselves to prepare for their guests. Once alone, Sreana knelt by the bed, smiling at Dini and at the sleeping baby. Then she reached out and gently touched the child's forehead with her fingertips.

"Parni, my sword and my life are yours. In the dark and in the light, I will always be there."

Dini gasped, reaching for Sreana's hand. "She has fathers for that."

"She has fathers to protect her from everyday things, like snakes and boys," Sreana responded. "I will slay the scariest of monsters for her."

Dini sniffled, squeezing her hand tightly. "You honor us with your devotion to our child."

"She is my family, too, Dini."

Sreana stood once she heard the men greet Rana and Duncar, moving to the side, smiling like a proud aunt.

~   ~   ~

Later that evening, in her hovel, Sreana whispered a prayer to Sera, thanking the god of hearth and family for Dini's healthy baby. She would gather a gift in the morning before tending to the duties of the day.

~   ~   ~

Days blurred together. Sreana sat on the log, feeling drained. She lazily poked the fire with a stick, her eyes unfocused. It was late in the evening and she didn't even have the energy to hone her sword, something she usually did to relax. Pirco and Darner bounced around like the happy fathers they were, helping Dini with feedings and diapers. They also assisted Sreana with the Talented children when they could, but she spent more time teaching than she had expected. Sreana tried not to complain, knowing that the two men wanted to spend as much time with their daughter and it had helped keep her mind off of other things.

Even with the joy of Parni's birth, exhaustion consumed her, but she assumed it was from stress. In addition, she still found herself unable to sleep at night. Eating also seemed to be a hardship, especially with the stomach acid that kept rearing up after each meal. Her body's inability to settle back into a routine frustrated her.

Jya materialized, eyebrows furrowed. The jahla sat next to her, with an expression on her face like she needed to say something but didn't know how. Sreana frowned, knowing it had to do with how horrible she looked.

"Do not worry, I am just tired."

Jya shook her head, then ran her hand along Sreana's abdomen. As the jahla cradled her stomach, Sreana felt the color drain from her face.

"No, I can't be," Sreana whispered. "It's not possible."

"I feel the life, my friend," Jya admitted. "It grows stronger every day."

Jya smiled, a mixture of sadness and fondness, as she wrapped her arms around Sreana's shoulders as the woman's face crumbled. The jahla rocked her as Sreana began to sob.

CHAPTER 49

Early in the morning, she dressed for cool weather, saddled her horse, then rode out of town along with a few others. The ride itself was long, but as they came up over a hill, the ocean greeted them with its cool, salty air and glistening blue tides. They tied their horses to a hitch upwind of the docks, where fresh water and hay would keep the animals happy. Sreana made her way down onto the creaking wood of the pier, where she met a weather-worn man layered for the cold, wet environment.

"Good morning, Trehan," she greeted her childhood friend. She hugged him until he clapped her heartily on the back. "Reporting as requested."

"Are you sure?"

"Why wouldn't I be here?"

"Sreana," he said softly, leaning back enough to look her in the eye. "We would understand if you sat this one out."

"I lead by example, Trehan."

"You've been through a lot. And you look like you haven't slept in weeks."

"I can't just sit my hovel, not doing anything. I need the sea. Let me get on the water and remind myself who I am."

She slipped out of his arms and headed down the pier. He sighed hard, then followed her up to the seiner. The crew loaded crates and other containers, stacking them on the deck. They headed out before the sun even crested the horizon. As the boat rode the waves, Sreana stood at the bow. She breathed in deep, letting the salty air fill her lungs and warm her heart.

Trehan found his nets by the fuchsia marking on the buoys, then started shouting orders. Sreana moved to one section of the boat, and with the command, leaned over the edge and started grabbing the rope. Several people joined her, pulling the nets onto the deck, fish flopping and splashing them. They dragged their catch to the hatch in the middle and let the fish slide out and down into the hold. With one done, two men tossed the emptied net into a container and the crew moved on to the next.

Trehan's nets were cleared quickly. Cheers and proud exhalations filled the air as men and women leaned against the edges, the sun finally beaming down on them. Trehan thanked the volunteers for their hard work before he and his crew secured the hold.

Suddenly, a large splash bounced out of the water and hit her. She peeked over the edge and an eahzal stared up through the glass of water. Sreana leaned over, smiling, and the eahzal grasped the edge of the seiner and pulled herself up. They both sat on the edge, face to face, and the eahzal blinked her large black eyes.

"Thank you and your people for the help."

The water nymph smiled with pride, then it turned into curiosity. Furrowing her eyebrows, she glanced down and reached for Sreana's stomach. Sreana opened her jacket and held the cold hand against her shirt. The smile widened, this time with joy. The eahzal freed her hand, then caressed the other woman's face in congratulations before bowing her head. The nymph slipped back into the water, disappearing into the deep. Sreana stood, looking over at Trehan who had watched the scene but wisely said nothing. Seeing that he would keep her secret, she gave him the signal to head back to the pier.

As they docked, Sreana helped secure the seiner before jumping onto the pier. She had completed her portion of the job, walking away as the next group arrived. Different shifts of helpers from each community participated throughout the day to make sure no one got overworked. Those who didn't pull nets would step in to assist in moving the fish from boat to processing areas. Then another group would process. She left Trehan and his men to manage the next steps.

She stood at the top of the pier, gazing over the buildings that lined it. Though they were still in their original positions, they all showed signs of damage from the invasion. The burnt shack at the head was her Momma's business. She had managed the pier, deciding who could dock where and for how long. Sreana remembered how her Momma would kiss her Papa in that doorway every morning. Every day, she would pray to Dranar for the sea to have mercy on the boats so he would come home to her.

The building a little further down was where her Papa and Uncle would manage their fishing business. There, they would prepare, clean and store their catches. They provided a place for other fishermen to do the same and bundle their catches as well to keep the supplies and food moving smoothly.

Then she chuckled as her eyes made their way to the other end, where the beach came up the small hill. Sreana would play and swim with the eahzals there. Her Papa would yell at her every time, but the next day? She would be out swimming again.

"My lady!" someone called out.

Startled out of her memories, she looked toward the voice, seeing three men standing on the shore with a small boat beached halfway. She furrowed her eyebrows in worry, then one man waved her down. As much as she wanted to leave, Sreana knew she had to deal with the issue at hand.

By the time she arrived, they had gotten the boat on the shore. Frowning, she walked around it and evaluated the damage. It looked like a small part of the plank running along the side, under the water mark, had ripped off and caused damage to its surroundings. It wasn't original, seeing that the other parts were one full piece of wood.

"Looks like a mend that failed," she said, running fingers along the tattered side.

"What am I to do, my lady?" the fisherman asked, voice quivering. "All I have is this boat."

Sreana looked over at the other fisherman. "Unless you have other thoughts, I can only think of two. Mend the old boat again or commission a new one?"

"That would be our options for Videran, my lady," the oldest man responded.

She returned her attention to the heartbroken fisherman, Videran. "I assure you, either way, you will get back on the water. We will move quickly however you decide. If you want to go with a new build, I will work with the jahlas to find the best wood. Is that amenable?"

"Oh yes, my lady, yes," Videran replied, bowing his head repeatedly. "I promise to get back to you in a couple of days? I must speak with my children."

She nodded, and with that, she left the group.

Then she started down a road that didn't lead back to her hovel, walking about a mile away from the bay.

~   ~   ~

Gutted and burned buildings lined the eroded, uneven dirt road. A few buildings had collapsed roofs, others had holes with singe marks dotting the sides. A modest bathtub precariously hung out of a three-story window. And from behind every building, nature had reached out and surrounded each with vines, limbs, and grasses. Homes, businesses, whatever still stood had all been taken back by nature. Places like her old township, that had seen so much pain and violence, they had become hallowed. Sedorans had decided to let nature take them back in hopes the spirits would rest. Thankfully, because they had evacuated everyone quickly enough, her current township had never seen such slaughter.

But all that was left of her childhood township stretched out before her.

Duncar had lived down the road, Pirco just past his place. Mirna had lived across the way and Trehan had lived at the other end. She laid her hand on one wall of a two-story home at the center of town that had been ravaged by fire and the outside was nothing but a tortured skeleton. She noticed a bouquet at the doorway, withered and gray. Someone must have come through a while ago, laying flowers in remembrance.

Sreana stared at the shell of her family home, then carefully entered through the front door's burnt frame. Standing inside the entryway, she trembled. After closing her eyes for a few breaths, she cautiously moved along the front room and into a small bedroom that had been hers.

Sreana caught sight of herself in the broken looking glass. The spiderweb cracks made her image multiply and fragment, giving her a deconstructed look. In one shard she could see herself in profile. Her hand ran along her belly as it hid under her tunic and she felt tears threaten.

She wished whole-heartedly that her mother was still alive. She would have given anything to speak to her about this new development, just like she had the first time. Even feeling her arms around Sreana's shoulders would have been a great gift.

She lost herself in a fantasy as her mind reconstructed her home. She dreamed about her parents babysitting while Sreana dealt with the family's fishing lines. She imagined Alarn teaching her little girl how to hold a sword properly. She smiled at the thought of her child swimming with eahzals and dancing with jahlas, even if her father would grumble about it under his breath like he did when Sreana had been caught doing just that. Even the image of her daughter pulling lines with her, being a daughter of the craft just like Sreana, warmed her.

The fantasy dissolved without warning. Glancing at the crumbling walls, it hit her that she had none of those memories to make. It would be Sreana, alone, navigating parenthood. She frowned, lifting her shirt to see in the warped reflections the small bulge forming. It almost strained against her scar, as if willing the skin to smooth out. She wondered what she had to offer this child now growing inside her. She had her hovel, her lea... but was that a good enough place to raise a baby? And without a father...?

She thought of poor Jya, having told Sreana the one thing she had prayed to hear again and something she had hoped to hear with Gregor by her side. Another dream dashed. Jya had held her lovingly, comforting her like she had comforted the jahla throughout all the past hardships, while Sreana broke down completely.

Sreana couldn't hold it in anymore. She again let her sorrow flow out of her in sobs. When it felt like she had expelled all of it, she fought to catch her breath.

Thankfully, Jya agreed with Sreana's hesitation in announcing the pregnancy. Sreana had held off the first time and it turned out to be the best decision she had ever made. She knew she would have to tell Duncar soon, however, because this pregnancy needed to be monitored by a healer. And he was the only one she trusted.

She knew then that she wouldn't do this alone. She would have Duncar, Pirco and his family, as well as an entire township happy to help her raise her child. Not to mention eager nymphs too. She wiped her wet face with her shirt sleeves, taking a deep breath.

Now, with everything having changed and not knowing what the future truly held, she feared Gregor finding out. She had started hearing rumors that he was packing up his chambers, preparing to leave. She didn't want him to stay because of her and the baby. She also didn't want to tell him because of how he felt about her kind. Their child would most likely have the same Talents. She wouldn't put her daughter through that. She would never let the child know that her father could never accept her.

She grimaced. She kept saying "her." She had no way of knowing. But Jya kept calling the baby "her" too and the jahla seemed quite sure of the gender.

The morning started to wear on her. Between the morning sickness and the hard work, not to mention her rollercoaster of emotions, she needed to rest. Returning to sleep in her hovel sounded like the best medicine for her woes.

She closed her eyes for a few moments, sending loving thoughts to the ghosts of her childhood township. She asked for guidance, support, even protection for the life inside her. Then she carefully stepped out the door, wishing her family and friends peace. But before leaving the area, she leaned over and touched the bouquet gently and it sprung back into a fresh bundle of flowers and herbs. By the warmth emanating in her chest, she knew the other bouquets left throughout the township had also burst back into full color. Content with the gesture, she walked down the road...

CHAPTER 50

Sreana worked on her next lesson, a move that could disarm their opponent faster than traditional moves. She stepped one way, while moving her staff to her side then swiftly connected it to the tree in her fake opponent's more tender parts: knee, hip, stomach, chin. Knocking the wind out of a person would definitely cause them to drop their weapons. She leaned against her staff, smiling with pride. Everyone would master the moves quickly.

Then speeding footfalls caught her attention. She turned, seeing Duncar and Pirco flushed from running. They must have sprinted from the tavern, or even the farm, she couldn't tell.

"Sella's community was attacked," Pirco managed to say. "They just sent a rider asking for help."

"What?" she demanded, confused. "A rider?"

"He says Carmanic forces overtook the Grenan army. They're now inside our borders."

Sreana almost forgot how to breathe. "Casualties?"

"A handful," Duncar confirmed, "some injuries too."

"Go, help with the injuries. We'll spread the word and get a message to Gregor."

Duncar nodded and started to leave when, from the edge of Sreana's lea, a bloodcurdling wail tore through the air. Sreana dropped her staff and ran to the trees, where she found Jya collapsed on the ground, screaming. Sreana reached for her and Jya flung herself into her arms, crying hysterically. She struggled against Sreana, as if trying to crawl into the other woman's skin. Sreana held her firmly, trying to understand what happened. And then it hit her, such grief and pain meant only one thing.

"Oh gods, they killed their jahla."

~ ~ ~

Ranthel strode onto the King's balcony, glancing quickly into the bedchambers and saw a line of trunks being filled by gloomy looking women. He hated seeing His Majesty packing up but he understood from Rana that there was a good reason. When the King looked up at him, he knew the look on his face showed that he brought bad news.

"Your Majesty, Jamos and his senior ministers have escaped. Queen Vehla believes they are heading here, to exact revenge on you and to crush the Sedorans."

His anger rising, Gregor leapt to his feet. The thought of those who had wronged the Sedorans from the beginning now returning to harm them again boiled his blood. He wanted to run out the door and search for Sreana but stopped himself.

"Thank you, Ranthel. We'll need to tell the Sedorans."

"Yes, Your Majesty."

Suddenly, multiple, heartbreaking shrieks broke the stillness in the forest around them.

~   ~   ~

Sreana sat on the ground, leaning against one of the logs, with the catatonic jahla in her lap. The nymph had stopped her screams hours before, but her silence was just as unnerving. Helpless, Sreana could only ensure that her feet stayed covered in dirt while Jya laid in her arms, keeping her connected to the soil that helped her thrive, while wrapping her in a blanket to keep the cold night from affecting her.

Duncar had rushed to Sella's community with a few others to help with the wounded while Sreana strengthened their own security. Pirco followed afterwards to find out what had happened so he could report back to Sreana. Garol and a few other riders were disbursed to other townships to warn them of possible attack.

Her stomach twisted at the thought of someone betraying them. They had tried to keep the jahlas as secret as possible, but anyone who watched long enough could have figured it out. Unless they killed the jahla on sight, not knowing anything more than something inhuman had to die. All she could do was wait for word from Sella's township to know what really happened. That burned her as her impatience festered.

Footfalls brought her out of her thoughts. Pirco approached, the color still missing from his face. He kneeled beside her, so he could look into Jya's blank face and caress her cheek. When she didn't react, his frown deepened.

"Duncar arrived at the fork at the same time as Gregor's men," he reported. "Most went to the border while a handful followed Duncar. They are working on the wounded and counting the dead. It sounds like there are only a few, since they were able to fight back quickly and efficiently."

"Small miracles. But one death is too many." She felt Jya stir against her, as if coming back to life. "Jya? Oh, my friend, you should return to your tree."

Jya sobbed. "But I will not hear Jena's voice."

"I know, but you will hear your other sisters. You need to hear them, grieve with them."

Jya stared at her, fresh tears rolling down her face. Then she nodded, absently, and glanced around as if trying to remember how to move her body. Pirco immediately picked her up, carrying her back to her tree. Sreana watched, helplessly, the memory of the jahla's painful screams still making her ears ring. Once he got her settled, Pirco returned to Sreana, sitting hard on the ground next to her. She leaned over and rested her head on his shoulder, which made him copy her.

"We haven't lost a jahla since the first days of the invasion," Sreana whispered. "I forgot how much it hurts."

"Hurt doesn't even describe it."

"Who was Jena's connection?"

"Sella's daughter, I think. They were lovers as well."

"They will need to keep an eye on her. We know the types of thoughts that cross our minds when we lose someone so close." She sighed, heartbroken. "I want to grieve, but I just keep thinking about strategy."

"What do you mean?"

"They effectively took out our communication to another community. Somehow, they figured out the jahlas and what they did for us. We've been exposed."

"I am even less reassured now."

"We can't count on the jahlas for now, not while they grieve. We will have to utilize other resources to stay up to date."

"Horse messengers take too long."

"I know. We'll need to figure out alternatives."

Pirco chewed on his lip for a moment, then asked, "Did you mean it? That you have accepted your Talents?"

She sat up and stared at him. "Of course I meant it."

"Then maybe it's time that you lead everyone, not just us. I saw the jahlas come for Jena's body. They're not only afraid and heartbroken, they are angry."

"We promised them we would never weaponize them."

"We did. But that doesn't mean that they don't want to fight. A jahla has been killed. We need to include them and the other nymphs in any decisions." Pirco shrugged. "We have protected them for so long, the enemy could assume that they are lambs. What will stop a slaughter?"

Sreana frowned, deep in thought. Then from behind them, the firepit burst to life. Sreana and Pirco jumped to their feet in surprise. Before their eyes, the fire changed from chaotic flames to a human shape.

"Reshepha?"

The saehwa bowed in respect then stood tall. "Good evening, our friend. We wish our visit were for better reasons."

"Me too. Are you and your sisters safe?"

Pirco glanced between Sreana and the saehwa, eyes wide, but wisely did not interrupt.

"We are. We are all helping our jahla sisters. We came to ask if you needed us to step in? Be your eyes and ears?"

"We would be honored," Sreana answered. "But not many can speak with you."

"We need not speak. We will watch and listen and tell you anything you need to know. We can travel easily through the fires you light."

Sreana bowed her head. "I would be beyond grateful."

"Consider it done. All of us, every nymph, will help any way we can." Then Reshepha dimmed her flames and disappeared in a flash of light.

"What was that all about?" Pirco asked.

"The other nymphs offered their help."

Pirco rubbed his face, the shock wearing on him. "What now?"

"You go home and get some rest," Sreana responded, then lifted her hand to stop his argument. "I need you tomorrow, not tonight. Go. Kiss Parni and hug Darner and Dini for me."

Pirco, too exhausted to complain, nodded and started home.

~   ~   ~

She didn't know how much time had passed when another pair of riders arrived. But she never expected Gregor. He dismounted but kept his distance, while Rana turned his horse back to the road to find Duncar. Alone, the dying fire flickered shadow and light along their faces as they stared at each other, speechless.

"Why are you here?" she finally demanded, trying to keep her tone calm.

"I wanted to make sure that…" and he stammered, before taking a deep breath. "Grenan wanted to share its condolences over the loss of your friend."

She swallowed, hard against the knot in her throat. "Thank you, Your Majesty."

"And I am sorry to bring you more bad news. Those we sent back to face the consequences of their actions have escaped and are reportedly heading this way."

"So, we not only have Carmanic murderers in our borders, but Grenan traitors?" she inquired, shaking her head. "The day has gotten worse. When did you find out?"

"Just tonight. Before we could send you the message, we heard the death knells from the forest."

She furrowed her eyebrows. "You heard it?"

"Just the sound of hundreds of hearts breaking."

She glanced away, toward the trees, her mind still in turmoil over the events of the day but now the news of Castle Guard and ministers... She shook herself. "Um, what about your armymen?"

"The regiment that was attacked has been switched out and moved to the castle grounds for medical attention. Every single man was injured and two died."

"I am sorry for your loss as well."

"Kasar and his men are scouring the countryside for the invaders. They have been ordered to show no mercy."

"I have my friends keeping a lookout as well. But it doesn't feel like before where they landed like locusts. Their intent feels... focused, taking out not just a township but also their jahla. Does that mean they are coming for me? For my friends? Or for you?"

"Whoever they're targeting, we should prepare for all possibilities."

"Agreed."

They stood in awkward silence.

"You should go back to the castle, it's not safe for us both to be in the same place at the same time."

"Once Rana returns, we will head out."

He watched as she wrapped her arms around her torso. He wanted so badly to hold her, to reassure her, but he didn't know if she could tolerate his touch. It had been months since they had seen one another, been near each other. But when he saw her grief shake her again, he had to offer. Hopeful but helpless, he reached out a hand. Tears welled up in her eyes and grasped it, letting him pull her into a hug.

"I am so sorry for your loss," he whispered against her hair.

She sighed hard against his shoulder. She felt the safety and reassurance in his embrace, even if it was just a lie. However, she had to recognize that the man she loved came to her side at a moment's notice. Not the King, the man. He wanted to check on her, and as badly as things had ended, she couldn't doubt that he still loved her to a certain extent.

A loud crackle from the firepit made her jump, then she stiffened and stepped back. Gregor let her go without hesitation, having realized the reassurance she felt in his arms had expired.

She met his eyes and saw all of his emotions reflected there. The adoration and sadness tore at her heart. She wanted to tell him. How their doubts about the damage their old wounds had caused were unfounded. How he was going to be a father. Everything. But as the tears ran down her cheeks again, she knew it would be a mistake. He was still a King and she was... she was the villain he had taken into his bed. She would never be anything more than that.

It was her job to protect her Kingdom, for her people and her child. The only thing they had left between them was working together to defend Sedora. Murderers and invaders were in their borders again. That was the only thing that mattered. And she could hide her heartache behind her grief.

"We will follow your lead on this, Sreana," he stated, after clearing his throat. "Grenan will support you and your people in every way, and we will follow your orders. This is your Kingdom and you must make the decisions you feel are right for your people. All of your people."

She wiped her face with a sleeve and tried to catch her breath. "Thank you. We have to negotiate this new situation carefully, but until we have more information, we are all blind."

"Then let's concentrate on seeing better?"

"That is my plan."

They heard roof beats, announcing Rana's return. Solemnly, Gregor mounted his steed, leaving her alone in her lea.

CHAPTER 51

After Gregor left with Rana, Sreana finally got some sleep once Pirco relieved her that morning. When she stirred a few hours later, she stayed in her lea waiting for word from the nymphs while Pirco and Duncar organized their community for possible threats. Reshepha appeared just as they returned, stopping both men mid-step. They stared in awe, still not used to seeing the nymph so close, while Sreana conversed with her.

"They set up camp and have not moved since entering Sedora," Reshepha reported. "But our halha sisters listened to them talk while they pretended to be a pleasant breeze. The invaders will head toward the castle and take out the Grenans before moving onto us."

"Strategically, that makes sense," Sreana replied. "They think we are still heavily dependent on our Grenan allies for protection."

"They know that you and the King are no longer aligned. The stories of your separation make them believe we will not protect them and that it will be easy to kill them."

Sreana sighed, thinking. "Can you ask your leaders to meet with me? I would like to discuss something with them or whoever they wish to send as a proxy."

"I can extend the invitation for you."

"I appreciate that. And thank you and our halha friends for your diligence. You honor us."

"What affects you, affects all of us, our friend. We must protect each other now."

"Agreed."

"Another thing, our friend. They know you lead the Sedorans. They do not say your name, but it is obvious they talk about removing you from power quickly."

Sreana took a deep breath. "Good to know. Can you promise me something?"

"Of course."

"Keep that to yourselves?"

"We shall."

"Thank you. I will keep the embers hot until you return."

Reshepha bowed, then her flames flashed into the air and she disappeared. Duncar cleared his throat. "What news?"

"They're going after Gregor first," Sreana replied. "Did Mirna agree to take in our most vulnerable?"

"Without hesitation," Pirco answered. "And said to send any Grenans in need of sanctuary."

"Good. We need to start moving everyone now. I've also asked to meet with the nymph's leaders to discuss their participation. But for now, we need to update Gregor. We also need to ask him if there are any Grenan citizens we need to send to the Temple."

"I'll go," Duncar volunteered. "Gives me a chance to help with their wounded."

Sreana nodded. "Thank you."

~   ~   ~

Sreana had Pirco help her move the small table from her hovel to the firepit, where she laid out a map of Sedora, with certain roads marked out and one highlighted by thicker lines. She secured her lea with fighters, on the ground and in the trees, to protect the nymphs as they manifested. Each leader, who she had met while in hiding, stood, hovered, or floated around the table.

"Thank you for meeting with me, I appreciate your consideration," Sreana began, glancing around at the nymphs surrounding her. "We have again been invaded. The Carmanic army has returned, with the help of Grenan agitators who were banished from our borders. We know they are willing to destroy us, but this time, we are prepared for their savagery. We know our enemy, their strengths and weaknesses."

Her eyes landed on Jayna, leader of the jahlas, who looked drained of her natural beauty by her grief. "I know you are angry. Heartbroken. We all are. But that was a catalyst when the Carmanic Empire invaded our borders before and it must be one now. I have been told that you too tire of the death and destruction others visit upon us. So I say to you this time, don't hide. Fight with us."

Sreana ran her hands along the map, flattening it so the saehwa's glow could highlight it better. "I ask that the jahlas control the invaders' forward motion. Keep other paths hidden," and she ran her finger along the marked road on the map, "and only let them move along the roads we wish them to move down. We know they will head to the castle to attack the Grenans first. I ask that the night before the fight, that the saehwa set their camps on fire. They will have campfires, which you can use to send sparks onto their tents. I ask that the halha to help the saehwa, bringing the right amount of wind to stoke those flames. We want them annoyed and exhausted. Miserable."

She shifted her attention to the other side of the table. "And we know we see better, move better in the darkness than our invaders. We know the territory. We ask that the aetha find a way to hide the moonslight to help us. I believe the halhas can come up with some ideas to help with that. If they succeed in neutralizing our Grenan allies, keep them confounded and lost when they head toward our townships. That will allow us to thin their ranks until we're capable of taking them out. And since the jahlas will guide the invaders, we will leave the route to the bay open. We know there are ships waiting to come ashore. I ask the eahzals to take them out if they succeed in defeating us. However, if they fail and retreat, feel free to make a point."

She folded her hands in front of her, waiting for any questions. When no one spoke, she glanced at each nymph, seeing their agreement in her plan. "Let us make sure that everyone knows that Sedora is no longer weak. That it is no longer a victim. This time, we will prove to be a force to contend with."

CHAPTER 52

As the sun began to rise, those from her township who could fight gathered in her lea, all nerves on edge. The nymphs reported that the Carmanic invaders were finally packing up their camp and heading directly toward Gregor's castle. Their enemy did not seem aware that they were being led to their destination by the nymphs' influences, so they were reassured their manipulation had not been found out.

Sreana shared her final orders and, with a smirk, "Hold the line."

Everyone nodded and repeated the phrase, then began to move out. Everyone had a job to do and, for Sedora, they were willing to put their lives on the line once again. But there was just one more thing she had to do.

Sreana grabbed Duncar before he could walk away. "Duncar, I need you to promise me something."

He furrowed his eyebrows in confusion.

"Promise you will let me go."

His face crumbled and he choked, his emotions strangling his voice. But he had to understand. She cupped his face with her hands, making him grasp her wrists.

"If it is my time, if Death finally decides I should no longer vex her, let me go."

"I do not know if I can," he responded, a sob escaping him.

"Yes, you can. I want you to. I didn't give you this permission last time and it was so unfair to you. This time, no heroics from you, do you hear me? I do not expect you to waste such precious time in your life trying to save me, or worse, save me in a state where you have to give up everything to care for me. This is your life. You live it, with Rana and everyone else who survives." She ran a thumb along one of his cheeks, wiping away his tears. "Do not misunderstand me, I will not put my sword down and let it happen. I have too many plans to ruin." She grinned, something she hadn't done in weeks. "And as long as my body allows, I will take out the ankles of our enemies even as I lay dying on the ground. But I accept if Death takes me. I want to see Momma and Papa, Uncle and Alarn."

He couldn't speak, but nodded solemnly as more tears streaked his face. She pulled her cousin into a tight hug, sighing relief.

"Be safe," she whispered. "Fight hard. Hold the line."

~ ~ ~

That afternoon, she followed Rana up the grand curve of stairs, until it opened up to the massive hallway. As she joined the King on the balcony, Sreana caught a glimpse of the bedchambers and saw a line of trunks. Hearing rumors was one thing, seeing the truth made her heart quiver.

She approached Gregor as he stood near the railing. She bowed as any courtier would, knowing both Gregor and Rana hated watching her do so. When she straightened, she saw them frowning, disappointed that she had regressed back to believing that she was nothing more than a commoner.

"Thank you for the audience, Your Majesty," she said, voice soft. "I wanted to ensure that you had no questions about the plan or the intel we provided."

"My lady, thank you for your concerns," Gregor replied. "However, both your men and mine have been very detailed regarding the situation. You believe they will be here before sundown?"

"Barring any new orders from their commanders, that is correct."

"Then we will be prepared for their arrival. Thank you for giving shelter to our vulnerable population."

"The Temple of Dranar is the most fortified. The priests will protect your people with their lives."

"That is reassuring to hear," Gregor responded. "We will always be grateful to the Sedorans."

Sreana bowed again. "We will begin our watch."

She started to move away but Gregor grabbed her by the arms. "Sreana, wait. I can't let you... I didn't... I... I never apologized to you."

Her eyes widened in surprise, then she glanced away. She caught Rana turning away, to give them privacy, before Gregor cupped her face, making her look back into his eyes.

"I am sorry, Sreana. I am sorry that I considered the words of ignorant and possibly jealous men over the woman I had gotten to know and love. I am sorry I broke my promises to you. I am sorry that I tried to command you like a King would his subject and ignorantly threatened you with Grenan law. I am sorry that I made you believe you were only something I kept close to amuse me. And I am sorry for what you went through. I do not deserve your forgiveness, but I owe you so many apologies."

Her hands clasped his wrists, her cheerless eyes staring into his. She tried to say something, but no sound came out. She blinked away the tears that threatened, then whispered, "Thank you. I mean that. Thank you."

"Thank you for hearing me out."

They stared at each other, words escaping them again. She saw his adoration for her, even if it was veiled by hurt and worry.

"I don't know what to tell you," Gregor whispered, "knowing that you are going to a fight I cannot join."

"When we faced our enemies separately, we always told each other to hold the line. It was our way to say not to give up, not to let the foe win."

"Then Sreana, hold the line."

She nodded, her fingers squeezing gently. "Hold the line, Gregor." Several breaths passed as the silence held them, safe and sound, until reality intruded. Voices of armymen from the courtyard below reminded them what awaited them. "I have to go."

Reluctantly, Gregor released her. She stepped back, hesitating, but before he could say anything else, she turned on her heel and strode toward the stairwell. She paused again for a moment there, then turned back toward Gregor and Rana.

"I do have one ask of you, of both of you."

"Ask anything," Gregor replied.

"If I fall, please make sure Duncar doesn't do anything foolish."

She watched as both men's faces crumbled. She knew the thought of losing anyone hadn't quite crossed their minds, but knowing that Rana cared about Duncar and that Gregor still had some love for her, it was important that they knew her wishes and would help her cousin keep his head.

"We will honor your wishes, my lady," Rana answered, voice cracking.

"Thank you. I will send word if anything changes." And with, she disappeared down the staircase.

CHAPTER 53

Mounted on her stallion, Sreana waited with her strongest fighters. Beside her, Duncar and Pirco sat upon their own horses, their impatience radiating off of them. In front of her were trusted men and women on foot. The silence almost drove them mad until they heard the familiar sounds of armor creaking, saddles squeaking, and haunting exhalations. The Carmanic invaders appeared around the bend, all funneled per Sreana's orders to approach the main gate. The trespassers looked annoyed, angry, and even a little tired. Sreana let a smirk break across her face as she knew the nymphs' harassment had done exactly what she had hoped.

As the foreign army lined up in front of Sreana and her group, they kept enough distance to ensure they did not immediately appear hostile. She found that ironic, considering why they were there. As their enemy settled in and waited, Sreana felt the hairs on her arms rise up.

"Something's not right," Sreana whispered.

"What do you mean?" Pirco asked, voice soft as well.

"They don't hesitate."

"No, they don't." Duncar cursed under his breath. "They're waiting."

"Gregor?" Pirco inquired.

"They had planned on taking him out first," she responded, gritting her teeth. "To weaken Grenan resolve. Throw them into chaos so they cannot provide us support."

"He can hold his own."

"Not if he's up against that Carmanic general."

"You really think he's…?" but Pirco's voice faded when he saw the look on Sreana's face.

"They got in another way."

"It's a trap," Duncar warned.

"Yes, it is."

"If they take out both of you…"

273

"Hold the line," she replied.

"Hold nothing back," Pirco answered. "Leave no survivors."

Sreana nodded, then turned her horse toward the castle. As the stallion galloped past the gates, chaos laid in front of her. She dismounted once she arrived at the stairs, sending the horse away and darting down the main hallway as former Castle Guards attacked Grenan armymen. She ducked and hopped around them, avoiding entanglement in their clashes. Before she made it to the stairwell, someone blocked her path. She recognized the snarling face of the Castle Guard, the one that held her while the other had threatened to harm her. He growled at her and swung his sword. She jumped back, then drew her own.

"I had hoped we'd finish our business," she taunted. "Apologies, I no longer have your other dagger."

He roared and charged, bashing his sword against hers. She blocked his blows easily, then let their hilts catch and lock. Face to face, she laughed at him, which only angered him more. She pushed free, then initiated her own attack. She drove him back until he stumbled into the doorway of the stairwell. Before he could regain his footing, she drove a dagger into his abdomen. He cried out in pain and stared down to find his own dagger driven in up to the hilt. He never saw her palm it off of him. As he started to collapse, she pulled it free, sheathed her own sword, and ran up the stairs.

She bolted down the hall, until sliding to a halt on the balcony. She saw Gregor leaning against the dressing table, his sword laying on the ground and blood smeared across his cheek. The hulking man in front of him had his morningstar drawn back, ready for the death blow. Seeing Gregor bleeding and in pain caused a rage to flash. Again, these murderers came to take everything she loved, cherished. Her anger infused her muscles and honed her focus.

Sreana charged, jumping onto the killer's back and stabbing him in the shoulder with the dagger. The man grunted, staggered a few feet back, then dropped his weapon. He grabbed her by the shirt and pulled her over his shoulder, tossing her away like a toy. She barely missed the door frame, landing hard on her shoulder and rolling along the balcony. She stopped on her side, facing the railing, and groaned in pain.

Then from behind her, a pleased growl as she heard the dagger clatter onto the floor. "The gods have smiled on me. You are still alive."

That voice sent a shiver down her spine, and with dread clutching her stomach, she pushed herself up onto her knees. She panted, trying to ease the pain of her landing, and wiped the blood that dripped from her nose. Then she climbed back to her feet to face the subject of her nightmares.

He sauntered out onto the balcony, glancing her over with malicious joy. He towered over her by the length of a horse's head, his shoulders too broad to let him walk straight on through a doorway. His grotesque sneer showed off his missing teeth, while a scar ran along his scalp and created a large bald part in his straight, dark blonde hair. His pale green eyes reminded her of the slime that dripped off of untreated, molding cheese, while his tanned skin seemed sewn together by the scars that ran haphazardly in light bands. He had retrieved his morningstar, the spiked ball on the end dripping with other victims' blood, maybe even Gregor's.

"They said you died escaping prison. I could not believe you would be so easily killed."

"I couldn't die," she responded, her voice steady, as she unsheathed her sword. "Not without a rematch."

Another pleased, guttural sound. "I have waited too long for one."

They gauged each other at a distance, her sword in front of her and his morningstar at his side.

"I am under strict orders, about you."

Her eyebrows popped up. "Do tell."

"I do not get to keep you. I am to kill you on sight."

"That's so? Well, what about your men? If you fall, what will your men do?"

The Carmanic general sniggered at the idea, before answering, "Our Emperor was clear. This is all or nothing. They are under orders to retreat if you or that irrelevant King best me."

She rolled both of her shoulders in unison then a click of her tongue. "They have a long trip home, let's not keep them waiting."

He happily obliged, raising his morningstar and taking a swing at her. She jumped back, the massive spike on the ball's head barely missing the tip of her nose. She exhaled, annoyed, then waited for his next move. Blocking a direct hit would do her harm, so she waited for the opportunity to disarm him.

He lunged forward, swinging toward her torso. She spun away but not far enough. He grabbed her again by the shirt and lifted her, then threw her across the balcony. She lost her sword because of the momentum and crashed against the heavy curtains. She grabbed onto them, causing the material to rip at the top but they saved her from an unforgiving drop onto the hard floor. Winded, she planted her feet on the railing while keeping clumps of curtain in her fists. She shook her head to regain some sense, aware that he was watching her. He took great pleasure in toying with her, just like all the other times.

After dropping the ripped material and letting it flutter down to the courtyard, she jumped back down onto the balcony. While she waited to see his next move, knowing he assumed she was completely unarmed, she took stock of the nature around her. The tingling in her fingertips confirmed that she had control over the vines of ivy that encased parts of the castle's walls.

He began to stomp towards her, dragging his morningstar behind him, causing sparks to fly. She stood her ground until the very last moment and, with a hope that they had fixed the rods properly, she jumped back onto the railing, grabbed the draw rope for the now absent curtain and ran. She sped toward him then hopped, letting the curtain hooks propel her along the pole. Surprised by her flight, he missed his chance to grab her but she didn't waste her opportunity. She kicked his weapon out of his hands then used the contact to push her faster along the pole. When she set her feet back down on the railing, the friction slowed her to a stop. She looked over her shoulder, noticing that his morningstar had clattered over the rail. She jumped back down onto the balcony, her foe glowering at her from the other end.

Seething, he strode back toward her, reaching out to grab her again. With her sword laying behind him, she had to calculate her next move deftly. Then out of the corner of her eye, she saw Gregor's staff. She mustered her intent as her eyes fell on the ivy that stretched along the wall behind the general. She ordered the plant to lash out. As if thrilled to be recruited, it burst away from the walls, reaching long tendrils that wrapped around the monster's arms. Surprised, he thrashed around until the vines fell away. With him distracted, Sreana darted over to the staff. She grabbed it, swirled it around her, keeping him at a safe distance, then slid into a combative stance.

The general chuckled darkly. "Little girl, little stick," he hissed. "I will break both."

He rapidly approached her, his grin sinister. By sheer instinct, she hit him in the knee, the hip, stomach, then the face. Startled, he teetered backwards and she swept the staff under his feet. At the same time, the ivy attacked again on her orders, wrapping tendrils around his throat and yanking. With a screech, he toppled over the balcony's railing and a dull thud indicated a fatal landing.

She didn't take time to check her work, spinning on her heel to run back into Gregor's bedchambers. As she crossed the threshold of the doorway, she saw that he still leaned, dazed, against the dressing table. Then Sreana felt the blade penetrate her abdomen. She gasped, looking over into the eyes of her murderer. The glee in Jamos' expression wasn't a surprise. He pushed it in deeper and then twisted, normally a fatal blow.

Sreana started to laugh, even through the pain. "You aimed for an organ I no longer have."

Jamos' eyes widened. Vines started to climb up his legs, around his torso, reaching up and around his throat. They wrapped tighter and tighter until the struggling breaths stopped. Then he collapsed, dead. She stared down at him, face blank, then heard her name. She looked up and saw Gregor limping quickly over to her. He grabbed her into his arms and her knees gave out. He helped her to the ground, heartache in his eyes.

The world went black.

~   ~   ~

From below, Duncar and Pirco watched the rematch on the balcony. When it looked like the Carmanic general had the upper hand, it took everything in them not to rush to help. But they had a line of Carmanic soldiers just within earshot, waiting for their general to claim victory. Then Sreana brandished a staff and their hope rose. She struck quickly and efficiently, then sent the general tumbling over the balcony's railing. Pirco caught himself cheering, then defiantly turned his attention to the Carmanic forces.

The men looked confused, shocked, and angry. But even with all of those emotions flashing across their faces, they had their orders. The Sedorans expected them to rush their line; however, they turned away, marching away from the castle and following the path that the jahlas carved out for them. Pirco and Duncar glanced at each other, then gestured to some of their fighters to follow just in case.

Then they heard Gregor yell Sreana's name. The tone broke their hearts and they knew something terrible had befallen their friend.

"Duncar, go!"

Without argument, Duncar spurred his steed into a sprint.

~   ~   ~

As Duncar arrived, the Grenan soldiers were lifting Sreana off the ground and carefully moving her to the bed. Duncar pushed through when they stepped back, checking her wound. Gregor shook himself out of his stupor, grasping Duncar's shoulder.

"She came to my aid," Gregor stammered.

Putting pressure on her wound, Duncar replied, "She knew you needed her."

Two men and one woman rushed past Gregor, with a young man right on their heels. They surrounded Sreana and Duncar, murmuring hurriedly to each other. One of the men unhooked her belt to pull her pants down enough to view her injury. The woman pulled Sreana's shirt up in coordination with Duncar to ensure he kept a constant pressure. Whispering between them, they checked her wound, her breathing, and her heartbeat.

The head healer had Duncar lift his hands for a moment, examining her wound. "She should be bleeding more," Genj murmured, surprised. "The wound to the kidney would produce more blood."

"She no longer has that kidney," Duncar responded, pressing his hands back down on her wound.

Genj glanced up at him in surprise. "Tell me."

"The scarring you see is due to multiple infections. Among other things, I had to remove that kidney. What he stabbed was really just scar tissue and muscle."

"What a strange thing to save her life." As the healer ran his hands over her stomach, he stopped. Then he glanced at the female healer, a peculiar expression on his face.

She stood and approached their young student. "Fetch Tesayin," she ordered, softly. The young student nodded and brushed past Gregor.

"Genj?" Gregor inquired.

"I'm not sure, Your Majesty, let me get another opinion." Then he turned to Duncar. "We will treat this as we would any other puncture wound." Genj nodded to his fellow Grenan healers and they began work on the poultice.

"Do we know if the dagger was laced?" Duncar asked, swallowing hard. "The Carmanic Empire always poison their blades."

"The other wounds are being treated for poison as we speak."

"I doubt it's the same one."

"Where is this dagger now?" Genj inquired.

One of the armymen who helped carry Sreana to the bed produced the weapon. Duncar nodded to Genj, who took over the compression to her wound. Duncar stood and examined the weapon in the fading sunlight. Then he cautiously sniffed and cringed at the familiar scent.

"What kind of poison?" Gregor asked, recognizing the look on Duncar's face.

"We called it fatal flower. Smells like blooms but if not caught quickly enough, it kills most victims. We will need to add red clover, dandelion, and nettles to the poultice."

The two healers nodded, immediately adding the other ingredients. Once the poultice was ready, they placed it into Sreana's wound. Her body reacted to the sting and cold of the poultice, but she remained unconscious. Once it was secured, a dark-haired, dark-skinned woman entered with the apprentice. She shooed everyone away, and as he backed away, movement in the doorway caught Duncar's eye.

"Rana?" Duncar asked, rushing to his side.

Rana held his chest, where the bandage appeared discolored with blood, and chuckled. "I'm fine. I've had worse."

"Sit down, you stubborn fool."

"I'm more worried about Wenth."

Gregor waited until Duncar got Rana comfortable, before inquiring, "The horde?"

"They retreated upon the death of their leader," Duncar answered.

"What about those in the castle?"

Rana scoffed, flinching. "All I know is my opponent stabbed me, then he disappeared out the window by his ankles. The whole lot disappeared like magic."

Gregor sighed relief, then turned saddened eyes toward Sreana. Suddenly, he teetered. He blinked but the dizziness overwhelmed him and his eyes blurred. He felt someone grab his arms and heard Rana calling, "Your Majesty?" He shook his head and his vision cleared enough to see Duncar in front of him.

"Where are you injured?" Duncar demanded.

"I don't know."

Duncar helped him lean back against the desk, then lifted his tunic. A large bruise had started discoloring his abdomen. The healer touched along the skin then pressed along the King's lower ribs, making Gregor hiss.

"Broken ribs, maybe internal bleeding. Did you get hit directly?"

"No, he hit the table with his weapon and that flew into me. Knocked me against the dressing table."

"Cold compress, pain relief, and keep an eye on him," Genj suggested, which made Duncar nod in agreement.

Gregor waved their suggestions off. "I can handle the pain. What about Sreana?"

CHAPTER 54

That following morning, their world felt different. The Carmanic army had retreated and escaped, at least half of it did. All of the nymphs strategically took their places throughout Sedora to protect their people and Sreana's, becoming the visual representation of Sedora's strength. The message was clear to any aggressors. Test the Kingdom and face a wrath never seen before.

And for the first time, they were safe.

There was still uncertainty as the news of Sreana's injury spread. The wound seemed minor but the poison that lined the dagger had infiltrated her body. She laid unconscious for most of the morning, leaving everyone to pray and wait. Pirco had returned to the township to check if any other injuries were reported, but they were minimal, then he sat at the quiet firepit in despair. He heard rustling and saw Jya, her expression mirroring his heartache.

She kneeled behind him, her green eyes dark as she sobbed. "We can't hear her."

"We've lost her," Pirco responded, fighting back his tears. "If you can't hear her, she's gone."

The jahla frowned as if he misunderstood her. Then she grabbed a pile of mud and dropped it into his hands. "We can't hear her. We can't hear *them*."

Pirco rubbed the mud between his fingers, realizing what she meant. He shook off the mud, jumped onto a horse, and rode off toward the castle.

~   ~   ~

Pirco sped past the gates and almost fell off his horse when he arrived at the steps. He ran up the stairs to the King's bedchambers and almost collapsed due to breathlessness. "This is going to sound ridiculous, I know," Pirco panted, "but you need to get her to touch the ground."

Duncar sat next to the bed while Gregor laid on the couch near the fireplace, holding a cold compress to his abdomen. Genj stood by the dining table, redressing Rana's wound. They all stared at him confused.

Until, "Like last time?" Duncar demanded, surprised.

"Like last time," his friend confirmed.

Carefully, Duncar picked Sreana up and carried her down the stairs, through the hall, out the main doors, and laid her down in the grass along the gravel walkway. They waited, watched, but nothing happened. Pirco whimpered when he realized the suggestion didn't work.

"Maybe this isn't the right place?" Gregor asked. "Should we take her home, to her lea?"

Genj grimaced, then glanced over at Duncar. "I cannot recommend moving her any further but I am not her healer. I will defer that decision to you."

Duncar stared at his cousin, inhaling deeply. "She needs to be home."

"Get the carriage, it's the safest way to transport her," Gregor ordered Ranthel.

Ranthel nodded, then he sprinted off to the stable.

"You don't think it's too late?" Gregor asked.

"Jya wouldn't've sent me if it was," Pirco answered.

~   ~   ~

The carriage arrived, rattling up the dirt road as far as it could, Pirco right behind them on horseback. Then Gregor and Duncar exited, with Sreana in Duncar's arms and they strode into her lea. They made their way to the trees, where Duncar laid her down near Jya's tree. As Sreana's body contacted the ground, the grass underneath and around her quivered, the bright green fading to a sickly yellow. Then the strands of grass burst free of whatever ailed them and grew slightly as their vibrant healthy color returned.

Sreana stirred, a small moan escaping, but she didn't wake. However, she reacted to her surroundings, which gave Duncar hope.

"I don't understand," Gregor murmured, unsure if his eyes had played some trick on him. "I still don't understand why Jya said to bring her."

Duncar sighed, sitting back on his legs. "Sreana doesn't just talk to nymphs. She has a connection with them and, in turn, with nature. I think Jya wanted to see if touching Sedoran soil would help her fight the poison in her system. She had me do that before, when Sreana was wounded rescuing Alarn. It helped, but it's not a fix all. She still has to fight."

Duncar noticed movement and watched as Jya stepped away from her tree. She kneeled down, then caressed Sreana's forehead, her smile sad but hopeful.

"We can hear them now," she whispered, with Pirco translating. She raised back up and leaned against Pirco, who hugged her to his side.

Reassured, Duncar picked up his cousin again, then followed Gregor to Sreana's hovel. They laid her in bed, made her as comfortable as they could, then they were left to wait.

~   ~   ~

As the sun started to set, Pirco sent the two men out to sit and eat near the bonfire. He took over the watch, leaving the door open for anyone to peek in while keeping his eyes on her. He stared at his friend, heartbroken, as his hand stroked her forehead. Then he heard gasps from outside. He glanced up and saw movement from the tree line.

In a line, a jahla, eahzal, saehwa, halha, and aetha walked or floated into the lea and headed straight to Sreana's hovel. Each took their turn entering the home, laying an offering on her quilt. The jahla set down a hand-woven basket filled with pine cones. The eahzal laid a wreath of dried purple seaweed with white seashells tucked into the strands. The saehwa left a metal pan of cooled embers that smelled liked lavender and orange. The halha arranged smooth stones of transparent and yellow that were strung along a copper chain like a necklace. Lastly, the aetha gave a small bottle of dust that glittered like starlight. And as they did so, they each whispered something to her. Then as quickly as they appeared, they returned to the forest and disappeared from sight.

Duncar and Gregor rushed inside, shocked by the gifts left on Sreana's bed. "What just happened?" Duncar asked.

Pirco shrugged, stammering. "I could only understand the jahla. She said that her gift was to help Sreana in this world or the next. The others? I think the sentiment was the same." The men were left speechless. Then Pirco shook himself. "You two need to rest. You've been going since the attack. Get some sleep, I will stay with her. Relieve me when you wake."

~   ~   ~

Duncar didn't sleep much, with both Sreana and Rana on his mind. He finally gave up after a few hours and relieved Pirco. As he sat in one of her small chairs, he checked her wound again. He kept expecting her to get worse, but she seemed to stabilize after touching the soil and being tucked into her bed. Frustrated, he fussed over the bandage.

Gregor watched from the doorway and sighed, startling the healer. "Duncar, you know her wishes."

"I know. The wound looks good but…"

"No heroics, no miracles." Gregor sat next to Duncar, taking Sreana's hand in his. "We've done enough of that. Now, it is up to her. She has to decide. Come back to us or reunite with her brother, her children, and her other family in the afterlife."

"She told you?"

Gregor nodded solemnly. "We talked a lot during our companionship. She always feared putting you in the same situation as the last time. She didn't ever want to be a burden to anyone, but especially you. She told me before she held the line that she wanted you to live your life. One she saw you finally accept when you and Rana found each other."

Heartbroken silence held for a moment.

"You should go rest, Duncar. I'll stay for a while."

"She will be glad to see you," Duncar said, voice soft.

"Will she?"

Duncar hesitated.

"I know we still love each other," Gregor continued. "I never lost faith in that. But I betrayed her, took her trust in me for granted, and even though I apologized, I know I am unwelcomed in her life. I will stay until I know she is well and then return to Grenan like I promised."

"Even though…?"

"Do you agree with the midwife? About Sreana knowing before the fight?"

"She would have had signs before Jena's death. But her recognizing them? With everything going on, I can't know that."

"We both know she is not stupid. She didn't tell you or me but Jya knew." Gregor looked as if he was aging right before Duncar's eyes. "It is obvious that she does not want me in their lives. I accept that."

"I am sorry, Gregor. I wish things were different."

"So do I. But there are consequences to actions and I have to take responsibility for what I said and did. Part of that is accepting her decisions. Now, go, rest."

~   ~   ~

Gregor sat on the ground and laid his head on the bed, near her shoulder, while holding her hand. It was late and he had dozed off out of sheer exhaustion, snoring in her ear. Sreana stared at him, in awe of his devotion, but still unsure about what had happened. She cautiously glanced around. Her stove was burning, warming her home, but her door was left ajar. Why was she laying in her bed when she had been at the castle? She remembered the minister stabbing her, then everything going black as Gregor rushed toward her.

She tentatively touched her side with her free hand and felt the tinge of pain. She grimaced in response, then sighed. She reached over and touched Gregor's cheek, running fingertips through his beard. The touch roused him and when he opened his eyes, they met hers. His were filled with relief and joy.

"You're awake. How do you feel?" he asked, cupping her hand with his.

"Some pain but nothing I can't handle," she responded. "How did I get here?"

"The jahlas told us that you needed to be reconnected to the land. And apparently, the castle had turned into a piece of Grenan because of how long we've stayed, so we had to bring you home."

"Are we safe then?"

"Yes, the Carmanic regiment retreated to the port, just like you said. There, they loaded up onto a ship only to drown in the depths as their boat sank. Your people reported a terrible noise and then the ship went down within moments. The other ship left quickly after that. I assume to tell their masters what awaits them if they try to invade again."

"You do not mess with eahzals," she responded, chuckling darkly then cringing at the pain. "Any casualties?"

"Not on our side. Wounds, yes, but all treatable." Then he kissed the back of her fingers, like he used to when she arrived at the castle. "Thank you for coming to my side."

"You needed me."

"I did." Gregor sighed, searching her beautiful gray eyes. He wanted to ask her, wanted to tell her everything in his heart. But she was barely awake and nowhere near recuperated. It wouldn't be fair to press her in her current condition. "Rest. We will have to make an appearance once we've healed."

Her eyebrows furrowed in worry. "We?"

Gregor straightened slightly, grimacing. "Didn't know getting hit with a table would break a rib, let alone two."

"You should be resting in a bed, too," she chided, then she noticed the change in his expression. "What is it?"

"Nothing. Rest."

"Gregor."

He regarded her, solemnly, unable to hold it in anymore. "During the examination of your wound, they discovered you were with child."

"Did I lose her?" Sreana whispered, her voice trembling.

"So you did know?" he asked, staring at her in disappointment. "Jamos went for the kill, to puncture your kidney, which was far enough away not to injure the baby." Her hand still in his, he moved them to her stomach. Their palms cradled the small extension in her belly. "Our baby lives and thrives, just waiting for you to wake up."

She sniffled and placed a shaking hand over her mouth, trying to quell the sob.

"You will be under very strict instructions from the healers, you understand?"

She nodded, still speechless.

"Why didn't you tell me?" he demanded, his heart shattered.

"I didn't know how. I didn't know if you'd even accept her."

"Why wouldn't I?"

Sreana sobbed, searching his eyes for proof. She needed to see evidence that he had no hesitation accepting their child. She thought she saw it there, but he didn't know everything. He needed to, if he were to be the father she had hoped. She pulled free her hand and reached up before gently tapping her fingers against the rock. In the crevices, green fuzz started to materialize and cover the stone. Once it spread about the length and width of her hand, small purple blooms manifested. The moss and its flowers seemed to gravitate toward her fingers until she dropped her hand back down. She watched as his eyes widened in surprise.

"On the balcony, the vines, that was you?"

"I am the monster you feared."

"Sreana..."

"Elementals have more Talents than just talking to nymphs. Our child will be able to do the same things. Can you accept her for her differences? For her magic?"

She worried when he hesitated. "I will have to learn to understand," he replied, thoughtfully. "But I will accept my child however Talented she is. Just like I will accept her mother. I failed you, Sreana, and I cannot apologize enough. But if raising our child together is a start, then I will prove myself daily and will never leave your side again."

"But your people, they will never accept me, a Sedoran, not with the way they talked about me and what you call my kind. They proved we are incompatible."

"I can't believe that. I can't sleep without you. I can't think, breathe... I don't know how to live without you. I can't. I wish you felt the same."

"Do you think I'm alive?"

He raised himself up onto his knees, then cupped her face and made her lift her chin so their eyes could meet.

"The part of me that loved you," she continued, "breathed with you, that made my heart beat, it died the moment I left your bed that night."

"Tell me how to bring it back to life."

She shook her head. "We can't go back. I cannot live your life as much as you cannot live mine."

"No, but we can move forward. We know that we're physically compatible." That made her scoff. "We know we love each other. We can live each other's lives because we will combine them into a life of our own, together. For the sake of our child and for the sake of our love. But we have to work on us, here and now, to make sure no one can drive a wedge between us ever again. We deserve our happiness and we have to both make sure that is our goal in all of this. Not what others think. Not what others see. What we think, see. Us."

"What do you see when you look at me?" she asked, hesitantly.

"I see you," he answered, not quite reassuring her. "When I thought back on how angry you were, I realized how foolish I was in believing some stories that didn't have any evidence to support them. I knew who you were and that you were still the same woman I fell in love with. I had already accepted everything about you no matter what name was attached to your facets. I don't think you're a monster, I am not afraid of you. I... I find myself in awe of you."

He grasped her hand and moved it to his heart, laying his over her. Her breath shuddered as she exhaled, as if the rhythm of his heart ignited hers.

"This doesn't beat unless you're near me. That stillness, it reminds me that the best part of me is missing. If you cannot forgive me, if you hate me, then banish me from your sight and I will go back to Grenan tonight. But if you can forgive my ignorance, if you still love me, come back to me, Sreana, and we can bring each other back to life. We can be the family we have yearned for this whole time."

"You are a King and I'm..."

"My love. My breath. My heart. And I don't have to stay a King."

"Your people need you."

"My family needs me more."

She looked away. She wanted to believe him. She wanted him to be in their lives, to be the family they had dreamed of but thought was out of reach. Her eyes blurred.

The tears in her eyes almost broke him. He waited several breaths, but withdrew his hands and leaned back when he realized she couldn't respond. He cleared his throat, trying to free his voice from the stranglehold of his emotions. "Now that I know you do not want me here, I will return to Grenan. But know that I will never forget all the things you taught me. I will never forget what you mean to me. I will never let others' doubts affect me. I will never breathe again. And I will never love another. I will never break my pledge to you."

Their pain made the air hard to breathe.

"I can only hope," he continued, voice breaking intermittently, "that maybe you'll send letters, keeping me informed about her and the milestones that I will miss. Maybe permit me to visit? I do not wish to be a stranger to our child. But if that is too much, I will respect that too. But I beg you, please, tell her what was good about us. Tell this blessing of ours how much we loved each other. How I think it was our love for each other that helped bring her to us even though neither of us believed it possible. And tell her, every day, how much you both mean to me."

Seeing his heartfelt investment in their child made something click in her. She whispered something, which he couldn't hear, and his eyebrows furrowed in confusion. She reached out and caressed his cheek, then cupped his face and brought him in close. Then, in a louder voice, "Stay."

He squeezed his eyes shut for a moment, wishing that touch meant more.

"Stay," she repeated. "Stay for her."

Torn, he glanced down at her stomach, then ran his hand under her shirt so he could caress it again. "I don't want to stay just for her."

Before he could react, she slipped her hand behind his head and pulled him in. Lips connected and they fell into the embrace as if it was the only thing keeping them alive. Then she pulled on his shoulders, urging him into the bed with her. He had to help move her over to make room, then he laid on his side next to her. Kiss after kiss, they lost themselves.

However, their injuries didn't give them time to enjoy their reunion. When he instinctively tried to move into a more convenient position, she cursed against his lips while he hissed in pain. He ended up rolling onto his back, laying shoulder to shoulder with her. They stared sheepishly at each other, embarrassed by their discomfort. He reached for her hand, entwining his fingers with hers.

"Promise we will make this work," he begged.

"It's going to take time," she responded, choosing her words carefully. "We will both have to make some concessions. We have to agree to accept the good and the bad in both of us, even if they are misconceived sometimes."

"Then can we agree that if something comes up, and we bring to the other's attention, we are to discuss it instead of reacting to it?"

"I can agree to try."

"That's a start," he chided. "But if I make the mistake again of threatening you or ordering you, no matter who is around, don't run away. Thrash me immediately."

A sly smile finally crept across her face. "You might want to put that permission in writing so I do not get arrested."

"I will happily do so."

"Will you bring things up a little more diplomatically? You know you are a King."

"I am not a King when I am with you, remember? I am a mere man who loves you more than I ever thought I could love someone. And who can act like the biggest fool in two Kingdoms."

"Then the man needs to promise to work on his tact," she retorted.

"The man promises to try."

He leaned over to kiss her again, but a voice from the doorway complained, "You were supposed to call us when she woke."

Gregor and Sreana looked up to find Duncar standing there, his arms crossed.

"We're already in trouble," she whined, sarcastically, then started to laugh. That caused her pain and made her flinch and curse.

"I'm guessing you caught her up?" Duncar inquired.

"I thought it best if I prepared her for your rules," Gregor replied, then glanced back at her. "Do you need anything?"

"I could use some water," Sreana answered.

Gregor kissed her, then slowly rolled to his feet and headed out. Duncar took his seat next to her bed, checking her wound and sighing.

"You didn't take any heroic actions, did you?" she demanded.

"No, not with everyone reminding me every moment what your wishes were. It wasn't easy, knowing two lives laid in limbo."

"Are you sure I didn't…?" and her voice quivered.

"I am. So are the Grenan healers. You're far along enough to hear the little heartbeat with a sound magnifier." Duncar's smile widened as it turned sly. "Not hard to figure out the night you conceived based on that information."

She smacked his cousin's arm, making him laugh. Then she whispered, solemnly, "What about the poison?"

Duncar's smile faded and he lowered his head.

"There's only one reason why you'd bring me home."

"We think we caught it quickly enough to only affect you. But Genj and I will keep a good eye on you until the baby is born. Out of caution, you will have to limit some of your activities until you make it past the first trimester."

"I slayed the monster from my nightmares and saved my Kingdom from another infestation. I think I'm allowed a little bit of rest. What about Gregor?"

"Two broken ribs from what I can tell. Nothing time won't heal." He folded his hands. "And what I walked in on? Are you giving it another go?"

"We have to think about our child, what we want for her."

"You should know that he was adamant not to leave your side, no matter his discomfort."

She didn't respond, stretching her legs carefully. She lifted her head and glanced around, realizing that something laid along the foot of her bed. "What is all this?"

"The nymphs came and gave you gifts to use in this life or the next."

Sreana blinked, then laid her head back down. "I'll have to make sure to thank them for their thoughtfulness."

"At least we know why you survived so long in the bog," Duncar said. "As long as you are connected to the land, to Sedora, it will protect you. Even help heal you. I mean, we knew it helped to keep you touching the land when you got hurt rescuing Alarn, but I don't think any of us realized how special your connection is." He shrugged, eyes finding the moss thriving on the rock wall. "Like it or not, you are an Elemental. Actually, from what I was told about what happened in the castle, you are *the* Elemental."

She took a deep breath, those words turning her blood cold. She had to stay connected, with the land, with Sedora. Then she felt the warmth emanating from her womb, knowing that her child too would have the same connection and that it was a good thing. Sedora would always have its link to the people and the nymphs. Jayna had asked who would connect them, lead them, and Sreana knew it would be her bloodline.

Gregor ambled in, hands full of mugs and plates. "Here, I was told that you need to eat, as do Duncar and I. Habni's orders." Gregor set everything down on her table, then glanced over at Duncar. "Since she's awake, you should go check on Rana."

"Rana? What happened to Rana?" she asked.

"Injured," Duncar answered after another sigh, "but he's been tended to."

"Go see him, I am not going anywhere. At least for now."

The dark glare he gave her made her smirk. "I do not trust you to behave."

"She will behave," Gregor responded. "I will keep her under careful supervision. If I need help, I have Pirco, Habni, and several others that will gleefully wrangle her into submission. Go see Rana."

"Fine, but I will require a full report when I get back. And no more crawling into her bed."

With that, Duncar grabbed a mug and sandwich, taking a bite as he exited. She chuckled, groaning when the pain reminded her any movement was improper. She let Gregor prop her up a little more with a folded blanket slipped under her pillow, then he handed her a mug of water and she sipped cautiously. When that didn't cause too much discomfort, he laid a plate of sliced cheese and meats nearby and let her nibble. He sat on the chair instead of the floor, taking a bite of his own sandwich and sighed contentedly.

She frowned, concerned. "I guess we will have to figure out living arrangements."

"What? Our current arrangement displeases you?"

"Split between the castle and my hovel? Didn't that displease you before?"

He chuckled, taking a swig from his own mug. "I am quite aware now that you must be here, with all of your people. We will always have one foot in each of our worlds. Together, we will make it work." He glanced around, thoughtfully. "But we might consider building on."

They ate quietly for a few breaths, their understanding bringing a new contentment between them.

"Well?" she inquired, raising an eyebrow.

"What?"

"Are you going to get back into bed or not?"

He grasped her hand, kissing the back of her fingers. "Finish your food first. Then we'll defy Duncar's order."

CHAPTER 55

Once Sreana was able to move around, a call for a meeting with the community leaders came through the jahlas. Without prompting, they all agreed to meet at Trealle's. Sreana hobbled to the tavern, with Duncar and Pirco by her side. When they entered, the tables and chairs had already been rearranged and the other community leaders were present. And so was Gregor.

Sreana furrowed her eyebrows, but Gregor's expression told her to be patient. Everyone sat down, except Sreana and her friends, as they were left at the head of the table. No one spoke.

"Well, you called this meeting," Sreana chided.

"King Gregor had reached out to see what we needed after this last invasion," Dener replied. "Our discussions have led us to one conclusion. What we need lies outside our borders. We must draw up treaties with our neighbors to bring safety and prosperity to Sedora, because Grenan cannot shoulder the full weight of our future. To do so, we need to pick a representative to lead the negotiations."

All eyes rested on her.

"I am already in talks with the nymphs," Sreana informed them. "That will take most of my time and energy. Not to mention healing and teaching the next generation of Talented. Someone else will have to step in."

"We have determined that we need a permanent representative. A leader of leaders."

"A Royal Family," Sella clarified.

Sreana felt heat rise in her cheeks. "We promised never to go back. No more Royal Family, remember? They let us down. Left us to die. No, we can't do that to our people."

Each leader stared at her, unfazed by her anger.

"There has already been a vote in each community," Sella admitted. "Majority agrees that if it wasn't for you, Rathfeather, we would have suffered a worse fate. And I do not mean just recently, but even during the original invasion."

"Even before," Terga added. "The farmers have told me stories."

"And it is time that the rightful heirs return," Dener said. "We have been failed by the imposters. We have done our research, even though some of us are old enough to remember. We know who the true Royal Family is."

"And they were removed," Sreana snapped. "Twice."

"By a mistake we refuse to repeat."

Terga said, proudly, "Long ago, Elementals led this Kingdom into prosperity. Our Elemental will lead us again."

"Have we not learned that one voice is weaker than a crowd?" Sreana demanded. "I cannot be the sole decider of the fate of our Kingdom."

Terga snorted when Sreana's hot gaze landed on him. "Fear not, Rathfeather, you will not be without your detractors. We will keep you in line."

Sreana struggled with words, almost gasping for air.

"Let's make this official," Sella ordered. "All in favor?"

A resounding "Aye" from all the community leaders seemed to almost shake the building. Each leader stood up, then bowed to Sreana. "Your Majesty." Then, without another word, each left the tavern.

The only ones left were Duncar, Pirco, Sreana, and Gregor. Sreana turned around and stepped backwards until she felt the table and leaned against it. She still felt her breath stolen, unsure about what just happened. From behind her friend and cousin, she could see her lover's perplexed expression and she glanced away.

Silence held them, as Gregor continued to stare at her. "Royalty?"

"Not for a long time," Duncar replied.

Pirco glowered, annoyed, at Sreana. "You never told him?"

"Explain," Gregor requested, confusion tainting his tone.

"There were two brothers," Sreana responded, finally finding her voice. "One was Talented, the other a regular man. They did not see eye to eye on how to run the Kingdom. The Talented one walked away, because the people decided to follow the lead of his brother."

"We believe this is the origin of the fears," Pirco interjected, his frustration becoming somber. "Why people became afraid of the Talented. The one brother turned our people against the Talented one to win the throne."

"My great-great grandfather never admitted that, but he honored the people's decision and he walked away. He moved to the ocean and never looked back. Not even after his brother was overthrown by the Garadni Royal Family, who left a cousin in charge, whose descendants eventually betrayed us to the Carmanic Empire."

Gregor nodded, thoughtfully. "Then the Rathfeathers are the true Royal Family of Sedora."

"So they believe," Sreana grumbled.

Gregor stood and approached her, a sly smile breaking through. "It will be my honor to negotiate a proper treaty with the Queen of Sedora."

"No, no I can't be called that. I am not a Queen."

Pirco jumped in. "Doesn't matter what we call you, Sreana. You are our Leader. Always have been. There's never been any doubt about that." Then he looked over at Gregor, eyebrows furrowed. "Wouldn't a treaty be automatic if you two got married?"

"Only as long as we are alive. We need to think beyond that. For both our Kingdoms."

"And I don't remember accepting a marriage proposal," she retorted.

Gregor grasped her hand, entwining their fingers. "Yet."

"How can I be an effective leader? I don't know if I can leave Sedora now. Not with my connection."

"Make them come here. I think it will benefit any ally to see what Sedora has survived and what it has done to thrive."

"I guess I need to start making a list." She sighed, hard. "But first, I need to absorb what just happened."

~   ~   ~

That night, as Sreana sat near the bonfire, she had burned through all of the excuses and reasons why a Royal Family would be a choice worse than death. However, everything she thought up was squashed by the faces in the tavern. They had no doubt and no qualms with their decision.

She caressed the cover of one her books as it laid in her lap. A book full of words written by her father documenting their family history. She closed her eyes, remembering what he had told her about their heritage.

His displeasure in speaking of the incident that tore their family apart and put their Kingdom in the hands of outsiders never outweighed the pain and grief that reflected in his eyes. Her Papa and Uncle took up the stead that their father and grandfather created without hesitation, to keep their fiefdom prosperous and their Kingdom thriving, but they had hoped their children – Alarn, Sreana, and Duncar – would find their own way in the world.

However, she had spent her life keeping their Kingdom standing. She had kept so many secrets from her family about what she did, how she manipulated Canor and others to keep their duty to Sedora... What she did to keep the invaders from murdering more of their people... How many men she had killed... But she knew her Papa was proud of her, for everything he knew and didn't know about.

She felt Gregor sit down next to her, making her look over at him and see his bewildered expression. "Royalty."

She scoffed. "It feels like a betrayal accepting that title."

"Why?"

"We fought so hard to regain our Kingdom and we all promised not to allow any more pretenders on the throne." She grimaced, hugging the book to her chest. "Well not literally, that was destroyed during the invasion. The invaders lit it on fire and catapulted into the King's castle."

"But if the bloodline is true, then you are no imposter."

Sreana sighed, watching the flames dance. "My great-great grandfather walked away. He left it all behind. Why should it be me to take it back?"

"All of the stories you told me gave a small window into your life. But every story told to me by someone else, be it Duncar or someone from another community, each one has backed up what I knew before we ever met – that there was a leader. Someone who brought the Sedoran people together in good times and bad. It was you. They settled any doubt of that just now in the tavern. Why fear a title when it only confirms who you truly are?"

"Titles change people. Power changes people."

He grasped one of her hands, entwining his fingers with hers. "You have your detractors," he reminded her. "They will not let you lose yourself and neither will I."

Silence.

"Is there anything else I should know?" he inquired.

She snorted. "I think it's best to come to terms that there will always be something else."

"I'll have to work on that."

"This might help," she added, handing over her book. "Some light reading."

"About?"

"My family. My father wrote it all down."

"I will take good care of it," he promised, holding it close with his free hand.

"And I hope that you will help me with the diplomatic side of things. Seeing no other Kingdom came to our aid… I think my type of tact will ruffle many."

"It will indeed, which could be useful, but I will be by your side all the way. It is my duty, remember? Not to let Sedora fail?" He reached over and touched her chin, making her meet his eyes. "And it is my duty to you, as your companion, to not let you fail either."

"What if we can't work it out? What if we cannot be companions?"

Gregor sighed, not wanting to admit the same concerns. "We will make whatever changes necessary if that were to occur. But why prepare for something that is only a possibility and not quite a reality?"

"Because it already was a reality."

"And yet we stood by each other's side to reject the scourge in your borders. And you saved my life even when we were not companions. And now, we are expecting a miracle that we will put before us every time. I think we can work things out when needed, no matter our status."

He leaned in, slowly, until their lips met. They cherished the tender moment until a giggle tickled her throat.

"What?"

"Duncar will have to tell Rana."

Gregor furrowed his eyebrows for a moment, then the image of a terrified Duncar trying to explain his royal heritage to an oblivious Rana made him laugh too.

"Oh to be in the room..."

CHAPTER 56

The wounds healed.

And the news of Sreana's ascension to the throne spread throughout Sedora as did her work with Gregor and the nymphs. As old treaties flashed to ash, new treaties brightened the future. The agreements with the remaining nymphs were finalized quickly after the Carmanic army failed their second coup attempt. The Talented children became ambassadors for their specific nymph, while Sreana confirmed that she would be the conduit for all. Sabira was officially announced as her apprentice, ensuring that everyone knew Talents came in different shapes. This openness about their abilities caused more Sedorans, of every age, to step forward out of the shadows and claim their birthrights as the Talented.

A treaty was also negotiated between Sedora and Grenan, with Sreana and Gregor as the respective representatives. The two Kingdoms became strong allies through their agreement, allowing their citizens to move freely between their borders and relocate if desired. Those Grenans who chose to stay in Sedora also learned with the children about the nymph that would reside nearby. Gregor and Rana both sat around Jya's tree, and even though they didn't understand a word, they saw the connection between nymph and Sedoran, realizing how special and how advantageous the relationship really was, banishing all doubts.

As for Sreana and Gregor, they found their way together as companions and eventually as spouses. Once they wed for all to see, she gained the title of King's Consort in Grenan.

But in Sedora, she was Queen.

And Sedora prospered under her guidance.

And her child, a screaming baby girl name Szaeja, became the next in line.

~ The End ~

EPILOGUE

Justice came swiftly.

For their aggression, the Carmanic Empire faced consequences never seen before by their people. Treaties were shredded and the Carmanic Empire was deemed irreconcilable. No other Kingdom would trade with them and they were left to fend for themselves. It became a hermit country, barricaded behind their border by the neighboring Kingdoms.

And even though peace spread far and wide… those in the banished Empire made plans…

APPENDIX

Nymphs

Jahla (ja-lah) – they represent earth

Eahzal (eh-zall) – they represent water; also work as messengers for Dranar

Saehwa (say-wah) – they represent fire; also work as messengers for Sera and Hendar

Halha (hall-hah) – they represent air

Aetha (ay-eh-thah) – they represent celestial

Gods

Dranar (dray-narr) – God of Mercy and Empathy
Sera (sar-rah) – God of Hearth and Home
Hendar (hen-darr) – God of Sorrow and Grief

Sayings

"Hold the Line."

"May the gods keep your nightmares to themselves."
"And may they give you dreams worth dreaming."

"I pledge to you my faithful heart and undying love."

ABOUT THE AUTHOR

Living among the cacti and coyotes in Arizona, Kassandra spends her free time writing. Besides entertaining her two Dobermans (that's the breed you pick when you're a cat person, right?), the author enjoys photography, hiking, traveling, music, visiting ghost towns and staying in haunted hotels.

www.ingramcontent.com/pod-product-compliance
Lightning Source LLC
Chambersburg PA
CBHW022021240626

47154CB00007B/2202